Corrupted Flux

Book Three of The Flux Catastrophe

Jonathan Weiss

Helixic Books

Print ISBN: 978-1-7642069-4-5

DEDICATION

For Ryza.

Rest well, my old friend.
Because your destination
Was a long journey.

And for my wife, Kayla, and anyone else who has put up with my chaotic aspirations.

CONTENTS

Chapter One

Through The Cracks

The scattered bones of a dying industry lay in the path of Ryza's slow approach. Three days of scouting had revealed a route through the maze of rusted iron trenches that sprawled across the barren rock. It wasn't the most direct way to his target, a decrepit outpost that he and the other two ex-conscripts with him had tracked a band of smelters to, but it was the only one Ryza's fraying wits allowed him to take.

The path had been found by Elya. She was the taller of the pair that'd made the journey with Ryza, and as a Reythurist with crystalline blue eyes, she was gifted with a magic common to the air itself. It was this that'd allowed her to take to the sky each day, searching out the route. Ryza's stern warnings for her to keep her distance, to not take risks, had always been lost in the blast of condensed air that launched her upwards, leaving him to pace mindlessly among the piles of discarded scrap metal he was more likely to control, himself.

The difference in the way that the three of them were born to handle their magics was stark. With what Ryza had so far experienced in his fraught lifetime, he was the only one among them to know there was less separating them from their magical origins than it initially seemed. The echoes of magic left behind by those-of-glass, the ancient people who'd populated the land eons before, sounded far louder in Ryza's head in the wake of what he'd witnessed beneath the town of Iroka.

If that even was magic...

The thought alone put Ryza's mind on edge, and he sped up his pace to allay the resulting nerves. Keeping low within the bounds of the ancient trench, he could barely see the glut of metal and machinery that looked over the land ahead. If he was fast enough, he'd reach it before Elya or Vhoze, who were approaching in a similar fashion from the other side of the trenches.

The pair were all that was left of the remaining conscripts that'd survived Revance's fall and similarly disastrous cleanup that still trusted him enough to follow him on these bounty hunting missions.

Probably because they don't know just what I did.

Where they'd once fought with the entire might of a walking fortress at their back, all that was left for them now was to track down the last of the escaped smelters and flux traders that no longer belonged in the world that their hideous industry had created. It was a challenge that Elya always took to with glee, which was why it was good to have Vhoze's tempering instinct to hold her back.

In his right hand, his sawn-off rifle swung low at his side. It was far from the first one that he'd owned. He'd been through seven in the past three months, a count he was certain of because each new one required him to spend an entire afternoon with the weapon secured into a vice as he slowly hacked off the majority of the barrel with a long-suffering handsaw.

Every time one broke or misfired, there was no chance of repair. Not because there was a lack of parts or means to do so, but because the rifles were so abundant across the Droughtlands that it was far easier to simply replace them.

Bit like me, really.

Ryza silenced the temptation to chuckle at the thought. It had now been nearly a year since the loss of his left hand, the very event that had necessitated the shortening of his chosen weapon. Others well knew, or quickly learnt, not to make cheap jokes of the result, and Ryza felt a strange urge to hold himself to the same standard. He had to carry himself equal to others if he were to carry a rifle with them, and there were plenty of them to go around.

After all, the two main wielders of clunky weapons were gone and scattered. The walking fortress of Revance had become a mass of shattered slag, trapped in the infernal heat of an oddity known as a rebel sun, another remnant from those-of-glass. Ryza had carried the rebel sun back into the heart of the mess and down into the flux-tainted tunnels in order to purge the place of it, almost losing himself along the way.

Without Revance to fight back against them, the smelters had little need for arms of their own. The problem was, the rest of the Droughtlands had little need for them as well. Molten flux had become far more volatile in the wake of Revance's fall. It was now near impossible to store it, let alone shovel it into corpses to create the autominds needed to control the factories that had produced the rifles.

A chain that had been broken at every link.

It was something Ryza should've been happy with, but while there were still smelters left to hunt, he would know no rest.

Not until I find this smelter.

Word was generally a slow thing to spread across the rolling dunes of the Droughtlands. Between the shantytowns and sandstone cities, the mines and the high-mountain fields, there was little reason to travel. Little to see along the way, and little to be gained at a destination other than a small pouch of reels for the goods carried there, most of which would need to be spent for the journey back.

It was another thing that the volatility of flux and Revance's fall had changed. With no factories to feed and no smelters to fight, many places simply lost their reason for being. What good was there in extracted ores from the ground if there was no one coming to collect them? What good was a furnace if it were to burn on empty?

This lack of trade had stoked a new kind of movement. People. Armies without arms, marching in their hundreds, sometimes their thousands, from their freshly abandoned towns and onwards to the tall walls of Breggesa, the largest city in the Droughtlands.

A year ago, it would've been rare for the stories and sightings carried with them to swap across mouths and ears. But now, they formed a gossiping web of rumours to help Ryza and the other ex-conscripts track down the last of the smelters and their flux-trader masters.

As Ryza readjusted his grip on the rifle's handle, he winced at the knobbly discomfort of a poorly placed rivet under the ball of his thumb. A replacement was never as good as the original, but a rifle was one thing he couldn't do without, even if the damn thing threatened to leap from his hand each time he fired it.

Only going to be a problem four times today.

His ammo satchel bounced off his chest as he forced himself into a jog. It was light. Just as light as it had been when he'd set out from their camp on the outskirts of Breggesa's reaches, but the unremarkable journey here didn't make Ryza feel any more well-stocked for the fight he was imagining.

Even if it had been the goal of those aboard the walking fortress of Revance to purge those who ran the automind-powered factories, it was impossible to get around the fact that they were the very place all their munitions had come from. Their success could only lead to a plunging deficit in their supplies, meaning that the last flux trader would need to be defeated with practically bare hands.

Perhaps someone was out there making more rifle slugs themselves, labouring away at the tedious yet dangerous process of funnelling precise amounts of blast powder into even more precisely sized brass casings, but they'd likely have the good sense to keep the products of their work to themselves, if only to protect their meagre supply.

This left Ryza and the others to rely on the dwindling stockpiles older than they were. Munition dumps that were buried in a time when Revance's clashes with the smelters could be measured in days, not minutes. The results of those battles only produced more corpses. More stock to be turned into autominds. More capacity for the factories that had armed both sides of the fight.

Ryza paused at a corner, pretending to check each empty direction down the trenches as he allowed himself to shudder. The idea of a corpse made to walk again was just as disturbing today as it had been when he'd first been shown them fourteen years ago as a small boy. Of course, how was it possible to explain to such a boy the thrill of power that it was to have an extra mind with which to control machines?

Ryza started walking again, his vision half-blind as he tried not to think of his father's business, or just how close he'd come to carrying on his legacy. He carried his father's green eyes, his father's gift as a Kretatic, an ability to control metal, warping it into semi-autonomous contraptions named arcanites, and the same limits shared by all Kretatics that only so much metal could be held inside their minds at any one time.

A limit that autominds helped surpass.

He stopped and shuddered again, leaning his shoulder heavily against the side of the trench. There were no corners to blindly glance down this time, no way to continue to delay his approach. He gathered himself. The memories of his father may be paralysing, but the thought of not being the first to the inevitable fray was far more motivating.

The rusted tops of the outpost came into view as Ryza wound his way further through the trenches, and he forced his gait into a low crouch. One thing Eyla hadn't been able to discern from her airborne scouting runs was who'd originally built the place. Its original purpose was unclear.

Three squat, rounded structures marked the bounds of the installation. The walls were interlocking plates of once white metal that warped around their frames like loosely layered belts, peeling away at some points to reveal dark hollows within. They'd survived sandstorms, looting, the general wear of time, and the constant rust that plagued the Droughtlands. Their longevity was a worrying sign.

The only other thing that had lasted this long in the constantly burying desert were the skyscrapers left by those-of-glass. Even calling those towers of dark windows and perfectly machined windows by the name of "skyscraper" was a forbidden piece of knowledge Ryza knew not to share with the two ex-conscripts travelling with him. Doing so would prompt them to ask all sorts of dangerous questions about the mysteries that lay buried below them.

But despite these structures looking nothing like skyscrapers, they were still just as unnerving.

Elya had estimated each structure to be ten metres tall and twice as wide, but as the nearest one loomed over Ryza, he'd wished he'd let her scout closer to the damn things. Thirty smelters would be able to comfortably garrison each one as if it were a fortress, and smelters weren't the type to just do things comfortably. And that was before he thought of what else could be hidden within them.

Atop the nearest structure was another trophy of expertly crafted metal. Ryza wasn't sure if it was an alloy or something the people of the Droughtlands were yet to rediscover, but being near it unnerved him. A Kretatic could often sense a metal's presence innately. It rang out to them like the end of a bell's chime, yet this thing was silent.

It was a round plate double the width of the building itself, its surface slightly sunken while the supporting pylons pointed its centre towards a spot in the midmorning sky somewhere to the southwest. From a distance, the ridge-welded seams running along the underside of the shallow dish that connected the composite plates of steel glinted in the day. Strangely, they glinted just as brightly at night. Now that Ryza was close to it, the midday sun pounding down on it, the shallow dish looked utterly inert.

It lent credence to the theory Ryza dreaded admitting. He'd first thought this place was a scraped-together installation made by the smelters as they'd attempted to restart one of their hellish factories. But he'd seen too many patterns in the architecture that had made an almost explainable amount of sense.

Almost.

There was the way that the pipes stretched over Ryza's head as he squatted in the trench, arranged in rows of four as they spanned out from one building, almost reached another, and then turned back. Not only was it nigh purposeless for the pipes to loop so far from their point of origin, but the sheer weight of the metal had no way to defy gravity as it did, no supports to keep it from crashing into the trenches below.

And yet it did.

Then there were the nonsensical routes the trenches laid across the land. Ryza had heard of similar arrangements running through mining towns, where buzzing conveyor belts ferried streams of ground-up rock along to nearby refineries. But the only thing under Ryza's boots now was the thin mesh of metal keeping him from the sandy ground, another inch below that.

The second day they'd spent observing the installation, Ryza had attempted to map the trenches, but had woken on the third day to find they'd all shifted. Simply changed their routes to a better liking without having the courtesy to wake him in the night and tell him his map was now useless. Either that, or he wasn't quite the cartographist he'd led himself to believe.

There were plenty of places in the Droughtlands where the mundane was still something that defied all sense of reason and purpose, and Ryza would be a fool to deny it now. In the past, more scholarly minds had attempted to assign meaning to such places, yet this had often led to catastrophic results.

It's how molten flux was discovered, after all.

He couldn't help recalling his meeting with that old scholar and the way he'd all but thrown him out of that small hovel he'd taken refuge in upon finding out that Ryza had come from Revance's ranks. That scholar was likely dead now, along with thousands of others who hadn't escaped the tunnels of Kyrea.

And I'll be joining them if I don't fucking pay attention!

While he'd been lost in thought, Ryza's pace had grown gentle, and he hadn't realised that the trenches had led him into the midst of the three structures. He was among the guts of what appeared to be a machine yard. All was silent around him. He'd witnessed firsthand the bizarre, unbound magic and the indecipherable technology that could be found in similar places. Even something as small as an ill-timed breath could be enough to trigger a horrifying effect.

The trenches could shift while Ryza was still sneaking through them, leaving him buried in whatever mix of sand and rock came to replace the gap. He was sure plenty had died that way before, but the commonality of such an end didn't make it any more appealing. Either way, Ryza had looked down the barrel of worse fates. Mustering his quiet bravado into action, Ryza moved a few steps along and started making his way out of the trench.

A set of low-hanging tubes had twisted in their course to run parallel above the trenches, low enough that Ryza could reach them. They were a copper colour, unpolished and somehow unscratched, considering their age. He waited for a quiet to come after the sound of his bootsteps had died out, then stretched up to quickly give a series of soft taps to the pipes with the muzzle of his rifle. The first three were utterly silent. Only the fourth made a dull clang. Ryza tapped it again, making sure the sound wasn't a fluke, then stowed his rifle and reached up to grab it with his right hand.

His shoulder creaked and popped as he hauled himself upwards, but he didn't let his dangling feet come anywhere near the walls of the trench. The leverage would make the action easier, but this bit of the trench didn't look right. There wasn't a speck of rust on the walls, the first clear patch Ryza had seen so far.

Over the lip of the trench, his boots landed with a pair of clunks. He was standing on a surface of metal grating that covered flat rock an inch below it. Ryza scanned his surroundings. There was little to see. The remains of ancient machines surrounded him in well-organised blocks, patiently waiting for someone to maintain them.

They looked like workstations, designed for a crew of a lone worker to modify a part in some forgotten way. All the tools and instruments hung over the empty yet dust-strewn desks on curved rods that arched like the tails of scorpions. Ryza wondered why the work would need to take place outside, but then again, maybe this place wasn't always "outside."

As he began picking his way through the workstations, his rifle once again drawn and held across his chest, he was reminded of being back aboard Revance. The heat of the forge rooms was exacerbated by the tight, wrought iron confines that contained the cramped halls, so perhaps it would be a relief to be working under the sun.

A comfort to some...

On the whole, Kretatics weren't strangers to their work having them be sequestered beneath the ground or far away from the sky. But that didn't mean others had to like it. Curiktics, like Vhoze was, bore eyes as yellow as the sun, betraying their affinity for light and fire. It was only natural they'd loathe to be away from sunlight, but at least they didn't fear such a thing.

That was the superstition of Reythurists. They were afraid of dying away from the sky. An old belief, where a Reythurist that perished underground, or even under a roof, was destined to do the exact same in the next life. It was a fear of both a dreadful end and a certain fate that chilled them, something that Ryza had only found out in brief, jarring lessons, and only once he'd already lost two Reythurist friends in such a way. It pained Ryza too much to think of their names.

Today will not make it a third.

He pushed the thoughts aside. Dwelling on them would only make them burrow deeper within him, and his mind was a crowded place. In the shade of one of the ancient workstations, Ryza squatted until he could fall back that last inch to sit down, landing on his haunches. He couldn't keep blundering through this place with such a busy mind. What if there was an ambush? As vulnerable as it made him, he needed to focus on devising a plan.

The smelters had to be around somewhere. The last town Ryza and the others had passed through assured them this was the only place to go for miles, and Elya was resolute that she'd seen movement around the large shed with rippling walls at the centre of the installation. If Ryza's reckoning was correct, it would be nearby, even if it was just out of sight.

And yet, there was no sign of them. Idly, Ryza brushed the gathered grains of rust from his boots. He started to wonder why he hadn't found anything to shoot at but promptly stopped as the puffs of debris from his boots simply disappeared as it passed through the metal grating. He peered through to the dull orange surface of rock below. Not a single piece of rust, not a single stray rivet, lay there.

Strange...

He stood up, readied his rifle, and proceeded forwards. The machine stations formed waist-high alleys for him to skulk in, but there still didn't seem to be anyone to hide from. The blown pools of amber-coloured sand hadn't been cleared from the small crevices where they'd been gathered, so he doubted anyone had figured out a way to put them to use. Perhaps they were too afraid to touch anything that lay outside the squat, semi-walled structures the massive dishes rested on.

A clear strip of walkway lay between the rows of machines and the nearest wall of faltering white panels. The walkway was raised about a foot from where he stood, circling the structure's perimeter. Ryza waited to step onto it. Observed the mesh of grey metal for irregularities, then checked for sentries and nested watchmen with patient rifles. Even looked for the slightest haze in the air that seemed wrong. But nothing was wrong. Nothing out of the ordinary at all.

That was what worried him the most.

Three quick steps took him across the walkway and into the nearest rip in the structure's wall. The interior swallowed him in darkness, and he forced himself to wait again as his eyes adjusted to the gloom. A clearing had been gouged into the centre of the large room. The ancient machines had been ripped from their housings to make way for rows of improvised cots that bore bundled and thrown-aside coverings. Between them were overturned crates that held only the crumbs of the food they'd once transported. The floor, a mesh like outside, only held loose piles of discarded clothes that'd become too tattered to wear.

Ryza walked slowly among the scene, his rifle lowered but his ears still twitching. There were far too many clothes. Enough to cover twenty or thirty people, if they all weren't laying in shredded tatters under each of the cots. The way they'd deteriorated didn't make sense, either. They weren't frayed at the edges, but instead in strange lines across their lengths that Ryza could only discern by leaning down until his nose was practically brushing against the thinning fabric. He pulled back and kicked a shirt over. It crumpled and then lay flat on the grates. The grid-like pattern ate away at the rough cloth, perfectly matching the flooring under it.

Ryza lurched backwards, dancing quickly off the grating until he found something more solid to stand on, not caring that his boots were making more noise than he had in the past three days. He found sanctuary on a low strip of railing near the room's edge and made sure to balance carefully as he checked the soles of his boots.

He'd only been walking on the grating for a matter of minutes, yet somehow the leather there was already beginning to deform. Part of him wanted to take one of them off to check on the foot within, but that would be another ordeal he didn't have time for. For now, he just had to trust the leather was thick enough for the short time he was to be here.

At least it explains what happened to the rest of the smelters.

They must've just fallen asleep in here one night and melted through the ground itself. Would it have been painless? It had to be, otherwise the screams of the others would've awoken the survivors. Only a few would've been so lucky, worked out what would've happened to their comrades, then moved their lodgings to the safer chambers above. As Ryza moved nimbly towards the stairs, jumping between the vacant feet of the machine frames to avoid the grating itself, he hoped that Elya and Vhoze had worked out to avoid the grating as he just had.

The stairs to the next floor of the structure's internals were mercifully solid, and Ryza slowed his pace again as he climbed. They only took him a few metres from the ground, but the wind was whistling through the place like he was on the edge of the sky. A missing panel in the internal wall at the upper landing was likely the source for this. He paused at the edge of it, standing so only half his face was touched by the streaming sun.

It afforded him a good view of the outpost. He could see the squared-off warehouse Elya had been going on and on about. The hastily erected structure was wedged between the other ancient ones. It seemed stupid to even try to fit such a thing there, but there must've been a reason to do so.

Its walls had been cobbled together long after the skins of these other structures, but rust had already eaten through them like scattered shots from rifles. Nevertheless, its exterior was complete, hiding whatever new type of factory the smelters would have been assembling within. Ryza swore to himself. He probably should've investigated that place first.

The heightened view gave him a better look out over the trenches. Large, flat panels of metal had been laid over the top of them. It was rare to see such large sheets of unbroken metal, especially when it was going to waste out here, baking in the sun. Elya hadn't mentioned them after her last flight over the outpost the previous day, so they must've been put there this morning, acting as some kind of road.

Or an escape route.

But Ryza didn't get another moment to survey the scene. His only warning of an interruption was a sudden clanging of boots on the stairs, and before he had a chance to turn and raise his rifle, a tackling force yanked through his waist. He was sent hurtling through the gap in the wall, his shins catching painfully on the edge before he careened towards the ground. There was a screaming in his ears as the grating rushed up to meet him, but he didn't know if it was his own or his attacker's.

He curled just before he hit the ground, bouncing off the grating like a thrown ball. It didn't hurt as much as he'd thought it would. Now sprawled out, he could see why. The fall had only been a bit more than a metre. Even so, it had knocked his senses loose, and it took him a bit too long to realise that his back was now on metal grating and his rifle was no longer in his hand. His attacker didn't give him a chance to remedy this.

She thrashed towards him like a many-limbed beast, rising to her feet and lunging forwards from the ground. It landed her squarely on his unguarded chest. The sudden advantage caught her between raining punches down on him and attempting to throttle his neck, the indecision resulting in an ineffectual assault. Ryza only needed to weakly bat the assault away with his left arm, saving his right to grope for his rifle.

The smelter was wild, rageful and hungry for violence. Her head was bald, not as if she'd shaved it but as if she'd pulled every last hair out herself, leaving behind stretches of angry red welts in rows down her scalp. Her clothes were tattered like the other items that Ryza had found, and more rash-covered skin showed through underneath. Ryza had seen, fought, and killed plenty of smelters in his lifetime. This had to be the most world-ravaged looking one.

Though she wasn't a smelter anymore. There was too much flux to trade, too many autominds leftover, and too many people with the good sense to stay away from the volatile liquid metal.

Still, have to call them something.

The thought felt all too serene to Ryza as his scrabbling right hand finally found something that wasn't rusted floor grating. The grip of his sawn-off rifle felt perfectly familiar in his right hand, but his finger was nowhere near its trigger as he swung it viciously at his attacker. He couldn't see it, but a deeply satisfying crack of metal on barely covered bone came to his ears as the side of the shortened rifle collided with the smelter's arm.

She screeched in pain, and Ryza swung again, his blurry vision only just allowing him to hit the same spot on the woman's forearm, this time breaking one of the fragile bones within. She lurched away from him, freeing his chest so he could suck in a strong breath to replace what had been choked out of him. He rolled to his feet, shoving the smelter out of her kneeling shock, using more force than necessary to make sure she landed in a crumpled heap in the trench next to their scuffle.

Another hard snapping sound came from her. Her screams ceased. All that came afterwards was a soft, pitiful moan as she rolled onto her side, her left forearm now entirely snapped in two. Her breathing quickened as she saw the splintered points of bone and marrow that were threatening to pierce the skin. It was currently bent inwards like a second wrist placed a few inches below the first as she tried to cradle it.

Ryza jumped down into the trench with her, ducking in case a plucky shooter that'd heard the fight was about to plug a hole in his back. At least that would be a quicker death than whatever had happened to the rest of the smelters. He could already feel the skin of his back tingling from his short time on the grating.

The smelter's other hand shuddered and shook. It was hovering an inch from an attempt at correcting the broken limb, and Ryza found himself feeling queasy. It was unusual for a few reasons. He'd seen plenty of violence like this before, most of it inflicted by his own hand, but he'd never stopped to morbidly ogle the product of his work. Why should he now? There wasn't even any blood involved, aside from the few scrapes and scabs the smelter must've had before their tussle began.

The smelter's moans had died out, her breathing just as hard as Ryza's as she gathered her resolve. With a pre-emptive scream of agony, the smelter grabbed her shattered arm at the wrist and straightened it. She looked up at Ryza as she held it in place. Her yellow eyes were desperate and afraid.

Ryza felt his head shake, an instinct carried out to tell the smelter that suffering like this would do no good. He didn't often have mercy for smelters. He used to think that the kind that became smelters were the kind that'd steal sand out of an unwatched pocket. But this felt different.

The smelter relented a few seconds later with a breathless gasp. The broken arm flopped as it was relinquished, the bone once again threatening to punch through her battered skin.

The nausea wasn't coming from Ryza's stomach. It was coming from the battered hunk of scarred flesh that formed the nub just below his left elbow. How it was possible for his limb to disgust his gut was a question for better-honed minds than his, but now he knew exactly why the sight sickened him.

'Near enough what happened to me,' Ryza grunted down at the smelter.

'What?'

He nodded down at his left side. His current greatcoat, a patchwork of repairs and leather scraps that were nothing like the original item he'd received aboard Revance, had suffered a similar injury. His left nub poked out from the shortened sleeve, drawing the smelter's look of utter disbelief. Maybe she was realising she'd just been single-handedly bested, despite having begun her ambush with twice as many working arms.

Or maybe it's because she's figured out who I am.

The lack of a left arm wasn't Ryza's only distinctive feature. Being able to carry on fighting while refusing a metal replacement was, along with his overgrown mane of burningly red hair. They were rare things, and his time aboard Revance had allowed him to carve out a brutal name for himself.

She was scrambling away in terror now, yelping each time she tried to use her crippled arm to push herself further across the grime-crusted floor. Ryza kept his pace slow as he moved with her, making sure that his shortened rifle swung in time with stride. She hit the wall of the sunken metal trench, finally in the shade so only the glow of her yellow eyes was left to show her fear.

'Bloodfist,' she whispered.

'That ain't my name,' Ryza said. 'It ain't who I am anymore.'

'Then... Then... Then who are you?' the smelter asked, twisting to the side and curling up.

Good question.

Ryza knew the smelter was playing for time. Her whimpering wasn't forced, but it was the only thing holding back the merciless reputation she was assigning him. She was utterly pathetic, and the worst part of it was that it wasn't through her own doing. As Ryza's eyes focused enough to see through the stark shadow of the afternoon sun, he could see the youth that'd been stolen from her.

Maybe she was younger than him. Even if she wasn't, she must've been when she had been given the same impossible choice Ryza'd once had when he was a boy.

Make the autominds. Or become them.

In the months since Iroka, Ryza's view of the smelters had somehow softened. Even if it were only slightly. Their choice would've been just as impossible as his. They'd all chosen wrong. All likely had looked back and wished they'd chosen death instead. It was a fate Ryza had become all too adept at meting out, but he'd come to realise he couldn't go on like that or he'd end up massacring half the Droughtlands.

'My name's Ryza,' he eventually said. 'You got a name as well?'

'They call me Foll.'

Ryza glanced down at her arm. 'Breathe through it, Foll. I've had worse.'

'You ain't killing me?' she asked, sounding unsure if the question would prompt a sudden and final answer.

Ryza wrinkled his nose and shook his head. 'You wouldn't be worth the slug. I came here with four of them, and I'm leaving with four of them.'

A pair of rifle shots made Foll jump. The low grumble of clanking metal that followed made Ryza do the same.

'What's that?' he said quickly. 'Your lot got motors?'

But Foll hadn't heard the question. Her jaw was quivering, half from shock and half from disbelief.

'They're leaving me. Without me, they're...'

Another wave churned in Ryza's stomach as she continued to stammer. The fear of being abandoned had inhabited his nightmares ever since he was small, in one form or another. First it had been his father's threats of leaving him to rot out in the dunes if he didn't pour the flux into the vials right. Then, as a conscript of Revance, the well-drilled warning that the metal collar around his neck would drive its spikes through his flesh if he fled the walking fortress.

Even once it had been destroyed and he'd lost nearly all ability to sleep, the nightmares had been replaced by sleepless nights of watching conscript after exhausted conscript wander off into the wastes the battle for the fortress had left, braving the dangers of the flux they were sick of cleaning up for a chance to be away from him. One last dream haunted him. One last abandonment to leave him every night.

Holm.

THE FLUX TRADER

E LYA HAD INSISTED THEY go with him. Vhoze had held her back. *Vhoze was good like that.*

With the other two conscripts begrudgingly caring for the captured smelter, Ryza had set off alone after the mechanical abomination that'd burst from its rust-shackled womb. The massive machine was little more than a cloud of obscuring dust, and the brief glimpse Ryza did manage to catch only showed him the endless sets of wheels kicking it up.

Ryza's first thought had been to pilot the lead-better they'd used to get here as a means of pursuit. He'd quickly quashed the idea. By the time he'd sprinted back to the point just over the horizon where they'd left the vehicle, their quarry would be long gone. Besides, they'd need to burn every last drop of oil they had reserved in order to get back to Breggesa. Wasting it here would force them to walk a considerable distance on foot.

This had left him to pray that whatever else was stored in the shack-like warehouse also had a working engine. If he was lucky, it would be a faster one than what he was about to chase.

He approached the walls of the warehouse quickly. His rifle was raised, and a spare slug was clenched between his back teeth in case he needed a quick follow-up shot. If the smelters had already left one of their number behind, they might as well have left a whole army. He slowed his boots as he moved towards the door, lunging slightly with each step to keep them away from the rusted grating that was becoming unavoidable.

The door was unlocked and hanging ajar by its last hinge, but through force of habit, Ryza readied himself to kick it in like he'd been taught. He reared back on his right foot, temporarily planting his left against a section of the wall next to where the latch would be as he mustered his strength into a body-tensing breath. Then, as one, he exhaled sharply, lifting his boot again and forcing both the power of the kick and his entire balance into the metal.

It slammed into the floor with a clang, and Ryza staggered in after it, waving his rifle around like a torch warding off rodents, but the only thing that moved was his shadow, cast in from the light at his back. He swept through the warehouse quickly enough —the place was picked clean as it was— and stowed his rifle as he approached the ramshackle vehicle sitting in the far corner of the room.

It's like they left it just for me.

At least he thought it was a vehicle. It had wheels, three of them, two spread on a wide axle at the front and a larger one stretched out on an arching support strut at the rear. Under that strut was an engine, though it was unlike anything Ryza had ever seen.

It was a long, solid block of metal, some kind of confused, improvised, and now nameless alloy, that was punctured at arbitrary intervals by inert pistons and valves that were arranged with no care for ridiculous concepts such as friction or alignment. If he leaned in close, he could smell how fresh the welds were between particular sections of it, as if it had been pieced together that very morning.

The last thing it needed to actually be a vehicle was something to steer with and a seat in which to do it from. Ryza had to crouch down in front of it to spot the mixture of rods and levers that poked out from under the front axle. These controls could only be accessed if he were lying flat on the large, scoop-like carriage that covered the majority of the vehicle's face.

Ryza glanced out the large hole the previous departure of this warehouse had created. The vehicle was nothing but off-cuts, potentially with the thought of creating a lightweight scrap hauler. Either that or a machinist with nothing better to do. As Ryza lowered himself into the supposedly intended piloting position, he couldn't help but laugh under his breath at the absurdity of the contraption. It was like trying to drive a lead-better while strapped to the front of its armoured plate.

He quickly found he needn't have been so dismissive of the smelter's engineering. After pulling three of the six levers his right hand could reach, the rickety vehicle's engine sputtered into life. The front of the motor was positioned between his boots and served as the only way to keep his body from sliding off the tilting plane of metal he was lying on. Its high-pitched, whining action forced him to clench his legs tighter around it, the sudden vibrations making his teeth chatter like misaligned cogs.

The feeling only grew worse as he threw a few more levers, kicking the engine over a couple missing gears until it found one that'd been installed. It lurched into action. Ryza only had seconds to find the steering vane as it picked up speed, and his grunts of exertion were lost as the engine popped and banged even louder. There was a clash of steel as the vehicle's right wheel clipped the edge of the warehouse's wall. Ryza glanced at it, his worry for it being damaged allayed when he saw it was a round plate of solid metal.

The vehicle jolted and jumped as Ryza attempted to manoeuvre the hefty wheels across the bridging paths that'd been laid out for him. Occasionally, one of his wheels would swing out over the voids left by the trenches, but he'd already picked up so much speed that he cleared the gaps before the vehicle had a chance to fall into them.

He wasted a moment glancing back at where he'd left Elya and Vhoze, but the two of them were already specks in the distance, the outpost itself quickly shrinking to a similar size. He was going concerningly fast, though he didn't want to wonder how the smelters had created such an engine with what little resources and expertise they had access to. They were as industrious as they were reckless. He'd already seen what happened when smelters attempted to manufacture things in the places left by those-of-glass.

A factory of factories. Good thing it's gone.

With all the rubble and dust kicking up into his face, Ryza had to wedge the steering vane into a shallow turn to the left as he quickly searched the pockets of his greatcoat. First, he found his goggles. They were cracked beyond repair, the "beyond" of that owing to the fact he had become so stubbornly short of reels that he refused to have them replaced. He used the nub of his left arm to pin them to his forehead as he used his other hand to wrangle the leather strap around the back of his head. Once that was in place, he pulled them down.

He felt his breathing quicken, though it was hard to tell whether the quaking motion of the vehicle was more in control of his lungs than he was.

In the satchel at his waist, clinking off of the two remaining slugs in there, was a vent mask. He pulled it out and bit down on the strap, exchanging his jaw's grip on it for the slug that was tingling at his cheek. If he punctured the soft brass of the casing, he'd have a mouthful of blast powder on top of a worthless hunk of lead, but he stowed it back in his satchel without checking.

He hesitated before putting the vent mask to his mouth, using the excuse of readjusting the vehicle's steering vane to buy him a few more seconds to freely breathe the dust-filled air. Maybe he shouldn't bother putting it on. Maybe he could just cough his way through all the dust and grit that coated his tongue. But as he looked ahead at the near-sandstorm his quarry was kicking up, he knew he had no choice.

He put the angular metal mask to his mouth and pinned it there with his left, clenching his eyes shut as he tried not to go back to the dream he'd had where it had been a part of his skin. He failed. He could imagine Holm before him, his lover, naked with skin of silver, gouging her fingers between the steel and his flesh as she tore it from his face.

By the time he'd cleared the image from his mind, the mask's straps were secured and his breathing was now accompanied by the disconcerting *hiss-click* of the vent mask. They'd been given them in case they ran into any molten flux, quantities large enough that it turned into blazing flux. That was its volatile gaseous form that billowed out if it were gathered in more than a bucketful. But Ryza knew the masks would do little to protect him from it. He'd seen a woman in a sealed and armoured suit fall to the flux, so this mask would buy him seconds at most if he were exposed.

It's better than nothing.

As uncomfortable as it was, the mask was doing an adequate enough job of protecting him from the growing trail of dust ahead of him. After a few slipped or missing gears, he found another lever he could jam forwards. It urged the vehicle to skitter along the barren land even faster. In another minute, he would catch up to his quarry.

The vehicle plunged into the dust cloud, and Ryza was blind. He counted his heartbeats. They were faint against the thrum of the engine. After eight beats, he burst out the other side of the haze and discovered his newly commandeered vehicle had taken him wildly off course. His quarry was still a hundred metres ahead, even further than that to the left. He swore. Every extra minute of this pursuit added what he was sure would be another hour of trekking back to the others.

But he couldn't be annoyed for long. It turned out the whining motor of the rickety little vehicle was doing him a favour, as a massive rent in the ground had opened up to his left, forming a shallow, cliff-lined basin that nothing would've survived crashing into. He grunted as he forced the steering vane nearer to the rushing ledge, taking the vehicle a few metres closer to his target to get a better look at it. It made little difference. The damn thing was enormous as it was.

There were many orders of magnitude between the two largest vehicles Ryza had ever seen. The first was obviously Revance, a walking fortress that had once strode across the Droughtlands on four gargantuan legs while housing an army of thousands of soldiers, dozens of vehicles, and enough supplies to keep them battling for months at a time.

The second largest was a treadhulk, which was a boxy mass of armoured plates that could carry twenty and little else, transporting itself around on four sets of interlocking treads that were just as efficient as Revance's soldiers when it came to severing stray hands or daring fingers. Revance would've carried eight of them in its motor pool alone.

The hulking construct before him was no match for Revance, but it still left Ryza dumbstruck. He only became aware that he'd forgotten to breathe the whole time he'd been staring at it when his ears registered the distinct lack of a *hiss-click* from his vent mask.

Four carriages sprouting batteries of whirring treads held up the massive vehicle's hindquarters. Ryza would've thought it overkill, but the exposed gaps in its armoured back showed clustered bulks of machinery and equipment that would likely weigh more than the sum of their parts.

As the basin dividing them narrowed and Ryza strayed closer, he realised what he was seeing. It was a factory. A *mobile* factory that could be taken anywhere safe from the taint of the useless flux in places like Kyrea or Iroka. That was the most recent problem with flux. It was a substance that only existed to please the wants of those that witnessed it, so when all that flew through the air was superstition and doubt, it was all too happy to contort itself to those terrifying shapes, making it useless for the old ways of industry that had propagated it so much.

The motor screeched between Ryza's knees as he urged it to go faster, pulling level with the trundling factory but still keeping fifty metres from its right flank. Even at a quick glance, he'd spotted half a dozen silent gun ports at its rear, but he was sure they wouldn't remain vacant for much longer.

This side of the factory exposed more of its guts. The armour plating only extended up from its belly to a metre or two of its ribs. The next seven metres of its height was an open cross section filled with more machines, more dormant forges that would eventually be unpacked, more covered trays of raw materials, more scurrying smelters, and the one thing Ryza dreaded seeing most.

More autominds.

The huddle of corpses swayed with the whipping wind and quaking motion at the factory's highest deck. Ryza could see the iron cables at their necks. They'd been tressed across their scarred and filthy bodies to bind them together as a single bundle of compressed, sickening misery. Molten flux dripped from the wounds that'd taken their lives, leaving the smelters operating the machine below to dance and twist out of the way of the deadly stuff as it fell.

Volleys of cracks broke out over the whinging hum of his vehicle's motor and the deep trembling grinding sound of the factory's treads. The smelters had noticed him and had far more ammunition to spare than he did. Puffs of sand and thrown dust shot up from the ground in front of him, and Ryza frantically started pulling levers in order to reduce his speed.

His vehicle slowed, gradually veering left as it did so for a reason Ryza couldn't work out. Soon he was behind the massive factory again, and this time the smelters had made it to their firing positions. Ryza hesitated as he reached for the handle of his rifle that was tucked under his chest. He still had a few runes on his right wrist from the expedition into the tunnels below Iroka.

He hadn't been able to bring himself to use a single one in the three months since, not for an aversion to the magic that'd led to so much destruction, but instead because he wasn't even sure it would work.

The fateful expedition had been the second time he'd had a brush with the unbound magic that'd wiped out those-of-glass. But then again, he wasn't fully sure if it had been their magic and not just the product of the molten flux's mimicry of it, or if none of it was real at all and—

A slug pinged off the armoured covering that Ryza was lying on, so close to his hip that he was sure it had punched yet another hole through his tattered greatcoat. Ryza brushed aside his indecision and grabbed his rifle, levelling it at the closest gunport his vehicle continued to drift across the factory's rear.

The batteries of clanking treads threw up a fierce haze of dust, but squinting through his goggles, Ryza waited patiently to see a movement. Another pair of shots struck his vehicle before he had a chance to pull the trigger of his own rifle, but when he did, he was rewarded with the sight of a splatter of blood and a dropped rifle tumbling down to the speeding ground.

As his vehicle continued to drift, he wedged his rifle under his chest, broke it open, and stuffed another slug in, snapping it shut to repeat the action once he'd found his next target. After firing a third slug, his vehicle had well and truly crossed out the other side of the factory's wake. Shots were still impacting the ground around his fragile little vehicle, but they were coming at a frequency far more relaxed than before.

Ryza jammed his final slug into his rifle and holstered it. The red markings on the outside of its brass casing meant he was to save it to kill something that he knew could not be killed by normal means. He shuddered at the memory of the last time he'd used such a munition.

It was a fight in itself not to think of doing so again.

The sound of another screeching motor joined his, and the two oil-fuelled screeches battled in the air as Ryza looked up at his little vehicle's sudden rival. The rolling factory was on to him. At the very peak of the factory's canopy was a bulbous turret. He recognised the exact one; it had once hung upside down in between Revance's right legs to deter skirmishers.

Now it was the right way up, the configuration of its plated armour doing little to protect the smelter manning it. Its original gun, a low-powered mortar that dropped crater-blasting shells, was gone, replaced with something that fired much smaller munitions.

Ryza's eyes went wide behind his goggles, and he ducked, covering his head as best he could with his right arm as the smelter's motorised weapon spun up to its firing pitch. While it wasn't an exact copy, it was similar to the weapon that Ryza had retrieved from the hands of a traitor in the flux fields of Iroka, which had been re-engineered into something the ex-conscripts dubbed the "R-Three."

Carrying its own motor and fuel tank, its array of rapidly spinning flywheels propelled endless streams of lead pellets down a thin barrel towards its intended target. It had never been accurate, but why should it need to be? A hundred pellets were coming along with it.

The lead pellets hammered down on his vehicle's frame, stinging as they struck Ryza's back but not bringing with them enough force to penetrate the reinforced leather of his greatcoat. Range was the one drawback of the R-Three. Beyond twenty metres, it was more of an annoyance. The whine of the smelter's weapon died out of the air, and Ryza twisted onto his back, pulling out his rifle as he went.

Between the jolting path of his own vehicle and the swaying motion of the factory, it would be a miracle if his next shot hit anything, let alone the narrow slit in the protective turret housing that the smelter was cowering in. Even then, Ryza would need to either hit them directly in the gut to set their innards alight or get even luckier and have the incendiary slug ricochet around the confined metal space, impact the fuel reserves of the smelter's weapon, and cause an explosion that'd incinerate them.

Ryza pulled the trigger. The rifle kicked down hard at him, driving his wrist painfully into his chest as a trumpet of fire escaped the muzzle. Somewhere within it, the slug roared forth, threading between the metal slit of the turret, clanging off the rusted roof, and then homing back down for the very same fuel tank that Ryza doubted it would ever hit.

The roof of the turret was catapulted into the sky as the pillar of fire propelling it momentarily put the sun to shame. More explosions rocked the factory in a chain of blasts that slipped back and forth across its flanks.

Still on his back, Ryza flinched with each shockwave. His rifle had been knocked out of his hand from the first, so all he could do was grope blindly at the levers just past his head to find the one that would get him away from the moving factory before it was nothing more than a crater. He pulled the first one his fingers found and got lucky again. His vehicle jerked, threatening to throw him off, and veered further to the left as one final explosion rocked the metal monstrosity.

A cloud of silver mist joined the billowing black smoke as a storm of junk, fragmented machines, and broken autominds were thrown skywards. They thumped and splattered around him as his vehicle valiantly carried him away from the carnage.

Once the chaos had stopped, Ryza set about kicking his vehicle's motor until the fuel pump came loose and it died out. Its wheels halted in seconds, and Ryza was almost bodily thrown to the ground, only saved when his left boot got tangled in a transmission line. He didn't waste time tearing the vent mask and goggles from his face and vigorously massaging the biting marks that the metal rims of the protective had made.

'I hate wearing these fucking things,' he said under his breath, the words merely a means to exercise out the stiffness in his jaw.

There were many ways that the events of Iroka had changed him. Many of them he was yet to discover, but of the few he had, the first had been that anything even slightly touching his head was enough to trigger a sudden and volatile rage in him that he struggled to quell in the days afterwards. The quirk was the only one that he'd been able to trace a cause to, for it reminded him of being trapped in the tight confines of the vent suit, the heavily armoured garments that he'd worn into the tunnels under Iroka.

The vent suit was supposed to protect him from the unpredictable effects of how much molten flux was down there. Despite emerging from the ordeal physically unscathed, he'd since spent a lot of time wondering if he really had escaped the flux. As he dismounted the rickety vehicle and looked back on his path of destruction, his eyes found another way to add doubt to his survival.

Bodies still stood where the autominds had fallen. But they weren't the autominds themselves. Their flesh and corrupted blood was splattered across the sands in the small craters they'd made on impact. No, the figures that stood in their place were far more intact than they should be, and with silver eyes they stared.

Looking at me.
Looking like me.

CHAPTER THREE

RETURN

THE DAY WORE ON slowly as Ryza made sure to walk the roughest, rockiest path back towards the outpost. It added maybe another hour to the sunsetting journey, but it didn't bother him. Not as long as it was bothering the flux trader that he'd captured, hogtied, bound, gagged, blindfolded, then unceremoniously stuffed into the sack he was dragging across the sharp ground from over his shoulder.

Despite the flux trader being the only survivor, many pairs of eyes had watched Ryza go.

My eyes.

The factory had been a tangle of wreckage to pick through in his search for his quarry. He had wondered how such an enormous construct had been able to move with nothing but motors alone. The truth he'd found was that there were more than engines driving it. It had all been controlled as an arcanite. Perhaps multiple arcanites, judging by the remnants he'd found of crude, interlocking hooks that'd kept massive sections of the vehicle together.

Multiple Kretatics didn't stand a chance at forcing their control on a shared arcanite. Their magnetic resonances, signature little notes of each Kretatic's own method of controlling metal, would duel and feud, unable to make peace with each other before the contraption had fallen apart. But that didn't matter if the contraptions were only held together by means of physical force instead of a magnetic one. This had all been aided by the batteries of autominds that Ryza had found lying limp and dormant as he'd picked his way through the tilted halls of the wreck.

Like those that'd been explosively ejected from the factory's upper tier, the flux had escaped these worn corpses too. It had wasted little time manifesting into the rows of identical likenesses of Ryza himself, only missing a few key differences.

For one, the way they stared. Their heads tilted and turned with each of Ryza's movements, their silvery eyes flashing as temptations at the corners of his vision for him to return their gaze, yet he made sure not to. Each time he'd been met with molten flux since Iroka, since losing Holm to—

She was already gone!

His violent thought cut off any attempt at grief, and he yanked at the handle of the sack he was dragging, adjusting his grip so the rough cords cut harder into his shoulder and back as means of a distraction. This was one of the few times he almost wished the second difference between himself and the likenesses in the flux did not exist. Ryza did not need to look them in the eye to see that they had both their hands.

There were some days where he could still feel the fingers at the end of his left, twitching and tingling. But these moments were uncommon. If he was lucky, he could now go weeks without feeling the inwards twist of the flesh at the end of his left nub.

This imperfection, whether it lay with him or with the imitations in the flux, told Ryza that they weren't simply copying him, nor the idea he had of himself. It was the ideas that the flux fed off, ideas of the living, or at least what it thought was living. It was how Maligar had conjured his own image into the face of the molten flux, manifesting it a thousand times over until it had been tainted with the thought of what had been his first death.

It was also the idea that was creating all these inert statues of Ryza, all these altered copies, was using them for the same reason, if only for the opposite outcome. The last words that Ryza had uttered as he'd tried to untangle the subject came to his mind.

Creating a version of her from the version of me that's a version of how she sees me... She'll be fucking unstoppable.

In the three months since he had said them, he'd tried to add as little to the idea as he could.

Because that's what she wants.

The tip of Ryza's shadow reached the dusty, beaten-up armoured plate at the front of their lead-better, and he joined it a few minutes later. Vhoze had wasted a rune to summon a glow orb and wedged it in the front bumper of the lead-better. He was sitting next to it, his skinny backside perched on the metal rim, his bones hooked in enough that he could sway from side to side with the coming night's breeze. His arms were crossed and he looked impatient, but then again, under the unruly mop of hair he'd viciously tried to cut with his own knife, his sharpened eyebrows and yellow eyes made him look like he was on the verge of constantly shouting.

Vhoze wore a greatcoat similar to Ryza's, but he'd at least gone to the effort of finding similar patches of leather to repair the inevitable holes that'd occurred. Vhoze was a conscript Ryza had seen the least of in their short time aboard Revance, but it turned out it was because he'd been quickly recruited into the cooking brigade of the fortress.

As the ex-conscripts' numbers had dwindled in Iroka during the ill-fated cleanup, Vhoze had soon become their only cook, and once a replacement had come in the form of the Scythes, the other conscripts had forbidden Vhoze from picking up a roasting spit again. Still, he was a decent, if cautious, shot with a rifle, two characteristics Ryza valued having around for hunts like these when it came to keeping folk like Elya in check.

Elya was some distance away from the lead-better, just beyond the reach of the glow orb, and stood on a pile of rocks that framed her gangly shape against the coming night sky. She was squinting, waiting for the first stars to appear, murmuring to herself as if they'd tell her which way would take them home. She was a more experienced soldier than Vhoze, and while none of the other ex-conscripts could claim to have had as many run-ins with smelters as Ryza, she would still try to find ways to make it seem she was close.

She had a fraying hedge of short, tainted blonde hair that ran across the spine of her skull, which flowed into smoother strands as it grew towards her ears, not that she'd let it get that long. She kept her knife sharp so she could trim it with gusto as if it were some kind of morning ritual and had even offered to do the same to Vhoze and Ryza. They'd both refused for vastly different reasons.

The last face Ryza's tired eyes saw was that of the smelter turned prisoner, Foll. She was sat in the rear tray of the lead-better on the other side of the glow orb to where Ryza was approaching from, so it had taken him a while to make out the sullen look of surrender on her face.

Ryza threw the sack aside and kicked it for unnecessarily good measure, producing a grunt from the bastard within, and moved to the lead-better to inspect his first captive.

Her left arm was swollen and red within the tight bounds of the bronze rods that were keeping it splinted in place. She winced as she shied away from him, shuffling to the other side of the lead-better's tray. Ryza let out an exasperated sigh and walked around the vehicle, catching her by the scruff of her coat before she could do it again. Aside from the usual cuts and aged bruises, she looked reasonably intact.

'You know we don't have enough food for her,' Vhoze said, two steps away from Ryza's shoulder.

'I know,' he replied.

'Doesn't seem like you to spare her. Why?'

Ryza didn't look back at him. Foll had just looked from Vhoze to her broken arm and had tried to shift again to hide it but was still caught in the grip of Ryza's right hand.

'She can tell us things,' Ryza muttered.

'Like what?' Elya called over from her rock perch. 'I'm assuming that's a flux trader in the bag, ain't it? They can tell us everything. Besides, she ain't said a thing the whole time you were gone.'

Foll muttered something, but seemed to regret it, trailing off halfway through.

'What?' Ryza snapped.

She shook her head, and Ryza realised his grip had been tightening on her clothes. He let go, and Foll scootched away as he'd expected.

'They ain't asked me nothing yet,' she muttered as she went.

Ryza threw his hand out in frustration as he turned back to the two of his companions, momentarily speechless.

'You wanted us to talk to a smelter?' Vhoze asked incredulously. '*You?*'

'I've been gone for hours! You've had nothing else to do with yourselves!'

'That's the truth of it!' Elya strode over, grinning until Ryza stared her into a halt. 'What? Nothing is all we did on Revance. Fuck, it's all we seemed to do in Iroka until the Scythes came along and turned the place into glass.'

'We didn't do *nothing*!' Ryza spat.

'We might as well have,' Vhoze replied. 'We were just sitting around waiting for someone to come and tell us what to do, and any time we came up with that something ourselves, we just made it all worse. That's what we're doing now, isn't it? Just puttering around out here because someone told us to and then puttering back until we hear it all again. That's what we're going to do now, because I don't see why you'd drag a sack that big back here for nothing.'

'Ryza thinks he's always dragging a big sack,' Elya cried out.

Vhoze laughed, and even Foll surrendered a small, whimpering chuckle, but Ryza kept his composure. There was an indignant rage sparking inside him that he was fighting to suppress. When he next spoke, it was through a set of clenched teeth.

'Doesn't matter if we made it worse. What matters is that we got to make that choice. That we had control over it.'

'That's a metal mouth thing, ain't it?'

Foll's voice was small owing to her still being huddled in the tray of the lead-better, but Ryza's ears had twitched at the slur. He'd been called it many times before, but it barely affected him now. There were more important, more personal things to lash out about.

'Why?' Ryza asked her, moving back to the lead-better to glare down at her wispy yellow eyes.

'Because I ain't one of you. But I was a smelter. I ain't denying it. But I heard tales about you. Who you are and what you were meant to be, so don't go thinking you're any better than me.'

Ryza's fist clenched on the lip of the lead-better's tray where it'd been resting, but Foll's train of thought mercifully diverted from where he was afraid it was going.

'That's what your lot want. That an' the flux traders and all of 'em that're making machines. Control. Take all the metal you can, then when you run out of that, you move on to the folks that gave it to you.' She nodded to the sack that was still laying in the dirt. 'That's what he was like.'

'The flux trader?' Vhoze said quickly.

Vhoze made for the bag to open it, but Ryza stepped quickly into his way. The man in the sack groaned softly, and Ryza gave him a harsh kick to shut him up.

'I need to check he's alive,' Vhoze said, holding Ryza back from delivering another kick.

'If he survived that, he'll be fine,' Eyla said, nodding off to the horizon from where Ryza had come.

Dregs of black smoke still wafted through the early night sky, occasionally blocking a star or two as they dissipated. The others would've seen the factory's chain reaction of explosions from here. Ryza could imagine the distant plume of fire and flux. It wasn't hard to imagine. He'd seen it before. In dreams and in life.

'Reckon I can guess why you wanted to go after them alone,' Elya said cooly. 'They do it again?'

'They?' Foll asked.

'The flux,' Vhoze said.

'Don't tell her!' Ryza snapped at Vhoze.

'Give it up, Ryza!' Elya retorted. She pointed rudely at Foll. 'Smelter! She knows flux!'

'Not the way you do. Not the way I do.'

Ryza let himself draw a deep breath, hiding behind the suspense of his dual statements. He looked back at Elya. 'Empty minds, remember?'

She groaned. 'Not this shit again!'

Ryza ignored her as she walked off, turning to Foll.

'Tell me what you saw out there. What you did for *him*.'

Ryza jabbed a thumb back at the man-shaped sack that'd slowly curled in on itself. Foll watched it with wide eyes, drawing her injured arm closer to her chest.

'It was a factory we was building. But it ain't like what was in Kyrea. I grew up there. They were big things. Filled the tunnels as long as they were making something people wanted, then just abandoned when no one was buying no more. Left the autominds behind. This thing was different. He kept saying we were too dumb to understand it, an' he was probably right. He said he wanted the flux to be the machine. To be any machine. To make anything, that's how that whole thing got built out of nearly nothing in only a few weeks.'

'Where'd you get the metal? That place,' Ryza pointed back towards the outpost, 'was pretty much intact.'

'Dunno.' She stopped, fear suddenly in her voice as she failed to take in her next breath. 'Some of us started pulling off scraps, but they kept reappearing the next day. Must've been something that place don't like though... Woke up one day and half of us were gone. Couldn't figure out why until I found one of 'em halfway in the floor.' Foll stopped herself, hesitant to say her next words because then she'd have to relive them. 'She was still asleep.'

Ryza heard Vhoze swear under his breath, but he didn't want it to distract Foll, and he pushed on with his questions.

'Where'd the flux come from, then? You've probably seen it's all messed up.'

'Yeah,' she said quietly.

She met his eyes again, and there was a hint of recognition from a time far before today. She tried to shuffle away in a panic, but her clothes caught on an ill-placed rivet, trapping her in place.

'Yeah,' Ryza replied, a slight snarl in his voice. 'Me. But why didn't it happen here?'

Foll shook her head quickly.

'Why?' Ryza barked.

'I dunno!' Foll cried out. 'He said... he said he'd got new flux! Told us all that and wouldn't stop telling us every day, but I—'

Elya had returned, though her impatience was still on display. 'Fuck, Ryza! Let's just ask him!'

She made quickly for the bagged prisoner, but Ryza dashed in front of her. They tussled for a moment, Ryza at an obvious disadvantage.

But he was used to it by now. He stopped parrying away her hands for a moment, pretending to be bested so he could plant his back foot hard in the ground as his right hand snatched for the front of her collar. He felt both of Elya's hands reach his shoulders, but it was too late for them to do anything. Ryza shoved her back as hard as he could, throwing her to the ground where she slid among the rocks for a metre or so.

Elya found her feet just as fast as she'd fallen. She only got a step into it, however. Ryza's right hand was resting on the handle of his sawn-off rifle. He didn't have a slug in it, but the example set by the still-whimpering Foll proved it was just as effective as a cudgel.

'I'm sick of this!' Elya shouted, her voice echoing off into the night. 'You ain't got no secrets! We all know your hands ain't clean! All of what you did down in Iroka! You didn't think that we would, did you?'

Ryza didn't have an answer. At least not one he could say, because she was right.

'Revance didn't fall apart because of anything you did. It fell apart because you tried to control it!'

Ryza felt himself flinch hard enough he nearly staggered sideways as Elya kept ranting.

'You tried to control everything you knew about the Locusts, everything you knew about the flux, playing games so we would all listen to you because there's something you weren't telling us. I reckon this smelter's right. Controlling machines ain't enough for you metal mouths. You gotta control the people, too.'

'Elya!' Vhoze shouted.

'I'm right, ain't I?'

'You are, but...' Vhoze trailed off and looked at Ryza. 'She is.'

'Now open the *fucking* bag,' she spat.

'No,' Ryza replied.

'He ain't gonna hurt us!'

Elya tried to sidestep around Ryza, but he was just as fast, still blocking her.

'But if you open that bag, I'm not going to be able to stop myself from hurting *him*.'

'Why?'

'Because he is my father,' Ryza growled. 'And I am his son.'

Chapter Four

The Refugees' Fear

R YZA WAS NO STRANGER to tense, silent rides in the back trays of lead-betters in the company of those he'd rather strangle until his fingers pierced their throat. He wasn't a stranger to a lot of things these days, but he couldn't find a reason to remove himself from being a friend with the brutal act, either.

The driving duties had been designated between Elya and Vhoze, who were taking it in hour-long shifts each. While they drove, they complained about how hard it was to keep the poorly maintained vehicle hurtling forwards in a straight line when the steering vane was bent in three places. While they rested, they rebuffed the driver's moaning by loudly declaring they hadn't had any sort of trouble with it.

Whenever Ryza grew sick of it, he turned to them and told them to go faster, or to orient the lead-better's path up a long hill. This did little to make their journey more efficient, but it least it made the engine roar a bit louder so that between it and the clattering of Ryza's teeth, he could momentarily block out the incessant whining of their voices.

They'd been travelling for two days now, driving through the hours of sunlight and attempting to rest once it was gone. Ryza wasn't sure which irked him more. The slow progress or the inevitable delays.

He'd tried to be patient with others. He really had. The fact that they'd made it this far was proof enough, but he still missed his original squad. At least what was left of them. There were many important reasons they couldn't journey with him on these long-winded hunts. Important things that needed doing at the sides of important people, leaving Ryza feeling more unimportant than ever as he'd watched them go, journeying off to Breggesa or on some other stately venture.

Better them than me.

He felt no envy for them. Those important people had important, and often complicated, questions, and that was something Ryza had expressly been told to avoid. Hunting down hefty bounties on the scattered remains of flux traders and smelters avoided these complicated questions. Sitting in the back with a wounded smelter and his own father bound and gagged in a sack, Ryza was battling with the most complicated question he'd yet faced.

What if I just killed him?

The proposition wasn't a recent one. It didn't bear relevance to when he'd dragged the man out of the wreck of his ambitious mobile factory, but instead to a time long before that. The time when Ryza had first escaped him in Breggesa.

He counted out the months under his breath. It wasn't all that long ago. Possibly only a year at best since he'd seen the man. Ryza had lived many lifetimes since, had many brushes with the ends of those lifetimes, and ended many lives in doing so. Even then, he could still remember the dead of night on the eve of his escape.

His father's manor had been a small one. It didn't have an excess of rooms like the others that were crammed into Breggesa's core. They weren't necessary, he'd said. The mercenary guards had no quarters of their own, instead residing in a house nearby, where they rested in between rotating rosters outside the manor's front door. There had been no kitchen, cooking pit, or metal stove, for food was brought in fresh from the nearby markets, and the only place to eat it was at a small bench on the ground floor where Ryza's father spent little time anyway.

The manor had been little more than a transient bed for a flux trader who was often busy overseeing the factories he had stakes in. To Ryza, it had been a loosely welded cage. It was a dull place to be, so he'd quickly learnt to slip past the guards when they swapped shifts, but only when his appointed tutor wasn't due for a lesson.

Ryza could remember lying awake at night in his bed —the one of two in the room that his father shared with him the few times he came to visit— plotting the perfect, violent escape he'd never have the guts to execute. He'd dreamt of inflicting carnage in so many ways that he still felt a coward for running away without carrying out a hint of it. Now he had the opportunity to carry out the original vision, he couldn't find the will to do so.

He'd been in the back tray of the lead-better for hours, facing backwards with his spine wedged against the low wall separating him from the driver's bench. His right arm was crossed over his chest, his hand clenched tight around his left nub, and the heels of his boots were planted for stability in the jagged gaps in the tray's floor.

In the back left corner, Foll sat much the same, though the frequent bumps hit by the lead-better broke her dour composure. She kept casting furtive glances at the bound man in the tray's back right corner, as if she were worried that he'd see her. Ryza knew that look. She was tired, which made it worse. The arm had kept her from sleeping overnight, as well as the worry of what would happen to her next. It was like she already knew.

Maybe she's wishing I'd put her out of her misery.

Conversely, Ryza had little worry for her. Perhaps some sympathy, but that was hard to think about when he could only stare at his father. He couldn't make out his features through the thick material of the sack he was bound within, but the midday sun would have him baking by now. They'd been travelling for almost eight hours that day. There were still another two or three left to go before they reached their destination.

Ryza could tell from when he'd looked over his shoulder a few minutes ago and had spotted the outline of Breggesa's walls through a gap in the dunes. They were coming at the city from the north but were set to pass by it without stopping by. Their destination was an outpost of their own that they'd set up some ways to the southeast of the city. It was the home base of the League of Revance. Despite

Ditric's organisational efforts, it was an easy place to overlook.

As the lead-better drew closer to Breggesa's walls and the rolling red sand dunes gave way to the fresh shanties and slums that pressed upon them, Ryza finally broke his silence.

'You ever seen it like this before?'

Vhoze and Elya didn't answer. They couldn't hear him over the thrum of the lead-better's motor, which didn't matter because the question had been directed at Foll. She didn't even look at the cluttered hovels Ryza had nodded towards.

'Where I came from,' she eventually muttered back.

'Gets bigger every time,' Ryza said idly. He paused for a moment, then Foll's words finally registered in his mind. 'Came from here? People have only been coming here since...'

Ryza trailed off. Foll had looked up at him with a broken expression, one that pleaded for a forgiveness she would never admit she wanted.

'Since Revance...' Ryza eventually said.

He glanced out towards the camps again. Calling them camps was generous. It implied that everyone there had a tent to sleep in, but the reality was that most shelters were just ditches that'd been burrowed into the hard-packed sand on Breggesa's outskirts. A few spots of blue canvas still showed through in between the low, ridge-like earthworks that had churned up the land.

They were the detritus of the Scythes' —and of Breggesa's— original attempts to corral the refugees that'd travelled here. The effort had only remained a heartfelt one for a month or so. The people had come in waves, each one started when their town had either been obliterated by the molten flux's new and bizarre behaviour or abandoned when the work and reels had ceased.

To those within Breggesa's walls, this mass of abandoned peoples was a problem without a solution. Maybe they liked to keep them on the outside because gathering them on the inside would be like locking them in a prison without a ceiling. Then again, with nowhere else to go, the walls might as well be on all sides than just one.

The spiteful, righteous part of Ryza had been looking to berate Foll for what she'd taken part in creating, if only for his still-restrained father to hear it without having the chance to talk back, but she had once again reminded Ryza that, like him, she'd been left with little to no choice of how her life was meant to go.

Might as well yell at someone who had a choice.

Breaking from his stiffly wedged seat, Ryza struggled briefly to tear open the sack that contained his father. He emerged with a spitting indignation, shaking the remnants of the canvas away from his head as Ryza pulled the rest from his body with scratching blows.

Ryza couldn't bear to look at him for long without having to glance away for a few moments. His crop of rust-coloured hair migrated in an orderly manner between the thinning ranks at his temples to the gruff curls at his chin. His teeth were bared, the set clean and complete, ready to summon a unique, snarling putdown for the circumstance. Ryza couldn't even meet his green eyes. He didn't need to. They were identical to his own, according to the last time he'd looked in a mirror. That had been an accident that Ryza still hadn't shaken the feeling of in the month since.

His father blinked at his surroundings, found them unsatisfactory, then turned his ire to Ryza.

'Your hair has become long enough that it's ridiculous. You shall cut it.'

'This was a fucking mistake,' Ryza muttered under his breath.

'I agree,' his father shot back.

Ryza was already fuming. It was made worse when Elya twisted in her seat, leaving Vhoze to drive in peace for once.

'Damn, ten words in and now I finally get why you're like this,' Elya said to Ryza.

'Fifteen,' his father replied.

'He got a name?'

'Aphtus-Hast,' his father said. 'Though you won't have heard of me.'

'And I wish I hadn't,' Elya said with a raised eyebrow. 'Why'd you get him out now, Ryza?'

He nodded sideways towards the nearing shanties of refugees. 'Because I wanted him to see that.'

'Squalor?' Aphtus-Hast challenged. 'You think I don't know what squalor looks like, Ryza? Where do you think I came from?' He finally looked his son up and down properly, his eyes lingering for far too long on his left arm. 'You race to get there yourself.'

'I'm nothing like you!' Ryza hissed.

'You're right. You are a mess. A dented barrel of rage and resentment. Yet you manage to carry all that without killing me at the first chance you find. You're a coward, Ryza, and you've become that way because you haven't had anyone around to hone you.'

'What?' Ryza said, taken aback by the stream of admonishment.

'You've always been headstrong, stubborn, and stupid. That's why you need someone to control you. To make you as you should be.'

It had been months since his temper had flared like this, and his father was lucky he didn't have a slug in his rifle to waste him with. Ryza lashed out with his right arm, not at his father but over the shoulder of Vhoze in the driver's seat, seizing the brake lever and pulling it hard.

The lead-better's gears crunched and squealed as the vehicle skidded to a halt. There were screams and grunts of pain and discomfort as they were thrown forwards from the sudden stop, but Ryza didn't wait for them to subside before he'd seized his father's neck and leapt from the tray of the lead-better.

Aphtus-Hast choked as he protested, but Ryza ignored it. With his feet planted on the ground and his knees wedged against the still-hot wheels under the lead-better's tray, he pulled hard at his father's throat. It felt like his father's skin was on the verge of ripping as the man fell bodily from the tray and landed face first in the red sand. The man kicked quickly to his feet, hissing and cursing, swinging his cuffed hands left and right to regain balance and stave Ryza off, but both were useless.

'You want to see what control gets!?' Ryza screamed close to his father's ear.

The man recoiled from the barrage of sound as if a rifle had gone off next to his head. Ryza felt his whole body jolt with satisfaction before screaming at him again.

'What your control led to?'

He seized Aphtus-Hast by the scruff of his formerly regal cloak and raised him properly to his feet, using his still off-balanced momentum to steer them both in a staggering gait towards the nearest cluster of idle refugees.

They'd watched the unfolding spat with a nervous curiosity. Now it was coming towards them, they weren't sure if they should retreat or stick around for the show. The ones with children chose to do the former, but most stayed as a loose semicircle.

Ryza shoved his father into the centre of it, then planted a heel-led kick into his back to knock him to his knees. Aphtus-Hast collapsed with one last gasp. He remained upright for a moment as he struggled to regain his breath, then fell sideways in a puff of orange dust.

Ryza was quick to stand over him, planting his boot on the side of his jaw to really press his cheek into the sand.

'Look at them!' he roared. 'Look! This is what you've done! All your reels destroyed all their lives! Left them as nothing better than used-up autominds to count their days outside the walls of a city that won't let them in!'

Looking up, Ryza glanced between the assembled faces of the refugees, waiting for them to draw closer, to throw stones, to do anything to start the violence that he wanted so dearly to unleash.

But they didn't. They just watched Aphtus-Hast writhing in the sand under Ryza's boot without a hint of recognition for the flux trader's face. It was only as they looked to Ryza that they began to grow scared.

It confused him. Meeting their eyes only changed their expressions from caution to a terror they'd known before they'd even met Ryza. It warped the black tattooed bars that'd been freshly impacted down the sides of their faces. It was a straight line between their left eye and the corner of their jaw that curved as their mouths shot open with cries of alarm.

Those with the strange mark were the first to panic. They fled towards the nearest barricaded gatehouse that was set into the mighty walls of Breggesa. It wasn't long until the unmarked among them did the same, leaving Ryza alone to berate his father as he attempted to hide his puzzlement.

'Your work destroyed—'

Aphtus-Hast thrashed from the ground, bucking Ryza's boot from his neck and throwing his words away. He twisted to his feet and towered over Ryza the way only a father could when scolding a son who'd finally matched his height.

A rivulet of blood ran loosely from his bottom lip, and he spat it at Ryza's feet. 'At least I taught you to strike fear with authority.'

Ryza swung his fist as hard and as wildly as he could into his father's guts. Aphtus-Hast did his best to avoid it, but the blow still knocked him back to the ground. He hit the dirt again, and Ryza allowed himself a small leap into the air as he swung his right foot backwards, priming a stomp that would shatter the man's skull once and for all.

He never got to deliver it. A gust of wind raced across the sands as Elya rode it towards him, catching him in midair and tackling him to the ground. Ryza thrashed against her, but she locked her grip firmly around his torso directly under his right arm. He could only flail and scream as Vhoze came along to roughly help Aphtus-Hast to his feet.

His father spared him a dissatisfied glare before allowing himself to be taken back to the lead-better. Elya's grip didn't relent until his father was firmly bound in the back tray. By then, Ryza had all but exhausted himself. He might've thought himself as a great deal stronger than Elya, but it was moments like these that he couldn't deny the advantages of an extra six inches of height and an intact left arm.

When she let go, she got up and dusted herself off, with no offer to help Ryza get to his own feet. She just watched with crossed arms, her feet braced in case he tried something else. However, glancing past her to the bloody gashes that Vhoze was tending to on Aphtus-Hast's face gave Ryza enough satisfaction to be placated.

'The fuck was that?'

'You know what,' Ryza grunted.

He tried to move past her back to the lead-better, but she shoved him back.

'You almost lost us our bounty. The Scythes want the flux traders alive.'

'Yeah?' Ryza retorted. 'And I want him dead.'

Elya swore, and Ryza could see Vhoze quietly echoing the sentiment.

'Ditric warned me you'd be like this. I thought after the first two we brought in you'd be able to keep yourself on a leash.'

Ryza shook his head as a manic grin took over his face. 'And you wouldn't believe how close I was to losing it.'

He tried to step past her again, but this time she'd had enough. She planted both hands on his chest and shoved him to the ground. He landed on his back with all the grace of a concussed toddler and felt the strange need to lie there for a moment before he tried to get up.

'Can't turn him in like this,' Vhoze called over from the lead-better. 'I've got to get him back to base to fix him up properly. Head's bleeding. No idea how bad. No idea if it'll get worse or—'

'What?' Elya called back. She waved at Breggesa's walls, the path to the nearest gatehouse now cleared of terrified refugees. 'The city's right there!'

Ryza sat up in time to make out Vhoze shaking his head. Aphtus-Hast was slumped forwards in the back of the lead-better, his head rolling back and forth on his shoulders as Vhoze tried to keep him upright. Beside him, even Foll looked worried.

'No good,' Vhoze replied. 'Could be hours until we get him to the Scythes. I wouldn't trust them not to keep the reels for bringing him in alive if he's about ready to die anyway. They barely handed over the bounty for the last one, and it figures. Breggesa don't have a reel to spare with the amount of people flocking here.'

'Fine,' Elya said. She turned back to Ryza. 'But you ain't coming with us.'

Ryza could only frown at her. His head was still ringing from the shove; he must've hit it on a hidden rock.

'Slim bet if we'll make the trip back without you trying to kill him again, and then there ain't a chance he'll make it through the night with you out the front of his cell.'

'Then how am I meant to get back?'

'You do what you need to fucking do,' Elya said as she made her way back to the lead-better. 'Walk it off.'

He didn't start walking until the lead-better had long faded into the distance. He couldn't. Not while his father's leering, bloodied face was looking back at him.

Chapter Five

The League of Revance

L ONG AND LONELY WALKS were another thing that Ryza was well-acquainted with. His first had been after he'd gotten lost in a cave taken up by the smelters and had been forced to race against the deadly metal collar around his neck to get back to Revance before the hefty device shanked through his neck. The reason he'd gotten lost was still too hard to think about.

The many lengthy journeys by foot that'd occurred since had often begun with a lead-better, either when they suffered an inevitable mechanical failure or simply ran out of fuel. As a green-eyed Kretatic, it would've been well within Ryza's realm of expertise to use a few choice axioms to get the cantankerous vehicles moving again, but he'd never done so for a number of reasons.

The ink used to paint the runes that made up the axioms was precious. Far more precious than the delicate vials of molten flux he'd grown up associating the axioms with. It was even more precious than his own life, according to his father.

His father was the other reason why Ryza had refrained from controlling the machines. While the tutors hired by Aphtus-Hast had attempted to teach Ryza the ways of enchanted magnetism, they were no match for the constant aura of doubt and faithlessness Ryza's father exuded.

It makes sense, in a twisted, fucked up way.

The events of the past year had given Ryza a new perspective on the doubts of others. The power they held and the way they overrode any of his own hopes. It was something that he'd almost thrown from his aching back, but laying eyes on his father once more had brought the weight of his own perceived incompetence crashing down on him.

It didn't matter much, Ryza decided as he trudged around the perimeter of Breggesa's walls. He was giving them a wide berth. This would add a few extra hours to his dimly lit march, but he couldn't stand the prospect of more terrified refugees. He knew why they were scared of him, and it wasn't for anything he'd done himself.

I think...

In the days following the fall of Revance, Ryza had thought that the flux was behaving as strangely as it would ever get, but the reports of recent months had proven him wrong. Word of such anomalies came as trickling rumours at first, whispers that were to be dismissed with sideways glances and muttered questions about the sanctity of the speaker's mind.

But as more towns blighted by molten flux began to report more of the same story, a familiar visage formed between them.

Mine.

He'd never seen it happen up close until the destruction of the moving factory the other day. Before that, it had been a spectacle he'd only been allowed to view at Kyrea, from behind the distant cordon that marked the place for total abandonment. It was a boundary set up by Vorric and the Scythes as they'd attempted to contain the mess there, with an army of silent guns to enforce it, but there were plenty more reasons to stay far away from Kyrea.

The unleashing of molten flux in its fluid form alone was enough to force the abandonment of a town. Within the metallic liquid were legions of tiny machines, created not by a Kretatic, but instead by those-of-glass. It was one of the many baffling gifts of either magic or technology that they'd left behind following their extinction countless eons ago.

No one could tell which of the two it was, not even Ryza. All he'd known was that these tiny machines must not be controlled, a warning given by a voice older than the Droughtlands itself.

Others hadn't heeded that warning.

The first to ignore it had been Archarus, a scholar from the Academy of Breggesa who, more than seventy years ago, led an ill-fated expedition into the heart of the place where molten flux was thought to have been created. Ryza still didn't know exactly what had happened, but the discovery had taken Archarus beyond the usual axioms of the Droughtlands, sending him stumbling into a moment of magic known as pure resonance. A single second where everything was possible because it was impossible to determine what wasn't.

The result had left Archarus as a shadow dancer, a spectral being beyond time itself that could only wait for the end of the universe. It was in this form, deep in the guts of the very same ruins, that Ryza had first met Archarus. Since then, he'd appeared with taunting irregularity, goading Ryza to fulfill the goal of his failed expedition.

To live beyond pure resonance with the aid of molten flux.

Archarus had told him that the flux's mission was simple. "To want as they want." Just as every person carried an inherent will to live, every inch of their body carried with it a drive to grow and heal and multiply. It had seemed that this is where molten flux's tenacity and self-replicating traits had been drawn from, and it had been enough to shoddily repair a damaged body.

Even as it did so, it still wasn't perfect. Each of those tiny machines within the metal liquid was only making a guess at what its role was to be as a part of the larger whole. For each of them that got it wrong, ten more got it right, and that was how they created a facsimile of an intact body. Yet they couldn't fully mend a mind. That was left empty.

A Kretatic's limit was defined by how much metal their mind could bear to control at once. Generally, something the size of a treadhulk would render a person comatose. The invention of autominds changed this. An empty, spare mind could be assigned to bear the strain, and suddenly the Droughtlands had given way to sprawling factories controlled by lone men.

Of course, it had also created an unending appetite for corpses to fill with molten flux, but that wasn't something the flux traders worried about. Lowlifes like the smelters were all too happy to "make" as many corpses as was needed.

It was what the economy of the Droughtlands became centred around, warping with it the perception of molten flux. All those who walked the surface of these burning red sands expected molten flux to behave in a consistent way as it was used to create automind after automind, therefore the miniscule contraptions within the liquid metal were all too happy to oblige. As long as there were plenty of people around for the molten flux to please, it knew all it needed to know.

Until it didn't.

Ryza looked around, surfacing from his trudging trance for a moment. The sand dunes around him were tall, tall enough they blocked out the view of Breggesa's walls, and he thought he was lost for a moment. He quickened his pace as much as his aching knees would allow, cresting the next dune to pant with empty lungs. Breggesa was still there. Firelights crackled around its walls in the various shanty towns, chaotic in comparison to the steady illumination of the glow orbs within the city.

Would the flux still behave as it once had if brought among the ranks of those who were questioning it? Or was there a new expectation set for it? One that tainted it like it had tainted the Droughtlands? It could explain why his father had decided to build a mobile factory. The flux in the autominds there must've been the last of that which was "pure" in the Droughtlands.

Perhaps that was also why he'd gone to such great lengths in preaching to his smelter companions that it was pure. As long as the smelters believed it, Aphtus-Hast's own doubts for the stability of his molten flux might not even matter. As long as he kept his distance from the dangerous ideas that mass civilisation held, the flux would behave as he wanted it to.

Ryza looked around as he descended into the trough of another dune. There wouldn't be another soul for miles out here. Would that be enough for the flux to only believe him? If not for the catastrophic consequences, it might be a question best solved by the scholars at the Academy of Breggesa. Perhaps they had tried it and destroyed the evidence in order to stop the flux from becoming more volatile.

That was how molten flux was when left well alone enough. It was something Ryza found out in the months he'd fruitlessly spent trying to clear it from the valley of Iroka in the wake of Revance's fall. Due to Tyrag's insane plan to control the walking fortress with batteries of thousands of autominds, the valley was left covered in pools of flux larger than ever thought possible.

This was due to another strange behaviour that was expected of the molten flux. Gather more than a bucketful and it exploded into a cloud of noxious silver gas, infecting the lungs and skin of all that it passed as it searched for new ideas to draw from, new minds to analyse and respond to.

This form was known as blazing flux and was something that should've happened in the valley of Iroka the day the wreckage of Revance had settled there. Its bent and twisted frame, its many fallen and battered chambers, had all been filled with pools of molten flux and little else, leaving the remaining survivors to puzzle at how it could possibly exist in such a form as they slowly drained it into the sands below.

It was only when a contingent of smelters outnumbering the former conscripts seven-to-one had attacked that the flux finally behaved as expected. Their surety had overridden the ex-conscripts' befuddlement, and the resulting plumes of blazing flux were visible from miles around.

Ryza's own understanding of why it did this was as shaky as his legs were feeling four hours into this damn trek. The Academy of Breggesa's more militant wing, the Scythes, seemed to have had a better understanding of it, Their leader, Vorric had explained it to Ryza with an example of hand drawn, overlaid maps.

The various plottings of Iroka that he'd asked Ryza and the other ex-conscripts to produce from memory had formed an accurate representation of the lay of the land. One error had been cancelled out by the correct details left by the others, much as the machines within the flux carried out their own guesswork. The problem came when each of these maps was divided and a traveller who'd never visited the town of Iroka was asked to copy a perfect map out from memory. It would likely still serve to help make the maps produced by the ex-conscripts more accurate, yet if repeated enough times, it would pollute the pile from which the map was being redrawn.

That was why the flux *had* to disperse itself in such a violent way. Why it must not be controlled. Otherwise, it began a cycle of poorly copied impressions that would make the flux itself more and more useless. It was because of this very problem that the second Kretatic to control the flux had made himself known.

Maligar.

The name felt bitter on Ryza's tongue even though he hadn't spoken it. The grandiose man had once been the leader of the Locusts, the clandestine sect within Revance's corridors that'd helped Tyrag plot his mutiny. In the battle between Tyrag's Revance and the ex-conscripts desperately garrisoning Iroka, Ryza had faced Maligar in a fight to the death. One he'd almost lost, owing to Maligar having somehow enriched his body with molten flux. It should've turned him into an inert automind, yet he'd somehow found a way to control the flux within his body and become nigh unkillable.

When Maligar had been felled, Ryza had hoped that would be the last he'd see of him, but he'd been proven wrong. Three months into the cleanup of the flux in the valley of Iroka, Maligar had shown his face again, his body clad in silver rather than flesh, as he'd emerged from the automind corpse of Tyrag that was left over from the battle.

The flux that Ryza and the others drained into the ground had collected in an enormous tunnel created by those-of-glass. It was a place Maligar had been using as a sanctuary to sustain himself in his new form. Whether it really was him or just a manifestation of the flux was one that gnawed at Ryza to no end, only for him to realise that the answer didn't matter. He could be both or neither, but it didn't change what effect his presence was having on the flux itself at Iroka.

According to Archarus, the flux had been born to respond *only* to the whims of the living, yet here was Maligar, living within the flux itself, his very presence causing the flux to look inwards upon its own kind as it continued to guess at what it should become. When one of those tiny machines got it wrong, the life it looked at in order to correct itself was the one that Maligar believed he possessed within the flux, forcing the liquid metal to copy itself again and again until it barely resembled its original form.

When Ryza and the others had ventured into the tunnels below

Iroka with the intent of destroying them, he finally discovered how Maligar had been delaying the inevitable corruption of his own essence. Maligar and countless copies of him bragged to Ryza as they showed him the strange replicas they'd created of a skeleton from the time of those-of-glass, the body of the man that'd somehow led to the creation of molten flux in the first place.

It was using that skeleton's mind, or at least the endless copies of it, that Maligar had created a series of lives that wouldn't lead to the flux's corruption. As impressive as it had been, Ryza had put a stop to it with the help of a thing Vorric called a rebel sun, another gift from those-of-glass, that burned hot enough to turn Iroka and its surrounding sands to superheated slag.

Ryza tried not to question how he'd escaped the tunnels with his mind still intact, because he knew it would lead to an answer he didn't want to dwell on. Because he'd had help. Help that was now creating statues of him wherever it could in order to sustain itself just as Maligar had with his ranks of skeletons.

But it's working.

He paused again at the top of another dune. Breggesa was far at his back now. One last sloping hill lay before him, and he wondered if it was even worth climbing. Light was beginning to build in the sky to the east, there just over the ridgeline ahead. Once the sun rose, maybe one of the others up there that were waiting for him would simply drive down in a lead-better and save his legs the last steps of this long journey.

Ryza stood there for a few more moments before he sighed and forced his feet into motion. Elya had been right. He'd needed to walk it off, and he wasn't quite done yet.

The ridge of the enormous hill gave way to a half-hearted attempt of a perimeter wall that Ryza passed through unchallenged. There was no guard posted to patrol the propped-up lengths of corroded iron. Some panels of it fell away, leaning desperately low to the sand. Their lengths were too short to accomplish the depth they needed to be planted for stability and the height they needed for any kind of protection, so they were left to fail at both.

There wasn't really much point fixing them. Who out there would want to attack a scrapped-together group of battered ex-conscripts calling themselves "the League of Revance"? Who would be bothered to?

There'd be little to gain. The row of leaning shacks that served as their sleeping quarters only contained rusted cots and weary, ill-disciplined soldiers. At the end of the row was a larger structure, its interior sunk half into the ground to save on how much metal went into creating its walls. A soft yellow glow escaped from the patchwork cracks of its shell, and Ryza could see small bursts of fire flare up occasionally through the open doorway.

Even at this hour, a Curiktic had enough wounded on their hands to be busy. Their ability to summon flesh-searing fire was all the healing their bedraggled army could afford. Anything more and that would require them to head into Breggesa proper, but that required spending the reels that constantly disappeared into the fuel tanks of their vehicles.

Ryza stopped outside the motor pool. Both words didn't belong in the name for the place. The only thing that had a working engine was the lead-better that Ryza had just been kicked out of. It sat at the front of the rank of ill-maintained vehicles, and Ryza felt himself grin with satisfaction at the crusted-up blood still present in the back tray.

At least I made that bastard bleed.

Two other vehicles had languished in the sun since they'd been brought here. Their second lead-better was in pieces, most of the useful ones having been sold for parts to repair the first. A treadhulk was the only other thing that made up their motor pool.

More like a motor puddle.

Ryza chuckled to himself and kicked the front tread of the massive machine. He'd been strict that it was not touched or looted like everything else they brought in, though it also meant it wasn't going to be touched for any other reason. It guzzled oil like a bottomless pit in the ground, and they were yet to set out on a mission where their target was slow enough for the grinding pace of the treadhulk to catch up to and big enough to necessitate the broad cannon that sprouted from the rear of its canopy.

Ryza moved on, slipping past their hollow armoury before the quartermaster noticed him and instead towards the little cabin that he'd built outside the base on the other side from Breggesa. It was positioned close enough that he'd hear any commotion that came from the base, but far enough away that they wouldn't hear any commotion that came from him.

It was a shack like the rest he'd passed on the way through the walls, made distinct both by its isolation and the row of three stone-pile graves that were growing next to it. Ryza stopped before them and chewed his upper lip. He knew that lying down wouldn't force him to sleep, so why bother in the first place?

Instead, he wandered in a slow circle around his shack and the trio of graves. His boots shuffled through the sand, kicking up the rocks that had fallen from the graves and occasionally discovering new ones. Ryza collected them all, stopping only when his pockets were overflowing to return to the burial mounds. Each stone was placed carefully so it was wedged between two others, painstaking work that had to be done from his knees, but Ryza never compromised.

The others had never questioned why he did this. Maybe they didn't care. Maybe they already knew why. Either way, they seemed to know to leave him alone while he carried out his odd task.

At least most of them do.

His ears twitched as a heavy set of boots approached. He didn't turn. He already knew who it was.

'Always thought I'd add a few rocks myself one day, but I still ain't sure who all these are for.'

Ryza set the pebble in his hand down in the sand and swivelled on his knees to look at Ditric. She looked as tired as he felt, the usual machismo and eagerness for a scrap gone from her yellow eyes. She'd even stopped bothering to shear her hair down to the skin. It resulted in a brief spray of black strands that pointed straight up, looking prickly to touch, though it wouldn't be the only jab one would receive if they tried. Her hands were stuffed in the pockets of her chalk grey robes, garments she'd unwillingly taken up in place of a greatcoat like Ryza wore.

She raised her eyebrows at him after a lingering silence, and Ryza nodded, giving her the permission to come closer, not that she needed it. Out of respect, she still stopped a few steps back from the grave and waved for him to keep placing stones.

'Surprised this is the first thing you do after walking all night.'

'Not long left to get any sleep in,' Ryza grunted in reply.

'Tah. Feel the same.' She paused for a few heartbeats. 'I reckon I've guessed who one of those graves are for, but you ever going to say about the other two?'

Ryza sighed as he hesitated. The question had thrown his focus, and three rocks had tumbled from the grave he was restructuring.

'Never had a body for them, so it's the best I could do.'

'Who? We buried Gry as best we could, didn't we?'

Ryza shut his eyes, and he felt his balance swaying him forwards, but he resisted. Gry had been one of his four original squad mates aboard Revance when they'd been conscripts. Probably the worst fighter out of the five of them as well, but he'd made up for that in smarts. It was why it was all the more tragic to Ryza that he'd been killed. He should've been a scholar within the Academy of Breggesa, maybe even one among the ranks of the Scythes, but instead he'd been stabbed in the back in the depths of an undercity by a traitor he couldn't have seen coming.

'It ain't him. It's Calict.'

He saw Ditric nod out the corner of his eye. She hadn't been there to know him, but that hadn't stopped Ryza from regaling her with stories of him as if she had. Calict had been another Reythurist, like Gry, who'd been Ryza's right-hand man when it came to the cleanup attempts at Iroka. He had faith in Ryza's mission, to the point that he'd laid down his life while Ryza had run like a coward.

'And the other one?' Ditric asked.

Ryza looked from the one on the left to the one on the right. It felt ridiculous to say, but after all they'd seen together and on their own, how could this top it?

'It's mine.'

She sniggered at him, and he felt his shoulders crumple.

'You ain't dead,' she said, coming closer to clap her hand down on his shoulder.

'I don't know that,' Ryza said quickly.

'Yeah? But I do.' She clapped her hand down on his shoulder twice more, one for each syllable. 'A-live.'

'You don't get it.'

'Vorric tells me I'm not meant to. Not because I'm dumb, but because... Shit, you know better than me anyway.'

Ryza shrugged her hand from his shoulder and stood up.

'Is it molten flux stuff or pure resonance stuff?' Ditric asked tentatively.

'Still don't know what the difference is, and I think I need to keep it that way.'

'Right. Means the third one is...'

Ryza still couldn't bring himself to say her name.

'She still in your head, huh?'

Ryza looked up, purposely blinding himself with the first signs of sunrise so he wouldn't have to meet Ditric's eyes. 'I don't think she ever left.'

CHAPTER SIX

DOUBT, REGRET, AND GUILT

DITRIC WAS NOT ONE to leave a proverbial stone unturned, but it seemed that Ryza had stumbled into a rare such day. She stayed with him for a while longer as he worked through his improvised ritual of stone-stacking, moving them from one grave to another in order to achieve mounds that unconsciously hoped would last for decades to come.

Maybe I should make them out of glass instead.

Ryza wasn't sure why he wanted them to last. He wasn't even certain that was what he wanted in the first place. But these days, it was the only thing that brought him a sense of peace, and the days away from the graves strained his nerves to a breaking point. As he stood up and dusted loose sand from his knees, he decided that was the reason why he'd lost his temper so violently, and not the myriad of others currently surrounding him.

As he walked with Ditric back into their meagre camp, he spotted a few of them. In the centre of the collection of their hovels, a clearing was marked by a metal post that'd been driven deep enough into the sand that it had hit rock. Affixed to it was a sign, its knife-scratched markings reading "League of Revance." The way Ryza understood it, a league was an organisation made up of proud and willing members, but the few ex-conscripts who'd joined him and Ditric on their petty venture were anything but.

Much like Ryza, there wasn't much of a place for them in a version of the Droughtlands that lacked Revance. There was no one else to give them orders, and even the few that could, taking the form of elite mercenary houses as old as Revance had been, wouldn't be giving the kinds of orders they were used to.

There was no clear enemy to fight, only rich nobles to guard. How those clients had come into their money was a topic that was taboo, so Ryza could only assume the worst. This had left the League of Revance to hunt down the other dubious nobles whose fortunes weren't large or flexible enough to hire competent mercenaries. All that resulted from these ventures was a sack of reels and a battered sheet of parchment detailing the next bounty.

There was no visceral sense of satisfaction that'd come from dealing a blow to smelter operations. No notion of doing good for the Droughtlands as a whole. Just an ever-shrinking pile of reels that was only good enough to buy a dozen or so slugs to hunt down the next bounty.

It's pathetic.

The thought chimed in Ryza's head off the back of his last, then repeated as he dipped into the armoury to resupply himself. He wasn't even sure why they'd bothered to construct shelves. He walked quietly past the quartermaster, who was snoozing in the corner, and rummaged through the lone crate of munitions they had left. The various slugs clinked against each other as he squeezed each one between his forefinger and thumb, testing the width of them for the few that would suit his sawn-off rifle.

After finding three, he looked back to the quartermaster and realised they weren't that at all, they were just another of the ex-conscripts that hung around the base, waiting for a mission that would send them out. Now he thought about it, Ryza couldn't remember if he'd even asked Ditric to assign a quartermaster when they'd set up the base a few weeks ago.

He shrugged to himself and left the armoury, doing his best to kick the endless drift of loose sand back out over the entryway's threshold. There wasn't much point having a quartermaster anyway. The only duty that could be assigned to them would be to sort the various slugs in the ammo crate before demoting themselves ten minutes later once it was done.

Ditric watched as he slipped two of the slugs into his satchel, raising an eyebrow as he loaded the third into his weapon.

'No bounties today and you're thinking of going out already?'

'Can't be too careful,' Ryza replied.

Ryza followed Ditric as she set off again, despite picking up the distinct impression that he wasn't meant to be. Her path took her to their infirmary, twenty paces away at the other end of the base. She stopped outside it, her hand pressed against one of the only doors they had that still worked.

'Who you planning on using it on?'

Ryza grunted in response.

'Can't let you in with me if you're—'

'I'm not planning on using it,' Ryza said dryly.

Yet.

Ditric held out her other hand to him and nodded to it.

'Give it.'

'What?'

'Rifle. Now.'

'You don't trust me?'

'I ain't having you do some Bloodfist shit in there.'

'I'm not the Bloodfist,' Ryza snapped back. 'Never was.'

'Yeah? You're sure acting like it. Don't matter how much you say it. Elya told me all about what you're getting up to out there. Just wish I thought she was exaggerating.' Ditric nodded to her outstretched hand again, a note of weariness now in her expression. 'I don't need more shit to deal with, Ryza. I've already got Vorric breathing down my neck for letting you piss off on your own looking for flux traders. He says I should be with you.'

'Then he can send some of his precious Scythes with us next time,' Ryza spat.

He hadn't intended the animosity, nor had he meant it to be directed at Ditric. If it weren't for her, the League of Revance's base would've only been his shack and his little set of graves.

At least she hasn't abandoned me.

His reticence softened, and Ryza handed over his rifle. He felt naked without it and off-balance without the weight of it in the holster at his hip. To make up for it, he subconsciously shifted his satchel to hang closer to his right and firmly clutched the small bag like it was a weapon. He could feel the brass casings of the two slugs inside squeaking and grinding against each other as his grip shuffled them around.

Satisfied, Ditric pushed through the door, and Ryza followed her into the room. It was always a bit warmer in here, but not enough to make him uncomfortable. No, it was the kind of warmth that would send him into a slightly nauseating sleep, a sensation not helped by his plodding journey through the previous night.

There were four beds in here, three of them bearing actual, supportive padding. Most of them hadn't been used much. If one of them was wounded badly enough to warrant it, it was often on ventures that would have them die halfway through the days' long journey back, if they couldn't be patched up on the spot.

Any lasting injuries that made it here were minor, and often in the realm of what Greely, their best healer, could care for. He was as skilled with healing fire as Ryza was with a rifle, an accolade proven by the nub of scar tissue just below Ryza's left elbow where Greely had sealed the grievous wound. In the year since, the only time it had given Ryza trouble was due to factors that were far, far beyond the nature of Greely's cauterising efforts.

If the health of one of their number continued to decline after his ministrations, they'd have to be ferried into Breggesa proper where the increasingly thin patience of the Scythes' healers would see to them before sending them back.

Their only member who'd made that journey multiple times was Avesta. She was always the first person Ryza saw whenever he walked into the infirmary. The bed she'd requested each time she'd returned from the city they'd taken to calling "big bricks" had a perfect view of the rest of the encampment if the infirmary's door was left open.

In the early morning, as Ryza followed Ditric into the infirmary, he found Avesta as she always was: fiddling with some contraption she said would make the lead-betters run better and in the company of a friend. Today it was Elya, and Ryza knew she wasn't at Avesta's bedside for the sake of pity. It was something Avesta had forbidden them from doing. Ryza understood why.

Ryza met Elya's eyes sheepishly. He knew she'd consider them "even" after his long trek back, but he still felt guilty that it had to be her that needed to quell his temper. Aside from Ditric, there were few others left who could put him in his place, but he wanted to become a man who didn't need such treatment in the first place.

And I'm failing at that.

As Elya looked back at him, it was with an air of tense caution. Her arms had been crossed as he'd walked in, but he saw the distinct movement of her elbows as she'd readied herself for another brawl. Ryza gave her a small nod, and she relaxed, allowing him to approach the other side of Avesta's bed, an action he was taking to put off the inevitable.

'Heard you've had a long journey,' Avesta said brightly to him.

Ryza shook his head. 'I feel like we all have.'

'Lizard shit,' Avesta said. 'You probably walked more in one night than I have since...'

She glanced down at her torso. It was still bound in bandages that were stained a deep, earthy red. Remnants of the wounds she'd earned in Iroka months ago when she'd been caught by surprise by a new weapon of the smelters.

Instead of firing heavy, solid slugs like the rifles Ryza had been first introduced to aboard Revance, the smelters' motorised guns spurted barrages of tiny lead pellets that'd peppered her flesh like a thousand knives. Avesta had nearly died on the stretcher as they'd carried her back through the wasteland left by Revance's wreckage, and Ryza had been the one to pull all the metal out with an axiom of his own.

Hopefully all of it.

Despite Greely's best efforts, and the even better efforts of the Scythes' healers, Avesta still hadn't fully recovered. It was as if the pellets were still dancing around inside her body. Multiple magnetic pulses of the wounds by more adept Kretatics than Ryza had failed to find a single piece of stray metal, yet he still lay awake at night wondering if there was a pellet he'd missed. Even if he hadn't, if he had successfully extracted them all, there were still other reasons to be so sleepless. At least this was a reason he could talk to.

'How're you feeling?' Ryza asked weakly.

'You know how. Tired of being stuck here.' Avesta handed him the gizmo she'd been fiddling with, a strange combination of pipes, valves, and spindly filters. 'Do me a favour and stick that in the oil pump of something that needs it.'

'What will it do?'

'Dunno. Something. I'll tell you when Greely lets me get out of here to find out.'

She chuckled and Ryza joined in, but the sound felt stilted in his throat.

'You found a big one, Elya says,' Avesta murmured to him.

Ryza looked up at Elya with a twitch in his face, but she stared him down. It was fair that she'd told Avesta. It was the only way she heard about things anyway.

'He'd better be worth the reels,' Ryza said. 'Where's Foll?'

'Vhoze is keeping an eye on her in one of the other bunks. She wouldn't sit still while she was near *him*.'

'She still scared?'

'Yeah,' Elya said with an unidentifiable wince. 'I'm starting to think I shoulda let you stomp him, the trouble he's been giving Greely.'

Elya nodded to another of the occupied beds, and Ryza finally stopped avoiding looking. There was his father, trussed up in shackles and leering at him with a face of fresh scars. He was talking to Ditric as she questioned him, but he didn't break from Ryza's gaze. He knew it was torturing him, and the only relief Ryza could draw was the damage he'd done to the bastard already.

And I ain't done yet.

Ditric's questions didn't stop as Ryza walked up to the bed, even as Aphtus-Hast's head turned to follow Ryza's approach. Greely was perched on a stool next to him, still working with a mixture of flame-jetted fingers and jars of chunky poultices to heal Aphtus-Hast's scratches. A part of Ryza wanted to order that he stop, but he knew Greely wouldn't listen to him. He just had to take comfort in the raised folds of welted flesh that were left behind by the process.

The most distinct of them all was a curled, pinched section of his left cheek from where Ryza had first kicked him. Ryza could almost pick out the distinct pattern left by the tip of his boot. It oozed and dribbled pale droplets of blood whenever Aphtus-Hast spoke in response to Ditric's questions. By the looks of it, Greely hadn't been able to seal it up with axioms alone and had resorted to sewing it shut with a thin length of copper wire before it split open worse. This left Aphtus-Hast's face in a constant, lopsided sneer, something he didn't need help maintaining.

The rest of his wounds were more manageable for Greely, yet numerous enough that he appeared to have worked through the night just to reach them all. He yawned as he sealed up the last wound, then looked to Ryza with an almost resentful expression.

'You have no idea the amount of water wasted on this prick because of you,' Greely muttered.

'He never did understand efficiency,' Aphtus-Hast remarked.

'Fuck off,' Greely replied as he left.

'I promise I'll be worth the reels!' Aphtus-Hast called after him. 'I'll see to it that you're compensated well for your ministrations.'

'From where you'll be? Not likely,' Ditric said.

'You think I'll be friendless in Breggesa?'

'I think you'll be in the ground.'

'Along with my other compatriots you've so dutifully gathered before me? It'll be quite the reunion that you've organised for me.'

His father's wit was quickly draining Ryza's steadied temper, and he could feel Elya standing close behind him in case it broke again.

'How does it feel to be the one that's imprisoned?' Ryza shot.

From the low cot, Aphtus-Hast still found the gall to smirk up at him. 'Why?'

Ryza nodded joltingly to his father's wrists and the rusted, short-chained shackles that bound them. 'What do you think I mean? You raised me under such a life of terror that I was born a prisoner. A slave. A fucking automind! The only day I got to decide what to do with myself was the day that I fled.'

'A short-lived day it was,' Aphtus-Hast sneered back.

Ryza almost gasped. He hadn't been expecting this, but when it came to his father, why would he ever expect him to back down? Before he or any of the others could cut him off, Aphtus-Hast continued, his tone enough to command the patchwork room.

'The whispers I heard of your shambling path pieced together the tale of a boy straying from one master to the next, always looking for someone else's thumb to burrow under lest you catch sight of the length of your own shadow. You found Revance and the collar it burdened its conscripts with, but by the sounds of it, it was exactly the type of leash that you needed in order to thrive.'

'What the fuck is he talking about?' Ditric spat.

But Aphtus-Hast continued unperturbed.

'Perhaps you thrived too much, biting the hand that fed you and destroying the very thing you needed to survive. It wasn't until the Academy of Breggesa saw fit to send out the Scythes that you found a new master to obey. Vorric was very adept at influencing you with you without knowing it.'

'No he wasn't,' Ryza said, rising to Aphtus-Hast's goad. 'He didn't—'

'Didn't he?' his father said, interrupting without needing to know the rest of Ryza's words. 'Even now you are controlled, and you don't even know it. You are unarmed.'

'How do you—?'

Aphtus-Hast looked at the sawn-off rifle that Ditric was holding by the barrel in her right hand. 'Not a way to hold a weapon you're familiar with, is it?'

'I took it so he wouldn't kill you,' Ditric growled at him. She leaned in closer, tapping the sawn-off rifle against Aphtus-Hast's bloodstained chest. 'And if you say another word, you're going to wish I controlled him as much as you think I do.'

Aphtus-Hast held Ditric's tense stare for as long as he could, then burst out with gargling laughter. He kept laughing as he looked around the room, meeting the eyes of all the others as if he could infect them with his mirth, but no one else succumbed.

'It's nothing but children's tantrums, isn't it? Imagined threats to be carried out by imagined actions that you're all too afraid of the consequences to act on. No, Ryza, I think you'll find you're still the prisoner here. For what is a captive if not one who cannot take the actions they crave? You wish to kill me and yet you cannot. Even as you walk these days of your life, you are walled in by what I sense is...

Doubt? Regret? No... Something else...'

Ryza was already shaking his head, knowing what word was about to come next as his father's lips twisted into a victorious leer.

'Guilt.'

CHAPTER SEVEN

SLOW RIDE

BEFORE RYZA COULD EXPLODE in defensive rage, a buffeting of opened hands and a slamming of the infirmary's door had him stumbling out into the sand-swept base. Ditric followed him closely, pushing him again for good measure. Ryza regained his balance as he spat with indignant furore.

'Did you hear him?'

'Tah, I did. He was fucking with you, Ryza. Just can't believe it worked.'

'No, what he said, that's something no one else has said to me, no one except—'

He cut himself off abruptly. All his time away from Ditric and the others that'd been there from the start meant he'd lost track of who he'd told what. Did she know about Archarus? About what the shadow dancer had said to Ryza when they'd first met? She couldn't, no one could, so how had Aphtus-Hast known those exact words?

'That you feel guilty? I barely know how to read, and I know that he read you like a fucken book. Why else are you out there stacking stones on graves that ain't got bodies under 'em? We all feel guilt like that, Ryza. I do. I'm sure Ruka does, if we ever fucken see her for more than two minutes.'

Ryza held in a retort. Maybe Ditric was right. Maybe he was being paranoid.

But being paranoid is the reason I'm still alive.

'He knows something,' Ryza said, keeping his voice quiet in case those inside the infirmary heard him. 'Something he ain't telling us.'

'Then that's a problem for the Scythes,' Ditric hissed back. 'We're taking him and the other one you dragged back over to Breggesa today. If they question them or torture them, I don't care, as long as they're out of your reach so you stop making this shit up.'

Her last words tweaked something in him, something he still couldn't quite find the buried root of. Ryza stopped himself from snapping back for a moment, opting instead to pace the stretch of sand outside the infirmary. Ditric had thrown the door shut behind her but had neglected to latch it, so there was just a sliver of the room's internal light creeping out to fade in with the early dawn glow on the sand.

'I'm not making it up,' Ryza eventually affirmed. 'I know what I saw. It's real!'

'Then what's "it"? Huh? Can't say? Vorric tell you not to?' Ditric let out a sharp sigh. 'I get it. I don't actually, but you need to get this. If I can't know, you gotta stop acting like I'm meant to. Got it?'

'Fine. But I'm coming with you.'

He held out his hand for his rifle, but Ditric kept it stashed in her robes. She shook her head.

'If I'm right, you'll need me there.'

'Right about what?' Ditric asked.

Ryza remained silent, his hand still outstretched. Ditric started nodding at him, a frustrated sneer on her face.

'Can't tell me, can you? Or don't you even know?' She chuckled darkly. 'That's how it always is with you, isn't it? Bad feelings producing bad things. Literally.'

'Give me my rifle.'

'Fine. But if you use it the way I think you're going to, the next slug's going in your skull.'

The engine of the lead-better burbled and gasped as Ryza manoeuvred it out of the base and through the course of rocky pillars that lay between them and the main trading routes. He'd felt honour bound to oblige Avesta's request to install the strange gadget into the workings of the vehicle's engine. It also gave him another reason to hold over Ditric as to why he should come to Breggesa with her. If he were the only one who knew how to pilot the lead-better now, how would she be able to refuse him?

Ryza didn't agree with the way Avesta's addition changed the pitch of the motor, masking the usually guttural roar he found comfort in, but if it really would do something like she promised, be it saving oil or preventing a breakdown, they'd be able to stretch the sack of reels they were about to collect a lot further.

The mechanism's installation had taken an hour of fingernail-bruising repairs. By the time he had it working, Ditric was threatening to injure a whole lot more of him. She'd made no offer to help, so perhaps she was hoping he'd fail so she could take out her frustrations. Once again, Ryza couldn't blame her.

Working on the guts of the machine had brought a strange calm over him. Even if he wasn't controlling the metal's magnetism directly, he still found solace in all the motorized workings as he tightened and greased them. The work a Kretatic could do with axioms could only go so far. At some point, they'd need to understand how all the parts fitted together or risk them grinding down to the point of uselessness.

In a way, the world around him had become a bit like that. Maybe there was some combination of axioms that could put an end to the flux catastrophe as they knew it, but it would surely leave behind a mess far greater than what Ryza had faced in the wake of Revance's fall.

Part of that mess was revealed as the rolling dunes parted, giving way to a view of Breggesa's towering walls. They were approaching from the eastern side of the city, where the refugee camps were sparser but still evident in their bulk. It didn't matter if molten flux was purged from the world tomorrow or in a decade, they'd still be there looking for a home in places that didn't have the room to take them in.

Ryza pulled on the steering vane slightly as the lead-better drew closer to the city, easing it towards the denser patches of the camps near a gate further to the north. In the seat next to him, he felt Ditric watching him with a raised eyebrow.

'You lost?'

He chuckled and shook his head. 'Just want them to see it.'

Ditric glanced over at the other two passengers in question, both of them bound and nestled in the rear tray of the lead-better. Foll was only lightly restrained. Greely had forbidden them from putting her injured hand in a set of box cuffs, but she was so docile, so resigned to her fate, that Ryza thought she might willingly walk herself down to Breggesa without their accompaniment.

Pity almost got the better of him, until it was snubbed out by the thought of their other prisoner. Greely had also forbidden them from restraining Aphtus-Hast too harshly. Ryza's father now lay on the rocking surface of the lead-betters tray. He was bound, gagged, and trussed up to the point he had as much free will as an automind. The way he was secured to the vehicle meant his eyes were only just high enough to see over the jagged lip of the tray, the perfect height to look up at all the famished faces they were about to pass by.

Now among the camps, Ryza dropped the lead-better's pace to a crawl. He was tempted to force his father out of the vehicle and parade him before all these lives he'd ruined, but Ditric would likely give him the same treatment on the way back for such theatrics.

Ryza contented himself with looking deep into the eyes of all those they passed. If they held his gaze, he nodded back to the restrained prisoners, hoping to direct their attention there. If he was lucky, they'd recognise his father and attack, climbing aboard the lead-better to beat Aphtus-Hast like Ryza craved to. Of course, he'd help Ditric repel the frenzied crowd eventually, but he'd make sure to savour the moment.

But no such thing had a chance of happening. Few people could bear to look into Ryza's eyes for longer than a heartbeat. Just enough time to recognise him and scurry away. Ryza swore to himself.

News travelled faster than their engine could carry them, so when they ground to a halt at the gateway into Breggesa, the nearby shanties were almost deserted. The refugees that stayed to watch only showed their faces through little gaps and tears in the scrap metal they'd used to fortify their homes. None of the faces Ryza could see had that distinctive black mark down the left side. He made a mental note to ask Ditric about it later but held his tongue as four members of Breggesa's guard waddled out from their posts towards the lead-better.

Like the city they supposedly defended, their armour was unwieldy, inefficient and ineffective. Shingled layers of dull grey metal hung in layers like a dress from their shoulders, running low enough to their knees that made moving faster than a brisk walk impossible.

Haphazard garments of chainmail were worn underneath, acting as the only protection to their arms and shoulders. Whatever inertly dyed fabric worn below looked to have been provided from each guard's own closet. There was no other way to explain the tattered state of those rags, but Ryza knew his own clothes weren't in better shape.

The only protection for their heads were wide-brimmed helms of thin metal that protected them from the noon sun and little else. With it being morning and the sun streaming in from behind the lead-better, the leader of the four guards had to squint into the light as he decided between approaching Ryza or Ditric.

They chose the latter, and Ryza swore under his breath, a sound loud enough that the lead guard flinched on the other side of the lead-better's chassis. Ditric commanded the guard's attention back to her. As their bureaucratic negotiations dragged on, Ditric made sure to keep her shoulders flared and puffed out, entirely blocking Ryza from the conversation.

He knew she'd said these words a hundred times before to guards with worn wits. Staving off the tides of refugees day after day was something that degraded their souls, so they had little comprehension left over for anyone that approached with big words.

Thankfully, Ditric can make threats with little ones as well.

Ryza could've sworn he'd heard the clinking sound of a clandestinely slipped handful of reels before the lead guard gave the yelping order for the gates to be opened. A racket of grinding chains roared over Ryza's only chance to complain about the bribe. Nevertheless, Ditric acknowledged the sentiment with a quick shake of the head as she leaned across Ryza to restart the lead-better's engine herself.

Ryza let the vehicle roll forwards as the enormous doors embedded in Breggesa's wall slowly split in two. A narrow, twisting street was revealed beyond. It was cluttered with carts, merchants, and travellers fortunate enough to get the right visitation tags stamped into their metallic pass sheets before Breggesa's guard had destroyed the embossing stamps themselves in order to stop the city from becoming even more overcrowded.

The barricaded checkpoints set up on almost every street corner didn't help the matter. Their foundations of small, interlaced stone bricks protruded like growths from whatever sturdy dwelling was unfortunate enough to be positioned in such a tactically important spot. The bricks had been stacked to around waist height and then filled in with hard-packed sand, creating an artificial plateau from which the conscripted guards could oversee traffic. Where the brick platform ended, low walls of reclaimed iron continued their purpose, forming a thin barricade around the heightened platform.

Ryza eyed one off as he gently steered the lead-better past it. For a moment, he thought he recognised some of the metal as having once belonged to a treadhulk he'd seen aboard Revance. He dismissed the thought quickly. Maybe he was imagining it.

Maybe I'm imagining a lot of other things, too.

Ryza only had a vague sense of where he was supposed to be guiding their path towards, and Ditric's barked directions were invalidated at almost every turn. What she'd sworn was a clear street from her venture into the city a week ago had become a dead end. Slums and shanties spilled out of opposing buildings and connected in the middle, creating a tented bridge of squatters across the passage that Ryza didn't want to barrel through.

In other places, markets had sprouted with no intention of vacating. The trade being held in their bounds looked so raucous and so desperate that it would likely continue long into the night and beyond the next morning. It was a miracle that the merchants profiting off them could even get their goods safely to their stalls to be sold.

The lead-better was constantly slowed by the dangling bodies of young street urchins and those who'd graduated from such a thing, becoming young vagrants instead. They wedged their feet in whatever axle or rail they could ride on, clinging to any part of the lead-better they could reach that also wasn't in range of Ditric's slapping hands. Her calls for them to leave off the vehicle were ignored as if they'd been shouted in a different language. Giving up, she then stood on her seat so she was high above the crowd, waving her own rifle in the air as she bellowed threats to the hangers-on.

Only those that she had the stomach to kill relinquished their grip and scattered off into the crowd, leaving behind the most junior of the street urchins. Ryza turned to look at them with an emotion that he couldn't decide was pity or shame. There was a girl outright sitting in the tray next to a still-petrified Foll that couldn't have been older than six. The urchin gawped up in awe at Ditric as she waved her rifle again, grabbing her little hands in front of her chest as a poor mimicry of holding her own weapon.

'Ryza! We need to ditch this thing. We still ain't anywhere near the Academy, and we won't be until night at this rate.'

'You wanna walk?' Ryza said in disbelief.

'I don't *want* to, but look at that!'

Ditric pointed ahead, and Ryza half stood from his seat to see better over the crowd. Once again, the street had simply ended. It was as if an entire building had been dropped in the middle of it with only enough room on either side for walkers to pass in single file like they were going through a tunnel.

But it wasn't a building. It didn't have any doors or windows, or any sign of habitation. It was just one gigantic slab of grey stone.

'Fuck me that's a big brick,' Ryza said.

'And there's more after that,' Ditric replied. 'Takes about a hundred men to move one.'

'A hundred?' Ryza looked around. They'd probably passed thousands of idle hands on their trundling drive into Breggesa so far. 'Then why are they still here? There's plenty of people around to help move—'

'A hundred men and the reels to pay 'em,' Ditric answered

pre-emptively. 'They got the people, but they ain't got the reels.'

'What do you do when you run out of reels?' Ryza muttered under his breath.

After making sure his rifle was secured firmly in its holster against hopeful pickpockets, Ryza hauled himself out of the lead-better. He swatted away the first dozen or so children that rushed up to him as they begged with rapid hand-to-mouth-to-stomach gestures. They didn't relent in the slightest, so he let them swarm around his back like a buzzing blanket as he reached back into the lead-better to unscrew whatever felt important in the fuel line's connection.

He came away with a valved sprocket and a sprocket-laden valve, pocketing both in his ammo satchel as he moved to the rear of the lead-better. From across the tray, Ditric gave him a nod. They'd be able to retrieve the lead-better eventually. Even if someone did manage to fire it up without the missing parts in Ryza's satchel, the only place they'd be able to drive it would be straight into the foreboding face of the grey stone brick dead ahead.

Ditric's grunt of strengthened exertion was audible over the frothing babble of the crowd as she hauled Aphtus-Hast's limp body onto her left shoulder. She swayed for a few moments as she found her balance, swatting away at beggars both to repel them and adjust her centre of gravity. Now steady on her feet, she again slipped her rifle from her shoulder where it was strapped and swept the muzzle of the weapon across the crowd ahead, sending them scattering.

Ditric roared after them in a boisterous tone as she walked forwards into the first clear square metre of cobblestone that Breggesa had seen in months.

'Yeah, now you know what a rifle does! And don't worry, we got plenty of slugs! We know how to load 'em with one hand, as well!'

She turned to throw Ryza a smirking wink, a motion she had to exaggerate to see past Aphtus-Hast's rear end. Ryza chuckled back. He'd had a gutful of people making snide jokes about his arm, thinking they were being clever, but Ditric was the only one he didn't lash out at before they reached the punchline. The way she made them, they were never exactly about him, but he still couldn't put into words what was different about it.

Ryza had an easier time helping Foll out of the lead-better. With only her hands manacled in front of her to a worn leather belt at her waist, she was a great deal more mobile than his father currently was.

More compliant, too.

She walked by Ryza's side without resistance, barely even needing his hand to be gripped on her shoulder to guide her. Breggesa's unhoused dregs continued to circle and beg, speaking in solemn yet rapid voices as they pleaded for a reel to be spared, only stepping back or out of the way at the last moment as Ryza pushed through to catch up with Ditric.

He craned his neck lower once he did, attempting to catch whatever look was currently in Foll's eyes. She didn't meet his gaze. She didn't need to. There was nothing there. Just a hollow acceptance of her fate as it unfolded before her. Ryza was half tempted to shove her off into the crowd to see if she'd pick herself up and find her way back to him from how dejected she was.

Ryza had never expected a smelter to be so docile. In his time aboard Revance, the smelters he'd fought had thrashed and wailed to the very end. Perhaps the devastation that the flux's new behaviour had wreaked on the Droughtlands *had* been the end for most smelters. There was no longer anyone that wanted the corpses they'd killed, no one that wanted them for anything else, and so the smelters themselves had nothing left to want for.

The thought stopped Ryza in his tracks, and it was down to Foll tugging on a handful of his long coat to get him moving again.

'Nothing more to want,' Ryza whispered to himself. 'An accepted fate and nothing more to want.'

CHAPTER EIGHT

INNER CITY

A STOP BEFORE ANOTHER street-corner redoubt was Ryza's last taste of Breggesa's frothing crowds. The overlapping din of minced words, the endless stench of living waste that trailed in their footsteps, and the staring eyes that were fixated on the missing portion of his left arm disappeared once Ditric successfully argued their way into what Ryza knew to be Breggesa proper. The people that thronged and gathered in the outer layers of the city weren't what he grew up among, yet he still felt a strange solidarity for their blight.

There, they were already crammed into their dwellings by the scarcity and desperation that'd brought them within the walls decades ago. When such buildings had been erected long before then, their four or five storeys had been thought to be ample living space for a historically expanding city. Now there were tales of after-the-fact renovations that introduced new floors and ceilings through the middle of these rooms in order to create two, even if it meant one would only be able to crawl on hands and knees within them.

Ryza had also heard stories of such constructions collapsing, crushing all those unfortunate enough to have been allotted the lower portion of what'd once been a high-ceilinged room. Looking up at the un-glassed windows of the buildings surrounding them, Ryza could see that this still hadn't dissuaded the practice.

Turning back from the guard's raised post, Ditric nodded for Ryza to follow, and he did so with Foll in tow. The crowd around them sensed action. They flocked towards Ryza and Ditric as they pressed their backs as best they could to the low gate of retaining steel that bisected the street. Ryza looked across at Ditric, but Aphtus-Hast, who was still on her shoulder, was all he could see. His father stared resolutely back at him with a tense and unflinching expression. Ryza turned away from it first.

Didn't even last three heartbeats.

There was a grind of metal chains and a chorus of warning shouts as the wall behind them began to lift into the air. The desperate crowd flowed like a wave of loose sand towards the new breach in the street, attempting to duck under the gap before it was even a foot from the ground. They were met with the vigorous prodding of guards armed with blunted iron rods. As the gate raised further, Ryza could see a phalanx of legs from over his shoulder. There were no less than twenty guards working to hold back the crowd.

At the other side of the street, the furthest point from the raised street-corner lookout, there was a break in the defences and a few of the rabble burst through. Shouts followed them as they fled into Breggesa proper before the earsplitting crack of rifles began to pursue them instead. Ryza's right hand flinched towards his holstered rifle, but he kept it in its resting place, gripping the handle tightly.

The unseen rifle shots were enough to momentarily pacify the crowd, and the gate was hoisted even higher, stopping at approximately chest-height. The phalanx of guards skittered forwards under the gate, roaring at the crowd without a hope that it would make them back away. Ryza, Foll, and Ditric with Aphtus-Hast on her shoulder were absorbed by their impromptu battle line and rushed back through the gate before it was abruptly dropped on anyone's limbs that were foolish enough to be reaching under the divide.

Ryza ran his eyes along the bottom of the gate as he held his breath. He released it. Thankfully, no one had been caught by it.

The guards that'd hauled them through the gate spent a few seconds congratulating each other on another job well done before a shout from their leader snapped them into action. They rushed into formation, two columns of rigid postures and upturned chins, and another barked order sent them jogging along an arterial alleyway towards another gateway where their services were required.

Ryza felt a strange impulse to go with them. He couldn't put his finger on why. Maybe it was the unquestioning authority they had, or the lack of decisions they needed to make. One of the many things he'd missed of his time in Revance despite having initially loathed it. Or maybe it was because their departure had left him and Ditric in an utterly empty street, spare for the three bodies that lay bleeding ten paces down it.

Ryza looked from the corpses to the guards in their raised bunker, but they were too busy engaging the crowd on the other side of the gate. He looked back to the corpses again, an uncomfortable sense of injustice curdling in his guts.

'Why'd they...'

Ditric grunted inquisitively at his question as it trailed off, then looked at the corpses herself.

'Run through like that?' she said. 'I forget you ain't been this far in Breggesa for a long while. To them, it's good eating in here. Slip in, hide in the dark corners, and grab what these people call scraps, because to you it's better than water. Doesn't matter if you eventually get caught and thrown out. As long as you're staying on this side, you've got a belly full and a head that you can rest. It's what Ruka told me she used to do. In a way, I reckon it's what she's doing now.'

Ditric let out an odd, resentful grunt, but Ryza's question hadn't been answered.

'No, I don't care about that... Why'd they kill them?'

He didn't get his answer instantly. Ditric gave him a soured grimace and nodded for him to start walking. They left the barren street and its abandoned corpses behind before she next spoke, though it was from Ryza's right, so the body of his father was in the way of her words, muffling her voice slightly.

'Yeah. I don't like it neither, Ryza. But it's been getting common. I'd fight the guards on it, but there's only one of me and about a thousand of them. All of them walking around thinking they're worn down from holding the line, from fighting the hungry and the lost, people they'd be like if they didn't have a rifle of their own.'

They turned a corner, and Ryza suddenly felt very out of place.

It was like they'd wandered into an entirely different city. The streets were clean. The crowds that walked up and down them were orderly, their conversations measured and civilised. The market stalls they patiently queued up for were well-stocked and as varied in colour as they were in the nature of the goods displayed in them.

Most of all, Ryza noticed, there were little to no guards on patrol. No street-corner bunkers that were built up like siege-worthy ramparts. The few armed and armoured men and women that Ryza did recognise stood with patient stances. It was a discipline that only broke when one of the well-dressed Breggesans tapped their shoulder and began to whisper to their ears while casting disparaging gestures towards Ryza and Ditric.

'Don't know why you're bothered by it,' Ditric jabbed. 'With the killing you've done, you'd be a fucken inspiration to the Breggesan guards.'

'I didn't kill people that were running away,' Ryza growled back. He shoved Foll forwards by a few steps so she was momentarily in Ditric's view. 'There's your proof.'

Ditric barked with booming laughter, and from her shoulder, Aphtus-Hast joined in by chuckling tauntingly through his gag.

'Let's not fucken lie to ourselves, Ryza. You love it when they run. I know I do. Still remember coming into what was left of Iroka with the Scythes and burning all those smelters to a fucken crisp. Don't tell me that you wouldn't've done the same, alright?'

Any chance that Ryza had of answering was muted by Foll. She'd taken a single, horrified glance back at him before spinning her head back to face as straight ahead as she could, her neck stiff as she continued to walk in front of him. Her mouth wasn't gagged like his father's was. She could've said something. But she didn't need to. Ryza knew that look. He'd seen it on countless faces before he'd jammed a needle into the back of their necks and turned them into autominds. He knew what it meant.

Is that what'll happen to me?

He forged this resurfaced guilt into scorn and tried to focus it towards his father as a malevolent glare, but once again his nerve failed after three heartbeats.

'They always end up killing people every time they open those gates, then?' Ryza said quickly, hoping this would change the subject.

'You actually want an answer or do you already know?' Ditric replied. 'Of course they fucken do.'

'You'd think they'd find a better way to do it. To work the gates, or to let people through. What happens when any of the people in here want to get out? How does anything get in here without having to slog through all that?'

'Doesn't matter to 'em. Know why? Too many people.' Ditric paused for a moment, grunting as she transferred Aphtus-Hast onto her other shoulder so she could look Ryza in the eyes, along with his father, who was now facing forward. 'Enough faces all at once and they all start looking the same when they're on the wrong end of a rifle. Pull the trigger and another is already in the way, so it's like you didn't even kill no one in the first place. That's what the fall of all these factories has done to Breggesa. Filled it with enough people that there ain't no such thing as a person anymore.'

'What'll happen to them all?' Foll asked, her voice catching Ryza by surprise.

'Ha! Five words and you've already asked a better question than Ryza! Shame you're a fucken smelter, eh? That's what the big bricks are for. There ain't hardly anywhere left in Breggesa to build something that ain't already got something built on it, 'cept the sky.'

'Skyscrapers,' Ryza said softly.

He still remembered the first time he'd heard the word. He'd been standing before the very ruin left by those-of-glass where molten flux had been discovered with Maligar's arm around his shoulder, the prelude to his grand plan of mutiny fresh in Ryza's ears.

'Towers big enough to hold everyone, if they ever manage to get 'em built,' Ditric said brightly. 'You'd be able to fit the folk from Iroka, Kyrea, and Breggesa combined in the city after that.'

'And that ain't going to be too many people?' Ryza asked.

Ditric shook her head dismissively. 'At least they'll have somewhere to live, y'know?'

But as Ryza cautiously turned his attention back to the other passersby on the street, he felt these new residents of the future wouldn't be welcome, just like he felt.

It had barely been a year since he'd fled Breggesa and his father's practically mechanical upbringing, but it was a lifetime that had erased all other traces of the identity he'd been running away from. He felt uneasy walking these streets. All this empty space and all these windows to overlook it made it a tactical nightmare, if he were to be expecting smelters or some other form of attack.

At least back among the crowds there was a sense of order among the chaos. That it was driven by a common, understandable instinct, rather than the inner sanctum of Breggesa. Where he stood, order seemed to be held in place by an unspoken set of rules that had either changed in the time that Ryza had been away from the city or that he'd simply forgotten as he'd embraced his role in Revance's lowest ranks.

The city changed again as they neared its centre. The buildings grew squatter and less congruous with their neighbours. Their architects had likely come from different eons, or had they shared a common time, disagreed on what made a beautiful structure. The only running theme they had agreed on was that of intricacy. It showed through in every crease and ridge of the pillars that upheld a dwelling's eaves, or in the lines and wrinkles etched into the busts of ancient faces that protruded from high walls.

Even the scents began to throw Ryza off-balance. They were no longer of human origin, like those in the crowded outer layers of the city or in the refugee camps beyond the walls. Delicately wrought iron lamps stood at the occasional street corner. They were only as tall as Ryza was, their sputtering flames open to the air as their heated colour alternated between all manner of purples, blues, and whites, depending on what bound-up parcel of herbs or satchel of finely ground minerals had been deposited in the trays just below the flames. Some smelt airy and light, and others came as a hazy aroma that flowed uncomfortably deep into Ryza's sinuses.

He tried not to walk near them as they passed. They only reminded him of the smell of blazing flux, a sickeningly sweet scent that he'd had to endure for the months he'd spent trying to clean up Iroka. Even the slightest whiff of something similar made him feel like he was waiting for the flux to gather in his lungs, wondering how much of it would be too much until he turned into one of the many autominds they were trying to clear from the battlefield.

Then again, the smell was better than the heavy feeling of his own breath from within a vent mask. He shuddered at the thought, imagining all too distinctly the *hiss-click* the valves made each time he inhaled.

The air began to clear when they reached the edge of the Academy of Breggesa's grand campus. With it now being midmorning, the scholars had taken it upon themselves to pace quickly between the various halls, dormitories, and sandstone-bricked laboratories as Ryza and Ditric attempted to ferry their prisoners down the main plaza.

It was strange to be hauling captives among such an otherwise civilised group of people, but if there was any unspoken discomfort for the scholars, they had no right to act out against it. It was Vorric himself, head of the Scythes and the person Ryza suspected was now pulling most of the strings in the Academy, that had put such a particular bounty on the heads of flux traders and their smelter lackeys.

Some way ahead, Ryza spotted another group of mercenaries that were just as laden with prisoners as he and Ditric were. There were four or five of the armed men and women, and they'd cleverly stuffed all their captured smelters into one of the caged carts that was often used to transport autominds.

The irony is too obvious to even enjoy.

There was a hefty amount of reels in play for bringing in so many at once, all likely from the same gang of smelters. Vorric's continuing philosophy of gathering as many perspectives on the one matter applied to his interrogations, though with the amount of smelters that'd already been brought in, he'd surely have enough accounts by now.

Ryza glanced to his father. The strain of being carried on Ditric's shoulder for so long was starting to show in the vein bulging from his forehead. This was the one mind Vorric would value the most, even if it was the one Ryza wanted to smear across the brickwork before there was a chance for it to be spoken.

The enormous hall at the end of the plaza was their destination, and they reached it just as the other set of mercenaries disappeared through its well-guarded and administered front doors. Ryza had been to this place before, but he couldn't help gawking at it. He was used to gargantuan constructs, but those had been made of metal, either by

Kretatics or by peoples long extinct.

The First Hall of the Academy of Breggesa was something else. It was stone. Nothing but stone. The most inert thing in the Droughtlands, something Kretatics couldn't control, Curiktics couldn't burn, and Reythurists couldn't blow away. The seams between each section in the supporting columns of the Hall's façade were invisible for how precisely the masons had carved them. The windows were inset with completely clear panes of glass, a feature rarely seen for how difficult it was to work out impurities in the stuff.

By the way Ryza had been told it, the First Hall had been here from the moment Breggesa was given a name and would likely remain standing until long after that name was forgotten. Contained within it was a maze that rivalled that of Revance's guts of rusted corridors and ladder chutes, although this one was made up of hallowed passageways and grand, spiralling staircases.

Navigating the interior without an experienced scholar would take so long that Ryza would likely emerge a scholar himself, if he tried. But he didn't need to worry about such a pleasant fate today. A familiar face was already making their way from the entrance and down the wide marble steps towards them.

Ryza felt himself smile. Ditric could have her reservations and resentments, but that was all because of the way she thought things should be, not what they were.

'Hello, Ruka,' Ryza said.

CHAPTER NINE

THE ACADEMY OF BREGGESA

RYZA HAD LOST COUNT of the weeks that'd passed since he'd last seen the other remaining member of his old squad. There had simply come a day when she'd headed out to Breggesa from their upstart little camp and simply never came back. There was never a hint of a farewell, so Ryza had assumed she had not departed them at all. It was easier than adding her to the list of people that'd left him with a lingering sense of abandonment.

'Where's Vorric?' Ditric called out, her tone cool.

'Busy,' Ruka replied, matching Ditric. 'We all are. What've you brought in? The usual?'

'Nope,' Ditric said.

Ruka forced out a disgruntled sigh. 'Fine, just dump 'em in through the doors and I'll make sure the reels get sent over to—'

'We need the reels now, Ruka, or we ain't going to have the slugs to bring in the next bounties. Besides, we got something more than a smelter.'

With an unceremonious shrug, Ditric dumped Aphtus-Hast to the ground. He landed with a harsh thud, but his groan of pain was ignored by Ditric as she rotated the strain out of her carrying shoulder.

Ruka looked between Aphtus-Hast and Foll, settling her eyes on the latter. Ryza shook his head before Ruka could say anything, and he nodded towards Aphtus-Hast instead.

'He's a flux trader,' Ryza said quietly. 'And he's my father.'

Only her recent training kept Ruka from gasping out loud. The shock made her pause for a moment, but afterwards she was back to her old self, snapping orders at bulky-shouldered Academy guards to come to her aid.

Their uniforms seemed to be a confused hybrid of that worn by the Scythes and what the Breggesan city guard was equipped with. Their armour was composed of the same layered plates of grey metal, but they were complemented underneath by the azure-blue robes that marked the Scythes. Ryza spotted green and yellow eyes among their number, so he guessed that they weren't as exclusive in their recruiting as Vorric was in the ranks of his personal band of warrior-scholars.

Four of them picked Aphtus-Hast up like he was a coffin and started towards the doors of the First Hall, while another two seized Foll by the arms and tried to manhandle her along as well. She cried out in pain as the grip on her left crunched up her injured bones, and Ryza shunted the offending guard away, taking over the grip at Foll's upper arm instead.

He looked at Foll, expecting her to look back with reluctant thanks, but she only stared straight ahead, still resigned to her fate. She dragged her feet as they proceeded up the steps to the doors of the First Hall. When they crossed the threshold, Ryza and the other guard were practically carrying her. Disappointment wasn't the word that Ryza would've used to describe what this left him feeling, but he couldn't put his finger on what word he'd use instead.

He brushed it all out of his mind. He wasn't there to do anyone any favours. He was there to finally make his father pay for what he'd done. For what his father had made him do.

The interior of the First Hall bustled just as vigorously as the outer reaches of Breggesa. Groups of conversing scholars were split apart like mined rocks as the guards carrying Aphtus-Hast pushed through them, only clumping back together once the trailing parties of Ryza, Ruka, Ditric, Foll, and the other guards had passed by.

The rooms that held the Academy's interrogations were close to the First Hall's entrance, but another snapped order from Ruka steered them straight past them. Down the missed hallway, Ryza caught a glimpse of pandemonium.

Cages had been built against the walls of the hall itself to hold the excess of captured smelters, and that hadn't even been enough. Some of the more recently arrived captives had simply been chained to the outside of the bars, free to kick and gnash their teeth at the Academy staff that had to deal with them until one of them had the common sense to reply with a sharply jabbed iron rod.

'When are you going to tell us to just go out and kill these bastards?' Ditric asked Ruka. 'Just pay us for that and we won't have to bring back all these smelters for you to deal with.'

'And start another corpse trade? Not happening,' Ruka said.

'Another what? What do you mean?' Ryza said.

'You got a way to tell if a dead body is a smelter or not? If we ask for corpses, we'll get corpses, smelters or not. That's what Vorric said anyway.'

Ditric gave a dark chuckle. 'You've been saying a lot of what he's said, ain't you?'

'Ditric, save it,' Ryza hissed. 'Never thought I'd be the one telling you to pack it in.'

Ruka had the good sense not to prod Ditric further while she was fuming, instead turning her attention back to Ryza.

'Must've been a hard one to bring in,' she said, nodding ahead to Aphtus-Hast.

'Alive? Yeah.'

Ruka nodded. 'You sure you want to be here for all this?'

'I need to see it. Besides, I have to talk to Vorric. I reckon you already know why.'

'I do. He wants to talk to you for the same reason.'

'Is this flux stuff again?' Ditric said, her temper now controlled. 'Thought we were meant to be keeping you away from that, Ryza.'

'And that's what Vorric told you both, huh?' Ryza shot back.

Neither of them could reply to this, so their stilted conversation was surrendered to the foggy babble that echoed through the passages of the First Hall. The sound seemed to intensify as they were led up staircases to one of the upper floors. Less grandeur had been imbued in the architecture here, favouring instead a more utilitarian design.

Doorways were squared off with the ceiling, which in turn met in the middle above the bare passages with a simple angled join. Windows and natural light were reserved for the rooms that the passages gave way to, so the walkways were lit with weak glow orbs. The shadows they cast were brighter than the light they gave off, at some points.

The room Ruka eventually led them to had once been three separate chambers. When Ryza passed through the doorway, he spotted the remnants of the knocked-through walls protruding slightly from the floor and ceiling where the space had been expanded. Desks, standing walls, and metal cabinets had been jammed into any space they could be placed, leaving a narrow circular walkway which busied Scythes navigated around as they consulted and compared all manner of papers and parchments.

The four guards carrying Aphtus-Hast deposited him in one of the few unoccupied chairs and departed, making their way back to their post with the two others that'd escorted them up here. This left Ryza alone to support Foll as she swayed on her feet. He struggled to balance her, but Ditric stepped in to help, grabbing her other arm.

Vorric was ensconced in the middle of the administrative chaos. He was the maestro of three different conversations, silencing one by darting a hand into the air, his fingers shaking slightly, as he turned back to the other two, seemingly talking out both sides of his mouth.

'You weren't lying about being "busy." What are you trying to do with all this? Is this another version of Vorric's trick with the maps?' Ryza asked Ruka.

She looked up at him, half perplexed, until she realised what he was talking about. 'It looks like it, but it ain't anything that easy. Apparently, this many Scythes is usually all the Academy needs to deal with everything people end up pulling out from the ruins. With the way molten flux is now, it's not enough.'

'The way it is now, huh?' he said under his breath. A few of the Scythes had broken from their busyness to stare at him. One in the distant corner of the room was even looking between him and a roughly sketched portrait they'd happened to be holding when Ryza had walked in.

'And that's why you've stuck around to help out?' Ditric said.

'More'n that, Ditric. I get to be something now. You have any idea what that feels like when you start with nothing at all?'

Ryza glanced unconsciously at Foll. The smelter was limp in his grip. If she'd had a chance to join Revance like Ruka had, she wouldn't be facing down whatever unknown retribution the Academy was about to mete out for her.

Maybe I should've just killed her to save her the trouble.

'I don't need to know,' Ditric eventually replied. 'Plenty of folk in Breggesa already do. Now see if you can hurry Vorric up before I go over there myself.'

Ruka only obliged out of a sense of duty, not friendship. Ryza had seen enough to glean that the two had grown distant in the months since they'd left Iroka behind. It was as if there was no common mission in their minds, no greater purpose, just a constant, overwhelming wave of things to manage.

While Ditric had been tied up trying to get the League of Revance a shred of legitimacy, Ruka had been in deep with the Scythes, a fact that showed when Vorric halted all three of his conversations on Ruka's approach. The lead Scythe listened intently as she spoke, the others that were talking to him moments ago listening along with him, so commanding was his presence.

Ruka must've chosen her words wisely. Vorric looked up from her so fast his neck almost snapped. He surged past the Scythes that barricaded his path and mantled over desks where they stood in his way. When he reached Ryza, he was out of breath, but he didn't need to say anything yet. He looked from Ryza to Aphtus-Hast and back again and again, disbelief and worry straining at the sides of his face.

'You found him? I thought...'

Ruka caught up to Vorric's side. 'It is him, isn't it, Ryza?'

He nodded, suppressing the snarl in his voice as he spoke. 'Without a shadow of a doubt. Aphtus-Hast. My father. The flux trader that helped plot the downfall of Revance.'

The entire room fell silent. The Scythes all knew there was little in this world that would leave Vorric dumbstruck like this, and anything that could do so was to be closely and cautiously observed. Ryza could hear them breathing. Hear the scraping of their chairs as they gathered closer. Hear them shuffling their feet to get a better look.

The tense serenity was punctured with a soft, echoing chuckle. It was muffled, coming from behind the gag that bound Aphtus-Hast's mouth, but no one motioned to remove it.

'What about her?' Vorric said, looking at Foll.

'I caught her before I caught my father. She was one of the smelters working under him.'

'Is she important?'

'Her name is Foll,' Ryza replied.

'Is she important?' Vorric repeated.

Ryza looked at her, and Foll finally looked back. There was a pleading in her eyes. The expression he'd been waiting all day to see. But now it was here, he wasn't sure what to do with it. If he said she was important, would that mean a harsher treatment as a prisoner? An interrogation involving torture for knowledge she did not possess? But on the other hand, if Ryza said she wasn't important, he was sentencing her to a similarly uncertain fate among the chained masses of the rest of the smelters.

The privilege to make this choice suddenly felt like an act of inhumane cruelty. It was different from killing a smelter in battle. There, he knew exactly what happened when he pulled the trigger of his rifle or drove a knife deep into one of the bastards' ribs. It was a fate he was giving that was within his control. One that both he and his opponent had accepted the responsibility for when they'd started the fight in the first place.

'I don't... I don't know,' Ryza eventually said.

An uncertain answer in the face of an uncertain fate.

Saying it felt weak to Ryza, but it was enough for Vorric to motion to two of the nearest Scythes.

'Special holding cells. At least until...' Vorric looked at Aphtus-Hast as Foll was snatched from Ryza's hands and taken away. 'Until we know what he knows.'

Ryza's pulse quickened as Vorric withdrew a knife and brought it close to Aphtus-Hast's cheek. He hoped that Vorric, an expert with a blade, would slip, dashing it across his father's neck, but no such error happened. A simple flick of the blade cut through the bindings that held Aphtus-Hast's gag in place. He spat out the wadded hunk of cloth, wordlessly working his jaw as he returned to staring at Ryza.

'You are—?'

'I am,' Aphtus-Hast said, cutting Vorric off. 'Yet my son gives me too much credit in the downfall of Revance. I believe that remains his doing.'

'How do you know that?' Ryza snapped. 'You weren't there! You didn't see what Tyrag did or what happened afterwards! Where were you? Where? Holed up in one of your other manors? A factory? Tell me!'

'Ryza!' Vorric barked.

Vorric held up a hand to him, a gesture that did little to steady Ryza's sudden temper.

'You had your informants, I assume?' Vorric asked Aphtus-Hast.

'Of course I did. Not that I needed them. A rust-haired boy was rumoured to be leading the last resistance against Tyrag's little mutiny? Who else could it be?'

Vorric left Aphtus-Hast's side and approached Ryza instead, keeping his back to the flux trader as he whispered softly in Ryza's ear.

'He wants to get under your skin, Ryza. Don't let him.'

'No shit,' he hissed back. 'Why else do you think I brought him here? I want to get rid of him and get the reels I'm owed.'

'Then leave the questions to me. I don't want you to get aggravated like you did back when we had Cardan in Iroka.'

Vorric turned back to Aphtus-Hast, pulling up a chair to sit opposite as he waved for another Scythe to note down their words.

'We know a great deal about who you are, Aphtus-Hast. That's been the benefit we've drawn out of the chaos of rounding up so many smelters. We have so many stories of you that we can sort the fact from the fiction, though I wish a great deal of what I've heard wasn't true.'

'And what have you heard? I'd be happy to correct your records, if you'd give me the chance to gloat.'

'I've heard that you didn't keep your hands clean like many of the other flux traders. That you controlled every element of your organisation by a pattern of personal demonstration, and raised Ryza here to do the same.'

Aphtus-Hast glanced to Ryza with a smirk.

'My one failure I'll claim responsibility for.'

'You don't regard being captured as a failure?'

'I regard it as an inevitability. You said it yourself. Your efforts in "rounding up" all the smelters you could find and those others that were associated with them were becoming all too successful. To the point, by the looks of it, that you've simply run out of places to put them all. I wonder what justice you will decide suits this criminal mass that you've gathered? They range from the killers and the corpse haulers down to the peons and the lackeys who were born into places where they had no other choice, yet you've painted them all with the same brushstroke as equally evil.

'Killing them all would be a punishment far too severe for the desperate ones like Foll, who you just dragged off, yet you can't fully investigate and admonish them all individually.'

'You are correct,' Vorric said in a measured tone. 'It would take a lifetime. Marked with the same brush as they may be, they are not your concern, and I recognise your efforts to distract from yourself. If you wanted to blend in with the smelters that we've already gathered to save yourself a greater punishment than they'll receive, I'll tell you now that it's a futile effort.'

'I am not a man of futile actions. Something you know from last we met, Vorric.'

Ryza's brow tweaked with a flash of anger. 'You met him?'

'I've met many,' Vorric replied quickly, not breaking his gaze from Aphtus-Hast. 'Many people before I met you, Ryza. Many faceless men that only deserved to be forgotten.'

Ryza went to retort again, to tell Vorric that he should've known to slit the man's throat from the very first moment he'd come face-to-face with him, but Ditric grabbed his arm to hold him back.

Vorric continued as if he hadn't been interrupted.

'Your actions were not futile, Aphtus-Hast. They were effective. Too effective. Thanks to yourself and other flux traders, the paralict of molten flux is now so ingrained across the Droughtlands that we're facing the prospect of never being able to get rid of it. The measures we had to take to contain the spread in areas like Iroka and Kyrea were beyond extreme.'

'But it wasn't my actions, Vorric. The trade of molten flux was measured and cautious. We even had our own scholars researching its properties to further discover how to safely handle it. Why else do you think each of us were so heavily involved with the running of the factories that employed automind-assisted arcanites? A single rash action would've destroyed the industry we'd created. We stood to lose more than anyone else if the flux escaped our control.'

'And yet it was always bound to,' Vorric said, cutting him off. 'The thousands of autominds and the roaring demand for more was always going to result in this outcome. Revance was always going to end up being destroyed when those aboard it realised that your industry was one better joined than fought against. You speak of moderation, but there was never a possibility of it while there were still more reels to be made. The fact of it shows clearly in the wake of Revance's fall. Cardan, another flux trader that—'

'I'm familiar with him,' Aphtus-Hast said. 'A good memory that made up for a poor instinct of when to stop.'

'He created a factory within a ruin left by those-of-glass, according to our reports.'

If Vorric was a less sensible man, he would've glanced over his shoulder at Ryza. But he didn't, continuing on.

'From what I now hear, even you were attempting your own operation of some kind.'

Now Vorric turned to Ryza.

'What did you see there?'

'It was a factory on wheels. Designed to steer clear of those that knew what the flux had become. That knew what you were.'

'And it would've been harmless, had you not destroyed it,' Aphtus-Hast replied. He looked at Vorric. 'Tell me, how will the Droughtlands survive without our factories? Where will the goods come from? Have you thought of that as you plot Breggesa's course forward? The amount of influence you hold over the Council is no secret.'

'Nor is it any of your concern,' Vorric said sternly. 'What is my concern is how you gleaned that this rolling factory of yours must be distant from the rest of civilisation. Why it had to be away from other instances of uncontained molten flux.'

'It's simple. Because we knew the flux to be tainted.'

'Why?'

'Those that see it in its tainted form will expect it to be tainted everywhere.'

'And how did you find untainted flux for this new operation of yours?'

'It wasn't found. We already had it. Stored reserves for such an eventuality.'

'Then my final question is this.' Vorric leaned forwards before he asked it, forcing the entire room to lean in with him. 'Why didn't that flux become tainted, as well? How did you know that it wouldn't? Because I didn't think you did. Because, of the thousands of accounts of how the organisations of the flux traders were run, not a single one mentioned scholars like you just have. No, they put together an image of a trail-and-error method of expansion. The resulting deaths were only beneficial to future business, because they created more autominds. There were no scholars, no research, no foresight. This story of yours is one told backwards, starting with what you believe we want to hear, and ending in an utter fabrication.'

'Why would you be so doubtful?' Aphtus-Hast replied. 'It's what you want to hear.'

Vorric's accusatory interrogation continued with gusto, but Ryza didn't process any of it. He was murmuring his father's last words under his breath, trying to get them to stick in his mind as an actual sentence that had been said, and not just one that'd been thought strenuously.

It's what you want to hear.

What was it about that phrase that was so jarring? Why couldn't Ryza get it out of his head? His hand instinctively began to drift to his holstered rifle, his mind catching up to it a moment later. It wasn't the phrase that bothered him.

It was a word within it.

Want.

He silently flipped the leather strap that held his rifle snuggly in its holster. The freed weapon sprung up slightly from the tightness of the embracing leather, the grip slotting perfectly into Ryza's hand, and he drew it out in a flash. Before it was even level, his finger was pulling the trigger. He didn't need to aim, instinct had already done it for him, just as his instinct knew how long it took for his finger to fire the rifle.

He'd imagined this target a thousand times before. In dreams and in waking. Now it was real and in front of him, he wanted nothing more than to strike and knew that wanting to do so would be more than enough to make it true.

The muzzle of his rifle barked and snapped backwards in his hand as the lead slug hurtled out the barrel. It seared through the air, the metal projectile registering in Ryza's Kretatic senses the split second that it flew. No one else in the room had a chance to react to it, not even Ditric, who'd been standing right next to him when he'd drawn his weapon, so all were taken utterly by surprise when Aphtus-Hast's neck exploded in a brilliant spray of silver liquid.

CHAPTER TEN

ATMOSPHERIC CONTAINMENT

THE MOLTEN FLUX BLOOMING out of the neck of Aphtus-Hast seemed to freeze in midair as Ryza waited for chaos to break. Vorric lurched backwards, his body halfway through a spin as he attempted to find the source of the gunshot. The Scythes beyond him, the ones that'd held Ryza in the backdrop of their gaze, lurched into fighting stances, though none were ready for what was about to happen.

No one except Ruka.

She'd been standing two feet to the left of Vorric, just beyond him so that Ryza would've been on the edge of her vision. She would've caught the flicker of movement as he'd drawn his sawn-off rifle and had spent enough time around him to know what usually came next. Her hands had moved quickly, marshalling axioms to summon a deflective wind that would've stopped the slug, but realising just in time it was too late for such a thing.

There was a snap like another shot had been fired, and every ounce of air was suddenly yanked past Ryza, throwing him and the others toppling like they'd been squarely kicked in the back. They were thrown across the floor or bent over tables, wheezing and gasping for breaths that would not come.

Ryza's eyes stung as he squinted to the middle of the room. Ruka was still on her feet, her right hand held out to the swirling morass of molten flux that was spurting from Aphtus-Hast's skull. Rune after sky-blue rune burned in her open palm, but she wouldn't be able to hold it for long. Ryza knew that a Reythurist's axioms came with a consequence to their breath, and if Ruka hadn't been fortunate enough to have a lungful in her when Ryza had fired his rifle, she'd be on the verge of passing out.

Something moved to Ryza's right. It was Ditric. She'd propped herself up on one of the tables as her legs wobbled under her. She had a bunched handful of fabric from her shirt pressed over her mouth for what little good it would do against the flux while her right hand was extended, streaks of fire rapidly gathering at her palm.

Ryza didn't have the breath to yell, to stop her, to do anything but watch helplessly as Ditric unleashed a burning torrent over all their stunned heads and directly into the heart of the molten flux.

A terrifying amount of molten flux had already emerged from Aphtus-Hast's body. Ruka's sudden vacuum had gathered in as one pressurised sphere about the size of Ryza's fist, but the trailing tendril of silver liquid that connected it to the slumped corpse was adding more by the second.

Ryza couldn't believe he'd missed it. Despite his constant and violent thoughts about what he'd do to his father, he'd never once dreamt that he'd actually find him. He should've never believed his luck. All along, it was the flux playing yet another cruel trick, giving him hope for vengeance and catharsis because that was what he so badly wanted. The charade had only been sustained by how much Ryza had yearned for it, and how all the others that saw him with his father in the days after his capture had known this, too.

It was only now that this copy of his father was among more eyes, more minds, more impressions of what he should be, that their clashing desires for answers had introduced inconsistencies into his character.

Ryza knew that there had never been scholars within the cartel-like ranks of the flux traders, but he'd believed it the moment Aphtus-Hast said it to Vorric because his father had sounded so confident in the idea. Yet the idea itself had only come about from the minds of the other scholars there, closed and full minds that only thought of the world as something to observe and transcribe. It was only logical that the flux would manufacture an idea that would play to their expectation of the world.

There'd been other lies, other things which Aphtus-Hast had said that should've tipped Ryza off, but none had been more obvious than those last words.

It's what you want to hear.

Molten flux was only stable when there was a common understanding of it, be it in the mind of one lone man or in that of thousands. Here, in this room of scholars, in a city of refugees, there was anything but consensus.

Ditric's gout of brilliant fire engulfed the swelling ball of molten flux just as Ruka's breath, and her control of the air that held the flux in place, failed. The silver liquid burst out in all directions, free of the over-compression and desperate to splash upon the unprotected skin of all those in the room, but Ditric's fire stopped this. At least temporarily.

There was a grating screech that Ryza had never heard before as the flux began to pop and snap like an out-of-control engine. Shards, spikes, impaling rods, and even groping limbs lanced out of every surface of the flux as it was forced to solidify. It crashed to the floor as a writhing mass of metal and fire, consuming every piece of furniture it touched as it burned. Aphtus-Hast's body was lost under it, but it had never been his body at all.

At least I got to be the one to kill it.

Now the others had had a chance to catch their breath, they let loose from their lungs a disjointed cacophony of alarmed cries and cautioning shouts. Vorric's voice was loudest among them all. He'd found his feet first, almost as if he'd been subject to sudden losses of air before.

'Vacuum! Vacuum! Burn all runes! Vent masks! Contain at all—'

His own axioms cut him off as he forced the air in the room to snap again. Ryza clamped his mouth shut and clenched his hand over his nose, but that didn't stop his ears feeling like they were being impaled with a skewer. Whatever Vorric had done this time extinguished the flames that licked up the side of the distressed flux. Without the stress of the fire, it reformed into a liquid, gathering as a massive, rounded bubble on the floor before Vorric.

The stonework beneath seemed to sizzle at the edges of it, but before it could burn through to the chambers below, it retracted. Ryza staggered forwards as the flux took a human form. It was as tall as he was. Its shoulders as wide as his. It was him.

His lungs pleaded with him to find a single breath of air, but he was too petrified by the likeness that was standing before him. It wore his clothes, its hair the exact shade of rusted red that his was, it was even clutching its own hand over its nose!

Vorric caught his eye as he looked between him and the apparition. Panic was there. Panic and indignation for having been caught unprepared, two things Ryza had never seen in the man before. The room swirled as Scythes evacuated, each one replaced by another that'd donned a vent mask and was ready with runes of their own.

Ryza wanted to run with them, but he knew what that would look like if he did. He needed to prove that he was the real Ryza before he could be confused for this sudden doppelganger, because if the flux's successful mimicry of Aphtus-Hast was anything to go by, it would be able to replace him with ease.

Ryza reloaded his rifle before anyone could stop him and levelled it with his own reflected face, squeezing the trigger before he could have a second thought. The bright muzzle flash stole his vision, leaving the last image in his mind as not his own face, but of Holm's, wearing that same maniacal grin that he saw every time she appeared in his dreams.

The second slug tore straight through her liquid-silver skull, spraying molten flux across the room and over the backs of the Scythes that were unlucky enough to be in the way. They screamed and thrashed in agony as the liquid metal burrowed into their skins, their terrible plights ignored as their allies stepped over them, wielding hose-connected cannisters that began to suck the rest of the flux from the air.

The flux put up a valiant fight against its captors, exploding into gaseous clouds of blazing flux that were stopped by Vorric's expert control of the air. The room was filled with the sound of more grating screeches as the Scythes' pressurised cases kicked up a notch, syphoning the rest of the flux out of existence.

Vorric let his control of the air finally lapse. He collapsed into the closest chair he could find, his chest heaving. He was dead behind the eyes as he stared at the husks that now stood on the other side of the room. The autominds that were all that was left of the Scythes that'd been hit by the molten flux.

Ryza felt for them. He really did. But he still didn't feel guilty himself. Guilt was a constant numb ache that he'd long grown used to. A necessary sensation to remind him that he was alive and that he was still real.

The Scythes were quick to assess and start rectifying the tragic scene without Vorric yelling at them. Even Ruka, sunk in a shell-shocked crouch in the middle of the room, couldn't bring herself to say a word. Ditric took a step, intending to go over to her, but hesitated and stopped.

There was still too much disbelief in the air to start mending the new grievances that'd sprung up between them. Eventually it was Vorric's weakened voice that broke their silence.

'Did you have to shoot him?'

Ryza weighed his words as he considered the question. If he explained properly, it would take him hours. Instead, he opted for something more cryptic, in keeping with the many similar answers Vorric gave to him in the weeks after they'd first met.

'I wanted to.'

'How long was it that you knew?' Vorric asked, his voice as defeated as his face.

'About as long as it took me to draw my rifle,' Ryza answered. 'You?'

'When he said he'd met me. I have never met him before in my life. He... It... must've believed that saying we had met was the answer we all most wanted. That you, Ryza, would've believed it the most.'

'I did. Be lying if I said he didn't have me fooled the whole time.'

Vorric sprang from his seat, suddenly pacing the room in the space recently vacated by the newly made autominds that'd just been ushered out.

'But Kretatics can detect metal. You should've felt it from the moment you found him,' he chided. 'And that goes for the rest of you! How did we let that thing in here? It could've killed us all! This whole city!'

'Yeah, but it didn't,' Ditric responded. 'It's like Ryza said. Had us all fooled. I questioned the bastard for hours, and he didn't slip up. Wouldn't have even thought of it after what Ryza said had happened. You've heard stories about how all the flux is turning into him. Why would it have happened to Aphtus-Hast, or whatever he was?'

'Doesn't matter why,' Ruka said in a low voice, still crouched on the ground. 'Matters that it happened. That's what we gotta think about.'

'Used us like it used those smelters to make the factory,' Ryza added. 'All those different minds to sustain a truth, just like with Maligar and...'

Ryza trailed off, and Ditric groaned aloud. 'Not her again!'

'No, Foll!' Ryza looked at Vorric, knowing his eyes were wide with panic. 'Where did you take her?'

Vorric's eyes shot open, too. He knew exactly what Ryza was thinking.

Ryza reloaded his rifle as he ran and Vorric dashed across the room. They both barrelled through the corridors of the Academy of Breggesa. Vorric was taking staircases in single bounding leaps both up and down, and Ryza surged forwards in his wake, bashing through unfortunate bystanders.

Vorric came to a skidding stop at the end of one final hallway. He was still hammering on the banded steel door when Ryza caught up a few seconds later. A narrow slat in the upper right-hand corner of the door slid open, and a pair of eyes peered out for a moment. On seeing Vorric, there was a scramble of activity on the other side and the door swung open, just in time for Ditric, Ruka, and a handful of the other Scythes that'd been present for the disaster to catch up.

Together, they burst through the doorway and crowded into the room, a difficult task considering there was only about a square metre of space to stand in. After taking into account the guard that'd let them in, only Vorric and Ryza were truly over the threshold. A set of mesh-like bars that sectioned off the rest of the room. Beyond it was Foll. She was bound to a stone bench by a dozen thick leather straps and still mercifully human.

The breathless ensembled stared at her. She didn't look back.

'Nobody say anything,' Vorric said quickly. 'Not a word. Not a whisper.' He glanced up at the half-stunned guard. 'Atmospheric containment.'

Before Ryza could ask what that meant, Vorric turned and started herding them out of the tiny cell with his arms spread wide to catch anyone that dawdled. His face was suddenly as casual as he could muster it, but he couldn't meet eyes with any of them until the door behind them was sealed shut. One of the other Scythes that'd come with had already set off to enact whatever procedures Vorric had ordered.

Vorric didn't risk another word until they were far enough away from the place they were holding Foll. This took them out of the First Hall and a hundred paces back down the plaza, where concerned scholars were clumping together. The glass of the room they'd just been in was shattered outwards, and a few who'd been nearby were now being treated for the minor scratches inflicted by the falling shards.

They're the lucky ones.

Would the Scythes or the Academy ever share the truth of what happened? Ryza knew he wouldn't, if it were up to him. Not only would it further fuel the very real fears of molten flux, but it would also undermine the confidence the city had in these people. From his time leading the conscripts after the fall of Revance, he knew it was the only way to keep control.

Vorric led them into a squatter building at the other end of the plaza. The stairs inside only took them further into the ground. When Vorric finally turned to face them, Ryza felt a strange, instinctual shake playing in his shoulders.

It's like being under Twin Rings again.

The room they were in felt more like an armoury than a place of learning, which Ryza found comfortingly familiar, at least. The rowed benches reminded him of the cramped briefing chambers that'd been aboard Revance. Ryza had only been on one mission that had necessitated a large enough contingent of conscripts to use the room. After that job, there'd only been enough of them to fill a single lead-better.

A similarly grim mood held the room as they waited for Vorric to address them. Ruka had positioned herself next to Vorric. It was strange to Ryza that Vorric didn't shoo her away. She was the youngest person in the room, yet Vorric was treating her like his deputy.

None of the other Scythes seemed to mind this. They'd taken their places on the sandstone benches with a weary tension in their postures. He tried to count their number but gave up. He'd been trying to figure out if this was all the Scythes that'd been in the room when he'd shot Aphtus-Hast, but since he hadn't counted how many there were in the first place, it was pointless.

Ryza recognised one of them as Caftor, one of the two other Scythes that'd survived the expedition into Iroka's chasm. He looked less stunned than those around him, likely because he'd seen far worse from the flux already. Ryza hadn't taken a seat. He stood near the barred door with his right arm crossed over his chest, his rifle tucked under his left in case he needed to use it again.

Ditric stood with him. At least she was upright and next to him, though with how heavily her back was leaning against the wall, Ryza wouldn't have been surprised if she fell straight through the masonry. She was staring up at the ceiling, shutting her eyes for periods too long to be defined as blinking.

A loud clunk from the other side of the door made Ryza jump. A small hiss filled the air, and Ryza felt his ears begin to ache. Vorric finally started to speak.

'Atmospheric containment,' he announced. He looked dead into Ryza's eyes. 'You have some explaining to do.'

Chapter Eleven

Stale Logic

T HE ASSEMBLED CROWD TURNED in unison, and Ryza felt himself go pale. The only sound was the scraping of Ditric's boots as she shuffled a few steps away from him.

'This entire room has been sealed off from the outside world. Not even our breath can escape this place, which is why this is the only place I can confront you on this, Ryza. If that really is you.'

'Me?' Ryza scoffed. 'Of course I'm...'

Vorric raised an eyebrow, and Ruka quickly copied him, stopping Ryza in his tracks. Now he understood what Vorric was implying. It was the very same doubts that he'd spent months in angst over in the wake of Revance's fall.

'It's me,' Ryza eventually said. 'I promise.'

'Then why are we getting reports of statues of you appearing in contaminated zones? What is your involvement in this?' another Scythe said.

'I agree with the sentiment,' Vorric added. 'Ryza, we need a full report of how you came across this... manifestation of your father.'

Ryza obliged them. He included every detail. His pity for Foll. The argument he had with Elya that'd led to him walking through the night to get back to the League of Revance's camp. And the words his father had said to him that he couldn't have possibly known Ryza had heard before.

'So, I had suspected something, I just couldn't figure out what,' Ryza concluded. 'I think... I think it's Holm's way of getting in my head.'

'Holm. Your former...'

Vorric trailed off, knowing the next word would be too painful for Ryza to hear still.

'Yes,' Ryza said quietly. 'Just like the way Maligar created all those versions of himself and the versions of Origin's skeletons to sustain himself in the flux under Iroka, I think that Holm's somehow using her copies of me to sustain herself somewhere, too.'

'Which explains the statues,' Caftor said. 'But it doesn't, because they have both hands, is that correct?'

Ryza nodded. 'Because they aren't me. Those statues are the versions of me that Holm thinks, or thought I was, or am. I'm not sure how to say it, but the point is that she thought I looked up to her. Saw her as powerful and strong and unstoppable, as if I wanted her to give herself over to the flux. I reckon that's what's going on in the "minds" of those statues. When they all showed up after the factory crashed, I thought they were there because of me, but maybe it was Holm messing with me again.'

Vorric digested this all alarmingly quickly, but somehow it was Ruka that spoke first.

'Then where'd your father come into it?'

'What?' Ryza said, dumbstruck.

'Guessing Holm never met him, right?'

'And? The flux probably pulled it out of my head when the factory crashed anyway.'

'Then how was he walking around before you showed up? You said that the smelter you captured told you that Aphtus-Hast was telling all the smelters that he had pure molten flux, but if he was flux the whole time, how was he walking around before you showed up?'

Ryza's head was suddenly filled with dreadful possibilities, each one more alarming than the last. What if Aphtus-Hast had already given himself over to the flux like Maligar had? But that didn't explain how the statues of Ryza would've appeared in the first place, would it?

Maybe his father had simply spent enough time around molten

flux that the flux itself had a good enough estimation to replicate him. But even so, how would the flux have known to create a copy of Aphtus-Hast long before Ryza was bound to come after him?

'It's an interesting prospect, Ruka, but let's not get ahead of ourselves,' Vorric said. 'We still don't have a working understanding of flux, nor a way to truly detect it. What happened just now proves this starkly. We cannot go about prescribing it plots and plans and personhood just because it presented us with such an image. That's what it wants. If I'm understanding our thus far gathered interpretations, it wants that because that's what *we* want. We're attacking this problem with stale logic. Our attempts to understand the flux haven't worked because we expect it to change, which means each time we come close to understanding it, it will change to defy us because we *expect* it to do so. Do you follow?'

Some in the room nodded, but most shook their heads like Ryza. Vorric attempted another explanation.

'I'll try to put it this way. Molten flux remained stable under the flux traders because we had a common understanding of the flux's properties. All of us. All across the Droughtlands, yes? In that time, the flux was only used in ways it was intended to be, in quantities that were well-regulated, by people who believed they'd mastered the process. It was only with what happened in Iroka that new conditions were introduced to it. Conditions that we attempted to observe, study, and learn from because we expected it to behave differently. Therefore, the flux did behave differently.'

'So, we aren't meant to learn from it?' another Scythe asked.

Vorric shook his head. 'It's too late for that. Too many have already witnessed the changing nature of flux and now also expect it to change more. Even if we managed to realign our own expectations to something more rigid, we'd still subconsciously wonder what could come next. As terrifying as it is, we now face a scenario where we don't know where flux ends and pure resonance begins. A dangerous question Ryza still grapples with.'

Ryza didn't respond right away. His face was twitching too much as his mind gnawed on Vorric's words. The others were now looking at him with trepidation, a new fear in their hearts for whatever explosive failure was about to occur in Ryza's head.

'I still don't know,' Ryza said.

'Good. Keep it that way.'

'But maybe Holm being in the flux is a good thing,' Ditric piped up. She had her eyes shut as she spoke, all brain power directed into parsing out the words correctly. 'We don't *need* to understand the flux. Can't, like you said. But we can understand Holm. Tell me if I'm getting this right, but the more of the flux that's... that's her, the more it'll behave like... I don't know what the fuck she's up to now, but it's better than it being *just* flux, right?'

'That's a good idea, Ditric,' Ruka said. 'We can find out what she wants and then stop her from getting it.'

'It's me she wants,' Ryza muttered. 'But she's already got all the versions of me she wants. She isn't going to get corrupted or "run out of ideas" like Maligar. Shit, even with me knowing what she is now, seeing more of me would only re-enforce what she's doing, right?'

Small clusters of murmurs broke out in the confused room, and Ryza wasn't sure he fully understood what he'd just said, either.

'We just have to keep you away from the flux, then,' Ditric said, clapping him on the shoulder. 'Find a nice little box somewhere far away to put you and we wait for it all to blow over.'

'You really think it would be that simple?' Ruka asked.

'It might be!' Ditric shot back. 'The only thing I've managed to get from all this is that you're all thinking about this too fucken hard!'

The room chuckled at her, and Ditric began to fume, but Vorric waved them into silence.

'Ditric has a point, even if it was crudely put. If we focus on dealing with the minds in the flux, then the flux may just take care of itself,' Vorric said.

'The minds? Plural?' one of the Scythes said.

'Yes. Minds. From what I've been piecing together, Holm isn't the only one "within" the flux.'

'Who else?'

'Origin,' Ryza answered.

He'd known the answer all along, but it hadn't made sense to give it voice until now. Ever since he'd found Origin, both the arcanite that represented him and the skeleton he'd once been, down beneath the ruins of those-of-glass, he'd questioned what version of the truth the little arcanite had been telling him with his cryptic little thoughts. Ryza had thought that Archarus' own musings on the topic had been to help, but they'd only made the fog of the truth denser.

Ryza had been sure that Origin, the being from the time of those-of-glass, was still alive through some miracle of forgotten magic, and it was this miracle that the molten flux was mimicking in order to give false life to the autominds it reanimated. The truth had changed over time, but Ryza hadn't noticed it doing so.

The disappearance of Origin the arcanite the night before the conscripts' showdown against Revance in Iroka was something Ryza had put down to the mysterious motives of the little contraption. When he had stumbled upon the thing again in the unnatural and endless lake of molten flux in the ruins, a hollow cavern where the bunker's guts had once been, he'd barely been surprised to find the arcanite busy at work.

Origin had been constructing a bridge from the cacophony of pointless factory machines the molten flux was attempting to construct and towards some impossibly far point somewhere in the distance. He'd only told Ryza that he was going away. Ryza hadn't even wondered where that was, let alone how Origin had gotten there in the first place. But why hadn't he?

Archarus had been helpfully by Ryza's side to share that Origin had made his own way back to this place from Iroka, but now Ryza thought of it, how was it even possible that Origin had crossed such a distance on his spindly coiled legs?

'There's a few things that don't add up about Origin,' Vorric said. 'But I think that's something for Ryza and myself to discuss in private.'

The Scythes didn't protest at the prospect of withheld knowledge. Even Ruka only tweaked a lip in restrained protest, a sign of how well-integrated into the Scythes that she'd become. Only Ditric voiced her displeasure, letting out a barely audible grumble. Her words were jumbled together, but Ryza didn't need to be able to discern them to know that the majority had been vehement profanities.

Another few minutes passed as Vorric doled out orders to the rest of his assembled flock. The commands were vague in nature, with little in the way of a deadline or a clear objective. These were things the Scythes were equipped to decide along the way, an implicit trust they traded with Vorric that made them far more efficient than anything Revance's conscripts had ever managed.

Ryza looked over to Ditric every now and then, wondering if she was taking notes on how she could run the League of Revance as the years wore on, but she seemed to be lost in another world. Ryza didn't begrudge her that. She was probably mulling over the endless list of palms to grease and ears to snag that came with the duties of running a mercenary company. Another thing the walking fortress of Revance had never had to deal with.

Rusty as the fortress may've been, the name that it had carried was untarnished. Now the mention of Revance elicited dark and disappointed mutterings, especially from those who'd had family in Iroka.

With the makings of a plan appropriately distributed, Vorric ordered the room to be unsealed. The air hissed and squealed again, and this time Ryza spotted the miniscule, vented grates in the upper corners of the chamber's ceiling. Ryza was rubbing his right temple as the heavy door swung open and remained as one of the last in the room, along with Ditric.

'You fucken make sure that we're still getting paid for bringing in whatever your father was.'

'You'll be paid,' Vorric called from beyond the doorframe, having seen the others off with fresh demands.

Vorric walked back in, alone this time. He'd dropped his steely mask of composure and now looked as gaunt as Ryza felt.

'I have to applaud your quick thinking again, Ditric. Had you not burnt the flux when you did, we wouldn't be having this conversation.'

'You can chuck in a few extra reels if you're that grateful,' Ditric replied. 'It was instinct. Ryza started shooting, I started—'

'I mean it, Ditric. My family is in this city. They, along with everyone else, would've been lost. I've been receiving reports of breaches of containment at the various places we've been forced to cordon, but we've never had an incident within Breggesa. It signals that it's time to take extreme measures, and I'll happily bankrupt Breggesa before we risk something like this again.'

'What about the refugees?' Ryza asked. 'There are thousands of them inside and outside the walls that don't have anywhere to live.'

Vorric let out a tired grunt. 'Another thing I've been nudging the Council to accelerate. Like everyone else, they just don't want to spend the reels to get the work done.'

'Then make 'em spend the reels!' Ditric snapped. 'Everyone's too tight with the reels as it is. Makes me think nobody has any.'

'Because no one does,' Vorric said. 'Our current estimate is that most stockpiles of physical currency were lost in the cordoned cities such as Kyrea due to the—'

'Flux traders,' Ryza finished.

Ditric's face lit up with a grin. 'Could go in and get them ourselves!'

'No, you couldn't,' Vorric said sharply. 'Besides, I'll be authorising a distribution of reels that'll make you forget about such a venture.'

'But you said everyone had run out.'

'And what do you do when you run out of reels, Ryza?' Vorric asked, coyly.

'Really?' Ryza shot back.

Vorric let out a stiff, unpractised, and mechanical chuckle. 'My poor jokes aside, yes. More reels. The guild in charge of their creation has warned me such a thing will destroy the shadow of a trade industry that the Droughtlands has left. I told them it's already destroyed, so they just instructed me to see that the reels were distributed to hands that are ready to spend them. There are other mercenary companies out there that we're targeting as a focus of this redistribution. I worry about greed overpowering these efforts and resulting in these extra reels ending up in vaults, however I have confidence you'll spend them well, as yours is one of the few that isn't trying to make a profit.'

'Oh, we're fucken trying!' Ditric said with a stilted laugh.

A Gentle Push

Ryza and Vorric saw Ditric off once they'd left the underground confines of the Academy's halls, but not before she'd verbally strong-armed Vorric into handing over any reels he had on his person as means of an advance on the promised payments. He didn't seem bothered by it, even making a joke that Ditric had done him a favour in lightening his pockets.

Even with the promise of plenty more reels to be coming her way, Ryza had the distinct sense that Ditric was thinking more about the rumoured vaults full of the currency buried away in Kyrea. They were just there and up for grabs, she'd kept whispering to Ryza as Vorric had distributed his orders, enough to build a new Revance, almost.

Maybe he shouldn't bother worrying. With the amount of molten flux apparently infecting the place, Ditric wouldn't stand a chance getting near it, with or without vent suits.

As Vorric led him back towards the First Hall, Ryza found it hard to listen to Vorric's words. Another niggling doubt had taken his mind. He knew Vorric was a man of martialled emotions, but how could he be this calm in the face of what had just happened? Ryza lost focus of where he was walking, and he knocked shoulder-first into a passing scholar, throwing them to the ground.

There was a short commotion as Ryza, Vorric, and others nearby rushed to help them up before they all went about their business as if nothing had happened.

Maybe that's what Vorric's trying to do to trick the flux.

It was a disposition Ryza could not match, even if he tried. As they re-entered the First Hall, he imagined what other incomprehensible things had been seen by those they passed. He could recall Archarus' strange philosophy on the benefit of an empty mind versus an expectant one, but how could these people call their minds empty after all they'd supposedly seen? How did they avoid the questions that stopped Ryza from sleeping at night or the looming thoughts he could not speak of?

It was like everyone in the Academy of Breggesa was trained in a school of careful and selective ignorance. Perhaps that was why he and Ditric hadn't seen Ruka much since they'd all left Iroka behind them.

Vorric took Ryza up another flight of stairs as he maintained a meaningless conversation with him. They didn't go back to the highest storey where Ryza had first found Vorric that day. Scythes were already stationed at the landing of those stairs as others quietly worked to decontaminate the mess without causing a panic. If it were up to Ryza, he would've ordered a total evacuation of the campus, maybe even the whole city, but Vorric seemed to know better.

The corridor they were now in was deathly quiet. It was a narrow place without windows and a ceiling that felt three times too tall. If Ryza was to guess, it had been constructed as an afterthought. As if the First Hall had originally been two buildings with an alleyway between, and this was just a means to connect them. His only evidence for this was the jarring contrast in the stonework of the walls on either side. He brought up the theory to Vorric, eliciting another stiff chuckle.

'A good question, Ryza. But which of the two would really be the First Hall, and which is the addition?'

'The oldest, probably.'

'Would it? What if it was only called the First Hall after the two had become one?'

'Are you trying to tell me something?' Ryza probed.

Vorric stopped, and for a moment, Ryza thought he might actually get to the point and spare him his cryptic way of unfolding words. But he wasn't nearly as lucky. There was a narrow door embedded into the newer side of the wall made up of two heavily riveted iron panels. Rust had taken to it affectionately and spread out across the surrounding masonry at the hinges.

Ryza expected Vorric to knock, but instead the man placed a single hand at the centre of the door's face and leaned his weight slightly into it. Vorric's eyes were shut as he kept applying pressure, his eyes twitching beneath the skin as he searched for some unknowable sweet spot. Ryza glanced back at the door. There was no visible latch or locking mechanism, so it should just swing open.

Would probably open a bit faster if he just gave it a good kick, too.

But such force was unnecessary. Without a single sound, the door swung open. Ryza marvelled at the hinges as Vorric led him through. It was impossible for them to have been so silent. The rust had eaten away at them so badly that half had been missing! He looked to Vorric, who'd just shut the door behind him.

'It's one of the few paralicts we don't keep in strict containment,' Vorric explained. 'The report is in here somewhere. One of the early scholars of the Academy found this metal that only moved in response to a precise degree of force. I've no idea how they got it back here, but it makes for a discreet locking mechanism for this place.'

'But couldn't anyone figure out how to push it like that?' Ryza asked. 'Where are we, anyway?'

'They could. But they could more easily demolish the wall next to it. And if they've found the means to do that, then the Academy has a greater problem on its hands.'

Vorric moved past Ryza and threw a metal lever that was embedded in a nearby wall. A choir of metal clanks rang out in sequence, getting softer and softer as they receded into the distance. Each sound unhid a bracketed glow orb that was slotted into the wall that cast a vertical slat of near-solid yellow light onto the shelves opposite.

Ryza took a few steps into the now lit hall, his head swivelling as he tried to sight the ends of the narrow space.

Perhaps this was the walled-off alleyway Ryza had imagined. Despite its stretching length, the hall was only two metres wide. On one side, the side that held the door they'd just entered through, the wall was bare, holding only the arrayed glow orbs. The mouths of their brackets were like a metal lower jaw, and Ryza guessed they were all connected mechanically to the lever Vorric had just thrown.

The other side was a spectacle that could not be illuminated enough. Shelves of ancient steel stretched twelve metres to touch the ceiling. Ladders with rungs of narrow pegs poked out from the frames and into the walkway, offering the only means to ascend to the upper shelves.

An uncountable number of old leather tomes, parchments bound by ancient strings, and carefully filed scraps of paper lay before Ryza. He should've realised what they were before Vorric had thrown light on them. There'd been a musty smell that'd hit him like a gust when the door first opened, and Ryza guessed it had been building up for eons.

The rims of the sagging shelves were marked with some kind of scratched-out filing system that Ryza couldn't make sense of. Some of the shelves weren't marked at all. Those that held nothing instead had been cut and warped into crudely built-in tables and chairs up and down the height of the shelves. Ryza even spotted one at the very ceiling.

'This is the Academy of Breggesa's Archives,' Vorric said.

He began to walk along the shelves, running his finger over each scratched-in inscription as he passed, muttering under his breath like he was translating their meanings just from touch.

'And this place is just... empty?' Ryza asked as he followed.

Vorric looked at Ryza and then back to the loaded shelves.

'No one's here, I mean.'

'It's not forbidden knowledge, if that's what you ask. It's old knowledge. Expired knowledge. Writings and reports that were once thought of as fact that have now become little more than historical errors by the new findings which are kept in our main libraries. The Academy sets out into the Droughtlands to observe a true understanding of its nature, so what good is a misconception?'

'Is this about your maps again?' Ryza asked.

Vorric stopped in front of a particular shelf.

'In a way.'

He traced his finger over the scratched inscription at the shelf's edge a few more times, then did so with his other hand for good measure.

'I've suspected we've been missing something about the flux for a while now. Something I'm not even sure you've questioned, Ryza.'

Vorric began climbing the stumpy pegs, speaking between silent breaths of exertion. It looked like hard going. The rungs were barely large enough to hold. To stand on them, Vorric could only use his toes.

'Origin... I've wondered where he came from for a while now, but it was only what Ruka brought up as we discussed what happened with your father... Whatever that thing was... That I realised I had been asking the wrong questions of myself. That I hadn't—'

Vorric stretched sideways as far as the wingspan of his arms would allow and plucked a bound set of parchments from the upper shelves.

'—looked back far enough.'

'What do you mean?' Ryza said as Vorric began his descent. 'About him convincing the smelters he was real?'

Vorric's boots hit the ground. He walked over to one of the glow orbs and began gingerly leafing through the fragile parchments.

'Not quite,' he replied. 'Tell me, Ryza, have you ever wondered about the origins of Revance?'

'I found one of them,' he said, trying not to grin.

'I thought you'd say that,' Vorric muttered. He paused. 'Maybe there's another truth to those words... By any means, you were conscripted, yes? What story did they tell you?'

Ryza shrugged. In his first week aboard the walking fortress, it felt as though he was fed a dozen different stories, none of which lined up with the truth of who or what controlled it.

'That they just found an arcanite walking through the dunes and started slapping more metal onto it.'

'And you never questioned it?' Vorric asked quickly. 'Never asked what came before that?'

'Not unless I wanted extra duties.'

'Another reason why the Academy never could've helped Revance. They never rewarded inquisitiveness. They rewarded the opposite, in fact.'

Ryza paused for a moment. Now he was giving it consideration, there was a great deal of Revance's past that didn't make sense. Why had it been wandering the Droughtlands in the first place? Why that specific route between the outskirts of both Iroka and Breggesa?

'It was just left as a mystery to us,' Ryza eventually said. 'Besides, I had other stuff to deal with, especially after I found Origin.'

'But you weren't the first, were you? You told me you found Origin in a stash held by smelters, bound towards Revance after mercenaries brought him up from another undercity.'

Ryza nodded. 'Still remember what one of them said about the place. I know I've been down one, but it was nothing like what he saw. Said something about stairs that went down when they should've gone up—'

'What did he say?' Vorric blurted.

He quickly ruffled back through the parchments to the first one, his eyes darting from left to right as he read quickly.

'They'd been down there before you.'

'Down where?'

'Twin Rings. That's where they found Origin. Unless there's some other ruin that possesses a similar fracture relating to stairs like that, because that's what the original expedition that *found* molten flux detailed.'

'Wait, there were other ways down there?' Ryza said. His mind did a double take as he realised what else Vorric had said. 'That's where they found Origin!?'

Vorric stepped to Ryza's side to show him the face of the parchment, but the scratched writing was so decayed it was inseparable from the tanned texture of the parchment itself.

'But they still weren't the first, were they?'

'Were they?'

'Who controlled Revance? That whole time, an arcanite so immense Tyrag needed an army of autominds to hold it, but who controlled it before?'

'It was Origin,' Ryza said. 'As I know, he created it, he even said he made weapons for them. The bolt-locks I told you about, that's what Origin said Revance used to fight with.'

'And how old is Revance, Ryza?'

'Old.'

'Older than this,' Vorric snapped, shaking the faded parchments. 'Older than the expedition that uncovered molten flux in the first place.'

Ryza swore, and Vorric repeated the same under his own breath.

'Our understanding of the flux stands on a foundation that's false. It wasn't first disturbed seventy years ago. Either someone else was down there, or someone, Origin or something else, decided to come out and create Revance.'

'But why?'

'I don't know, Ryza,' Vorric said, his voice faltering slightly. 'But you understand how dangerous a question like this can be, don't you?'

'Don't lecture me about dangerous questions,' Ryza spat. 'I've asked them all and I've got back nothing.'

The chiding order had flared his temper, but there was something else in the air that was putting him on edge.

'But no one else can know this. It must stay between the two of us.'

Ryza felt the hairs on the back of his neck stand on end. He looked up as slowly as he could, keeping his eyes focused on Vorric but still aware of the silhouette standing in the hall beyond him.

Archarus.

CHAPTER THIRTEEN

ORIGIN'S ORIGINS

RYZA STAYED AS STILL as he could. He didn't even let out his breath, for fear that Vorric would feel the irregularity in the air he exhaled and detect that there was something far more terrifying than a question in their presence.

He bought time by looking between the parchment and Vorric, his mouth ajar as if the look of being on the cusp of a word would hold Vorric for a second longer. Just one more heartbeat to give Archarus an opportunity to disappear before Vorric saw him. They'd been through unimaginable peril together in the tunnels beneath Iroka. They'd seen impossible things that promised to drive men mad. Vorric had even hinted at seeing a shadow dancer himself, but Ryza could not stomach the thought of afflicting him with the sight of another.

He risked the quickest glance past Vorric, and his eyes snapped into focus on Archarus. His pale face was identical to the one that had once haunted Ryza's dreams, but now it was wearing an expression of dumbfounded shock. The look of a man kicking himself for having just found a searched-for pair of spectacles that'd been perched on his forehead.

But when Ryza looked back to Vorric, Vorric's gaze seemed just as distant as his own.

'Is this as it's meant to happen?' Vorric asked softly.

'Wait, you know he's there?' Ryza whispered back.

Vorric met his eyes again, another shot of panic setting in.

They both spun in a whirl, and Ryza's hand snapped to the grip of his rifle, but the only thing he found behind his back was the stretching gloom of the empty Archives. Ryza's breath strained to escape at his throat, but he didn't let it. Behind him, Vorric was silent as well.

Ryza turned again. Archarus still stood there in the distance, his form more distinct than the gloom that surrounded him. Vorric continued to stare at the shadow dancer, dumbstruck and unable to muster a word.

'Just go,' Ryza whispered. 'Please. Just go.'

'I can't,' Archarus replied. 'A question has been asked that I had not realised myself. Besides, what difference would it make?'

'You've been watching from the shadows,' Vorric said. 'Archarus, I take it?'

'And you do not fear me. I understand why.'

At Archarus' words, Ryza glanced over his shoulder again, but there was still nothing there.

'Why? What happened?' Ryza said quickly.

'I don't think I can tell him, can I?' Archarus said to Vorric.

'I'm unsure. That's what worries me most,' Vorric said.

'Can you both just cut the lizard shit? Why are you here, Archarus? And you, Vorric! You'd better tell me what's going on quick, because you just watched five of your people get turned into autominds and this has you more scared.'

Ryza waved his arm back at the empty Archive behind him, and for the first time in his life, he watched as Vorric crumpled slightly.

'I saw uncertainty. Something I've been wary of this entire life. Of all the things I've dealt with, the impossibilities I've seen, I've coped with the memory of them through a certainty that somehow they were meant to happen. That there was some unexplained, logical cause and effect that would follow the other things we deem natural law.'

'Yeah, well, we've seen a bit of that lately, haven't we?' Ryza muttered.

'But don't you see that we've put it all down to the flux? We've given it reason and logic, and the flux has responded to it in kind.'

Ryza stared at Vorric for a few moments longer in the vain hope that he'd get more of an explanation. He gave up, looking at Archarus instead.

'And you? Finally decided to help?'

Archarus looked away for a moment. 'If you'd permit me.'

'You're a shadow dancer!' Ryza burst out. 'Whose permission do you—'

He fell silent as he realised Archarus' question wasn't for him and looked back at Vorric.

'He's talking to your shadow dancer, isn't he?'

Vorric sighed. 'I supposed I've been too reckless in the clever little hints I've been dropping in your path. Then again, there's a part of me that wanted you to ask directly. A shadow dancer is a constant companion that makes for a lonely existence.'

'Loneliness. What a terrible fate,' Archarus said dryly. 'I'm here because you both stumbled upon a question I never had thought of myself.'

'Origin's origins,' Ryza said.

'To put it blithely, yes. The walking fortress of Revance was an established fact even in my time. But I never had the opportunity to spend enough time with both the fortress and with Origin while I was alive to detect and interpret his magnetic resonance. To connect the pair like you have, Ryza. I'd wager that you're likely the only living soul that's ever done so.'

'Sure, it's a mystery, but why do we need to figure it out?' Ryza asked Vorric.

'Because it implies that we were wrong about molten flux, and therefore the molten flux is wrong about itself. That it only behaves this way due to the conditions which Archarus, and then Rettic after him, found it in.'

Vorric waved the sheaf of parchments, making the oldest of them flap most prominently.

'The Droughtlands' entire understanding of how flux works, how autominds and controlling them works, stems entirely from one expedition and the experiments that followed. Yet somehow, despite all this, despite Revance itself being controlled by Origin, an immortal being so closely linked to the fortress, the fortress still didn't change with it. I don't know what that means, but perhaps that's the point. If you can discover the real truth, Ryza, the real origin, then you might just find a way to vanquish molten flux once and for all.'

'And it has to be me?'

Both Archarus and Vorric exchanged an uneasy look.

'You're afraid I'd doubt the flux?' Ryza asked.

'Of course we are,' Archarus said. 'I've seen what you've been through, Ryza. I began following you because I believed you would survive pure resonance with the help of molten flux, just like I attempted. After all you've been through, however, I'm baffled that you've yet to crack. It's as if you're surviving pure resonance out of your spite for molten flux.'

Ryza grumbled an inaudible answer as his head began to spin. He cleared his throat and tried to respond again, but nothing came out.

'Dangerous questions, Archarus,' Vorric said with a note of caution in his voice. 'I'm sure you want to put a stop to the flux as much as the rest of us.'

'Indeed. It can't kill me, but the prospect of an eternity watching a world of liquid metal makes me shudder.'

'So you're finally going to help me?' Ryza asked. 'No tricks? No games?'

'Yes. But you must understand that there's still things that I must keep from you. I've watched you grow volatile, Ryza. I thought that being faced with your father would be enough to push you beyond your limits, let alone having his death snatched from you.' Archarus paused for a heartbeat, his mouth half-open as he pondered the price of his next question. 'How do you feel about that?'

'I don't want to feel anything,' Ryza spat. 'It wasn't real. It was Holm playing with me, using my own mind, too.'

'But everything you felt until then was real, wasn't it?'

'Archarus, enough!' Vorric snapped.

'No,' Ryza said. 'He's right. It was real. But I need to feel these things, don't I? The rage and the anguish. I know they're mine. It's all that's kept me going since Revance fell. I live because I feel.'

'But what if the flux feels?' Archarus asked.

'Then it lives,' Ryza growled. 'And I can kill it.'

As resolute as their goal was, their first steps towards it were slow and tedious. Research was something Ryza wasn't nearly as adept at as Vorric or Archarus, but he was forced to take part in it anyway. Most of it was following Archarus' spectral image as he perused the archival shelves, muttering his displeasure at the number of closed minds all this written knowledge had created.

Wherever Archarus spied a book or article that might look promising from its outer pages, it was up to Ryza to ascend the spindly rungs of the shelves to retrieve it, as the shadow dancer was insistent on reminding him that he couldn't touch the pages, no matter how many times Ryza said he understood.

Ryza quickly lost his patience with the whole process. Standing with Archarus and waiting to be permitted to turn over the next page created a stillness that made Ryza's bones jitter in their sockets. He checked over his shoulder. Vorric had headed in the opposite direction along the stretching row of shelves, able to both read and retrieve without assistance. He was far enough away now that his own body was a silhouette, so surely it meant he was well beyond earshot.

'We're wasting our time,' Ryza whispered.

'This research is important. As much as I want to pity you and avoid heaping you with blame, we've seen the results of your... less-than-scholarly approach.'

'And I'm still not the one that went fucking around with molten flux in the first place,' Ryza hissed back.

Before Archarus could retort, Ryza wedged the book he was currently holding open under his arm and tore out the next few dozen pages, scattering them across the floor and then using the toe of his boot to space them out. Archarus gasped as the dust and grit from his shoe stained the ancient parchment, but not loud enough to draw Vorric's attention.

'There's your reading. I'm going to look for more.'

'You don't even know what you're looking for,' Vorric shouted from the other end of the Archive. 'Let alone what you're meant to destroy!'

'Well, it's got to be old, ain't it? Anything as old as Revance was.'

Ryza's confidence in this definition quickly waned. Like Vorric had promised, everything around him was *old*. Yet no matter how high he climbed the shelves, no matter how dusty the fraying tomes had become, they still held no reference of Revance's beginnings. All the words he found hazed and blurred before his eyes. Only after picking up the same book three times did he realise just how tired he was. The blood rush of the incident an hour prior was wearing off, along with it his ability to remain conscious.

Vorric was still far down the other Archives, and Archarus was still reasonably preoccupied, crouched over the scattered trail of pages that Ryza had left behind. They hadn't said a word for the past twenty minutes. If Ryza were to guess, they probably hadn't even looked at him, either.

Not like I'm doing much to help anyway.

He climbed slowly up to one of the desk-and-chair contraptions that was embedded in the shelves. It was a fight not to simply hang limp and fall asleep there and then, but he forced himself on to the thin metal chair and shrugged off his coat. It fluttered and flapped as he spun it around his arm into a bundle of creased leather. Putting it on the table, he lay his head down on it like it was a pillow and was pleased with how effective it was.

Better than a normal cot.

For a moment, it felt like he was falling from his perch up on the shelves, but his body stilled as darkness consumed him. He could feel his eyes squeezing shut, his eyelids squabbling to overlap with each other as he pushed further and further into his sleep. It was this semi-controlled way of sleeping that was the only way he managed to get any semblance of rest these days, but it wouldn't avoid the dreams entirely.

Like always, the silver sand was there, but at least it was not an island in a sea of molten flux. It flowed and breezed over the hills and dunes before him, stretching out to distant horizons he had no intent of approaching. He could see the beginnings of the flux sea there. Black stone blocks stood like pebbles among the lapping waves. The liquid crashed over them in sprays that disappeared into the air, and when the block re-emerged, they seemed to have shifted.

From the top of the hill he was standing on, Ryza could watch them with a curled lip. He knew what they were and what they had once been. But they were no more, so why did they still fill his mind?

'Because they're still real,' a voice whispered to Ryza.

Her voice.

Ryza's breathing stilled. He wasn't sure if he'd been breathing in the first place, but now he could only think of the sudden absence of air in his lungs. He didn't dare turn to face the speaker. He knew she'd come into view soon enough.

Holm's form took gracious, dance-like steps across his vision. She was far from him, ten paces or more, but her words came as if they'd been trickled into his left ear.

'They're real to you,' Holm said. 'Just as I am real to you.'

The shining silver liquid that clad her body dissolved, flashing him for a moment with pale, uncovered skin before strands of fabric and leather sprouted from her pores like fine hairs. They curled and weaved into patches, the patches then overlapping into garments, fluttering and folding until Holm was garbed in the very forge leathers she'd been wearing when she and Ryza had first met.

She approached him as a jagged weight began to grow around his neck. His hands snapped up to it, his left suddenly restored and made of flesh, and found coarse metal surrounding his throat. He scratched at it, gouged at his skin, anything to wrench the conscript's collar off, but Holm's next words stopped him.

'Please don't do that.'

Her voice was tired. Uncaring and frustrated. Exactly the way she'd sounded when they'd first met. She was looming over him now, and Ryza couldn't figure out how she'd become so tall until he realised that he was squatting in an odd half-crouch.

'Why?' Ryza said, his hands still gently pressed on the collar.

'Last thing I want to do is clean your corpse out of here. Even then, the smell of the blood...' She wrinkled her nose in disgust, and a small trickle of blood came from her left nostril like she'd just been punched.

Another few droplets appeared at the corner of her eyes like they were tears, then suddenly the lakes of flux at the horizon were a stark red. The blood rose up in waves, consuming the grey dunes and coursing through their troughs and valleys like newly formed rivers until Ryza was once again on the little island with Holm.

Now Ryza could smell the blood. All different kinds of it. The blood that seeped from an infected wound that'd become more bandage than flesh. The blood that got stuck deep in his nasal cavity after a smelter died on top of him. The blood that was his own, rushing out in furious gouts after Maligar had blown his left hand clean off.

He let out a gasp of pain as he relived the memory, and his left hand fell away. It landed soundlessly in the sand at his feet, and the detached fingers launched into their work. They grabbed and skittered at the sand, digging and burying itself deeper and deeper as the decapitated wound at the wrist pumped more blood than his hand could have possibly held.

But that blood was not like the rest. It spattered and splashed in individual droplets, unsure if it should be crimson or silver until the moment it hit the ground. Grey-green and purple scabs grew from it like weeds as it dried and coagulated. The now tiny island was soon covered in a reef of waving maroon grass. The sea of blood tried to retreat from it as one great wave, but it was too late.

The grass met the shoreline and the scabbing continued, turning the vast ocean into a lumpy plain of sharpened, scabbed edges and sore, infected flesh.

Ryza looked back to Holm. She was still mercifully human, but he knew it wouldn't last long. His decapitated hand was still thrashing at his feet, searching for something buried just below them. Ryza dropped to his knees and used his remaining hand to help it. He rapidly scooped out handful after handful of grey sand, fighting back the infectious blood grass, until his nails hit something hard.

Metal.

He looked up at Holm once more. She'd crouched down so they were face-to-face, her lips less than an inch from his as her breath roared across his skin like the gust of an open furnace.

'Makes everything rusty as well.' A smirk crossed her face which Ryza registered as her usual expression.

The shattered remains of his forearm's bones lanced out like a pair of thrust pipes, no longer pale and full of marrow, but hollow and made of metal. Powdered rust danced across them in jagged bolts, falling like sky-carried sand onto the ground inches below.

Once the seeds had been sown, the rust infected the bloody grass. Each blade collapsed like a toppled stone tower as jagged pillars of rust rushed to replace them until they fell as well. It made a shaking hiss in the air as it spread across the tiny island.

The scabbed mass that'd once been an ocean cracked and crackled as it tried to retreat like the blood it had once been, but once again, it was too late. The rust took to the vaguely fleshy flats and turned the skin to metal, then the metal to rust, then the rust into powder that dissolved all its form until it was no different from the orange dunes of sand that Ryza had lived and breathed all his life.

Rusty.

'That's what I'll call you! Because of your hair!'

Holm's cry was a joyous one that had her back on her feet, walking away in a taunting prance that beckoned Ryza to follow. He rose from his knees and hesitated, the sands before him once again grey.

'Origin,' he called out.

Holm stopped, frozen mid-step.

'Where is he?'

Holm turned, her face and her skin beneath her old clothes once again silver. Her smirk remained.

'He is here.'

'I need to find him.'

'Then point the way.'

'But I don't—'

Ryza felt a weight suddenly yank at his left arm. The left hand was back again, secured at the end of his nub like it had never left. But it wasn't his, nor the one he'd been given aboard Revance. It was the one Origin had made. The one Holm had instructed him to make.

'But I destroyed it,' Ryza said, realising what she meant. 'Origin destroyed it. Took his resonance from it.'

'Because that's what you wanted. He gave you what you wanted, just as I tried to give you what you wanted.'

'My father.'

She rushed back to him, grinning with glee.

'Ryza, I love you, that's why I know what you want!'

The words echoed from her mouth out of time with her lips, produced not from her throat here and now, but from the memory of their last fight before she'd given herself over to the flux.

'Why?' Ryza asked weakly.

Her lips moved, but no words came out. She smiled at him as if she'd just spoken, but the only sound was the soft whisper of the ethereal wind playing on the dunes of powdered rust.

'I never knew, either,' Ryza whispered back.

Chapter Fourteen

Ancient Rites

A GENTLE NUDGING SHOOK Ryza awake, but he still rose with a yelp. There was a rocking clang of metal and the world lurched under him before his vision returned, but the sudden rush of motion was halted when a strong grip seized his right hand.

Through the darkened blur, he could make out Vorric sitting across from him in the cramped table built into the Archive's shelves. His face was a strained grimace, not for the difficulty of stopping Ryza from cracking his head on the marble ground below, but a worn patience that he no longer held the capacity for.

Ryza shimmied himself back into his seat and rubbed the corners of his eyes with his forefinger and thumb. Vorric let him play out the motion before he even acknowledged that Ryza was truly awake. Instead, Vorric kept gently palming his way through the new collection of books and papers he had carefully arranged around Ryza's sleeping form. In his other hand, he held a glow orb high above it all.

'Would you?'

He passed the orb to Ryza. It felt warm on his palm, not for the light but the heat of Vorric's flesh. Ryza gripped it tight with his fingers as he suspended it in the place where Vorric had been holding it, leaving his thumb free to gently caress the glow orb's glassy surface with his thumbnail.

'Did you find something?'

Vorric hummed affirmingly but didn't go on right away. 'You were dreaming.'

'I was tired. A lot's happened. Surprised you aren't... aren't anything, really. You aren't scared or shocked or... nothing. Not until you saw—'

'What did you see?' Vorric asked quickly.

'Is Archarus here?'

Vorric twitched. 'He took his leave. Now, what did you see?'

A deep breath came and went as a sigh for Ryza. He didn't like reliving his dreams, especially not when they were so fresh. He could still taste the tang of the dream's rusted air on his tongue. It was hard to distinguish from that of blood, which had also been remarkably present.

'It was Holm again.'

'Should I be worried?'

'I don't know.'

'Good.'

Ryza frowned.

'If you said I should be worried, I would be,' Vorric said. 'If you said I shouldn't, I'd think you were lying.'

'Empty minds, huh?'

'That's what Archarus said the first few times I went to wake you. He decided it would be best if he wasn't here when you did finally rise. Dangerous questions, you know.'

'Yeah, I—'

'Tell me more of this dream.'

Ryza had to work his jaw a few times to reorient his ability to speak after the interruption.

'I could ask her things. I asked her about Origin. But she just said, "he is here" and that she wants to give me what I want.'

'Did she say why?'

'I wish,' Ryza said quietly.

Vorric didn't reply to this. The silence made Ryza feel like his boots were melting. Maybe his dreams were just that. Dreams. Completely inaccurate to the world he truly lived and breathed. But in the past, they'd rung true. Holm had shown him the black blocks of stone that'd turned out to be Maligar's method of sustaining himself within the flux, so what meaning could he glean from the reappearance of Origin's arm?

And Holm's love.

The thought made his stomach suddenly churn, and if his legs didn't feel so locked up for having slept in this uncomfortable chair for the past however many hours, he'd be scrambling for the door.

'What have you found?' Ryza asked tentatively, hoping that Vorric was done with his own questions.

'Archarus deserves a portion of the credit, but I've *found* a new way of thinking about our problem. We're looking for something from before the time of the Academy of Breggesa, so it's not as though a direct report will be found in here. More likely a study of historical finds and the subsequent interpretations. Even with that, we need to think like that time period long gone. Hundreds of years ago, now. A time fuelled by fluid belief more than solid fact. Archarus had me dig up some research on the rituals and practices of an old Kretatic sect from centuries ago. Good thing you slept so long. It's dense reading. Half the words written here aren't used anymore.'

'How long was I asleep?'

'Long enough I'll be making sure I get a meal in you instead of my child.'

'Oh. I'm sorry.'

The apology felt hollow in Ryza's mouth. He couldn't fathom the concept of a father looking forward to a meal with their child, let alone a father doing so after having witnessed the deaths of half a dozen men that very day. But Vorric, much like the rest of the Scythes he led, was an unshakeable man.

'This... cult. I don't know how else to describe it. It's the word used here, but it was a different meaning then. Less nefarious, it seems. They had specific rituals for their rites of passage when their children came of age. Travels that crossed the Droughtlands as they collected specific samples of metals to form materials for the last stage of these rites. A mask of some sort... They don't outline the details of it in these writings.'

'You want me to make a mask?' Ryza said.

The thought didn't seem as ridiculous as Ryza had intended it when he'd asked the question. A wall of iron to hide his face would at least stop people from recognising him. Staring at him.

Seeing me.

'Think harder about this, Ryza,' Vorric said, hiding his exasperation. He slid one of the parchments across, displaying a faded map that was little more than a set of squiggles.

'You want me to draw that again?'

'Wake up properly, for—' Vorric cut himself off. He held his breath as he cooled his temper.

Ryza could only stare blankly at the page. Vorric was right. He was still half asleep and felt like he would be for the rest of his life.

'This route is one of these rites,' Vorric continued. 'It is near identical to that which Revance followed.' He began pointing to various points along the squiggle. 'Breggesa. Scraplands. Kyrea. Iroka. Some of these places likely hadn't even been settled or founded at that point. It's likely there are cities along here we never knew of and no longer exist. But they still followed this route, all of them, when they came of age.'

Ryza looked back up at Vorric and shrugged.

'How old are you?' Vorric asked.

Ryza shrugged again. 'Not of age. Nearly was when I ran from...'

'You see what I'm telling you, though?'

'That you think that I can track down Origin by taking a big walk because some kids did the same thing a couple hundred years ago?'

'What was the last thing Origin said to you under Twin Rings?'

'You just want to get rid of me!'

'What was it?' Vorric pressed.

His patience straining, Ryza did his best to remember. But he didn't need to. Vorric was already rustling through his papers to find some other report he'd written after Ryza had come back from losing Holm.

'I'm going away. A command it must obey. It wants nothing else.' Vorric paused. 'I know he said these things to you as part of what you described as a conversation, but I've been looking over these phrases as their own complete statements. I could liken it to poetry if I were the type to enjoy it, but has it never occurred to you that there were other things that Origin was trying to communicate with you?'

'Maybe it did. Maybe I was busy at the time trying to stop Revance from getting taken over by fucking smelters.'

'But now! Think about it now! These dreams you have, you lend them credibility, so why not the actual words being said to you? I have a theory, and I don't like having theories, but I don't like a great deal of what's happened, so I'll bear it for the time being. This ancient cult of Kretatics formed specific rituals around something that either already existed and would go on to become Revance, or even had a hand in creating it themselves. Something happened along the way that involved Origin, and with the way you describe Origin's instinctive behaviour, it could be that he's returned to that very instinct.'

'And that's how I could find him? By following this path? Revance's path? Why can't we just scrounge up a few of the old conscript collars? Academy would've kept a few after Iroka, right? We get them working again, they'd point the way to—'

'It'd be no use,' Vorric said abruptly. The tone of certainty in his voice was far too sharp. 'The flux will interfere with it. Show you only what you want to find before you can really find it.'

'And you know that for sure?'

Vorric glanced past him, holding his gaze over Ryza's shoulder for a moment too long as if he were meeting someone's eyes.

'I do. Finding Origin will mean finding something incorruptible. You said he was still the same when you found him among all that flux under Twin Rings while the rest of that factory had consumed itself. It might just be that Origin is the key to overcoming whatever influence Holm has on the flux. A purity to flush out the impurity she's introduced.'

'If it really is her,' Ryza said.

'Do you believe it is?'

Ryza's jaw clenched in place.

He could not answer.

Chapter Fifteen

A Replacement

S ILENT SANDS PRICKLED AND whispered at the bottom of Ryza's boots as he shuffled along the ridge of another dune. The walking was unnecessary. The sleek buggy that'd propelled him deep into the Droughtlands —a parting gift from Vorric as Ryza had left Breggesa— was nestled in the sanctuary between a pair of harsh plateaus some way back.

He'd taken to calling it a drifter. It was fast, too fast to cross most dunes without carefully steering around the ridges lest he wanted to fling himself into the air. Whenever he drove, it was never in a straight line, always drifting left and right.

It was more than up for navigating the trail that his footprints had thus far left, but the action of walking still felt important to Ryza.

That's why it feels real.

A jagged and undulating outline of ancient metal scrap lay ahead of him. A border that marked the beginnings of the Scraplands.

Weeks had come and gone since he'd left Breggesa behind. Weeks where he'd not needed to say a word, let alone have it questioned the moment it was out of his mouth. Vorric had been the easiest to convince to let him go. All Ryza had needed to tell him was that it was what he wanted, a seemingly magical combination of words that had snubbed all protest from the usually imperious man. Something he'd never second-guessed.

Ruka had been harder to convince. It was only under Vorric's orders that she'd relented. Not the orders Vorric had given in the moment, but the advice Vorric had given her in the time when the two had first met.

Not why or how, just what it is.

These sage words were the very ones she'd relayed to Ryza in the days before he'd ventured back into the flux-riddled tunnels beneath Iroka. What had allowed him to claim victory over Maligar's thousandfold apparition.

By the time Ryza left, Ditric still hadn't been convinced. At least Ryza believed she never would have been. He'd left in the dead of night without saying farewell, knowing it was the only way he'd be able to do so without her doggedly following.

He'd told himself that she'd be busy enough. She was still intent on hunting down the cache of reels that Vorric had mentioned was hidden away in Kyrea. In the last conversation Ryza had sat through with her, she simply couldn't stop talking about the ways that those reels would be able to help the refugees still thronging outside of Breggesa's walls.

Ryza only saw this as a distraction but hadn't the heart to tell her as much. Until the flux was purged from Kyrea, Ditric's plan was little more than a dream.

He needed a clear head to find what he was looking for. To figure out what that was in the first place. Vorric's theories of the ancient rituals that'd followed Revance's path were all he had to go off to find Origin, but even if Ryza did find him, what would he say? What would he do afterwards?

No matter the answer, he was well-stocked for the undertaking. The drifter was unlike any vehicle Ryza had seen. It was built with parts that'd been freshly machined for it rather than cannibalised from the wrecks of its broken brethren. The two front wheels pulled it forwards like beasts hauling a chariot. The surfaces of them were coated with interlocking scales of metal teeth that grabbed at the sand as they spun forward.

The pointed nose of the drifter's fuselage housed an engine that Vorric had instructed Ryza to destroy if there was a risk of it falling into another's hands. It burned no oil like a conventional motor, but found heat and power from the shard of a rebel sun that the Academy's research team had managed to extract.

Ryza had seen the devastation that the full paralict could wreak on the land, so he'd taken the warning as another excuse to steer clear of civilisation. He had no need for such a visit anyway. The ample stowage compartment at the back of the drifter held enough food to last him a year, if he ignored his hunger, and the smooth struts that sprouted from the drifter's back were all too happy to hold the weight as it skimmed along the dunes.

The avenues of the Scraplands twisted and forked around Ryza as he made his way through them. Shifting piles of rusted and worthless machines lay strewn across the path, obstacles that were trivial for his feet but would likely twist the drifter's forward wheels into an irreparable state. The early morning sun shimmered and flashed overhead as inconsistent bars. The light would only catch and flare if there was a significant enough divot in the walls of detritus to allow it through, otherwise it was like Ryza was still walking through the night.

He slowed his pace as he continued onwards. He was no longer lost. He perfectly remembered the route that the lead-better had taken on his first expedition out of Revance. The words Holm had shouted over the engine's roar came to him now as leisurely whispers whenever he passed the spots he thought she'd said them.

Ryza let his eyes shut for a few paces as he reminded himself why he was there. It had been hard to remember his mission. The long, lonely days and the desolate nights had given rise to questions that'd swayed and warped his goal. Doubts that made him wonder if it was even worth it to continue.

Origin. I need to find Origin.

He turned a corner, passing under a grand bridge composed of some derelict mining machine, and a few more of Holm's words trickled into his mind.

It's hard enough adding to an arcanite that isn't your own, even harder if you've never met the maker.

Back then, her words had made Ryza question Revance's workings. Now they made him question a great deal more. Whatever he was dealing with was well beyond the realm of axioms and arcanites, but did Holm still see it that way? Were those gnashing little machines within the molten flux just more arcanites to her? And what of Origin? Was he even real?

He has to be. I have nothing else.

A few more minutes of trudging along placed Ryza at the gates to the scrapyard he'd fought his first skirmish in. He drew his sawn-off rifle and held it close to his chest, the side of the barrel resting against his jaw, ready to be swung into action. The place looked identical to how Ryza had left it. Untouched, in a strange way. Ryza paused. Why was a place where things were so often taken and left behind untouched?

Temporarily stowing his rifle, Ryza pulled out his vent mask and fixed it to his face. The rhythmic *hiss-click* that came with his first few breaths sounded weak, so he adjusted a few of the valves until each noise was more distinct, then drew his weapon again.

He moved forwards with caution, eyeing off the small jumble of shacks with suspicion. He approached one and nudged the door open with the toe of his boot. It was stuck. He kicked it harder, and it flew open with a rattle of tumbling bones. The squeaks and scurrying feet of the lowliest scavengers followed the sound, and Ryza leapt backwards from the doorway.

There was nothing in that room that could've ever been alive. Just the picked-clean skeletons of corpses that'd never been filled with flux. Ryza glanced away, catching sight of a few of the smelters he and his squad had dispatched the year prior. They'd been picked clean as well. Their clothes were torn only where the animals had become frustrated with the way they blocked access to their precious carrion. What little flesh was left on them was petrified and encrusted with sand.

But why has no one else come here?

Ryza looked at the walls of scrap beyond the hut for any other sign of habitation but found nothing. It was hard to focus on the individual pieces that made it up. The browns and rusted greys that coloured each torn and wrecked form made it all blur into one, a signal to an onlooker that it would be too hard to discern what the scrap had once been.

Out of spite, Ryza approached one of the scrap piles. He could remember when Holm was digging through the scattered metal with a disinterested sneer. He kicked over a nearby piece, revealing a complex mechanism of elongated gears and smoothened hammers. Any possible use for such a thing escaped him, but he couldn't help but be impressed that they all moved perfectly in concert when he pushed one section of it with the toe of his boot.

'Who left all this shit?' Ryza said under his vent mask.

A strange, existential dread came with the question. A great deal of things in the Droughtlands were manufactured from similar panels of scrap metal, yet where it came from was rarely spoken of. It seemed as taboo as the ruins left by those-of-glass themselves. Ryza always guessed that that was who'd left behind all the debris, but now he thought about it, the form of the scrap had nothing in common with the sleek beams of steel and stretching panes of glass that he'd seen in Twin Rings that made up the skyscrapers.

Even if it were, why was it here on the surface? Almost everything left by those-of-glass was buried by eons of sand, yet all this scrap metal was exposed to the sun for it to rust and waste away, turning to a powder indistinguishable from sand. Was it the remnants of the ancient Kretatics Vorric had spoken of?

'What if it's always been here?'

The sound of Holm's voice made Ryza spin with his rifle raised. A figure stood at the doorway of the nearest hut, and Ryza didn't wait for another hint of recognition before he pulled the trigger.

BLAM!

His rifle kicked in his hand, throwing his arm up to the sky as the cloud of fire burning at the end of the muzzle followed like a lit flare. Over the ringing in his ears, he heard a faint *ping* as the slug bounced harmlessly off the wall of a distant shack. His rifle clicked and snapped as he rammed another slug into its breach, but the figure was gone.

Ryza kept his rifle levelled at the spot he'd seen them, breathing hard through his vent mask as he tried to listen for more over the incessant *hiss-click*. Had he really just seen her? Had he seen anything at all?

He began moving forwards, pausing outside the shack before taking a quick step into the doorway. His rifle shook in his hand as he swept it over the piles of skeletons, but none moved. None gave him the excuse to fight.

The next few shacks were similarly desolate, and it was only as Ryza kicked in the door of the last one that he accepted the sinking feeling of doom he knew he had to confront. He looked to the mouth of the cave. The narrow passage that led to the abandoned smelter lair where Holm had first tried to kill him.

The very place she was standing now.

Ryza lowered his rifle as he approached. He knew it would do no good. He stopped five paces from Holm.

She looked back at him with curiosity. An innocent longing as if she'd never seen what had happened beneath Iroka between Ryza and Maligar. At least this time she was clothed. She was wearing the exact same forge leathers she'd come to this place wearing, her neck bare of the iron collar that Ryza had seen there when Maligar had conjured his imagination of her.

But her skin was still silver, pulsing and flashing as the morning sun finally came down into the little valley of ruin. Sometimes it made her look golden, and Ryza might've been able to delude himself that it was her real, sun-kissed flesh, but he knew better than that.

Holm was gone. Her mind was gone. This was an echo. He just couldn't be sure if it was from her or from himself.

Silently, she turned and delved deeper into the cave's opening. She walked with precision and care. Her hand was raised as if it were resting on an invisible shoulder. Ryza checked the valves of his vent mask and followed again into the darkness. There was no sputtering oil lantern to light the way, so Ryza holstered his rifle and searched his pockets, withdrawing a small torch he'd cobbled together a few days ago.

He'd had to allow himself a few runes to get it working, nothing that actually gave him control of the metal, just to put a hint of magnetism into the necessary pieces. He gave the small tube of metal a quick shake, making sure he didn't smash the fragile glass bulbs on either end against the cave wall, and it emitted a low green glow.

The light caught on Holm's metallic skin, and Ryza felt he was back in Iroka's tunnels again, watching the odd green glow of the walls as it caressed her form. Holm looked back as Ryza had the thought, a small smirk only just discernible by his torch's light.

She waited for him at the foot of the path before it was due to slope upwards. He met her silvery stare and knew she would not continue until he was by her side. He hesitated. There was nothing stopping him from simply leaving. He could go, walk back to the drifter, and continue his journey without a second thought, but there was a sincere look of tempting mischief in Holm's eyes that told him he'd regret it.

I want this. I want to know.

With Holm walking on his left, Ryza proceeded up the path and into the cathedral-like cavern. He glanced down at her hands as he went, spotting that her right was hanging at somewhere his left would've been. Looking up, he met Holm's eyes.

'What's in here? Flux?'

Holm didn't reply. She only pointed ahead.

There, on the plateau she'd once pushed him to his death from, stood another figure, though not one of flux.

Ryza approached him as his thoughts began to dissolve, feeling like they'd dribble out his mouth if he breathed wrong. The figure was a perfect reflection of him, down to the horrified curiosity hidden under his vent mask. He was even missing his left arm, exactly as Ryza was, something he was convinced Holm would never accept.

'Why'd you bring me here?' the figure suddenly said, his voice identical to Ryza's. 'What do you mean by showing me... showing me this?'

Though the question wasn't meant for him, Ryza answered by drawing his rifle and firing it directly into his clone's chest. The copy collapsed as he grasped at the wound. Silver flux poured from the ragged hole and over the copy's bare hands, and he screamed as the flux took hold of his flesh. It steamed and burned like spilled acid as it spread up his arm, the molten flux unable to discern itself from the flesh it had created.

Ryza reloaded with mechanical precision as his clone thrashed and screamed. He knew those howls of pain. Those were the very ones he'd made himself when Maligar had shot off his arm. Ryza snapped his rifle shut and fired it into the clone again, this time unleashing one of the specialised incendiary slugs he had with him.

His clone exploded into an infernal pyre with one last scream. His body fragmented and took root in the stone floor of the cavern's plateau as spines of blackened metal shot from the remains. The spikes crackled and snapped as they continued to split and grow, burning harder as they reunited with each other.

Soon the false corpse was a mass of flaming needles, spilling enough light to fully illuminate the cavern. Nevertheless, Ryza stowed his rifle and retrieved his dropped torch before turning to Holm.

'Where's Origin?' Ryza asked flatly.

Holm's expression was tweaking with frustration as she struggled to understand.

'You don't even want to know why I showed you this?' she retorted.

'Why?'

'Because I could—'

'No,' Ryza snapped, cutting her off. 'Why should I want to know?'

She took a step towards him, her eyes fighting back rage as she tried to plead with him.

'I'm trying to help you, Ryza! To find a way that you can run away from the world and not have it come looking for you. That was why I remade you. To stand in your place. You don't even have to stay with me, I just want you to be at peace!'

'So you'd use a fake me to take care of the real me? What does that say about you? What does that say about what you've done to yourself? Are you even real?'

'I'm here because you *know* I'm real.'

'And that's why you're leaving all those copies of me around. I know what's out there!' Ryza shouted through his mask. 'Have you seen the way people look at me? They think I'm one of your statues come to life! That I'm just one of your many. Doesn't make me feel too real, does it? You still don't want me, do you? You just *need* me.'

Ryza stowed his torch and drew his rifle once more, jamming another slug into it before snapping it shut and holding the muzzle against his chin.

'What happens when I die, then? How long can you keep making all these mimics of what you think I am before you start to forget what I really was?'

'Ryza, don't!'

Holm lunged towards him with a clumsy swipe at his rifle, but Ryza stepped away, aware that his heels were teetering on the edge of the plateau.

'You tried to kill me here once,' he snarled. 'What happens if you try again?'

'Then I'll destroy everything.'

Her words weren't a threat. They were a regret. A mournful muttering of a fate she knew she could not escape. Ryza hesitated and almost lowered his rifle, but he held it firm. Holm went on.

'You're right, Ryza. I need you. I'm the last thing stopping the flux from truly running free. The last expectation it has. If you're gone, it has nothing. That wasn't a problem before, back when we all just thought it was for making autominds. But now you've all seen what it can do, you're all braced for the worst, and the flux will be all too ready to give it to you.'

'Then why take me here?'

Holm shook her head, her grin back across her silver face. 'You came here, Ryza. You expected to find me here.'

'Then is this really you? This isn't just something the flux is pulling out of my head?'

'Who's to say it's not?'

'Me. I can. But I can't make that decision alone. Not unless I want to be certain of it.'

Holm took another step towards him. Her hand came up, and her fingers snaked around his wrist. There was a soft warmth in her silvery skin. And that slight coarseness of the overlapping calluses of her hand. Her grip was gentle yet irresistible, and she slowly pulled his rifle away from his chin.

'Then find Origin,' she whispered.

CHAPTER SIXTEEN

THE MEANING OF A LIE

RYZA WALKED AWAY FROM the scrapyard in a disturbed daze. He was too tired of all the doubt that came with seeing these apparitions of Holm to even question why the flux was waiting for him in that cave. Or why it was doing so as a perfect copy of him. Of course, Holm had been trying to tell him something, but he couldn't discern what. Maybe he should've stayed and asked her, but to do so he would've had to fight the overwhelming sense of repulsion that her presence elicited from him.

Hours dragged past him as he staggered through the mazes of the Scraplands. By accident, he got lost, then when he found his way onto a familiar route, he purposely turned around and got lost again.

Despite it making no difference where he did it, he needed time to process and subsequently forget what he'd just seen. The sky was an inky blue, the sun having long vanished, when he found the bravery to begin crossing the rolling dunes again. Night stole his view of the jagged line of debris from behind him before the horizon could.

His hastily created torch was little help in navigating back to where he'd left the drifter. The green light that ebbed from its core flickered more frequently as his own worries about it began to grow, until it failed entirely after another bout of percussive maintenance.

Opening the torch up and attempting to repair it wasn't worth the time, Ryza decided. It had taken him an hour to piece together the contraption in the first place. Having to use his bare feet to hold certain components in place while snapping them in place had delayed him, not to mention the fact he barely knew how these things worked to begin with.

It was something to do with the mix of copper and cadmium that was pressed into a ball and then encased in the central housing of the tube. Maybe it was in the way it interacted with the magnetism Ryza had imparted at either end, or the constant motion of it, that caused it to glow. Either way, it wasn't working now, so Ryza discarded and shambled on as his eyes adjusted to the stars.

It was hard to pay attention to the ground around him when the spread of stars above him kept drawing his gaze. They weren't individual pinpricks of light like he'd always thought. It was a cloudy mist, from within which a thousand little beacons glowed. A thousand little far-off lanterns that didn't even know where their light would fall. They were unthinking in their purpose, yet this only made them more confident.

These were the lights that smarter men than Ryza had spent lifetimes charting, watching for the slightest flicker or shift in their position, all while the world around them whizzed and rushed, carried by the ever-flowing waves of sand that washed across the Droughtlands.

Which was more important? As he walked, Ryza wondered if those stargazers of eons past had asked themselves the same. Which was the world to be paid attention to? The one above their heads or the one below their feet? Ryza's life had been dominated by the latter, a fact that was doubly true now that he knew the origins of molten flux. It had been hard to think of a life outside it, to find a meaning or a purpose for himself beyond the flux.

Ryza chuckled to himself, and a chirping chorus of buried bugs chattered in response. He could remember thinking a similar thing in Iroka, in the dark night before the impending battle against Tyrag's Revance. He could've never planned or expected what had happened next, but nevertheless, it had come with a purpose just for him. It had only been when he'd accepted this fact that he'd been ready to face the battle that'd ensued, so maybe the same needed to happen now. That the end of flux would not mean the end of him.

It would, however, mean the end of Holm. The end of the spirit lingering in the liquid metal, manifesting itself only when Ryza was alone and desperate. He chuckled again. She was a bit like a shadow dancer, in a way. An echo of a lost magic, a lost ambition, one that only lived on just to tease his mind.

Was this what those-of-glass had intended when they'd created molten flux? Had they known that they'd never be able to create a true replica for life, but they'd found themselves satisfied with the imitation of one?

That was the question Holm had posed to him again and again, not only in herself but now with what she'd presented to him in the scrapyard. She'd made the offer to him that he could live with her, to live a life where she could cater to his wants and desires just as the flux had catered to hers, but what good was this satisfaction when getting such things had left Ryza so hollow?

Perhaps Holm had thought she was giving Ryza a gift when she'd created the image of Aphtus-Hast. A peace offering for Ryza's soul. After all, he'd wanted nothing more to get his vengeance on the man who'd raised him to be so spiteful. For it to result in such a hollow sense of catharsis was an irony not lost on Ryza.

His father's death had truly meant nothing to him. After the hundreds that'd come before it, maybe he wanted it to mean nothing. A meaning the flux had been happy to provide for him.

By the time Ryza was back at the drifter, he'd almost forgotten the reason why he was out there. His search for Origin was no longer methodical. It was something that Ryza drifted along with, an assigned purpose to fill the void of his swirling thoughts. Even the idea of following the trail that Revance once walked was a distant, forgotten ambition.

Contentment is a funny thing like that.

He began digging out the sand that'd gathered under the drifter's forward wheels. It was still late in the night, and he was yet to sleep, so the sand would likely be back by morning, but his mind was still turning over. Not as an impatient engine trying to slot loose gears into place, but as the slow and constant roll of a motor that never once ceased.

Was this the way Origin now felt? A being who'd lived a life so long and so removed from his birth that there was no scale to compare the events of the day against? There was nothing more to want for him, not because he'd gained everything he could, but because it simply didn't make sense to want anymore.

Origin's last words to Ryza floated into his head, and he stopped what he was doing to hear them again, savouring the way they'd come as a deep throbbing tone from somewhere at the base of his skull.

You cannot destroy it.

Not until it wants something.

When it needs something.

'And that's why Origin can't be destroyed,' Ryza muttered under his breath. 'Because he wants nothing.'

Was the flux the same? It didn't want for itself, it didn't even have a self to want for, did it? It just had a simple command to attune itself to the wants of others. Even the gnashing little machines that Ryza had sensed with his magnetic resonance seemed trivial now. Perhaps he'd made them up, much like he sometimes wondered if he was doing with Holm.

Ryza gave up on clearing sand from the half-buried wheels and went to the rear of the drifter. He opened the large, circular door at the back of the vehicle's stowage compartment and climbed into the cramped space, his knees just balancing on the low lip of the compartment's floor.

A warm amber light illuminated the trussed stacks of supplies and papers that he'd set off with, and he had to be careful where he placed his hand so as not to snub it out. The light was coming from the rebel sun shard within the engine itself, piped in by a series of narrow, mirrored tubes that ran across the underside of the chassis. This meant the illumination came in narrow beams out of glass-covered vents and covering one would cast large portions of the space into shadow.

Vorric had sent him off with as many notes and records of ancient and irrelevant things as possible, in the hopes that they'd one day become more useful than they'd been sitting in the Archives. Ryza had dutifully spent his nights reading through them, though he'd stopped when he'd given in to the suspicion that Vorric had only saddled him with them as means to distract his anxious and isolated mind.

Ryza grunted softly as he climbed in further. He was looking for the only fresh report there, the one that Vorric had written in the wake of what had happened at Iroka. It had been the first thing Vorric had packed, and the last thing Ryza thought he'd need —he'd already lived it, after all— so the report had been buried under everything else.

'Has to be here somewhere,' he muttered.

But finding it would be impossible while the compartment was packed as tightly as it was, so Ryza simply shoved his fist in through a gap in the stacks and pulled out the first thing his fingers found. Holding this new stack of parchments to the light, he raised an eyebrow.

'Can't believe that worked.'

He shimmied back out of the stowage and knelt in the sand, using the floor of the stowage compartment as a table as he leafed through Vorric's report. One of the illumination pipes lay there underneath, so the writing looked like a set of veins on stretched, ancient skin.

Somewhere in the middle of the report, he found the other words that Origin had left him, at least what he'd been able to recall and recount to Vorric in the days that'd followed. He read through them a few times, muttered the words aloud as if it would give them more meaning.

Vorric's suggestion that this was poetry had been absurd, but now he could feel a certain rhythm to it on his tongue. A rise, peak, and fall in the sentences that made them so concise yet so expansive.

He kept coming back to one set of words in particular, the others that Origin had said to him in the self-replicating factory beneath Twin Rings.

I'm going away.

A command it must obey.

It wants nothing else.

Ryza mulled the words over. Read them backwards, reordered them, swished the sounds around in his mouth until they were unrecognisable and then said them anew.

He'd thought that this had been Origin's way of telling him that he was fleeing, but maybe it was something else.

'A command *it* must obey,' Ryza said aloud. 'It. Why it?'

Was Origin referring to the molten flux itself? Why would it obey a command, especially from Origin, of all things?

'But there is no *why*,' Ryza reminded himself. 'It just is. The flux does not ask questions or know what's right... it just... is.'

He focused on the third line again.

'It wants nothing else... A command, is that what it wants? Of course it does, what else would the flux be, otherwise?'

Ryza frowned. The conclusion didn't feel right, especially not with what Origin had gone on to say at the time.

'You cannot destroy it. Not until it wants something. When it needs something.' Ryza paused for a few heartbeats, waiting until his pulse slowed a touch. 'But all the flux wants is a command. It always wants a command. So it could always be destroyed? No, that doesn't make sense. Not that it needs to, but...'

Ryza swore to himself. He forced himself to look at the written words again, but they still wouldn't align in his mind. Maybe there was some immortal sort of wisdom that he was missing, one that he'd only unlock once he was as old as Origin was. Maybe it didn't need to make sense at all, maybe it just had to exist as it was, stuck in a strange illogical quandary.

'Or maybe...' Ryza's words stilled, holding back for a moment an admission he knew would shatter any sense of progress he'd so far made. 'Maybe the little bastard lied to me.'

Ryza snapped, shouting wordlessly as he swept the papers aside and slammed his fist into the bare metal where they'd been. Of course Origin would've lied to him! He was probably lying the whole time! What if Origin, much like Holm, was a manifestation of the flux itself? Yet another layer of defences that the flux threw up when fools like Ryza came searching for meaning and logic in a place where none could be immediately provided.

It was like how fire turned the flux into those brittle spines and shards. Just a ploy to delude him into thinking he'd won for long enough that he'd leave and the flux could go back to what it had once been. Because there was no way for the flux to "lose," was there? It wanted nothing in the first place! It was immortal, so even if it had to spend an entire lifetime pretending to be dead or broken or whatever other form it took to satisfy those it was tricking, it would spring back to its true self eventually.

And Origin was just one of those elements. The longest serving one that existed to placate those of the Droughtlands, including Ryza as he'd searched for a way to stop the mutiny aboard Revance. To Rettic as he'd attempted to figure out what Archarus had done, and then even Archarus when he'd mounted his first failed expedition. Probably all the way back to whoever or whatever had first created Revance, hundreds and hundreds of years ago!

After taking a few steadying breaths, Ryza collected and reordered the scattered papers of Vorric's report, turning back to the page of Origin's words. There was little trust he could place in them now, but maybe reading them with a distrustful eye would find yet another meaning in them.

Ryza paused.

'This is getting stupid,' he muttered.

Nevertheless, he scanned the words again. There had to be some tiny bit of truth to them, some tiny fact at their core, otherwise they would not work so well as a lie. He rested his focus on the lines about Revance. That was something real, at least. Something that really did happen.

These were called bolt-locks.

This is how Revance once fought.

They didn't need me.

Ryza chewed on his upper lip as he lingered on the last line.

'Maybe they figured you out,' Ryza muttered. 'Found you were a fake and threw you off. But that doesn't work, the fortress would've fallen apart if they thought that, right?'

He let out a soft groan. The only way he'd get a proper answer to this would be if he could somehow ask someone that was there, but they'd all been dead for a few hundred years.

'Unless one of them turned into a shadow dancer,' Ryza said.

'They didn't,' Archarus replied.

Ryza jumped at the sudden appearance of the shadow dancer's voice, hitting his head on the inner rim of the drifter's stowage compartment. He swore as he wheeled around, rubbing the sore point of his skull as he glared at Archarus. The shadow dancer was standing a few paces away at the edge of the amber light, his expression infuriatingly indifferent.

'You could've given me a warning you were going to show up like that!' Ryza snapped.

'I've been looking over your shoulder for the past ten minutes. I thought you were ignoring me.'

I wish I could.

'Besides, it's hard to search for another shadow dancer,' Archarus continued. 'Two rarely meet, because it can prompt a dangerous outcome.'

'But you're both dead, how can you...'

'Dead, yes. But we've still never discovered if we can still tap into pure resonance.'

'I thought you'd been trying this whole time?' Ryza asked. 'Wasn't that the whole reason you went looking for something like molten flux in the first place?'

'You're correct. I did try. Once, shortly after I became this way. I was warned against it.'

'By who?'

'Another shadow dancer. The same one that appeared with Vorric all those days ago when we met in the Archives.'

Ryza grunted dismissively. 'And I'm guessing you aren't going to tell me who they are?'

'Best not to think about it.'

'Got enough to think about,' Ryza said. 'You been listening to me, then? You think Origin's a liar?'

Archarus' answer didn't come immediately. Something Ryza was used to.

'Birds and cliffs?'

'The best way to put it,' Archarus said reluctantly. 'I worry about the effects of what I can tell you and the consequences of what I can't. The assumptions you'll make and the actions you'll take. Perhaps that's why the flux lies to us. It gives us the first answer we seek so we don't search deeper. So we don't begin to tangle with the questions that'd lead us to pure resonance.'

'And that's why you can't tell me if you think Origin is a liar or not?'

'Precisely.'

'Then why speak? Why show up only to say that you can't be seen or heard?'

'For the same reason as the thing that carries you forth on your journey. An instinct. That's the only thing that I know that molten flux cannot understand. An instinct is something that appears from nothing, an action that is not prompted by anything at all. It cannot be predicted or planned for, in the grand scheme of things, even if it seems like the flux has you trapped at every turn. It's your instincts that provided you victory over Tyrag's mutiny. Your instincts that shepherded you into the heart of Maligar's lair and brought you out again. It's now your instincts that will see to the total destruction of molten flux.'

'I know you probably can't answer this... but... how?'

'Because you are beyond pure resonance, Ryza,' Archarus said earnestly. 'You may have doubted it before, but do you recall what you said to me before you went back into Iroka? All this is pure resonance. Everything. You faced that existential question, and because you faced it with *instinct* and not *logic*, you did not answer it as I and many before me have. You found a sanctuary in doubt, and you turned that uncertainty into a certainty in and of itself. It created a distance, a distance in your mind between yourself and the conflict of ideas that kept you safe, proven by the fact you haven't exploded in a shower of fire and whatever else and simply turned into a shadow dancer just by hearing me say this!'

Ryza rubbed the inner corners of his eyes as he digested this, but his mind was already a spent force.

'Simply put, continue on your course,' Archarus emphasised.

'But I don't know what my course is... I don't know what I'm doing out here! I keep seeing Holm, or myself or... or... I don't know—'

'And that's just what you need to keep doing! Explore it! Just keep following that thread and you'll find an answer of how you can finally destroy the flux.'

'But what if there is no answer?'

Archarus smiled at him, a hungry grin that faded as the rest of him disappeared, leaving only his last few words.

'Isn't that an answer?' he said in a whisper. 'A certainty in an uncertainty?'

'Maybe,' Ryza said to no one. 'I just wonder what the flux will think of it.'

CHAPTER SEVENTEEN

ENSNARED

THE DRIFTER'S QUIET HUM was no match for the constant, skittering scraping sound its curved rear struts made carving through the dunes. Each one was a long blade, twisted so it wasn't the edge that made contact with the ground, but the flat. The other sounds rattling around the drifter's compact cabin included the rapid clicking that came from the scales of the forward wheels as they pressed into the ground, grabbed hold of it, came out the other side, and then were freed again.

There was also the ruckus of bumping cargo and supplies in the rear that made Ryza second-guess if he'd tied everything down correctly. Occasionally a puff of white fire would burst from one of the exhaust pipes sprouting out of what Vorric had erroneously called an engine, but Ryza was too scared of the inner workings of the machine to investigate the supposed fault further. Loosen the wrong bolt and he might just unleash the wedge of the rebel sun that Vorric had sent him off with, incinerating himself instantly and marking his grave with a glassy pit in the ground.

Still, all of this was lost to the rear blades and the way they picked up every bump and stray pebble. It was a sound that came to Ryza through the base of his spine and up through his back, leaving his ears free to search for the other noises in the thick desert air.

The drifter's cabin was as tight as the rest of the vehicle's design. The seat was barely the size of a bucket for Ryza to fit himself into, and the edge of the cockpit only reached his shoulders no matter how much he tried to nestle himself down. This left his head and neck exposed to the blasting waves of passing sand. His only protection were his goggles and the few extra rags of dense fabric that he tied to his face before setting out. After that, it was on his squinting eyes to spot the faint, shifting clouds of dust before he burst through them, and to ease the drifter's steering yoke accordingly.

The manner of controlling the machine was the opposite of how Ryza expected vehicles to work as well. There were only two pedals to work, both positioned under his left foot. The first controlled how exposed the rebel sun shard was to the rest of the machine's workings.

There was little it actually connected to. Mainly it just jetted an absurd amount of infernally hot air out of a series of vents arrayed along either side of the drifter's fuselage. The orientation and angle of these vents helped the speeding craft hug the ground as it sped onwards, but there had been times when Ryza had crested a dune and found the other side steeper than expected, resulting in a few panicked moments of flight. He never envied Reythurists after that.

The other pedal was supposedly connected to some kind of braking mechanism. He could only think vaguely of it because he'd never felt any kind of effect from it, not even when he'd viciously stomped on them the time he'd found himself racing towards the edge of a cliff. The drifter was fast. The only thing faster was probably a freshly fired slug. Even then, it would be a tight race.

It took his full concentration to pilot the drifter, yet his mind kept floating back towards the previous day, and he could feel himself frowning by the way his goggles cut into his brow that little bit more.

The only knowledge Archarus had saddled him with was a weight of duelling expectations. An impression that there was nothing in this world that he could truly trust except for himself, and that his complete and utter mistrust for himself was the only thing that was keeping him alive through all this madness.

Ryza fought to dismiss the thoughts as a few ridges of rocky spires loomed up over the horizon. They were a chalky red in the light cast by the morning sun behind him, a marker that he was only a day or two's journey away from where Twin Rings had once stood.

Ruins within ruins, now.

In hindsight, it was the only logical destination to begin his search for Origin, but he'd wittered away so much time stopping off at other locales along the way. Places where either he or Revance had once visited. It had been in the hopes that Vorric's theory of Origin's relation to Revance's first journey would prove fruitful, to steer his course away from where he knew he needed to go, but all Ryza had found was desolation and destruction.

The raided water pump where he'd found the mercenary claiming to have unearthed Origin in the first place had been raided once more in the intervening time. All the complex equipment had been broken down and hauled away as scrap, never to dredge up water again.

The few villages Ryza and his squad of conscripts had temporarily patrolled now stood as hollow husks to be eaten by the sands. Either the residents had been taken by smelters the moment they'd been left unguarded, or they were now among the many faces of refugees that clamoured at either side of Breggesa's walls.

Ryza had passed a few processions of these refugees on his way out of Breggesa. They formed slow, walking lines that stretched out for a number of intermittent miles, their faces as gaunt and downcast. They didn't look where they were going, only at the heels of those in front of them, for there was no hope waiting for them beyond that. It was more tragic than seeing a similar number of autominds, in a way. At least the autominds were dead. There didn't need to be hope for them.

At the very least, the refugees had no fear of being turned into autominds. There were enough corpses out in the Droughtlands as it was. The massive burial pits outside those deserted towns proved as much. And with the factories abandoned, that was where they lay, their flesh picked apart by winged scavengers until the sand covered them up for good.

Maybe that's how I'll find Twin Rings, too.

The spires continued to grow as Ryza rocketed towards them. The juddering motion of the drifter made it difficult to see very far ahead, so he could only estimate the safest path between them. Something with plenty of sand. Deep sand, preferably, so he wouldn't need to worry about shallow rocks. There was an opening to the south that looked promising, and Ryza gently veered the drifter towards it.

It began to look less promising by the time he was half a mile out. The brown shapes he'd mistaken for boulders pressed up against the trunks of either spire were too definite in shape to be utterly inert. They hadn't been weathered by wind or sand like the rest of this place because they were shacks.

If Ryza yanked at the steering yoke now, the best he'd do would be to crash headlong into one of the little dwellings. Instead, he rocked his foot back and forth on the exposure pedal, easing in a few more bursts of speed to his already roaring pace. Something didn't feel right about the place. The sight of interlocking wheel tracks on the sand as it whizzed by on his left proved it.

Ryza had been expecting pursuing vehicles to lurch out, misaimed gunshots to follow with them, all things that he knew the drifter would outrun, but when the entire span of sand between the two spires exploded upwards into a wall of dust, his guts twisted.

His foot slapped uselessly at the drifter's brakes as he fought to keep the steering yoke steady in his now shaking hands. The wall of sand didn't look solid yet. It was still falling and settling. Maybe he could punch through it before it solidified!

He ducked low into the cockpit so that his eyes were level with the upper protective rim at the fore and clenched his whole body as he hurtled towards the wall of thrown dust. The drifter punched through like a stabbing blade, but a jarring crash of metal on metal screamed out from the drifter instead of the smooth hiss of sand he'd been expecting.

Ryza felt something whip over his head as the racket continued, and the drifter felt like it was being slapped from all angles as it careened out of the dust cloud.

The drifter's nose became muzzled in a web of thickly coiled steel cabling. The rest of the net swept out from either side like a pair of dragging wings, but as the drifter continued uncontrollably on, these wings were ushered into a strangulating tail. The craft jolted and crashed as the net entangled more of its workings.

The front wheels were the first to go, the interlocking scales of their surfaces hungrily gnawing at the cables' threads, pulling them in and twisting them around the wheels' delicate axle. Despite the constriction, the wheels continued to spin with the ground beneath it, adding pressure to the cables laced across the nose cone. The riveted fuselage, though reinforced from the inside, began to deform under the bindings. Small gashes erupted across the lengths, bleeding fire and light instead of blood as the shard of the rebel sun became more and more exposed.

Ryza heaved left and right at the steering vane in an attempt to loosen the pressure, but the metal rod just groaned in his hand as it bent in two, unable to shift the wheels.

The drifter rocked and bounced as more of the steel net was pulled around it. Its lengths were slipping under the rear blades, threatening to snap them from their struts. Ryza gave up on the steering vane and pushed himself halfway out of the cockpit and was almost blown clean out of his seat by the rushing wind. His greatcoat billowed behind him like a sail, threatening to throw him clear of the drifter entirely.

Regaining control of himself, Ryza crouched low and tried to dig his fingers under the nearest section of wrapped cabling, but his fingertips only stung and bled as they scrabbled uselessly at the fused metals.

Fuck!

Ryza looked up and swore again when he realised there were more spires ahead. They were smaller, but at the speed the drifter was still travelling, just as deadly. He only had seconds before he hit one of them.

Still fighting against the out-of-control motion of the drifter, Ryza climbed fully out of the cockpit. The trailing net must've caught on something, because the entire craft was starting to veer rightward. The locked front wheels screamed against the diversion as they gouged sideways through the sand, and the drifter began to tip.

Straddling the fuselage, Ryza glanced wildly around. The banks of soft dune sand were growing shallower and more infrequent, but that was still better than the stretches of jagged stone the drifter was heading towards.

Ryza jumped, his path directionless, his only goal to get away from the drifter. He was still midair when the vehicle flipped like a rolling barrel. The violent motion coursed out through the rest of the net, whipping the trailing portions into Ryza's path and ensnaring him too.

FUCK!

The ground rushed up and walloped Ryza, knocking all sense out of his head as his limp body was dragged senselessly along in the drifter's crashing wake. He struggled to curl up against the tautness of the net as he bounced and smashed off the ground, coming to a stop an eternity later with a quiet groan.

He knew he needed to find his feet. To untangle himself, draw his rifle, and get ready to fight. But doing so was an agonisingly slow process. The net truly had him. He was knotted tight. It was a tangle of twisted steel and fresh welts that left his skin raw. His left leg had caught the worst of it. Something felt wrong with his knee; it wouldn't bend as he tried to push the cabling down his leg. A pained breath escaped him as a wide patch of blood began oozing through the fabric of his tattered pants.

'That might fucking explain it,' Ryza hissed under his breath.

The blood was spreading fast. The entire left leg of his trousers was crimson by the time he'd gingerly slid his ankle free. Droplets were forming pools in the shallow mix of rocks and sand beneath him, turning into a sticky paste that clung to the rest of his garments. Ryza shuffled back a few more feet from where he'd started, then drew his rifle from its holster across his chest.

He twisted to look around. Through his swaying vision, he couldn't see a sign of his supposed attackers. He could stand to better search for them, but just the action of planting his right elbow in the ground to start twisting to his knees brought a surge of acid into his throat. He clamped his eyes shut as he choked it back down. Even if he could stand, he'd probably be empty of both blood and puke in seconds.

His hearing came back to him at a ringing pitch that was an octave lower than what he was used to. The sparking and spitting wreck of the drifter sounded like the echoes of distant gunshots reverberating inside a metal drum. It now lay on its side, its sleek shape crushed and strangled by the net that'd cut through the metal. The crumpled nose cone was glowing like a forgotten forge and was beginning to deform further from the heat.

Ryza could either run away or try and fix it, but he knew both options would result in him being incinerated. Stifling another groan of pain, Ryza twisted onto his belly so he was facing the crashed drifter and began hauling himself, one armful of sand at a time, towards it. He threw his rifle aside as he went. The damn thing kept catching on the steel net beneath him, and there was no point trying to fight if the rebel sun was about to burn him to a crisp.

He felt the thud of his elbow slamming into the ground each time he pulled himself forward, hearing it clash over the metal and rock it struck. For a second, he thought he was speeding up, but then he realised the thudding rhythm was entirely out of time with his pace.

Ryza stopped and looked back over his shoulder before his eyes shot wide with panic. A figure was walking towards him, picking their way through the trail of tangled netting with huge, stomping strides. The sun was at their back, dazzling Ryza so he couldn't make out their form properly, but they didn't look quite human. Their shoulders were too bulky, and the top of their head looked like it had been squared off on an anvil.

Ryza could only lie there, fighting for his breath as the figure stomped past him and towards the wrecked drifter. His vision faded as he twisted to follow them, but there was something distinctly recognisable about the array of bulbous tanks affixed to their backs and the distant *hiss-click* that carried through the air.

Dark spheres began blotting out Ryza's vision as he continued to squint at them. The figure crouched down next to the nose of the drifter, pulling something long and cylindrical from their belt. The scene blurred further still, and the last thing Ryza could remember before the chill of nauseating emptiness took him was a flash so brilliantly white that it seemed utterly black.

CHAPTER EIGHTEEN

BOUND WITH BLOOD

IT WASN'T PAIN THAT woke Ryza up. It was the odd, rhythmic squeezing at his right wrist. Each cycle of tension came with a skewering rush of blood. But it didn't feel like his blood. At least the magnetic resonance didn't feel like his, instead coming to him as a distant, watchful feeling of caution and curiosity. The point where it entered his wrist stung with a constant ache of stretched-out skin, shaped like a circle that felt entirely hollow in the middle.

Hisses, both of voices and of little flames, came to his ears. It was difficult to tell them apart from the ringing pitch that'd captured his head from the crash, let alone make out what they meant. He opened his eyes, but blackness still remained, so he decided he'd lost the ability to open them at all. Ryza tried his mouth next. His jaw creaked where it attached to his skull, scraping open an inch before giving up.

Warm air stuck to his teeth as he pulled his lips back to breathe in. Very little air actually came, and he tried again, inhaling harder this time and noticing the coarse material brushing against his lips.

The squeezing at his wrist grew tighter, this time forgetting to relinquish its grip as the hissed voices overshadowed the flames.

'He's waking!' one said.

'Doesn't matter,' the other replied. 'Just keep him steady. If he moves too much—'

'I know what'll happen if he moves! We both bleed out!'

Done that before.

Ryza's next exhale came with a soft moan that burned in his throat, like his voice was either too new or too old. It prompted more panicked words as the squeezing at his wrist resumed more rapidly.

'I told you we should've tied him down,' the first voice said.

On instinct, Ryza tried to face the speaker, but his neck flopped as it turned, leaving his head slumped.

'There wasn't time,' the other voice muttered. 'It's too late, just take the hood off him.'

The pain at Ryza's wrist magnified suddenly, and his skin twisted as if it had been pinched. There was a rustle of movement over his head. It was like his skull was too small for his scalp and the latter was being peeled off.

He felt every fibre of the coarse material as it flowed across his battered skin. Strands of his matted hair caught in the material's grasped folds and ripped from his head, creating a wave of prickling pain to match whatever was happening to his wrist.

He was in a small room lit by a single, sputtering oil lantern. For a full minute, it was all Ryza squinted at as he came to his senses. He could feel the eyes of others on him, hear their laboured and impatient breaths, but he was powerless to make them out.

'Crash must've knocked him too good,' the second voice said gruffly. 'Or he's had too many knocks like that. Pretty sure I gave him one of them, a while back.'

Ryza lolled his head towards them. Though his vision was still a pointless blur, he recognised the voice just enough to force out his first word.

'Ditric?'

'What'd Greely say this was? Cognation? I don't give a shit, just don't move, alright?'

Ryza clamped his jaw shut and clenched it until it felt like his teeth were going to shatter. Somehow, this sharpened his vision a bit, and Ditric's closely shaved head came into focus. She wasn't looking back at him, however. Both her hands were hidden by a thin layer of lapping yellow fire. Her fingers danced across Ryza's exposed leg, tracing lines back and forth across the maroon tracks that'd once been wounds.

Ryza stared at the still-oozing welts until they seemed to extend past his skin and on to the stained cot he was propped up on. He was still piecing together how they'd come to be there. He could remember the crash, the fall as he'd tried to escape it, and then crawling away from it, but he hadn't fought anyone, had he?

He released his jaw, and his vision almost went with it. He could feel his head lolling around aimlessly as the scene began to fade before the pain at his wrist tweaked again and a firm grip fixed his head in place, holding his skull against the wall behind him.

Allowing himself a small respite, Ryza tried to count his heartbeats, but for some reason he couldn't keep track of them. Each beat seemed irregular, almost like there were two pumping through his blood lines.

Ryza clenched his jaw and found himself looking down at Ditric again. She was crouched low on a steel mesh floor, half straddling his leg as she continued to work on it. The level of concentration twitching on her brow was immaculate. It was like there was nothing in this world that could shift her vision an inch away from where it needed to be.

It was hypnotising. Ryza's own gaze followed precisely where Ditric's hands worked. She wasn't just knitting together his skin with her fingertips, it was with her nails, she was so exact. Her path weaved around each individual bloodstained hair follicle on his leg, leaving behind them a serrated trail of narrow scar tissue.

Ryza followed the line slowly back across his leg as it looped around his thigh and headed up towards his hip. Much like his bloodied leg, his torso was also uncovered, and Ryza tried to turn his head again, fighting back against the hand holding it in place.

It relented, and Ryza was free to revel in his nudity, spare for the crumpled and bloody rag that'd been thrown over his crotch.

'Oh...' he managed. 'Clothes...'

'When you're less of a mess,' Ditric grunted.

'But—'

Ditric finally paused her work and looked up at him.

'What? You worried about us seeing something?' She nodded to the rag covering his groin. 'Not the equipment we wanna work with anyway.'

We...

There was another person there. The realisation made the pain at his wrist triple, and he gasped in shocking, shooting pain as the grip around it tightened again. His gaze followed across his body, across the patchwork of scars old and new, down his arm and finally to the other hand that was clasped tightly around his upturned forearm.

'It hurts enough as it is, so you better not move no more.'

There was another squeeze, another sickening rush of invading blood, and Ryza recognised the other speaker. It was Avesta. She was sitting on a chair that was positioned high above him, the legs of it barely staying on the slanted table that raised it up. She was doubled over in her seat, her other arm held tightly around her chest and flexing in an alternating rhythm to the first.

Ryza tried weakly to pull free from her grip. His skin seared again, and both he and Avesta winced. Forcing his eyes to focus, Ryza leaned to look closer at his wrist. He'd only moved a few inches, but the sight he was rewarded with nearly made him fall from the bed.

His skin was burnt and scarred in a perfect circle, grafted and cauterised not to itself but to the underside of Avesta's own wrist. A messy spatter of dried blood was crusted around the conjoined wounds. Avesta squeezed at his forearm again, her grip circling a place on his arm a few inches up from the wound, and Ryza felt her blood gush into him.

'What are you... What have you done to me?'

'You lost blood,' Ditric said. 'She has blood.'

'Call it returning a favour, eh?' Avesta said.

Ryza looked back up at her. She'd barely been on her feet when he'd left on his journey a month ago. She looked just as pale now. Nevertheless, she was determined.

'Revance used to have tins of spare blood for things like this,' Avesta said. 'I talked to Greely about it a while ago. He said you'd just about drained out a whole 'nother man from what he'd treated you for.'

'Didn't have any of that out here... Wasn't expecting you to get so messed up by it all,' Ditric said. She stayed quiet for a while as she gently manoeuvred Ryza's leg into another position. 'This is gonna take a while, so if you've got questions, spill 'em. You always said something about beans…'

'We sure got beans,' Avesta muttered.

Ryza didn't bother correcting them. He wasn't sure what beans were himself. He'd just been too scared to admit it and face the ensuing mockery. A thousand questions rushed to his head, ricocheting around and bouncing out the other side without leaving a recognisable impression, so he stayed silent. It prompted Ditric to continue on.

'Just need to make sure your leg works right. Could burn it from the outside and be done with the fix, but I made that mistake with Ruka, and she still ain't walking right. Healing up the skin, layer by layer from the inside… takes a lot of time. You didn't want to stop bleeding, so I had to improvise a bit.'

'Where is Greely?'

Ditric chuckled softly to herself. 'Rather him be doing it? You ain't the only one. He's gone. Fucked off southeast to Basarod. Don't blame him. Only place not currently feeling the brunt of the flux. Maybe some places in the north…'

'And Ruka?'

The name made Ditric flinch. Her finger slipped, and a screaming bolt of pain shot through Ryza's leg, making it kick out wildly. The thrashing motion made his hand jerk as well, transferring the pain to Avesta.

'Fuck. Hit a nerve,' Ditric chided herself. She waited until Ryza's twitching leg had settled before she went on. 'Ruka ain't here. She didn't want to be, and I didn't want her either. There ain't many of us here, really. Us two,' she said, nodding to Avesta, 'Fynis, Berlic, Sarova, couple newer conscripts—'

The mention of Sarova's name finally made a thought stick in Ryza's head.

'Shit! Ditric, the drifter, it had a rebel sun, a piece of it, in the front, it could—'

'Sarova's got it,' Avesta said, cutting him off. 'We knew you were coming, Ryza. Been trying to catch you for a while.'

'You definitely fucking caught me. Couldn't have just walked up to me? Waved me down or something?'

Ditric shook her head. 'We had to know it was you. You and not... well, you remember what happened to your father, right?'

Ryza didn't respond. Not immediately, at least.

'Could've killed me, Ditric.'

'You were already as good as dead out here,' she replied.

'What?'

She glared up at him, the rage burning in her eyes not intended for him, but for many others who weren't there.

'Vorric lied to you. He lied to all of us. He's playing a game with all our minds just to get something that vaguely looks like control back. That's why he sent you away, because he's scared of you the most.'

'Me? Why? He was... He was helping me? I thought—'

'What *you* thought,' Ditric said, jabbing a still-flaming finger at him. 'He tricked you like everyone else did. I like you, Ryza, but fuck, you're gullible. I guess Vorric thought that was a good thing. That's why he sent you after Origin after filling your head with all these old stories. He wanted you to believe in something so you'd stop doubting yourself, and he wanted you alone so there'd be no one else around to tell you it's all lizard shit.'

'But I don't... I don't get it...'

'You're a bomb, Ryza,' Ditric stated. 'A bomb of pure resonance just waiting to blow. Why do you think you were going on all those hunts for smelters and flux traders after what happened at Iroka? Vorric was trying to give you purpose, to put off what he thought was going to happen sooner or later. He told me to start the League of Revance to let you do that. He gave us guns and supplies, but only enough so we could keep you hungry. Keep you wanting.'

'How do you know all this?' Ryza asked, still unsure if he should believe any of it.

Ditric stayed silent, so Avesta answered in her stead.

'Ruka told us.'

'Told us too late,' Ditric muttered. 'You'd already gone by then, hadn't you? Vorric had strapped you into that rocket and shot you out into the wastes where you wouldn't hurt no one when you ended up losing it. That thing you were driving? Ruka said it was barely a prototype! The Scythes had it made, but they weren't even sure it would start rolling without the rebel sun bits inside it blowing up.

Reckon that's what Vorric was betting on, that it would just blow up before you did and all they'd need to worry about would be a glass crater like Iroka.'

She sighed as she continued working on Ryza's leg. To him, it looked as though she was almost finished, but the consternation pinching at her cheeks said otherwise. He still couldn't feel anything below his knee, and it wasn't until Ditric started searing together another layer of sensitive flesh and sinew that his toes began to twitch.

'No, no it doesn't make any sense... Why should I even believe you? How do I know that this ain't just another play from Vorric? That he wants me to think—'

'Because we're your fucken friends, Ryza,' Ditric said. 'Dunno why you'd doubt that after all this shit.'

'Plus, you don't know what else Vorric's been up to,' Avesta said darkly. 'If Tyrag'd had half Vorric's wits, we'd all be long dead. Bastard's only gone and put all of Breggesa under his laws. Easy thing to do when no one had any control of it in the first place. He wanted us and all the other mercenary companies to help push the refugees into building the towers. I think we were the only ones that refused.'

'Kept telling us that it had to happen, that he'd promise to pay 'em, but it still didn't feel right in my guts,' Ditric said. 'Told him he might as well start putting collars on them like back on Revance. I didn't feel like we had much of a choice walking away from that meeting with him, it a day after you fucked off, by the way, and it only got confirmed to me when Vorric sent Ruka out to us to give us a last chance.'

'She's still working under him, then?' Ryza asked, keeping his voice low so Ditric wouldn't flinch again.

'Tah, she knows which way the wind's blowing. Fucken...' Ditric trailed off before she said something she'd barely regret. 'I mean, I get it. Only thing she's ever known is that she's about to starve. I wouldn't let go of being all important like she is now to the Scythes. Tried to tell her that it's probably only because of you, but...'

'She knows,' Ryza muttered. A twinge of pain from his leg rocketed across his body, wiping his next words from his mind. It took him a few seconds to find them again. 'A fucken net, though? You caught me with a net? Must've been hoping to get really lucky that I'd come this way.'

'Had plenty of ways to get lucky,' Avesta replied. She nodded to the wall of the small room over to Ryza's left, where a scratched-out map was hanging. 'We figured you'd come here eventually.'

The map was large, maybe a metre by a metre or more, composed of about a dozen different pages that'd been nailed to the wall to form one canvas. At its centre were two circles, one inside the other, that Ryza took to indicate the ruins of Twin Rings.

The surrounding lands had been charted extensively, with every bluff, butte, and peak indicated by a series of dotted lines that grew closer or further from each other to indicate steepness or elevation. Bars containing criss-crossing patterns stretched between most of them, forming an almost fully enclosing perimeter across the surrounding lands.

I could've drawn it out better, though.

'Fynis' idea. We weren't going to catch up to you, and we weren't going to chase you down, so we just had to go to where we knew you'd end up and hope you hadn't beaten us there, or gotten yourself blown up in the process.'

'Fynis...' Ryza rolled the name around in his mouth. 'He's on his feet again?'

'Oi,' Ditric snapped. 'You didn't like arm jokes, so don't start making foot jokes around him, got it?'

'Oh, yeah... You're right,' Ryza said sheepishly.

The last he'd seen him, Fynis and the other ex-conscripts that'd been injured in their final battle against the smelters were being ferried away by the Scythes' airborne dirigible fleet to safety before Ryza and Vorric had embarked on their final expedition into the doom town of Iroka.

'Ditric and a few others managed to pull him out of Breggesa right after Vorric ordered the gates be barred,' Avesta said. 'He'd told us all he was done fighting, but when he heard we were hunting you down... How many guards did he kill in the escape, Ditric?'

'Guards or bystanders?'

'His aim was a little rusty,' Avesta admitted. 'Don't know why they let him keep an R-Three and not me. I built half the damn things!'

'Yeah, and he built his own afterwards. And his damn leg. Makes me wonder if he was meant to be born a metal mouth like you two,' Ditric said.

'So you all just came out here to find me? Nearly killing me in the process?'

Avesta pretended to think for a moment. 'Yep.'

'Nothing else?'

'Nothing.' She held it in for a second, then laughed, and the way it pushed another burst of blood back into his veins made Ryza even queasier. 'Of course there's something. We reckon we can find Origin.'

'Do you!? Where?'

'Nowhere Vorric had you looking,' Ditric grunted. 'Now shut up, I gotta concentrate unless you want your toes to feel like fingers.'

CHAPTER NINETEEN

SEPARATION

WHAT LITTLE KNOWLEDGE DITRIC had taken from Greely in the last days before he'd headed for Basarod seemed to be precisely what she needed in order to piece together Ryza's leg. It took another two hours after Ryza woke up for her to be satisfied with her work.

Avesta used the time to fill Ryza in on all he'd missed, somehow keeping her rhythm of blood transfusion going without break. A good thing too, because Ditric had casually mentioned she had no idea what her improvised life support could lead to.

The tale of Vorric's crackdown on Breggesa was difficult for Ryza to swallow. It was one he believed, but how had a pragmatic man suddenly turned on his heel and declared himself ruler like that? Maybe it was the only logical solution, in Vorric's mind.

Ryza could still clearly picture the fear that'd strained across Vorric's face when Archarus had first appeared behind him. A fear not caused by the shadow dancer that'd been following Ryza, but by whatever had appeared at Ryza's back and subsequently disappeared before Ryza had been able to catch a glimpse of it.

It wasn't a thought that he shared openly with Ditric or Avesta. The mention of a shadow dancer would make the latter flinch, so for the sake of his wrist, he mulled it over himself.

Whispered folklore often decried shadow dancers as deathly omens, that the sight of one was enough to drive those unlucky enough to witness them mad. With what Ryza had learnt about pure resonance, it made perfect sense. It wasn't any particular power or effect of the shadow dancer that had this effect, but the gnawing questions that caused the victim to doubt their own existence. To ask themselves those dangerous questions about where normality ended and magic began. Pushing them closer to turning into a shadow dancer themselves.

It was an effect that Ryza seemed immune to despite his questioning. Archarus had said as much with his last appearance. Yet his words still planted a deep seed of worry in Ryza. What he'd concluded from his brief interactions with Archarus was that shadow dancers were unlikely to appear unless they absolutely had to.

Their own magic, a magic beyond axioms and runes, maybe beyond pure resonance and the magic left by those-of-glass, was one that influenced time. They could age or throw forwards pieces of the world on an instantaneous whim, yet the price they paid was far greater than what the living did for their own axioms.

It was to throw themselves forwards as well. As immortal spectres, the definition of a lifetime was one that'd been bent and twisted beyond its meaning from when they were alive. They'd already died their deaths, so all there was for them to do was to wait until the end of the world itself, but what happened after that for them? It was an unknown fear they must all carry, so it would only be with great necessity that they'd use their own magic and hurl themselves even closer to the end.

On the loneliest nights of the past month, Ryza had sat and wondered why Archarus had been yet to visit him. He'd only been able to assuage the feeling of abandonment by concluding that merely the act of appearing somehow cost a shadow dancer their time.

All this came together to make a shadow dancer's appearance a well-judged necessity on their part and a dire omen for those they saw it vital to commune with. Vorric had vaguely hinted at speaking to a shadow dancer before, that it now followed him as Archarus followed Ryza, so whatever in that moment had spurred not one, but two shadow dancers to appear must've been the pinnacle of a teetering catastrophe.

It was something Vorric had recognised and that Ryza himself had failed to see. Something that'd led to his unwitting manipulation at Vorric's hands, if what Ditric and Avesta were telling him was true.

He believes that's what he needs to do, and I was just a piece of that puzzle.

But it was a puzzle incomplete without the shadow dancer that Vorric himself cavorted with. A few of Vorric's words from their conversation after their venture into Iroka's flux-plagued depths now came to Ryza's mind. He'd asked what had happened to the rebel sun, the land-burning paralict that was to incinerate the valley like it had Twin Rings.

In time.

Vorric's reply had been cryptic, much like the other things he often said, and Ryza had thought little else of it. He'd just been relieved that someone else had the confidence that the plan was going to work, even after so much of it had gone so, so wrong. The chaotic blur of what Ryza had been sure were his final moments was an order of events that he was still struggling to pick through.

That was what those lonely nights had been good for. After he had checked his sandy perimeters around the most convenient outcrops of rocks or shallow caves where he'd hidden the drifter, he'd bundled himself up in the rear stowage compartment. It had been a cosy little place. The warmth emanating from the shard of the rebel sun at the front of the vehicle reminded him of leaning his back against a brick wall with an oven on the other side.

In that dim glow, Ryza had idly leafed through all the reports and papers Vorric had sent him off with, not absorbing a word until he'd read the surrounding sentence four times over, as his mind kept floating back to those eerie tunnels. The papers were only a distraction, a temporary impetus to make sure he didn't stay in that memory for too long.

It was almost painful to recall those times correctly. Times where he'd felt so close to death that he was beyond it, because the terrors he was facing had no concern for death, be it his or their own. Most of all though, it felt dangerous to tangle with those little recollections of how Holm had come to him.

She'd emerged from his severed arm as if she'd been birthed from the metal puck she'd left like a gift within his skin. She'd wanted him just as Ryza had wanted to be wanted, yet he'd had the heart-wrenching resolve to turn her away. Then there was Maligar's version of her, a diminutive, fearful conscript who'd been too terrified to speak, the very thing Holm had been trying to turn Ryza back into.

The final manifestation of her was the hardest to think of. That parasitic idea of how she'd killed Maligar that'd sprayed forth from the arm of flux that she'd given Ryza down there. She'd burned and screamed and stabbed and clawed at Maligar's face in a deathly dance mirrored a thousand times over as Ryza had lain dying in his failing vent suit. He'd accepted his fate, even tried to take it by his own hand, yet he'd failed. Maybe his mind had given up on creating memories by then, because everything that'd happened afterwards had been a nightmarish blur.

He remembered the lead-better as it had roared towards him. The carrier as he'd flown it up from the burning chasm left where Iroka had fallen into the tunnels below. Even the horde of tiny gnashing creatures he couldn't be sure were real or imagined when he'd attempted to stave off the molten flux from the inner machinery of the carrier.

Now he thought of Vorric and his shadow dancer, he discovered a new memory. A moment just after the lead-better had roared past him in the tunnel, when Vorric had scooped him up from his almost-final resting place. Ryza had been on his back, the vent suit's crackling hearing implements having long been broken. He couldn't hear what Vorric was shouting over the chaos, but there'd been a sharp turn in the lead-better's course, and Vorric had hurled the cannister containing the rebel sun deeper into the tunnel, where it had disappeared in a flash of blackened light.

Could that've been his shadow dancer?

It meant that wasn't the first time they'd interfered on Vorric's behalf. Maybe a second appearance had been enough to spur Vorric to overthrow Breggesa. The Academy was already a powerful force in the city, so it was possible that this wasn't as large a power grab as Avesta and Ditric framed it to be.

This final chunk of his thoughts felt safe enough to share, but

Avesta still shot it down, primarily on the grounds of what it would lead to. Power and control were not something that was given back, rather taken by force, and after the devastation of the flux catastrophe, the Scythes were likely the last true force left in the Droughtlands.

'When'd they start calling it the flux catastrophe, anyway?' Ryza asked.

'Dunno,' Ditric grunted back. 'When'd you get a collar put on you?'

'Very funny,' Ryza replied.

Ditric flicked one of the few uninjured portions of his leg with a flaming finger to punish him for his snark, but it barely made him wince. His entire leg was still a numb mass of tingling, burning aches.

'Whole thing's been a fucken catastrophe since then anyway,' Ditric added.

'Yeah,' Avesta said. 'I'd like to stab the guy who found the damn stuff in the first place.'

'Ryza had a chance,' Ditric said. 'Met him.'

'In Kyrea though, so don't go getting your hopes up. His name was Rettic. He was old. Really old. He's probably already dead with what I've heard,' Ryza said.

'It's only gotten worse,' Ditric said. 'Vorric sent whole swarms of refugees back with the equipment to try burying the flux. No one's heard from them since. Waste of metal.'

'They could've run away,' Ryza suggested.

Both Avesta and Ditric shook their heads. It was a grim thought. Hundreds more added to the grave of a place where thousands more autominds were buried. It was probably worse than Iroka by now. He just had to pray that Holm's essence or whatever she was now hadn't gotten into it, but judging by her appearance in the scrapyard, she wasn't limited only to where the flux was.

As Ditric finished up her work, she made sure to thoroughly brief Ryza on what she'd done, what sensations or markings to look out for on his finely stitched skin to indicate a breakdown in the scar tissue, and what range of motion he'd have for the first few days.

'Greely wasn't this thorough when he sorted out my arm.'

'What happened to your arm ain't meant to move that much. Maybe the skin and everything underneath can stretch a bit, but otherwise it's just... there. Plus, disgusting as it is, Greely would've had a fair bit of extra flesh to work with from the way he fixed it up. Here, what you've got is what I got, so I can't go cutting and trimming where I like. Now stay still, I need to get you and Avesta... well...'

The process of separating his veins from Avesta's was somehow more excruciating and more improvised than the past few hours of healing performed on his leg. Ditric first went to simply slice the wound open with a knife, but that was more likely to sever the rest of the veins in their arms. She then tried burning another axiom to begin searing the flesh apart, only creating a dense mass of connecting skin instead.

'Nothing else for it,' Ditric said with an indifferent shrug. 'Just gotta twist and pull, then hope that the bits I attached your blood lines will snap before the rest of them do.'

'What do you mean, "twist and"—'

Ryza never had a chance to finish the sentence. Avesta pulled, almost leaping out of her chair and into the ceiling as she yanked her arm away. They both screamed in panic and agony as Ditric roared over them both to shut up and give her their arms, both her hands ablaze. She seized both their wrists, cutting off the jets of spurting blood. The distinct sound of sizzling flesh hissed through the room along with Ryza's and Avesta's sharpened breaths.

When Ditric released them, they both shook as they collapsed from shock. Ryza simply fell backwards into the cot, the top of his head clanging off the wall behind him, but Avesta tumbled off the table she was standing on. She flailed as she rolled over the top of Ryza, accidentally kicking his freshly healed leg as she tried to regain her balance.

Ditric thrust out her arm to save Avesta from ploughing face first into the floor, but the movement hit her like a heavy punch.

'Better not tell anyone I did all that,' Ditric said, placing Avesta down at the foot of Ryza's cot. She glanced down at Ryza's wrist and sucked at her teeth. 'Don't want anyone trying it for themselves.'

'Fuck, Ditric! He just lost all that blood I put into him.'

Avesta was probably right. Ryza's vision swayed and darkened as he held up his right arm to inspect the damage. The skin was blackened and scabbed over where the blood had covered it, which was just about his entire forearm. Clawed-out tracks marked the site of Ditric's burning grip, another scar to be carried with the rest. Surprisingly, the skin on the underside of his wrist where Avesta had been connected was undamaged.

'There ain't enough rags in the world to clean that up,' Ditric said, nodding down at Ryza.

Ditric was definitely right. The mess and muck of blood and sand that'd covered Ryza a few minutes ago now seemed like a complementary layer of light warpaint.

'Bloodfist, bloodleg, bloodarm, bloodneck, blooddick, bloodfoot—'

'Oh, shut up,' Ryza moaned as he tried to wipe some of it off. His hand was so well-coated that it only swished the liquid gore around.

'Just go outside and roll around in the sand, then... I don't know, just scrape it all off,' Ditric said.

'I'm not wearing anything.'

'You're wearing half of me by the feel of it,' Avesta jabbed back.

She tried to stand, but her knees hadn't even straightened out before she dropped back onto the cot. The blood hadn't spattered across her brown greatcoat as badly as Ryza had copped it, but it still left a pattern of dark, camouflaging blotches across the right side.

Ditric gave Ryza a few minutes to gather himself before helping him to his feet, throwing his unbloodied left arm over her shoulder as she led him outside. Ryza kept the rag clutched across his groin for the first two steps, but dropped it when a tempting doorframe presented itself for him to grab on to.

It was early in the afternoon outside the small shack, a hazy day where the sand hung in the sky to ease the blare of the sun, but it still made Ryza cringe away. The sky was too bright, and the orange sand was all too ready to bounce it right up into him. The ground was still rough underfoot. The sand layer was even thinner than Ryza had first estimated. The strain of his scarred leg combined with the uncomfortably pointy rocks hidden beneath made it difficult to walk quickly, but Ditric was patient enough to keep a slow pace.

Each step with his left leg felt like an action prompted by a puppeteering amateur. Swinging it forwards brought a sensation of tangled and constricting string across it, but as it moved back with the step, it suddenly felt like all those strings were being yanked straight up towards his hip. They walked for another minute more as Ditric searched for a deep enough patch of sand.

Squinting, Ryza could make out the knobbly, towering shapes of the spires that he'd driven the drifter between. There was little to support them, so his foggy mind couldn't resist wondering how they'd come to be.

There were a few shacks at the base of each one, hastily thrown together little structures that looked like they'd never been occupied at all. Nearby were the remnants of the net that'd caught him. Most of it was gone, having been carried along by his careening drifter, so all that remained was an articulated post that trailed a few strands of ripped steel cabling from its bent and tired length.

The trail of the drifter's crash was marked upon the land by a wide streak of raked sand and rock that stretched almost to the horizon.

I must've kept going for a while. It's a miracle they got to me in time.

Over his shoulder, Ryza could see the lead-better that'd ferried him here, judging by the crusted patch of blood that stained the side of the rear tray. It sat alone next to the shack he and Ditric had emerged from, but a few more pairs of deeply gouged tracks sprouted off from the blank ground next to it. There must be others out there today, patrolling their traps and waiting for their prey.

Ryza hoped they wouldn't be back until he got his hands on some clothes.

Chapter Twenty

Ryz-Ain't

I T WAS AN EXTRA, grating punishment to his skin to wash the blood off like this. The handfuls of sand he carefully scooped from the ground at his feet had to be held carefully to filter out sharp pebbles and keep the finer grains within. It took Ryza a painstakingly long time to realise he was going about the task the wrong way.

He set aside the task of cleaning himself for the moment and spent a few minutes creating a larger pile of fine sand he'd already filtered. It sped up the process, but soon he was facing the next unpleasant step.

The sand had formed a coarse paste as it absorbed the drying blood that coated his skin. It caught on the hairs that were both fine and delicate, or curly and rough, yanking them out if he pressed the paste-like globs too hard against the external scabs. What remained after the cleaning process was skin so raw it was almost as red as when he'd started.

Ryza's instincts told him to work quickly. He felt vulnerable for obvious reasons and regretted not asking for Ditric to stay and watch over him for a while. Then again, the isolation gave him more time to think about how he'd relay the rest of his solitary journey to her and the others in a way that wouldn't make them doubt his sanity.

They probably already do.

It wasn't an unreasonable thing, Ryza thought to himself as he knelt down to better scrub the blood from his backside. He was going to look like a lunatic wandering back into the little gathering of shacks utterly naked. Ditric could've at least left her greatcoat behind.

Once he'd reached a sufficient level of cleanliness, he hoisted himself to his feet and began his slow, staggering path back to the shacks at the base of the spire.

The slow wind that was chilling places it rarely touched had blown away any sense of tracked footprints, so Ryza couldn't quite remember which hut he'd come from. He'd still been woozy when he'd been escorted from one of them, and the nearby landmarks of tangled net remnants and distant rock spires didn't help him pick between them as he ambled up to one of the doors.

There were two lead-betters sitting next to the huts now, so Ryza knocked with caution. There was an unintelligible response from within. Ryza knocked again.

'Quit fucken around, would ya?'

The voice was indistinct through the roughshod door. He couldn't tell if it was Ditric or someone else, but the choice of words was a common refrain for her. Ryza pushed the door open and almost immediately jumped back as a gale of swearing burst out in reply to his presence. The man in the shack knocked over the chair he'd been sitting in as he scrambled for the rifle that was propped up against the back wall, a surface of stone from the rock spire itself. His coat and travelling cloak whirled around him, throwing off waves of the day's dust and obscuring him in a haze.

The man stumbled as he snatched up his weapon, a red-tipped slug flashing in his hand as he jammed it down the breach before pointing the rifle squarely at Ryza's chest.

'Naked! That's a new one!'

'What? What do you—'

'You even sound like him,' the man muttered to himself. 'Never thought they'd get this close to the camp.'

Ryza finally recognised the voice, even though he couldn't make out the owner from within the comparative gloom of the hut.

'Fynis? Is that you?' Ryza asked. 'It's me! Don't shoot me!'

'Lizard shit!'

'It is him,' Ditric's voice bellowed from within the other shack.

The door to it was wrenched open, and she came storming out, hurling a greatcoat at Ryza before she went and snatched Fynis' rifle from his hands.

'Damn near used up all my ink stitching him back together, and I ain't having it wasted because you can't believe that—'

'It's the third one this week, Ditric!' Fynis complained.

As Ryza pulled the greatcoat around his shoulders, the two continued in an argument that spilled out of the small shack. Ditric was the first out, the still-loaded rifle in her grip, and Fynis followed close behind, making vain attempts to snatch it back. Every second step of his clanked and squeaked against the ground, making his posture sway heavily rightwards in his gait.

The golden light of the late afternoon glistened off the steel workings of Fynis' prosthetic leg. Ryza could only see a fraction of the contraption beneath the layers of Fynis' travelling garb, but he wouldn't have been surprised if the metal frame embraced his entire body. The leg itself wasn't connected where the original flesh had been severed. No, that just hung as a limp bit of hastily tied-off cloth with a void beneath it until the twice-articulated knee came into action. The joint moaned with its constant work, an army of strings and clockwork-tensed wires straightening it out whenever Fynis wasn't resting his weight on it.

A constricting frame around the very upper portion of his right thigh and a larger one around his waist, positioned much like a belt would be, kept the limb in place. The surface of them were adorned with an array of dials and wound-up levers that connected to the various cables that stood in for his leg's muscles.

What stood in for his foot, however, was far less complex. It was just an upside-down dome of studded steel. Ryza couldn't help looking down at his own bare feet to compare, and he found the solution to be an elegant one. Full of ankles, toes, and more joints to bend than entirely necessary, feet were a complicated thing. For what Fynis needed, there was no point trying to replicate that in metal.

It was a conclusion Ryza had arrived at following Revance's fall when he'd attempted to recreate a prosthetic limb of his own so he wouldn't have to use the one Origin had crafted for him. Although for all the fiddly little things that hands were expected to do, Ryza found it easier to simply do it with one and the help of his left nub, rather than waste hours mimicking it with metal.

'Y'know, I could've easily *told* you it was him if you'd just checked in with me when you got back!' Ditric snapped, her attempt at ending the argument. 'Why're you back so early anyway?'

'Something felt off in the air. Heat. Heat like a big day of sun, but I knew it ain't the season for it. Just got back to sit down for a second before coming to you and then that thing—'

'Ryza,' Ditric said bluntly.

'—comes knocking at the door.'

'It is me, Fynis.' Ryza paused for a moment. 'It's good to see you.'

But Fynis didn't seem convinced. He looked to Ditric again.

'Does he know?'

Ditric snorted. 'Whole bunch of things he doesn't know.'

'You know what I mean.'

Ditric shook her head.

'Do I want to know?' Ryza asked.

'What's that thing you and Vorric were always on about?' Ditric said to herself. 'Empty minds?'

'Half a mind to empty *his* mind,' Fynis growled. 'Look, we gotta tell him sooner or later. Another one of them is coming.'

Fynis pointed into the distance, in the direction of where Twin Rings would've been visible as a silhouette on the horizon if it were still standing, marking out a figure that was slowly walking towards them. Ryza squinted, but they still looked like a speck through the haze of the day's heat, and the low beams of sunlight didn't help.

Ditric was better equipped. She stowed the rifle between her ribs and her elbow as she used her free hand to rummage through a satchel hidden beneath her greatcoat. A few slugs, also red-tipped, fell from it as she pulled out a brass scope and held it to her eye. It was a finely tuned instrument, and Ryza guessed it had been "inherited" from her brief time with the Scythes.

She bared her teeth as she twitched the tip of the glinting scope left and right, eventually stilling when she properly brought the figure into her view. She sucked a cold breath in through her exposed teeth.

'Yeah. Yeah, that's one of them,' she said. 'You wanna do it?'

Fynis shrugged. 'You're the one holding the rifle. Go on. I'll keep an eye on this one.'

Ditric went stomping off to the nearest lead-better. She hurled the rifle into the rear tray as she got in and then gestured to Ryza that she was about to toss the scope to him. He was barely ready by the time it was sailing through the air, but before he could fumble it, Fynis had stepped in with a metallic squeak and snatched it out of his path.

The lead-better started with a throaty roar, something Ryza hadn't realised he'd missed with the drifter until this very moment, and trundled off towards the approaching figure. Its steel wheels spun and spat dust out behind it in vicious spurts as they attempted to gain traction. The trail of kicked-up sand eventually obscured the vehicle entirely. Ryza could only guess at how wide a path it was taking towards the figure until Fynis pressed the scope into his hand.

'You gotta see it for yourself.'

'And you aren't going to tell me until it happens, right?'

Fynis shook his head, and Ryza held the scope up to his eye. He had to tilt his head in order to prop his elbow against his ribs to keep a steady grip, but soon enough he had a wavering view of the figure in his sight.

They walked like him. Wore clothes like he'd once worn. Even had one hand, just as he did. But their face was still covered by a vent mask. There was no way to tell where the flesh ended and the steel of the mask began, or if it were the other way around. It was just one seamless blend of skin and metal just below the figure's eyes. Ryza used a free finger to twiddle at the scope's dials, tightening the view and getting an even closer look.

The eyes were the part he couldn't believe were real. It had to be a trick of the sun's setting light. Something was wrong with the scope, maybe. They weren't green. They weren't entirely filled with silver either. They were black. Black as a shadow dancer's were.

'But how can the flux do that?' Ryza whispered to himself.

'Same question we've been asking ourselves,' Fynis replied. 'Must've been happening before we set up our nets around these parts to catch you coming in, but ever since we did, we've been on a constant lookout for a version of you coming *out*. Of the ground, I mean. Other people have been seeing things looking like you all over the place as well, is what I've been hearing. Dunno if this is the only place they're coming from, but we can only hope we're helping put a stop to it.'

'From Twin Rings?' Ryza said softly, trying not to jolt the scope too harshly.

'Yeah.'

There was a pause between them as the lead-better ground to a stop in the distance, maybe five hundred metres away now. Ryza tilted the scope towards it, steadying his sight in time to catch Ditric leaping out of the rickety vehicle, rifle in hand with a vent mask secured on her face.

'You gone to have a look at the place yet?' Ryza asked.

'Not closely. That's why we've been waiting for you. Makes sense that you go in first.'

'Why?'

The rifle hung low in Ditric's hand, her grip around the barrel of the weapon rather than the trigger, as she marched over to the still-walking figure. The figure didn't turn to notice her, not even when she was within ten paces as she stopped and raised the rifle to her shoulder.

'Here we go,' Fynis said.

Ryza wouldn't have needed the scope to see the brilliant tongue of fire that burst from the muzzle of Ditric's rifle, or to take in with a sense of horrified awe what happened next. The burning slug pieced the figure straight through the side of their head, continuing out the other side as a solid spear of silver. Thorns branched off it like crackling forks of lightning, plunging into the sky or the ground as the original rod continued on, slowing in pace until it stilled, more than a hundred metres in length.

The original figure still stood there, its legs still actioned without producing motion, planted in place by the ever-expanding thorns coming out of the connecting rod. After a few more agonising heartbeats, the eyes of the figure dissolved from the pitiless black and into the silver Ryza expected from such an apparition. The clothes on its body, a battered greatcoat much like the one he wore now, bubbled and melted before wafting off as gas, revealing smooth surfaces of silver beneath where skin should be.

Like an acid was eating its way across it, the rest of the figure and the ensuing rod of branching thorns began to dissolve too. Eventually nothing was left, and Ditric was already back in the lead-better as its engine grunted and huffed towards Ryza and Fynis.

'Ditric figured it out,' Fynis said. 'At least she thinks she did. I think she did. There's a few different versions of you that come out. Don't know what day, but we know the times of days, roughly. She reckons, by the clothes you're wearing and the state you look like you're in, they're from different times you've been to that ruin.'

'Really?' Ryza said distractedly. He still had the scope pressed to his eye, his attention almost entirely focused on the spot where the figure had stood, even though there was nothing left to mark them.

Where had the flux gone, then?

'Something like that. She could tell you more, but there's even one of you that comes out with both hands. Don't get that one, you know? We've just been blowing them apart as they come. Got enough incendiary slugs to keep doing it for another month or two, but after that...'

'You don't know where the flux goes?'

Ryza finally lowered the scope to see Fynis shaking his head.

'I know why you're asking. After Iroka and all... But there ain't much we can do about it if it fucks off into the air like that. Shit, there's probably a little bit of flux in all of us and we just haven't realised it.'

'Yeah, well...' Ryza sighed. 'Best not to think about it?'

'I reckon,' Fynis grunted.

They watched as Ditric pulled the lead-better to a stop, almost crashing it into the other remaining vehicle, and she turned off the engine. The throaty, intermittent puttering died down, but it didn't disappear entirely. Ryza looked around and spotted another cloud of dust on the horizon coming towards them.

'They ain't coming at you in lead-betters, are they?' he asked.

'You saying that better not make it fucken true,' Ditric shouted as she re-joined them. She squinted at it, somehow seeing further than Ryza could've done with the scope. 'One of ours. Berlic, I think.'

'Those figures...'

'Ryz-ain'ts, we've been calling them,' Ditric said.

'Stupid name if you ask me,' Fynis muttered.

'Only coming during the day? You got people posted all around but they only come during the day? And you expected me to be only coming in the day too? What if I'd come at night? Who would've set off that net?'

'You were going to drive that fucken fast at night when you couldn't see nothing?'

Ryza grumbled in agreement.

'But yeah, the rest of 'em... only in the day. Dunno if Fynis filled you in, but I reckon they're bits of you. Echoes. You remember what we saw of Gry down there?'

Ryza nodded bitterly.

'Like that, maybe. More advanced of the flux. Don't know how they're getting out from under the glass from the rebel sun, but now you're here, we can go have a proper look.'

'Right now?'

'Tomorrow,' Ditric conceded. 'Get you some clothes, some food...' She looked him up and down, curling her lip with thinly veiled disdain. 'Get some more of the blood off you, maybe.'

FRIENDLY FORCES

TRUE TO HER PROMISES, Ditric told Fynis to help Ryza out with something that would cover the still-bare portions of his body. She muttered about having more important things to do, of which Ryza couldn't imagine, and wandered off, leaving him and Fynis to reacquaint themselves.

The pair of them went from shack to shack, raiding the belongings of the other members of the League of Revance that were out on their own patrols. It was something Ryza was hesitant of, but Fynis assured him they wouldn't mind.

'Rather see you wearing their stuff than nothing, they would.'

Fynis' own meagre wardrobe had been able to offer him a shirt with one too many sleeves and a pair of trousers with one too few legs, so Ryza pulled on the former and their search continued, tracking to another set of huts in the shadow of the next spire along. Ryza soon had a full, if mismatched, outfit, and had even found a spare greatcoat, allowing him to return Ditric's oversized one that she'd lent him.

On the way, Ryza felt compelled to ask Fynis about his leg, and what'd happened to him after he'd been carried off by a dirigible all those months ago. It wasn't easy for him to raise it in conversation, considering that Fynis had resisted doing the same for him, but he obliged Ryza's question anyway, telling the story in such an unrecognisable order that Ryza had to mentally chew on his words to make sense of them.

Fynis' trip hadn't taken him and the others to Breggesa first. The Scythes had set up a much larger staging camp a few horizons away to help fuel the operation occurring in Iroka. That was how they'd had such a limitless supply of staff, meals, and equipment seemingly at Vorric's beck and call. It was something Fynis had paid close attention to as he'd continued to recover from his injuries. When Ryza asked why, Fynis had tapped his nose with a knowing look.

'They might've been fighting on our side then, but what if they ain't one day? Saw it with Revance, didn't we?'

He did have a point, and Fynis' suspicious had turned out to be right. He and Avesta, both of whom were still too injured for the Scythes' healers to consider moving, had stayed there for another two weeks, while the others had been sent onwards to Breggesa the next day. When they'd eventually been ferried off to Breggesa themselves, Fynis had remained in their infirmary for a great deal longer than Avesta, who'd longed to be back with her own people.

But for Fynis, the calm and comfort afforded by his new arrangements had been appealing, and he'd even found a new talent working with a few Kretatics he'd met within the city, crafters for some kind of unsanctioned arcanite fighting outfit. His experience aboard Revance of welding the constantly breaking lead-betters back together had made him a valuable addition to these arena crews, who valued physical sturdiness more than magnetic enchantment, and in turn they'd assisted in Fynis' own efforts to push the limits on what a non-Kretatic could manufacture.

He'd first tried to replicate an R-Three, a goal he'd accomplished within three weeks from the small room he'd been allowed to keep in the Scythes' infirmary in the city, and had gone on to design his own prosthetic leg. Even Vorric himself had come to visit to check in on his progress, musing to Fynis that there was a certain inventiveness that came from not being able to summon magnetism from the metal itself.

'A future for industry in the Droughtlands,' Fynis said. 'All his industry, though. He ain't in it for the reels like the flux traders were. Something else in his eye. Kind of look I'd expect to see in the Locusts, if they were still around. It ain't power, neither.'

'It's necessity,' Ryza said.

The sun had fallen from the sky as they walked back to the spire where they'd started their garment-gathering trip. By the dancing lights of a few fires, Ryza could pick out the shadows of a few more lead-betters, signalling the return of the others. There was a certain trepidation in his heart at the prospect of seeing them again, and he wasn't sure who it was held more for. The old friends he'd run away from, or the new members of this motley crew who'd only heard tales of him as if he were some kind of mythic war-beast.

'Yeah, that sounds about right,' Fynis said, continuing the conversation, not noticing that Ryza had slowed. 'It's not like he thinks he knows best, like he knows it has to be this way. I dunno how much I can say about Vorric anyway. You were the one always talking with him, and I ain't seen him for about three months.'

But Ryza nodded. 'It's right, in a way. He's scared. Might be of the flux, might be of me. Just ain't sure if I want to find out.'

Fynis turned to look back at him, and Ryza realised his own feet had stopped moving.

'You scared too?'

Ryza wasn't sure how to answer. Both answers were lies, and anything in between them would be insufficient.

'Different kinds of scared,' he eventually said. 'Lots of them.'

Fynis sidled back to him and clapped an arm over his shoulder, fixing his face into a straight-lined grin. 'Got a lot on your head. Don't know how you went so long carrying it yourself, but we're here for you now, eh? Come on, let's get you a feed.'

The League of Revance's camp was now a much more substantial offering. The returned lead-betters, nearly a dozen in total, had been parked and arranged in a specific formation, almost like a grid with a few offset columns. Canvases had been unfurled from the vehicles' side compartments and conjoined with each other to form windbreaks and sand barriers to keep out the hostile night gusts. Braziers were laden with roasting spits of meat, and those sitting around them bounced the conversation back and forth like the sparks from the coals warming their knees. It echoed across the sky, only falling silent as they realised that Ryza had finally arrived.

They didn't reach for their rifles like Fynis first had, but they still rose with an air of readied caution. Only when Fynis slapped him heartily on the chest and loudly confirmed that it was him did they rush to greet him, deluging him with backslaps and warm greetings. The barrage of voices and accompanying faces was a struggle for Ryza to keep up with, let alone respond properly to, and by the end of it all, he was holding his old sawn-off rifle and he had no idea who to thank for it.

Ditric came out of the crowd last of all, her grin a weary one only held up at the sides by the excitement of the others, and snatched her greatcoat back from Ryza.

'It's a relief for this lot that they don't need to watch the nets no more. Probably be able to get moving soon as well. They're probably as sick of this place as I am, aren't we!?'

She called the last two words to the rest, and they responded with a cheer that dissolved into a chorus of swearing. They went back to their seats around the fire and resumed their conversations, albeit with a touch more spiritedness in their voices. Ryza could now count them properly. A bit over twenty of them, half of which he recognised.

'Where next?' Ryza asked.

'After we figure out how to stop all these versions of you from coming out of Twin Rings, or if it's even worth doing, we're going to Origin. Get him to stop this whole mess with the flux one way or another.'

'I don't know if it'll be that simple—'

'Fucken better be,' Fynis interjected.

'—but even then, how are you going to find him?'

Ditric nodded. 'Got a good way of tracking him down now, but I ain't telling you. Don't want you going off running into the night without us like last time.'

'I'm sorry,' Ryza said softly. 'I thought it's what I needed to do.'

'It's what Vorric convinced you that you needed to do,' Ditric replied. 'Vorric and that lot might have their own ends, and we might have ours, but... fuck, we're just trying to stay alive for long enough that we can start worrying about the next day. You going to be here with us tomorrow to do that?'

Ryza felt himself grin. 'Gladly.'

Ditric directed Ryza to sit his tired body down next to the largest fire at the centre of the camp. It had been dug out as a pit, filled with butchered carcasses of over-gorged and easily caught scavenger birds, and then reburied with another layer of smouldering coals. This made the final layer of covering sand glow a gentle yellow, emitting a delicious sizzling each time someone prodded an iron poker in to check on the meats.

The assembled members still with the League of Revance cycled in and out of the surrounding seats, flat patches of ground at least, catching up with him for as long as they could before Ditric barked at them to follow up on some other duty. Even if she forgot to say anything, getting too caught up in the idle reminiscing, Fynis was ready to give orders in her place.

This constantly drilled efficiency felt usual to Ryza. Aboard Revance, efficiency came in the form of necessity or threats of being thrown off the fortress. Out here, Ditric's authority rested on loyalty, but it seemed far more powerful than when she'd commanded the little outfit from outside Breggesa's walls. There was a purpose here. A greater goal that stretched beyond just waiting around for the next bounty to come in.

In between the words of reacquaintance, Ditric quietly confided her plans in Ryza like they were an unspoken proposition for him to be involved with them. To her, the League of Revance wasn't just about fighting or hunting down smelters. It was to be an effort that rebuilt the Droughtlands, righting the destruction that the path of the fortress had inadvertently caused. The new recruits among them hadn't joined simply from a will to fight or a need for reels, but because they believed in the mission as well.

Ryza only had the briefest of moments to interact with these newcomers over the course of the night, but it was enough to pass a first judgement of them. They were older than the standard crop that would've made up Revance's conscripts. Some might as well have been their parents. Their tasks were carried out with worn and battered hands that were held together by knuckles that'd grown almost unnaturally large, a sign of long-lived experience in whatever craft they'd been brought up in.

The jobs that Ditric and Fynis ordered them off to hinted at that. Some were builders and crafters, charged with maintaining the integrity of the League's lodgings, the huts that turned out to be far more thought-through than Ryza realised. Each shack was held together by a series of sturdy hinges and could be folded down and lifted into the back of a lead-better at a moment's notice. A few of these builders had been sent off to the other encampments to do just this in preparation for their departure tomorrow.

Another three or four of them were hunters and trappers that knew the land better than any of the rest, along with how to get a meal out of it. Most of all, they knew how to make it last. Bandoliers of salts and dried spices hung loosely across their chests as they tended to the firepits.

The rest had even more specialised roles as other masters of the lands, and even one that took on a more diplomatic role to trade with the local villages they passed. Despite being experts in their field, they seemed all too happy to take on Ditric's orders. According to her, they were the secret to the League's success so far.

'Wasn't ever the fighters that made Revance a force not to be fucked with,' Ditric concluded to Ryza. 'It was the people that supported them. That's where the Locusts got in. That's why they won. That's why cleaning up Iroka was always going to be a lost cause for you. Because you were nothing but gunners trying to fix something that you couldn't shoot at.'

'Even then, is it enough?' Ryza asked, making sure his voice was low enough not to be heard by others.

'Don't matter. People are going to like the idea more than they like the results. The idea makes the results, see?'

'I've seen where that thinking can lead,' Ryza replied. 'I didn't like it.'

'Lot of things not to like at the moment, Ryza. But we take the help we can get. Even had a Scythe show up to throw his lot in with us.'

'Who?'

'Caftor. Sarova reached out to him, actually. Figures the only other two that made it out of whatever the fuck happened at the end of Iroka would have a few things to share. He keeps to himself, mostly. Knows the others ain't gonna trust him, but I've heard half of his reasons for leaving the Scythes, and you probably already know the half of them that I don't.'

Ryza had little time to ask more of the former Scythe and decided it was a mission for the next day. Vhoze and Elya, the pair that'd accompanied him on the venture that'd resulted in the capture of his would-be father, had already been sitting around the cooking fire when Ryza had joined them and spent the time between Ditric's commands needling Ryza with questions about what happened on the day that'd been so disastrous.

Ditric had refused to tell them, and Ryza silently joined her on it, so the two were left to bicker among themselves as they unpacked the few rumours they'd caught on to. Out of the whole group, they were the only ones keen to speculate on the past, whereas the others simply accepted it with a grim, unspoken resolve.

Berlic and Sarova had dropped by next. They were less interested in Ryza's presence than they were consulting with Ditric as to what to do about the shard of the rebel sun they'd recovered. Salvaging it had damaged the only vent suit the League carried with them, a spare inherited from the Scythes' reserve camp that only Sarova could fit into, and the materials required to repair it sounded costly. Berlic had campaigned spiritedly for the cause of selling the piece of the paralict to repair the suit, but Ditric had eventually sided with Sarova in keeping it.

She hadn't said what she might have planned for it, but Ryza knew a cunning look in Ditric's eye when he saw it. It was something that bothered him late into the night and long into the next morning as he watched the League disassemble the remains of the camp and load it into their convoy. They set off as the sun rose, trundling towards the place where Twin Rings had once stood. Ryza didn't know what they'd find there, but he just hoped it wasn't something he'd already dreamt.

CHAPTER TWENTY-TWO

WORDS WITHIN GLASS

IT WAS TO BE a short drive. Ryza had ended up in one of the rear vehicles, a larger one that mimicked a treadhulk, despite being composed of two lead-betters that'd been welded together. It carried the bulk of the League's cargo, including the bundled-together remnants of the wrecked drifter. They'd offered Ryza a chance to go through it before they'd loaded it onto the rear tray, in case he could salvage something from its stowage that might be useful, but other than a few spare slugs, Ryza was content with it all being assigned as scrap.

All the documents, all the papers, all those hopes that Vorric had sent him out with were lies, or at least they were things he simply couldn't believe once he heard Ditric's side of the story. The facts didn't quite conflict, but it felt like a betrayal.

Ryza's driver was a man named Platus, who had a head flanked with crisp grey hair that seemed to stain the skin around it. Ryza almost felt strange sitting next to a man not carrying a rifle, but he supposed that was his own task in riding as Platus' passenger.

Ditric had told them there was little risk for ambush or attack out here, something she hadn't needed to say, considering the terrain was flat enough that they could spot anyone hiding in the shallow gullies from miles off. Ryza still kept his sawn-off rifle ready in his lap as he talked idly with the older man.

He'd had to ask the man's name three times before he was properly able to remember it. The same had happened with the other newer faces among the League of Revance's ranks, and even a few of the older ones.

It just seemed as though these people were from another world than the one that Ryza had been living in for these past months. They didn't understand what he'd done or what he'd seen. They just looked to Ditric and her orders and decided that she'd done the thinking for them as they carried them out. It made Ryza want to shrink up into a shell of himself and not talk to them, just so he didn't have to strain to remember just who they were, other than the blur of faces and arguing voices that they seemed to be.

One replaced another every time Ryza's own thoughts drifted off in the direction of Holm, something that was happening more and more with each day since he'd left her in that scrapyard. At least while he was cooped up in the slightly-too-small seat of the lead-better, he could force himself to focus on a somewhat normal conversation.

Platus had worked briefly with the Scythes, not as one of their number, as the Scythes at that point didn't take on Kretatics or anyone from beyond the Academy, but as an engineer for their fleet of dirigibles. He'd been part of a team charged with inventing lightweight engines to fit the flying crafts, but that work had been permanently delayed when Vorric had summoned the Scythes to Iroka.

He'd ended up joining the League of Revance shortly after the Scythes had seized power across Breggesa and had played a non-violent hand in Fynis' escape. With his own sons and daughters safely trapped within the city, he'd figured the sooner molten flux was dealt with, the better for them, and he had more faith in Ditric's unspoken mission than Vorric's carefully laid plan, after what he'd heard happened in Iroka.

Platus, along with Berlic and Fynis, were the ones responsible for keeping the various engines of the League's new fleet fuelled and running hot. Ryza did his best to understand the convoluted workings of the engine currently hauling them along as Platus explained it to him, but the intricacies of fuel efficiency and oil usage wasn't enough to stop his mind from lingering elsewhere.

Every trip he'd taken to Twin Rings had come with a devastating loss. With all he'd seen and all he'd done, and with all this doubt in his mind, he was certain there wasn't any way today could be different. Would Holm be waiting for him? Or something else? There was still the question of where the copies of himself were coming from and what they hoped to accomplish, two facts he wished Ditric and the others had gone and figured out for themselves instead of waiting for him.

The convoy suddenly began to halt, and Platus twisted the steering column so the enlarged lead-better veered sharply to the right as it slowed, narrowly avoiding the vehicle in front.

'Why've we stopped? We're not there yet, are we?' Ryza asked.

Platus pointed ahead, his gruff voice requiring a few attempts before it caught as words.

'Another one of you, apparently.'

Ryza didn't have a scope on him today, but he didn't need it to recognise Fynis' hobbling outline against the horizon as he walked up to the mindless figure. Fynis' rifle came up, there was a blast of burning shrapnel, and the figure exploded into a short-lived metallic abomination.

'Never seen it happen that close,' Platus muttered as the convoy ground back into motion.

'Why not?'

'Ditric and the others, all the ones that've met you, they take it upon themselves to do it. I think they'd ask the rest of us to leave it to them, if they ever figured out the words for it. Don't think they want us to see you like that, by my eye. It's fair. All the stories I've already heard about you, I wouldn't believe you're real either, if I'd seen things like that.'

'I am real,' Ryza said, more to reassure himself than Platus.

'I know that,' Platus replied calmly. 'But I wonder if the rest of your friends are having trouble remembering it. They always come back after putting slugs in those... what do they call them... Ryz-ain'ts looking all hollow. Like they've killed the real you.'

Maybe that's what they're preparing for.

It was a grim prospect, but it was one Ryza was sure he'd beat them to. He squeezed his rifle a bit tighter as the vehicle took off again, rocking and creaking under the thrum of its overcharged engine.

Looking over the landscape of half-hidden glass, Ryza stood alone. The others had circled the convoy and were waiting for him a few hundred metres back, allowing him to go first. It wasn't out of caution for themselves, but some kind of mourning respect for him.

Ryza looked back over his shoulder at them. It was like a little fort had been formed around their stilled wheels. It didn't hearten him. He'd come to the realisation that little did, these days. All of Ditric's talk of clear missions and rallying ideas was wasted on Ryza as long as there was no clear enemy for him to fight. To loathe and plot against. He wouldn't put it past Ditric to invent one for him. Vorric certainly had. Maybe her insistence that he be the first person to look upon this scarred plain was her way of making him invent an enemy of his own.

Though there wasn't much to see. Months of shifting dunes had done their best to cover the window to the still-burning undercity, but it only managed to encroach on the outer edges. Loose dust scattered and rolled across the smoothly undulating hills of shimmering glass at the centre, the foundations of another forgotten dune, and Ryza found himself compelled to approach them.

He thought back to the last dream he'd had. The last truly vivid one, at least. The disgusting landscape of flux, blood, scabbed flesh, and then rust upon which Holm had taunted him with words she'd said long, long ago.

Was this the landscape she, or the dream at least, had been trying to represent to him? Maybe the glass was the sand's way of scabbing over, the first stage of the land itself healing from a grievous wound.

The ground under his boots crunched less and less with each step.

A soft clinking replaced it as the glass became more exposed. Ryza's eyes stayed glazed over as he watched his feet move, one in front of the other, his focus on the distant yellow glow that sat far, far below.

It was the rebel sun, the devastating paralict that still burned away at the core of the world. Would it ever stop? The hairs on his shins prickled uncomfortably under his trousers as he imagined the unnatural blast of heat from it.

It was so bright.

Holm's words drifted through his mind as he tore his eyes away. A dark spot remained at the centre of his vision no matter where he looked, as if he'd been staring dumbly at the sun itself. He'd always suspected that the rebel sun hadn't destroyed her entirely. At least not the original version of her that'd given herself over to the flux. She must've escaped, the same way Origin had, and made her home somewhere else, somewhere far away from the prying, meddling minds that sought to influence her.

And I know how she feels.

Ryza let his course deviate as he made his way towards the midpoint of the glassy plains, wandering left and right, unconsciously relishing the little, childish challenges from the near-frictionless hills under his worn boots as they slipped about. There were still a few shards of the skyscrapers trapped beneath the glass. The very tallest points of those that'd lived above the surface that had survived the scorching puddle they'd fallen into.

Ryza stopped and watched each one for a while whenever he found himself standing above one. He waited for them to move, to float to the surface in order to follow some unexplainable instinct in his heart. But they didn't. Nothing moved. It was all a static image of a life once lived, never to be touched again.

It was only as Ryza wondered if he should head back to Ditric to tell her this trip had been for nothing, that something below his feet appeared to prove him wrong. It wasn't its slow and gentle movement that caught Ryza's eye. It was the shape of it. A rounded blob of some kind of grey matter slowly oozing up from the glowing depths of the glass, casting an upwards shadow that surrounded him in a dark blotch.

Its path didn't disturb the glass as it went. The blob shifted subtly to avoid the contrastingly jagged remains of the entombed skyscrapers. The circumference of the shadow shrunk as the orb continued to rise, and Ryza retreated until he was just beyond it, then slowly approached as the shadow tightened more and more.

Now only a few feet from the surface, Ryza could estimate the size of the rising shape was close to what a balled-up person would be, and that was precisely the shape that emerged out from the surface of the glass. Its form pushed through without cracking or chipping the flat, reflective plane. It stayed curled on its side, and Ryza's hand went for his rifle, gripping it but not yet pulling it from the holster.

This was how the Ryz-ain'ts were born, it seemed. The figure lay on the ground for a while longer, still on its side with its back to him, its ribs rising and falling in an imitation of breathing that sometimes swelled or collapsed too much. Ryza watched it with a sense of something nearing pity. This thing wasn't dangerous. He didn't even feel inclined to reach for his vent mask. He just let it hang limply from the strap around his neck like an oversized pendant.

Was this how the world looked upon him? Like some wounded wreck that'd emerged from one enormous catastrophe or another? Or was this simply the flux trying to make him feel that way? But as he looked closer, he realised it wasn't him that the flux was trying to represent, at all.

It was Holm.

The details of her were exquisite. Every hair and pore across the flesh on the back of her neck was raised and on end, sometimes twitching as she continued to breathe, in and out, at a rhythm that Ryza's own lungs yearned to match.

Her form continued to bloom. Her white-blonde hair came as a short, undisturbed wave that was pulled back across her scalp. Her clothes rose from the surface of the indiscriminately grey skin the flux had given her, manifesting as the tattered forge leathers she'd been wearing when she had abandoned Ryza and given herself over to the molten flux.

Ryza's hand twitched again, not for his rifle, but to reach out to her, to touch her shoulder and turn her over and look into her eyes just to see that defiant shade of green once more. But he resisted. He let Holm lay there for a while longer as he prayed that Ditric or one of the others wouldn't come over the ridge and see what he'd found. The privacy they'd given him was a hard-won privilege that Ditric wouldn't chance again if she were to know what was about to happen.

'Holm?' Ryza eventually whispered.

She didn't answer. Maybe she wouldn't. Maybe this copy of her was only enough to draw his attention and fix him in place, leaving him to wait until he died of hunger or exposure. But that wasn't to be.

Her shoulders shifted as she was taken by a particularly deep breath, the kind he'd watched her wake with many times before, and she rolled forwards slightly, pushing the ground away as she rose to her feet. She looked down upon herself before she looked at Ryza, dusting the imperfections from her impeccably created body like they were clinging grains of sand.

Even then, she couldn't shift all the faults. Belts lingered where they had no buckles to secure them. Stray hairs grew too long from places that should have none. Even her skin could not decide a specific shade of sun-beaten tan to portray, shifting colours as if under a moving light despite the stillness of the light above them.

It even reached her eyes. Her form, so perfectly human, could never look right as her irises flickered between her green and a shadow dancer's black.

Whatever's happening to her, I need to stop it.

'You don't,' Holm said, answering to his thoughts.

'I...'

No words followed for Ryza, and he could only clench his jaw, his teeth moments away from biting through his upper lip, as he held her stare.

'You took so long to find me,' she continued.

'To find you? What about... But you're...'

'I am me, yes. But I am not yours. Just as you asked me to be,' she said, venom in her last words.

'No... No, this doesn't make sense,' Ryza said quickly, his feet fighting to retreat. 'I've seen you. In my dreams, under Iroka, even just a few days ago in the scrap yards where you—'

'But was it me?' Holm snapped. 'Was it really me or was it just what you wanted to see? What the flux wanted you to see?'

'I don't... but what does that make you now?'

She shrugged, her expression shockingly indifferent.

'You don't care!?'

She shook her head, taking a step towards Ryza as her face stiffened into a stern look.

'I care, Ryza. But you shouldn't. I wish you fucking didn't. Every time I try to extend the reach of *my* flux beyond what's even left of this place, you or someone else seems to show up and start giving it other ideas. Why do you even think I did this? I was going to get rid of Maligar, but by the time I'd gotten anywhere close to Iroka, all I found was a big fucking hole in the ground and a thousand copies of me stabbing him in the face!'

'So that wasn't you?' Ryza said, still aghast.

'I did look pretty great there, didn't I?' Holm smirked, looking around at an imaginary audience. 'But no, it wasn't me. It was you, Ryza. And I see it in you now. Everywhere you go, you've been seeing me, haven't you? Doubting every little thing to the point that you're even turning the real stuff into flux.'

'Even the dreams?'

'The dreams? You really think I can reach into your head like that? Sure, the flux can reach your mind, but it can't change it! It can only feed you what you *want* to see, Ryza! I don't need the flux to read your fucken mind. Could do it just by looking at you.'

She took another step closer, squinting as she scrutinised him, her breath carrying a faint smell of sweetness that he knew didn't belong to her.

'You found your father. How did it feel to kill him?'

'How do you know I did?' Ryza shot back, taking another step away.

Holm allowed him the space but began to pace around him, observing him for any other twitches or tells.

'What else would you have done with him?' she asked. 'I've seen you kill for less, and with what you'd told me, I'd say you'd be right in ending his miserable life.'

'He was molten flux all along,' Ryza muttered. 'I thought you'd made him. That you were trying to give him to me to distract me.'

Holm stopped mid-stride, halted by her confusion. 'Well... I didn't. In fact...'

She leaned closer again, her nose less than an inch from his cheek. Ryza felt the skin there tighten as if it were trying to shrink away from her.

'He *was* real, Ryza. You doubted him. That's why you felt nothing from killing him. You doubted you would, just like you doubt everything else.'

When she stepped away, he turned to see her leering at him again.

'Archarus said I found sanctuary in doubt.'

She sniggered. 'But is that really a way to live? Is that how you'll put things right?'

'I don't know,' Ryza whispered.

'Of course you don't. It's the only answer you can give.' Holm drew a deep breath, one that Ryza could hear whistling through the air. 'That's what I'm trying to do, Ryza. That's what I've always been trying to do. Put things right. As they should be.'

'As *you* think they should be!' Ryza retorted. 'Do you even realise what that did to me?'

'What you did to yourself!' Holm shouted back. Her words didn't echo. 'I saw it in you every single day. That worry. Not just for yourself but for all of us. It was like a control. A rushing of your hands to right everything that you doubted. That was your way of controlling things, and I had to walk that line, otherwise you'd throw a fit and try to step in again! It was like I couldn't do anything on my own without you. It made me feel weak. It's why I had to do this. Sure, I'm probably just as guilty of it all, but this is what you wanted me to do. You *wanted* me to put things right.'

'But not like this! Why would I have ever wanted this!?'

'Why should it be about what you want?' Holm shouted back. 'It always has been! The flux just feeds it! Even Vorric feeds it! Just for once, Ryza, just once you have to think about what someone else wants. *Why* they want it! You think you already do, but you've only gone out of your way to give it to them in a way that satisfies you.' She stepped in again, leaning closer to leer as she continued to whisper. 'You're just like the flux, Ryza. You just want to please people so they'll leave you alone.'

Ryza's voice shuddered as he attempted to reply. He wanted to run. To draw his rifle and shoot something, either her or himself, but like

Holm said, he was afraid.

'What do you want me to do?' Ryza said, his voice quavering.

Her hands came out from behind her back, snaking towards his own and taking it with a firm, warm grasp. Ryza could even feel her pulse. Her magnetic resonance. The burning defiance he'd known and loved for those short few months that'd felt like a lifetime.

It's her. It really is her.

'Exactly, Ryza,' she whispered. 'I'm real. Always have been. And I'm sorry. About the way I was down there. What I said to you. Because you were right. I was like Maligar, in a way. I did want. But it was only a wanting that I'd tied so closely to yours. I thought you wanted to be fixed. That you wanted your arm back. I thought in giving that to you, you'd be... you'd be happy. But I never looked past the words *I* was hearing. The things *I* was seeing. I just believed it. I didn't doubt you the way that you doubted me, and I regret it, because it made me blind to the things you weren't saying. The secrets you were keeping.'

Ryza's throat was too closed-over to even muster a response, but he squeezed Holm's hand tighter. Her grip squeezed back. He could feel her tendons tightening, her bones beneath them, her knuckles and the edges of her nails under his fingertips.

'Ryza.'

Her voice was soft. He looked up from their conjoined hands.

Her eyes were green.

'I need you to stop,' she said. 'Stop wanting. To believe that I can do this and to do it without you, not for some reason of pure resonance or to manipulate the flux, but for your own sanity. I will put things right. I promise.'

'But you'll die. You'll destroy the flux and yourself with it, and you'll—'

She smiled at him. That manic, madcap smile.

'I don't need to destroy the flux, Ryza. I just need to control it.'

Her fingers bled through his grip until there was nothing to hold. Her smile remained on her face as she sunk back into the glass, her green eyes shifting to black as she slipped beneath the surface and descended until she disappeared entirely.

Ryza fell to his knees as he watched her go, his palm planted flat against the smooth glass as he willed it to sink through the solid surface so he could follow. He'd been wrong. He'd been so wrong, not just about her, but about everything.

He'd let all these dreams, all these visions of her, lead him on like they were an infallible compass, but all this time it had just been exactly what he'd suspected it to be. His own constant paranoia. A readied reflection to find sense in a world that seemed wrong, to find a place for himself in a world that felt like it was always on the verge of rejecting him.

Everything she'd said made perfect sense. It was his own father that he'd dragged in from the far-flung wastes as a common bounty. That he'd brought before Vorric and unceremoniously killed on a fleeting instinct. The flux had only come afterwards, when Ryza's doubts had manifested beyond the fabric of his own mind and into the reality he constantly ran away from.

When the shapeless blob that'd once been Holm disappeared from sight, he was only left with his own reflection to stare at. A warped and colour-drained shadow that he hung over with creases of misery imprinted across his face.

The copies of him that'd emerged were no mystery. They'd just been Holm's attempts at getting his attention, to tell him a truth that everyone else had been shielding him from. That he wasn't needed. That he wasn't special. That he wasn't the key to destroying the flux. That he was just Ryza, and he didn't need to be anything more.

Pure resonance has nothing to do with it.

Yet as this thought struck Ryza, his own reflection wavered. For just a moment, his eyes, those dim pits that shimmered a foot below the surface of the glass, had seemed black.

CHAPTER TWENTY-THREE

TO WANT WITHOUT WANTING

'YOU WHAT!?'

Ditric's response was predictably earsplitting. She began to pace before him, her path constrained by the tightly arranged defensive barricade of vehicles they were standing in the middle of. Her hands couldn't stay still, undecided as to whether they should cross over with her arms, grasp firmly at her hips or over her head in frustration, or reach for the rifle hanging at her shoulder.

The others, who had either been sitting astride the flanks of the vehicles or leaning against them as Ryza shared what had just happened, were equally shocked, but Ditric's dynamo of a reaction was drawing too much of their attention for them to even think about acting out in a similar way. Out the corner of his eye, Ryza saw a few of them hastily secure their vent masks, but the more experienced of their number weren't among them. They knew if the vent masks were needed, it was already too late.

'I'm never letting you out of my sight again,' Ditric snapped through grinding teeth, still not stopping her pacing. 'How do I even know it's the real you? You could be another Ryz-ain't!'

In a flurry of motion, she whipped out her rifle, jamming a red-tipped slug down its breach before the others could scramble for their vent masks. But Ryza didn't move. Not even as the dark pit of the gun barrel swayed inches away from his eyes.

'Nothing!?' Ditric roared.

'Doesn't matter,' Ryza said, his tone as indifferent as it could be as he attempted to look beyond the rifle's muzzle and into Ditric's eyes. 'If you expect flux, that's what you'll get.'

'What fucken sense does that make?'

'My father. Aphtus-Hast. He was real. He just blew up in flux because I believed he would.'

'And that's what Holm told you, was it? Why the fuck would you even believe her? After all this—'

A loyal rage tweaked inside Ryza. He shot his arm up, bashing aside the rifle before Ditric had even noticed he'd moved. The muzzle flared hot just beyond his right ear, and he staggered sideways as a burst of fire billowed out behind him.

Still off-balance, he lunged towards Ditric, hitting her almost side-on as she attempted to reload, and began to wrestle the rifle out of her hands. Two punches to the kidneys were enough to make her drop it, and Ryza narrowly dodged the thrown elbow that came in response.

He danced back a few paces, light on his toes and aware of half a dozen other rifles being pointed at him.

'Why shouldn't I believe her?' Ryza bellowed, the sound only seeming to come out the left side of his mouth. 'Why should I believe you? Or anyone? We could all be wrong! The more we want to be right, the more the flux will give us what we want. I've seen it now. I've tried so hard to understand it, but I never even thought about just giving up. What can it give us then? What "want" can it even see in that?'

'Ryza, she tried to kill us!' Ditric replied, still holding her battered right side. 'You don't remember that big fucken metal snake?'

'Because I thought that was what she was going to do. Then the flux just gave me what it thought I wanted.'

'You're saying that's *your* fault?'

'He's not.'

The new voice made them spin, and Ryza saw it had come from Caftor. He was standing in the shadow behind one of the more heavily laden lead-betters. After everything that'd happened at Iroka, Ryza hadn't had a chance to speak to the now former Scythe, and even after being reunited with the League of Revance, they hadn't crossed paths for long enough to share a word.

He looked older by a matter of years, not months. His blue robes had faded entirely to grey, but he still wore them, likely because they were better stitched than anything the rest of them were constantly having to patch up and repair.

'Then tell me, Caftor. You've been pretty fucken quiet about it all, just like Sarova, and I don't blame you, but we ain't got time to keep secrets. Not anymore.'

'It isn't a secret,' Caftor replied in a measured tone. 'It's sense. I've toyed with the idea Ryza has presented before, but I did not want to voice it. I wanted to see if he, or someone else, for that matter, could arrive at the same conclusion. That was how I'd know I was right.'

'And that idea is?' Fynis asked from the other side of the commotion.

'That we cannot truly know how the flux works without introducing an element of doubt into the understanding. And certainty... is not an absence of doubt. It's a set of truths. But how are we to establish any of these truths without the flux shaping itself in a way to accomplish our own notions?'

'Our what?' Ditric said.

'Our ideas,' Caftor continued. 'See it this way, perhaps: we thought we'd discovered that fire neutralises or otherwise disables the flux, forcing it into that form of recurring thorns, yet once it was left alone, it simply turned back to liquid. Even now, these mimicries of Ryza, when subjected to the incendiary munitions we are lucky enough to have acquired, now go from thorn to gas, to blazing flux, in a matter of moments. Off to find new ideas to feed on, in a way.'

'But all the Ryz-ain'ts have done that,' Berlic piped up from the driver's seat of a vehicle, his rifle still trained on Ryza.

'Precisely,' Caftor replied. 'Because we understand it that way, and as such, the flux seeks to maintain that understanding. It is a matter of stability.'

'To behave as expected so it is not forced to change,' Ryza said.

Caftor nodded, at first with vigour, but then turning solemn as he registered Ryza's hollow expression.

'The flux becomes more dangerous as it is forced to change. More unpredictable. It's something Sarova, Ryza, and I experienced firsthand. With nearly all of the Droughtlands expecting it to change, we can only assume it will take new and unpredictable forms and effects as time goes on and more people are exposed to these... these radical iterations. People will expect worse of it, and the flux shall provide. Another layer of pure resonance atop the one that already exists in this world.'

'Without the risk of turning into a shadow dancer at the end of it, either.'

Nearly all of them flinched at Ryza's words, but at least it bought him a few moments where he didn't have half a dozen rifles pointed at him.

'Then what the fuck do we do now, Ryza?' Sarova said from her seat next to Berlic.

He nodded to her but didn't speak for a few more moments. There were too many thoughts to chew on, and his mind was quickly becoming too noisy for him to see them all at once.

'I don't know. And I shouldn't know. That's something Holm was... something she is right about.' He brought his hand up to his face and massaged the bridge of his nose, pushing his thumb and forefinger back towards his skull until they were digging into his eyeballs. 'Caftor's right. We can't understand the flux. Neither can Vorric or anyone else who's out there thinking they're trying to manage this crisis. So we need to stop them before they make things worse.'

'Yes,' Caftor said. 'For all we know, it's very likely the Scythes' style of research is accelerating molten flux's evolution or iteration into stranger and more dangerous forms.'

Ryza nodded in agreement. 'Putting it like that... It makes me wonder if Vorric is aware of it himself. That he sent me away looking for Origin because he thinks I'm a walking evolution or something.'

'But what about Holm, then?' Ditric asked. 'If she ain't going to destroy the flux, what's she going to do with it?'

'Hide it. Make it invisible. Make it part of the world. That's why those-of-glass made it. They made it to be the same as magic so their people wouldn't doubt what they saw and kill themselves on the pure resonance that happened afterwards.'

'I don't trust her to do that,' Ditric growled, shaking her head. 'Not one fucken bit.'

'But I have to trust her,' Ryza said quickly.

Ditric responded by jabbing a finger into his chest, sending him stumbling back a step or two. '*You* have to, but I don't!' She began to pace around again, looking across the confused faces of her assembled army as she tried to impart some desperately needed confidence in them. 'Maybe Caftor's right. We can't understand flux, because it'll just turn into whatever we think and then we're back where we started. But we can still go to where *it* started.'

'The bunker's gone, Ditric,' Ryza said. 'Even before Vorric dropped a rebel sun on the place, Cardan's attempts at a factory destroyed anything we could've figured out from there.'

'Not what I'm talking about,' Ditric said. 'There's something better out there. Something older than the flux itself. That's what you said Origin was, right Ryza?'

'I... yeah, I guess, but—'

'Then he knows what it originally was! He can tell us what it was meant to be before metal mouths started fucken around with it. Then, if we can just get enough people to believe that, then maybe the flux will stop getting so crazy, right? That's what your little rules mean, right, Caftor?'

'I don't see why not.'

'Then you'd better fucken believe it!' Ditric roared. 'We just have to get Origin, figure out what the hell he's on about, then we can take it back to Vorric and—'

'Ditric, we can't go anywhere near Breggesa,' Fynis said, cutting her off. 'Don't even know if we've got enough oil to get there, let alone the slugs we'll need to bust into the place.'

'What if we sneak in?' another person offered.

'And what do we do if they don't believe us?'

The entire congregation devolved into a crossfire of doubtful questions that Ditric couldn't lift her roaring voice above, no matter how loud she got. The doubt had returned to their little group, and there was little Ryza could do to quell it, so he just slunk back through the gaps left by the parked lead-betters and kept walking until he was back on the dune that overlooked the remains of Twin Rings.

There was one question that hadn't been asked in the melee of uncertainty. What about Holm? If what she'd said was right, was there even any reason for them to find Origin at all? Then again, wasn't that all the more reason for them to do it anyway? Fighting back his own doubts, Ryza found some kind of middle ground to settle in.

It was entirely possible that Holm could find a way to right things from within the flux itself, but where would that leave the rest of the Droughtlands? And what was her version of "right" in the first place?

At the same time, Caftor was right. He'd put words to a garbled series of thoughts Ryza had struggled to assemble until now. It was an alarmingly real possibility that molten flux had spread its reach much further than could be perceived.

In those final days before they'd eradicated Iroka entirely, the valley had been an unending plume of blazing flux spreading out over the land. The flux could've settled everywhere and in microscopic pieces, waiting dormant for an idea to strike and call it into action.

Maybe that's what happened to my father. The flux in him just wasn't ready until I believed it was.

Ryza looked back at the gathered vehicles and the figures still arguing between them. It had to have already affected them. Himself included. As time passed, the commotion eventually simmered down into a well-reasoned debate of tactics and battle plans. Cooking fires provided heat within the group in place of terse words, and they seemed to settle into the night's rituals.

The will to join them was weak, so Ryza remained at his post. Perhaps they thought he was guarding the glass plains, waiting for another version of himself to rise from it and start stumbling across the dunes. But maybe that wouldn't happen anymore. The copies had served their purpose. They'd brought him to Holm and she'd...

'She's made her peace with me, but why can't I do the same with her?' Ryza whispered to himself. 'With me?'

He was still mulling over all she'd said. He'd gone straight back to Ditric after Holm had disappeared, so this was his first chance to think on it all without the suspicious glares he'd been treated to on his return.

It's a wonder Ditric even let me slip off again.

Yet Ryza was the most sure of himself that he had been in months. His paranoia, his constant doubts, they no longer felt like a disease or a death sentence waiting to be carried out. Instead, they felt like a comprehensive guidebook, touring him back through all the visions and interactions he'd had with Holm since they'd so catastrophically broken up their relationship under Twin Rings.

The version he'd seen of her in his dreams had been a spiteful, fleeting mystery of her former self. Yet that was only a symbol of the sense of abandonment Ryza had been teetering on the edge of for all those months they'd spent in Iroka. A belief that his partner, his love, would leave if he failed to understand the cryptic, incomprehensible signals that he believed she was giving him. Signals that, now he reflected on it, were his own fears made manifest.

It was in the most recent dream, the one he'd had in the Archives of the Breggesan Academy, that the Holm he'd been visited by had seemed... different. Her words were no longer her own, but echoes of things she'd once said. Despite it making little sense, he'd still tried to glean meaning from it, when he should've realised it meant nothing at all.

Even the versions of himself that were appearing in the molten flux were cast in a new light. It was like Holm had told him. The flux hadn't infected him. He was infecting the flux. It was producing reflections of him because that was what he expected to see, and now others had seen it, it was what they expected as well.

He was sure he'd had the realisation before, multiple times, in fact, but this was the first time the concept didn't terrify him. In a way, it was a benign truth. An inevitability that he could simply ignore.

But what about the copy of me in the scrapyard?

There was still something slightly unnerving about it. That copy had spoken with his voice, his face, yet it had bled with flux all the same when he'd punched a slug right through its chest.

Ryza ruminated on the memory for a while, even though it was against his best instincts. If this was the flux's way of giving him what he wanted, could it be true that he wanted to run away from the world?

No, the flux only thinks that. It's what the flux sees in me.

Thinking deeper on it, he did his best to remember what that version of Holm had said instead.

I'm the last thing stopping the flux from truly running free. The last expectation it has. If you're gone, it has nothing. That wasn't a problem before, back when we all just thought it was for making autominds. But now you've all seen what it can do, you're all braced for the worst, and the flux will be all too ready to give it to you.

Yet it hadn't been Holm that'd said it, if the one he'd just met out on that field of glass was to be believed. This left these words to have either come from a reflection in his own mind, or from within the flux itself. But which Holm was he to believe? The one that had told him she needed him more than anything else, or the one that'd dismissed him and said she didn't need him at all?

'The flux needs to want,' Ryza said slowly, parsing through each word's meaning as he spoke them.

'Why does it?'

The sudden appearance of another voice made him jump. He turned and saw Caftor and Sarova hiking up the last few steps of the dune to his side, the latter holding a plate of charred meat that she handed to him, the former holding a torch that did little to light the way. Ryza took the offered meal and sat down, motioning with a nod for the others to join him.

He perched himself on the very ridge of the dune, the dented metal plate balanced in his lap as he half-heartedly picked away the congealed strands of gristle from the edible flesh. Caftor sat next to him, still half in a crouch. He'd planted the torch upright in the sand, so it looked like a little metal worm with a glowing green head. The light of it couldn't touch anything more than a handspan away, but it still drew Ryza's eye.

Sarova seemed too restless to sit. She paced back and forth, stopping occasionally at one side or the other to kick away at the sand around her boot so she could watch it flow in little waves down the face of the dune towards the plain of glass.

'Ditric sent us up here,' Caftor eventually said. 'Wanted us to make sure we come back with the real you, if there's such a thing.'

He gave Ryza a soft, fleeting smile, the creases around his eyes tightening in a way that looked uncomfortable. Even by the night sky's dim light, Ryza could tell Caftor's skin to be a great deal greyer than when they'd first met those few months ago. He could only guess at what had happened in the intervening time, and what had led to Caftor abandoning the Scythes in favour of joining Ditric's expedition out into the barren plains.

'Just need Vorric here, then that's all of us who went under Iroka,' Ryza remarked.

'You forget Lucia,' Caftor said.

Ryza blinked. 'I did, didn't I?'

It was too easy to forget all those faces that'd once been vital to his survival. Even of those that were gathered at the bottom of the hill, Ryza would struggle to greet them as the allies they were. In a world that had gone so wrong, everyone seemed to be a stranger.

'No use,' Sarova said, returning from her pacing to sit on Ryza's other side. 'Still dunno what Vorric's like, but I don't think he'd talk about all that with us. Nothing to talk about. We all saw what we did, and then...'

She opened her clasped hands as if she were presenting something, but the only thing before her was more sand.

'I think the same. Dangerous ideas,' Caftor said. 'Still, I don't know if it will matter. It's all written down somewhere, ready to be forgotten. Unimportant, in comparison to whatever crisis tomorrow may bring.'

'What about Iroka?' Ryza replied. 'What about Holm? Revance? Any of it? None of it even matters?'

'I don't know if it does. I don't know if it ever did, at all.' Caftor looked out over the shining field of glass again, momentarily enraptured by the way it twinkled with the refraction of the stars above. 'We are... so small, and yet so... so instant. But then I look out over all this that we've attempted to study and understand and discern, and I wonder... I wonder what would be left behind of us.'

'Ruins?' Sarova offered.

'Maybe not even that,' Ryza muttered. 'We've destroyed everything we've touched.'

'Perhaps those-of-glass did so as well. That the remnants of their time that we see now are only accidents. I can only wonder what they created with the intention of being left behind for their, and our, future generations that never made it beyond the catastrophe like the one we face now.'

'Molten flux. Or whatever name they called it when they created it. That was the point of it. To mimic their magic so they could believe in a life they could live forever.'

'But that's what I mean,' Caftor replied. 'It's what they believed. What we believe now is different, and the flux responds to that. It's the "instant" nature of our lives that the flux feeds off. Forming itself as whatever thought or feeling we have in each fleeting moment, but leaving nothing else behind. I think that's why, when we find Origin, we can trust him. Because he was left behind. That through all of time, he never changed. He even, according to your statements, Ryza, fled in times of crisis.'

'How do you mean? Origin might not be old. He might just be another image conjured by the flux.'

'You say that he disappeared before you and your army of ex-conscripts fought the overthrown Revance, yes?'

'He went missing. I don't know that he left on his own purpose.'

'And his final words to you, that he shared with you under the very sands we stand on, were that he was going away?'

'Yes,' Ryza answered.

'But why would he do that?' Caftor challenged. 'Do you understand what I'm veering you towards?'

Ryza looked over at Sarova, expecting her to look just as confused as he felt, but there was instead a strange sense of pensive wisdom about the way she stared out to the skies.

'The flux wouldn't run,' she said slowly. 'Running isn't instant. It's confusing. Uncertain. When you run away, you don't do it because you know where you're going, but because you just have to get away from something. Molten flux, the way it is now, can't do that, can it?'

'No, it can't,' Caftor said. 'But please, go on, Sarova.'

She nodded as she spoke, the movements starting as a small rhythm until she gained momentum, hypnotising Ryza with this strange wave of communicating motion.

'The flux was made to be instant and certain, the two things we all are, or what we want to be, at least. We make decisions and we find reasons.' She nodded back to the assembled vehicles. 'That's what they're doing down there. If the flux doesn't match that, then it's not doing its job.'

Ryza felt like he was beginning to pick up the threads Sarova and Caftor were laying down for him, and Origin's words once again had new meaning.

'The flux can't be confusing. It reacts in the ways that we think it to be defensive, but it follows a logic that we can connect with,' Ryza said. 'You're right, Caftor. Origin running away confused me. I've wondered for a long time why he left and where he's going, and if he was made of molten flux, he would've given me answers.'

Caftor chewed on his next words before he spoke them, almost swallowing them instead.

'Vorric shared with me the words Origin had spoken with you. They were cryptic, and perhaps with that exact purpose in mind. To keep you guessing and reinterpreting. So that no single solid understanding can form. A space of uncertainty.'

'A sanctuary of doubt,' Ryza muttered, echoing Archarus' words. 'Maybe that's how Origin finds his freedom. All this time fighting against the flux has felt like running through a maze of impenetrable walls. Nothing but turns that lead to dead ends. Every time I think I understand it, there's another wall and I'm stuck again. But now I expect to be stuck.'

'And the flux gives you what you expect,' Sarova said.

'But we can no longer be swayed by what we see in front of us in lieu of what we already know to be true,' Caftor said. 'That is the flux's power. Pure resonance's power. It's what we saw, especially you, Ryza, beneath Iroka. I wonder if those blocks ever existed in those tunnels before we ventured down there, before your dreams could be read as expectations by all the molten flux that'd drained down into the sands after the destruction of Revance.'

'Maybe the tunnels weren't even there,' Sarova said.

'No, they were there,' Ryza said quickly. 'I felt them when we first arrived in the valley. Deep in the ground. I felt how hollow it was down there, and I knew they were not natural formations.'

'A known truth,' Caftor said lightly. 'Hold on to that, Ryza. It's what we'll need if we are to deal with the flux once and for all.'

'What do you mean?'

'The world existed before molten flux and will continue to exist after it, likely having forgotten about it entirely. The only question is how long that will take. Look again, Ryza, to the depths of what we have destroyed. These ruins stood empty and vacant of purpose or people for eons after they had been built, yet it only took the decision of one man and a weapon that we'd found almost entirely by accident to obliterate this place from the surface of the Droughtlands. How many years do you think will pass before it is no longer thought of? No longer remembered?'

'And you think we can do the same to the flux?' Ryza asked. 'Just forget about it all? Pretend it doesn't exist?'

Sarova snorted at the prospect. 'Bit hard to do when it usually kills anyone who goes near it.'

'Is that not what we think of the ruins left by those-of-glass?' Caftor replied. 'Places we have shunned and abandoned, where research carries equal prospects of learning and death? Perhaps molten flux will one day become another scar on the land. A place we don't understand, that we don't want to understand, but know that if we leave it well enough alone, it will not harm our way of being.'

Ryza shook his head. The idea was noble, but unworkable.

'But that needs us to change. To get to a point where we do cut our losses and leave it alone. I agree with you, Caftor, I really do. I now wonder if we'd just left Iroka alone after Revance was destroyed, it would have simply become a new ruin like you've said. But it's not something we can do. Not while Vorric is trying to contain the flux by finding meaning in it. Not while Holm is within it, trying to put things right. And not while I am still here, knowing what I know about it. I can make peace with my uncertainty all I want, but it'll be no use while the rest of them are out there doing the opposite.'

'So we gotta kill 'em?' Sarova asked.

Ryza allowed himself a low-hearted chuckle.

'I think we're beyond that.'

Chapter Twenty-Four

THE OLD NEEDLE

Another early morning start followed that night. It saw them trundling further north, this time with a solidified goal in mind. Ryza was riding at the front of the convoy with Ditric behind the wheel and Berlic squatting in the back tray as he tended to some kind of arcanite Ryza still hadn't learnt the purpose of.

Berlic, Sarova, and Caftor had returned to the camp last night to find a loose consensus on what the League of Revance's next move was. The three of them had huddled among themselves as they decided in quiet whispers whether they should introduce their own philosophising into the mix and potentially cause discord, but Elya, keen-eared thanks to her gifts as a Reythurist, heard the whole thing and had already filled Ditric in.

To Ryza's relief, the plan remained largely the same. They were to find Origin, just as they'd originally intended, and then 'figure it out from there,' as Ditric had put it. There were some mutterings about getting Origin to undo whatever the flux had done to Kyrea so she could pull the fabled cache of reels out of the tunnels' depths.

Even then, what was she planning to do with the reels? There was nothing left to spend them on. Even if she just gave it to the refugees she wanted so damn badly to help, what could they do but exchange the inert metal tokens among themselves for the nothing they already had?

Just another pile of useless metal.

Now he was sitting in the passenger seat behind the roaring engine of the lead-better, Ryza wasn't sure how they were even going to accomplish the first step. He twisted to look over his shoulder at Berlic, but before he could get a proper look, Ditric clapped a hand on his shoulder to force him to face forwards as she continued her unendingly keen lecturing.

'Gotta keep an eye out, thought you'd've known that by now. Good thing you didn't, we wouldn't have caught you with the net.'

'Yeah. Imagine that,' Ryza called back over the noise of the engine as he massaged his leg. The scars that wrapped around his thigh were largely painless, but the skin beneath was tight and tender. 'Besides, there ain't anything out here for miles!'

That was one thing Ryza was sure of, beyond the strange illusions he was ready for the flux to throw at him. He'd never seen land so flat before in his life. The sand itself had turned to a blinding white, making it easier on the eyes to look up at the sun rather than the plains that reflected it. Early in the journey, Ryza had thought there to be hills on the horizon, but the distant ridges turned out only to be the wobbling bars of heat haze rising up from the desert floor.

The occasional scrubby bush was the only thing that gave him any impression that they were moving in the first place, but even then, there was no telling if it was a large one in the distance slowly crawling across his view, or a tiny one right next to them that'd somehow ripped its roots from the ground and was now running alongside them like it was being carried by little legs.

Ryza had never been this far north into the Droughtlands. Barely knew of it in the first place. The tutors his father hired to teach him such things had considered the northern reaches a pointless subject. Maybe that was due to the instruction of his father. What good was there in knowing about a place without autominds or flux to make them with?

'But that's good, ain't it?' Ditric eventually replied.

'What?' Ryza said, having forgotten what they were talking about.

She waved across the vacant landscape and threw a sideways grin at him, her eyes obscured by sand-guarding goggles. 'Nothing out here,

I mean.'

'Wish it was that easy.'

'Can wish for a lot of things, Ryza.'

'Wish you'd tell me what makes you so damn sure you can find Origin, for a start.'

'He doesn't already know?' Berlic called from the back tray.

They hit a bump, the first one for hours, and there was a clatter of boots as he stumbled around. Ryza twisted and threw his hand back over the lip of the tray, catching Berlic by a handful of his greatcoat. He grunted as the fabric strained against his grip, and Berlic used the anchoring force to haul his balance back into the vehicle, dropping heavily into the tray to prevent another involuntary disembarkation.

Now that Berlic was positioned like this, Ryza had a better view of the arcanite he was so attentively playing with. It didn't have arms, legs, wheels, or gun barrels, so Ryza's first instinct had been to dismiss it without a thought.

The arcanite's rusted casing was a patchwork of bent and mismatched scraps of thin metal plates. Where each one met a corner, it had been folded, likely by hand, to conform to the shape. A few had been screwed up like pieces of torn paper and stuffed into gaps between larger plates, leaving even smaller gaps through which Ryza spotted whirring gears and connecting axles.

The only exposed feature on top was a needle-like dial that curved out of its housing like an uncombed hair, its tip pointing straight ahead.

'What is that thing?' Ryza asked.

Berlic looked up, his expression momentarily incredulous. 'What do you... I thought you invented this thing! That's what Ditric told me.'

'That ain't it,' she said. 'You mustn't've heard me right. I told you Ryza *told* me about it. Not that he invented it. Anyway, I just told you about the idea of it. You did all the inventing. You're good at that, but fucken listening?' She trailed off for a moment as she dramatically sucked at her teeth. 'Fucken invent yourself a better set of ears next.'

'But what is it?' Ryza asked again, his frustration beginning to grow.

'Origin detector,' Berlic grunted, his focus reunited with his machine.

'Real helpful,' Ryza shot back.

But Berlic hadn't heard the snark, or maybe he couldn't, now he was so fixated on his arcanite. Ditric took over for him.

'You told me about this,' she said, trying to jab at Ryza's chest without looking, instead poking him in the side of the head. 'You said it yourself. Mercenaries. Looking for Origin. They found him in an undercity or something by following an arcanite that rolled up with a dial on the back of it.'

'Tyrag's arcanite,' Ryza added.

He could still remember the distant terror on the man's face, back in that hut next to the abandoned water pump. He and Ferrick had just kicked in the door, finding that battered mercenary frantically scrambling away from them. But it hadn't been them he was afraid of. He'd told his story to Ryza as Ferrick had searched the rest of the shack, of the impossible places that the hunt for Origin had led them to. To this day, Ryza still wondered how Origin had ended up there, or how Tyrag had known Origin existed and needed to be sought out, but all who could give those answers were long dead.

Almost all.

'Yeah, well, something like that. Something to do with magnetic resonances. I didn't get it at the time and I ain't gonna pretend I get it now, but Berlic managed to figure it out, and now that little dial says we go north, so that's where we're going.'

Ryza looked back at Berlic as his jaw began to slowly lower in understanding. How could he have forgotten something so simple? He'd wasted weeks hunting Origin through the dictates of strange, lost texts that Vorric had dredged up for him when all along an obvious solution, a proven solution, had already passed him by.

'It's the magnetic resonance,' Ryza said. 'The magnetic resonance of Revance was the same as Origin's. All the Kretatics onboard knew it almost by heart. They'd know what to track down!'

'Seems it makes sense to you,' Ditric said with a shrug. 'Like the old days, eh? Following dials so we don't fucken die?'

'But... But Vorric said it wouldn't work!'

'Vorric lied to you! Tell him, Berlic. And tell me how long we got 'til we find that metal piece of shit!'

Her last words left her mouth in a raised tone, balled up and thrown over her shoulder as a demand for Berlic rather than idle conversation.

'Need more ink for that,' Berlic replied after a few moments. 'Another one of these arcanites or a whole lot more fucking about to improve this one.'

Ditric dismissed him with a snort. 'Probably would've found him in that time anyway.'

'But what if someone else has gotten to him first?'

'Then we'll deal with 'em.'

'What if it's Vorric and the Scythes?'

'If Vorric's best idea of finding Origin was sending you out on your own, then I don't think we've got anything to worry about.'

'We both know he did that just to get me out of the way.'

Ditric paused for a moment as she reconfigured her thoughts. 'Yeah, I did say that, didn't I? Anyway, he's going to be too tied up with whatever's happening in Breggesa right now. Worst thing about being in charge of anything. Can't go nowhere.'

Two entire days passed until there was even a hint of civilisation. The only movement detectable was the sun roaring overhead from east to west as its light cycled the sky through its various shades of blues, pinks, and oranges, and the slowly drooping needles of the lead-betters' fuel gauges.

If it weren't for those two things, Ryza would've been sure Ditric was playing a trick on him by piling them all into lead-betters each day and just making the engine roar without a single wheel turning beneath them. He scanned the horizons constantly, not out of caution, but out of sheer boredom.

Maybe there was a village just beyond them, or a ruin, or something else to break up the endlessly flat plain of white sand. So close, yet so narrowly avoided by the miracle of their path having taken them through the most nondescript piece of land in existence.

At least the nights could be more sociable. With little else to do, the newcomers hadn't exactly warmed to Ryza's presence, but eased their caution to him, nonetheless. He still struggled to remember their names and their stories.

It was difficult to keep them untangled from each other. He wished he'd done the same back when he was aboard Revance. All those conscripts he'd fought alongside were now just foggy memories, indistinguishable from one another despite the heroic actions he'd witnessed them carry out in battle before their deaths.

Of the newcomers, only a few were ready to replicate such deeds. A small crew of four mercenaries, friends of Ditric from her own days as one, had taken her offer to join the League of Revance, and seemed jovial enough that they didn't regret their decision. It was either that or be absorbed into one of the guard companies currently contracted to wrangle the mess that was Breggesa.

With the smelters largely scattered, that was the only paying work left for fighting men and women like them, not for a lack of need for their services, but because the city of Breggesa was the only one that could afford to pay.

'They promise they can,' one of the mercenaries told Ryza. 'Same worth as Ditric's promise, but I know her, at least.'

They, along with their rifles, brought the League of Revance's fighting force up to a strength of twelve. There were more travelling with them than that, but they didn't trust themselves in a fight. Neither did Ryza.

It wasn't much, but of the battles Ryza had been in, the smaller ones were the least deadly to come away from. He couldn't help but look out over their little camp, imagining a thousand more camps just like it spread out across the plains as part of their army.

Be enough to overthrow Breggesa.

It was a fanciful thought. He wasn't sure if Revance had held so many fighters at its peak. Or if there were that many fighting men and women left in the Droughtlands today.

The rest of the newcomers didn't seem to think so. They were constantly busy. The scouts among them took to the skies using what little ink they had to forewarn them of any potential threats, while the trappers and other land masters spent a good deal of the night scouring the sands for the few extra scraps of food they could produce. They seemed glad to be busy. Better than waiting for a fight, Ryza thought to himself.

On that second day when they finally did spot civilisation, Ryza didn't feel the relief he'd been waiting for.

It was his turn to drive the lead-better, with Ditric snoozing in the back tray with her arms crossed and coat thrown over her face, tucked into the corner of the space that Berlic needed the least as he tended to his machine. The fuel needle was what he watched as the lead-better's engine sputtered on, and it was only out the corner of his eye that he saw the other speck of movement he'd been waiting for.

They'd sent Elya up only thirty minutes ago, and she wasn't due back for another hour, so her early return meant news.

Good news or bad news...

Ryza glanced between her and the fuel needle for the next few minutes as she descended. Reythurists couldn't come down too fast, not from how high they were reaching. They called it "the thermic height," something only other Reythurists seemed to understand no matter how many times it was explained to Ryza. It was likely how someone felt when Ryza tried to explain the intricacies of arcanites if they weren't a Kretatic.

She kept flying as she came closer and closer, her face obscured by a thick leather mask with built-in goggles. It was the kind of thing that could only be worn for about ten minutes while walking on the ground for how scorchingly hot it kept the wearer's head. Ryza had tried it on that very morning to indulge Elya's playful banter before she was due to ascend and had felt like he'd shoved his head in a furnace.

Closing in on the still rolling lead-better, Eyla kept her arms outstretched like wings until the very last moment. She hovered over the vehicle as Ryza kept his foot steady on the engine's intake pedal, then she abruptly dropped, landing clumsily enough that she stomped right on Ditric's outstretched knee.

She roared in pain as she woke, but Elya had already scrambled to the front seat next to Ryza, looking innocent enough that Ditric began berating Berlic for a moment, only stopping once she noticed their scout's return.

Elya ripped off her sky mask and, still breathless, pointed ahead, indicating a spot on the horizon slightly left of their current heading.

'Village. Thataway. Small one, but better than nothing.'

Her finger was shaking so much the direction was as vague as a slumbering nod, so Ryza turned back to Ditric to wait for her call.

'Just do it,' she grunted, massaging her knee. 'Need to stop and figure out if I can still walk on this damn thing anyway.'

'Good enough for me,' Ryza muttered under his breath.

He slowly veered the course of the lead-better to the left, following Elya's still outstretched finger like it was the new dial directing him. It was another half hour's travel before the pinpricks of structures began to peek over the horizon. In that time, the lead-better's engine had developed a worryingly hollow cough. Ryza eyed the fuel gauge. The needle had stopped moving entirely.

Shit.

It didn't mean the oil tank was entirely empty. Lead-betters had never been built for precision like that. For all Ryza knew, it could be anywhere up to being half full. But that was a risk Ditric had discussed with them the previous night, and one she couldn't allow. If they were unable to find more oil, they'd be forced to abandon half of the convoy and siphon the fuel from the lead-betters they'd ditched into the ones they were still using, buying them another day or two's travel at most.

Let's hope they've got oil. And that they're friendly. Or that there's someone even there at all.

Ditric instructed him to draw the lead-better to a halt just beyond the small outpost's perimeter, and he obeyed while she roared the order to the other drivers. They formed the well-practised defensive circle that they always rested their machines in and dismounted.

Ryza left Ditric to stagger and hobble on her recently stomped-on knee, taking a few steps away from the stopped convoy for himself to get a better look at the village ahead.

There was a fair walk between them, but they were close enough that the residents wouldn't have needed a very attentive lookout to spot them. Ryza squinted, but that did little for his eyesight, so he turned and went back to his lead-better to rummage through the satchels and bags affixed to its flanks. He'd made his way fruitlessly through three of them before a creaking of metal at his left alerted him to Fynis' presence.

Ryza turned to greet him, but his attempt at a casual handshake instead found the scope Fynis was offering him.

'Looking for one of these?'

Ryza took it, muttering his thanks, and held it to his eye.

'You had a look with it yet?' he asked.

'Don't need it.'

Ryza lowered the scope just enough to see Fynis as he quickly tapped his temple, indicating his yellow eyes. Ryza couldn't be sure if sight that far was a gift of being a Curiktic, or if Fynis was simply trying to boast to him, but he pushed the thought aside.

The village had been built around the only raised hunk of land Ryza had seen that day. A rocky hillock with a pair of valleys splitting through it like the head of a well-manufactured screw. The shacks that'd been built into the shaded walls were sturdy and so deeply embedded that it looked like the rock had grown out around the metal.

Ryza held his breath as he adjusted the scope with his index finger, a fiddly operation with just one hand, but manageable, nonetheless. The glass within the metal tube blurred and then came into focus again, bringing him an all-too-close view of something dark grey. He shifted slightly, and the view rushed too quickly, and he realised he'd zoomed in a great deal more than he'd meant.

He adjusted the scope properly and got a better look at the huts. Calling them shacks was a disservice. Old and rusted, sure, but the rivets that held the sheeted metal to their girders lay in impeccably straight lines. The windows even had sills and intact glass. The huts were stacked in two or three tiers, narrow walkways connecting them, sometimes spanning across the valleys to form bridges three or four paces in length.

'See anyone?' Fynis asked after a while.

Ryza let his mouth hang open as he continued to search, ready to say the word, but also holding back a laugh at Fynis' expense. The poor idiot definitely couldn't see the place from here.

'There's one,' Ryza murmured, careful not to say it too enthusiastically in case he bumped the scope too much. 'Clothes on them look hardy... Face... can't see that. Covered. We should probably have ours covered... And... and they've got a scope of their own.'

'Think they're looking at us?' Fynis said excitedly.

Fynis' metal leg creaked as he waved broadly, swinging his arm over his head like a loose flagpole.

'Cut it out!' Ryza hissed. 'Don't know if they're—'

But to his surprise, the figure at the other end of his scope began to wave back. It was a slow, broad movement. The figure then turned and retreated back down into the warren of tiered huts before Ryza could discern more about them.

I hope they're still friendly.

Chapter Twenty-Five

Tentative Steps

A FEW HOURS LATER, as their convoy trundled away from the small outpost, Ryza couldn't help feeling a note of doubt alongside his surprise. The oil tanks for all their vehicles were now full to the brim, and an extra grumbling engine had been added to the rolling din, an ancient treadhulk whose stowage had been converted to hold a battery of large, mortar-flinging pipes.

Ryza and Berlic rode in the back of this vehicle along with Platus, their most experienced machinist, doing their duty as knowers of metal to check that the damn thing still worked. Ditric had ordered they carry out this task on the move. Wasted time was her only enemy, but Ryza had no idea why she was intent on fighting it.

The outpost had been nothing short of a stroke of brilliant luck. Not only was it the one place that hadn't been touched by the cascading effects of the flux catastrophe, but the few of them still there to guard it hadn't even heard that Revance had fallen in the first place. It came as hard news when it was shared, even if it was left out that Ryza was partially responsible for it.

The outpost, better known to its dozen or so remaining residences as The Northern Dump, was one of the many ammo stockpiles that'd once been supplied and maintained by leaders of Revance past. Excess supplies were stowed here in the event that a disaster or battle befalling the fortress warranted them, but Ryza supposed that in their case, it was likely a good thing they hadn't been called in.

They would've all just ended up in the hands of the smelters.

But the unfolding mutiny and subsequent disaster must've happened so quickly that word didn't make it to those guarding the stockpiles. Even then, what would they've done? Abandoned the cache of armaments, or arm themselves and go rolling out into the desert in search of their own enemies to fight?

The latter wasn't a prospect for the veteran soldiers of The Northern Dump. A smelter hit from a few months ago had left them as a skeleton crew. There'd been too few of them to afford to send a messenger to the other ammo dumps and without the means to call for help in other ways.

They'd settled in for a long wait. The League of Revance was the first friendly set of faces they'd seen since the hit that'd all but imprisoned them there, and once they'd been convinced of the plight the Droughtlands was stricken with, they'd agreed to join forces.

One of the stockpile's veterans, a Curiktic named Lasteer, couldn't help himself in battering Ryza, Berlic, and Platus with questions as he forced the modified treadhulk's engine to keep up with the nimbler lead-betters. Ryza did his best to answer, but it was hard to concentrate on forming a coherent sentence while making the most of the new infusion of water that the stockpile had provided.

It had taken the combined efforts of all forty-five of them to strip the stockpile's stores clean and load it onto their convoy, not for how much or how heavy the goods were, but for how securely they'd been secreted into the ground itself.

The shape of the mound that the huts were embedded in was not a natural one. Larger machines from ages long past had bored straight through the rock to create the intersecting pair of defensive alleys, rendering the place nearly impregnable to an attack. It was genius, in a way, and Ryza was glad he was never going to be on the assaulting end of a force trying to crack into such a thing.

With the barren plains of the surrounding lands, the only way to line up an effective shot at the defensive emplacements was to proverbially stick one's own head right down the muzzle of the guns that needed silencing. Assuming an enemy achieved firing superiority, the defenders could simply take shelter in the other valley that ran perpendicular to the one being assaulted, requiring multiple, coordinated attacking forces to move in as one, a feat an untrained band of smelters could rarely pull off.

If this was managed, the veterans guarding the stockpiles still had another avenue of retreat. The stockpile itself. The mouth of it was a hole at the centre of the two intersecting, artificial valleys, a deep one that'd presented itself as the main delay in getting things out, along with the sprawling cave network that'd been dug from the bottom of it.

Ryza had politely excused himself from going down there, calling on his missing left arm as a reason he wouldn't fair well on the numerous ladder trips required, and was allowed to stand back and watch with Fynis as the rest of them retrieved an armada's worth of supplies.

Along with what was likely the last few crates of rifle slugs that'd been produced by conscious, human hands, came a few other munitions that would set the League of Revance up well for a fight. A padded case of ancient, hand-thrown bombs was carefully lifted out by a series of ropes and shouts from those manning the pulleys. They were likely the only ones of their kind. They were too expensive to produce in the face of what a Curiktic could do with a few axioms, and too volatile to keep aboard Revance, and Ryza had to hold himself back from worrying about those riding in the lead-better that now carried them.

They also provided the group with a staggering half-cannister of water, along with the ingredients to turn it into ink for Curiktics and Kretatics. Older doctrines of Revance's operations, back when the recruitment processes of the fortress were more rigorous than having a neck to slap an iron collar around, dictated that those were the two most useful runic magics to be using in the face of a fight, leaving Reythurists to find their own ingredients.

Ditric had ordered the majority of this water be dispersed to the Kretatics as green ink, with most of it being used now by Ryza, Berlic, and Platus as they attempted to perform mechanism checks on the converted, mortar-toting treadhulk.

The vehicle had lain dormant for more than half a century, buried in a caved-in hollow to hide it from attackers if they were ever successful. Despite being older than the veterans of Revance that were guarding it, they were all too happy to assure them that it, along with its one-of-a-kind mortar shells, would flatten anything it hit, if they knew how to work it.

But the risk of a misfire would mean they'd be flattened, and not their target, so the three of them now took it in careful turns to control the separate mechanisms of the machine like they were arcanites. They gently actioned the decaying triggers and force valves, all while avoiding their control spreading to the engine or the rapidly spinning drive shafts that powered the constantly clanking treads.

Ryza barely trusted himself controlling the small, inconsequential mechanisms he was tasked with, but there were three things keeping his focus in check. The first was the way Platus had asked for his help with the task without a second thought.

Even painting the runes on his skin made Ryza's memory flash back to the tense preparations he'd made in the dirigible on the way to Iroka. The magic that those axioms had produced, the bizarre control it had given him not only of the metal, but of the molten flux that was gnawing away at it, had unnerved him to the point he didn't trust himself to control an arcanite again.

Sure, he'd used a rune or two for much simpler things in the time since, but the nonchalant way Platus had asked him, as if it were something he'd asked a thousand times before, made him temporarily forget his vow to never control another arcanite.

The second was his most recent conversation with Holm. As much as he did worry about what her version of "putting things back as they should be" meant, he'd still taken these words to heart and had thought deeply about what it would mean for himself if *he* were to put things as they should be. What normal would mean to him. This pattern of thinking had provided him with a dreamless, even restful, night's sleep for the past two nights, and he'd wondered where else this idea could be applied.

Getting Origin back. That's where.

This was the final factor in Ryza's newfound courage over his axioms. The veterans of The Northern Dump had reported a sighting of a lone figure trekking north across the plains at a rapid pace, too far away from them to have even noticed the stockpile. A trio of dirigibles had come along the next day, following their path, and another set the day after.

Comparing the veterans' drawn-up estimates with the direction of Berlic's Origin-tracking dial, Ryza, Ditric, and the others had only been able to conclude one thing.

'You think it really is a smelter?' Berlic asked Ryza. 'Even if it's only one... could it be one of our people?'

Berlic had just finished actuating the mortar battery's lateral rotational bracket. The squealing pitch of rust breaking free from the gears' teeth overpowered the low thrum of the engine and nearly made Ryza lose control of his own section of the mortar array. It was now Platus' turn to action the vertical brackets that catered to the weapon's long but pinpoint range.

This process had been going for some time, as the pair could only rotate their respective mechanisms a few inches before the other had to turn theirs, all while Ryza, with his sense of magnetic control monitoring the mechanisms playing off them, calibrated the various gears and triggers that would enable the two systems to freely turn in conjunction with each other.

It was a process better suited for a motor pool where they could strip the damn thing down, but without the prospect of one they could use until they eventually returned to their camp in Breggesa, this would have to do. It was the only way to truly understand the mechanics of the ancient war machine.

'Whoever it is, it sounds like they've got something the Scythes want,' Ryza grunted. 'Means we want it, too.'

'And that's the Academy guys, yes?' Lasteer called from the half-sealed driver's compartment.

'Bit more than that. Fighters,' Ryza said.

'We've seen them in action,' Berlic added. 'Vicious bastards. Could've done with them on our side sooner.'

'And they're not on our side now?' Lasteer asked.

'Apparently not,' Platus said. 'Berlic, your turn. Almost fully turned the thing.'

Berlic's brow nearly folded in two as he focused, and Ryza could feel his magnetic resonance sparking off his own bounds of control like an impatient wave as the enormous gears finally completed their full rotation.

Lasteer was saying something else, but Ryza blocked it out, instead concentrating on the series of clicking latches that were suddenly dancing somewhere deep within the mechanism. He felt his own frown deepen like Berlic's as he tried to keep track of them all. They had a purpose. He was sure of it. Otherwise, it meant there were broken parts on the loose in there, and that meant a broken machine they didn't have time to fix and a vehicle they'd hauled all this way for nothing.

'Turn it back a bit,' he muttered to Berlic.

He heard Ryza over the din and obliged him, but Ryza didn't feel the clicking again.

'Forwards...'

The same latches clicked once more, but now Ryza was expecting them, they seemed to come at a slower rhythm. They started near the centre of the turret's brackets, spreading outwards through a series of push-valves to the outer rims of the mortar battery. Ryza gently edged his magnetic resonance to those outer reaches, carefully feeling out each new piece of metal. If he accidentally hit the hull, he'd flood his control to the entire vehicle, and then his mind would be responsible for keeping the treads and the engine rolling, along with every apparatus that connected them. A single lapse in concentration there and they'd seize up, damaging the vehicle beyond repair.

'Do it again,' Ryza said.

'Me or him?' Platus asked, pausing his conversation with Lasteer.

'Him.'

Berlic actioned the lateral bracket back and forth once more, and this time, with his control expanded to the perimeter of the bracket, Ryza could properly follow the kinetic path of the latches. They led even lower into the guts of the treadhulk than he could've expected, and Ryza let his control follow cautiously along. He discovered a concealed box that the spinning driveshaft ran through, filled with differential gears waiting to clamp down and divert all that torque away from the treads and into...

Ryza snapped his control into a retreat before he accidentally activated something he shouldn't and instructed the others to do the same. Negotiating his way around the rocking vehicle, he found a rusted-over hatch at the foot of the mortar battery. With a few sharp kicks of his heel, it opened, revealing a series of dust-covered levers and cranks they'd been ignorant of up until now.

'It connects to the engine itself!' Ryza announced, still taken aback. 'This thing...'

He looked back over the complex loading mechanisms that ran along the lower lengths of the eight tightly packed mortar tubes. Suddenly they all made sense. Their initial thinking was that they'd need to hand-load each one, but the way this'd been designed, the machine did it all for them.

'This thing could probably fire a few hundred shells a minute!'

Berlic nodded to the weighed-down lead-better that was struggling along at their left flank, a dozen or more crates of mortar shells pushing its suspension to the limit.

'That should give us a few minutes of fun!'

Chapter Twenty-Six

The Standoff

THE RIDGE RYZA AND Ditric were sheltering behind was a narrow one. Barely more than a low wall of rock that creased up from the ground itself. They had to keep their chests pressed hard against the ground in order to keep their eyes and the tops of their heads the only thing visible between the crenelated pebbles, but even that made it feel like they were exposed.

Watchers being watched.

The rest of the League of Revance was hunkered down half a mile back down the hill, where a small valley had allowed them to jam their vehicles into a shady spot that wouldn't be touched by the sun until the following day.

It was early in the afternoon, four whole days beyond when they'd been resupplied by the now abandoned ammo dump, and they were once again running low on fuel. The past two days had seen the ground turn rocky and difficult to navigate, especially for their more waylaid vehicles, and Ryza had spent the time worrying that the delay would've lost them their hunted quarry.

This worry was now assured, yet there were still other hazards to contend with.

Ryza passed the scope back to Ditric and shuffled closer to the ridge, stopping only when the rocks grazed his chin. They'd been laying here for the better part of an hour surveying the strange terrain before them, but they were no closer to making sense of it.

The dial constructed to find Origin had led them to this place with utmost certainty. Earlier, when they'd first arrived here, Ditric had instructed Berlic and a few others to take the enchanted dial on a short scouting circuit across the land, staying out of sight, of course. The dial had twisted and turned steadily throughout the manoeuvres, proving this place to be Origin's current location.

Now we just have to go in and get him.

It was easier thought than actually done. Some kind of ruin sat in the boxed-in valley before them, yet it was unlike anything Ryza had ever seen or heard of. It had towers, glass walls bracketed in shining, twisted steel just like Twin Rings once had, but it had other things that overshadowed them.

'You still reckon it's metal?' Ditric whispered as she squinted down the scope.

Ryza had to let his eyes adjust back to seeing without the scope before he answered. The magnification on it was a miracle, powerful enough to see the creases and joins in the structures that stood a mile away.

'I ain't sure. It's white. It's rounded. No welds, no rivets, no joins... nothing.'

'But you still think it's metal after all that?'

Ryza nodded, a movement that Ditric felt through the rocks between them.

'I can practically taste it with my eyes,' Ryza said. 'You know when you see something and you feel like you've already got your tongue on it?'

'No.'

'Well, it's like that.'

'Better not be looking at me like that,' Ditric muttered.

Ryza ignored the jab and tried to make sense of the structure one more time.

The glass towers of the ruin were squat ones. Only the first tier or two were free of the ascending slope of sand that gathered in the dead-end valley. It must've been accumulating for eons in there. It started low at the mouth of the valley, getting higher and higher as the valley grew deeper, growing to be its own mountain at the very end of it. At least it would've been, if the valley walls weren't so high as to still surround it entirely. Climbing up there would be like climbing into the sky itself.

The uncovered remnants of the glass towers became buried by the orange sand of the hill around a third of the way into the valley, yet the tall archways of the strangely repeating structure resisted their fate right until the end.

It was hard to estimate the length of space between each archway. They were facing straight into the archways, and each one seemed to meet the sand around a hundred metres apart from the bases ahead or behind them. Each archway's two trunk-like legs curved forwards towards them as it rose out of the ground, twisting halfway up as they stretched to meet in the middle, continuing in one graceful flowing motion almost all the way until they joined, where their lengths suddenly went razor straight and merged at a jarringly sharp angle.

From there, atop those sharp archways, more complex creations were birthed. Seeing those complex tassels of wire only just convinced Ryza that they were made of metal. The impossibly smooth and whitened struts of each archway had thrown him off, but each archway wore a differing crown of rusted and forgotten machinery.

That high up, they'd likely been one of the few things created by those-of-glass that hadn't been probed, looted, or scavenged in some way over the endless eons since their time. Ryza had used a good chunk of his time with the scope squinting at the nearest one, discerning the intricacies of the narrow walkways and sprawling, finger-like antennae that bristled like hair from their bulbous forms. Some even carried sheets of gold as hexagon-shaped tiles.

A tempting prize protected by a hidden danger, maybe?

There had to be a reason why something so precious and so easily seen still remained in the place it had been installed. Gold had a value beyond its shining trinket-like qualities. An arcanite built with it, controlled with it, allowed for a quicker reaction from the Kretatic controlling it. The closest thing one could get to an automind's benefits without the necessity of a corpse. This philosophy had been in play around Tyrag's wrists in his last living moments as he'd controlled the entirety of Revance.

But it still wasn't enough for him.

Some invisible force would be at play around the peaks of those strange structures to dissuade the efforts of those who'd pillage from its heights.

Other, far more visible and deadly forces still lay between that, Ryza, and Origin. They'd spotted movements within the bounds of the ruins. Not anything discernible like a garrisoned force, but slight flickers of motion at the corners of buildings or within them and hidden behind the archways.

More metal, in Ryza's eyes, but whatever they were, they hadn't remained in sight for long enough to be determined. They'd looked strangely human, a concept Ryza was dreadfully familiar with when it came to metal beings, but they were far more solid than anything the flux had yet produced.

Another new behaviour of it?

Ryza shook the thought from his head. It could be something else. Arcanites set up by Origin himself to defend this hiding spot from his pursuers.

The trailing force in question lay in the sands between Ryza and Ditric and the valley of ruins itself. An encampment of the Scythes, larger than the force they'd brought to Iroka. Their fleet of dirigibles, a dozen or more in total, were strapped to the ground at the rear of their camp and as far from the valley as possible. Tents, surrounded by lightweight barricades, continued out of them in spread-out rows, forming a loose perimeter around the mouth of the valley.

Ditric had taken it upon herself to survey every inch of the valley's surrounding walls for any other outpost the Scythes may've setup up there, but an hour later had been left frustrated and with sore eyes.

'They still ain't gone in,' Ditric muttered as she focused the scope of the encampment. 'Looks like they've been set up here for... two days, maybe? Nothing. They would've already tried the ridges. Must've found something they didn't like about 'em. They're just going to wait him out.'

'They can't just wait Origin out,' Ryza replied. 'He's immortal. Don't know what makes them think they can wait anyway. It's like they're comfortable.'

'Tah. They should've found us by now. If I know Vorric, he'd have sentries all along this ridgeline.'

'Is he there?'

Ditric shook her head ever so slightly, careful not to disturb the scope at her eye. 'They all got vent masks on. Can't tell one from... Fuck me...'

'What?'

'There's someone I wasn't—'

'What!?' Ryza hissed.

'Ruka. She's here. In charge, by the looks of it.'

Ryza felt himself blanch. He knew Ruka was enmeshed with the Scythes, but to be leading this many of them? Then again, he and Ditric were leading their own little army, and there were plenty of other things with the Droughtlands that weren't as they should be. He shuddered at the thought of Holm's refrain and refocused his mind back on Ruka. Finding Origin was a hopeless chase, something Ryza suspected Vorric knew when he'd sent him out alone with the task. But it hadn't been something Ryza had known. Maybe Ruka hadn't thought it hopeless either.

Empty minds.

'She must really think she can find him,' Ryza breathed. 'She's basically done it once... no, twice before. We all did. Now she thinks she can do it again.'

'She's thinking wrong, 'cause we're going to get him first,' Ditric grunted.

'How? They've got... three or four times the—'

'Don't matter. We've done worse.'

Ryza gave himself a moment to fume at the interruption. 'Then what? What do we do once we've got him? We just ask him to—?'

'Doesn't fucken matter,' Ditric replied gruffly. 'If they want him, we want him, too.'

'And we just work out the rest later?'

He looked over in time to catch a shadow of a smirk lift Ditric's lips.

'Just like old times,' she said.

Ryza kept looking at her, unabashed for the incredulity he could feel spreading on his face, even though Ditric couldn't see it with how concentrated she was on the scope. There was a determination there that Ryza hadn't felt in himself for a while, the same determination that the two of them had just prescribed to Ruka.

Certainty.

Ryza wanted to shift his focus back to their surveillance, but a shuffling of feet on the rocks behind them turned his attention. He curled his torso to shy away from the ridgeline and caught sight of Avesta crawling up towards them.

'We've been working as quietly as we can, but the rest of the troops are still wondering if we're really gonna do this thing,' she whispered.

Before he replied, Ryza let her drop to her chest and shimmy up the last few feet until she was also level with him and Ditric at the ridgeline. The momentary shock on her face gave him pause.

'That's a lot of 'em,' Avesta said quietly. 'It's like they're expecting a fight, and not one with us.'

Ryza chewed his upper lip. She had a point.

'You managed it?' he asked.

Avesta nodded and turned onto her side with a wince, digging through the deep pouches of her resewn forge leathers to produce a small metal pipe. She handed it to Ryza, and he turned it over in his grip, taking note of the tightly wound webbing of wires and the button at one end that was embedded in a divot.

It left a powdered layer of rust in his hands as he turned it over. The nine-inch length of metal had come from the rear axle of the most dysfunctional lead-better that'd driven with them. The rest of the vehicle's carcass now lay just outside the shelter the rest were in, having been scavenged for parts and corrupted into a makeshift assault vehicle.

'Come on down, I'll show you,' Avesta said, nodding to it.

Ryza rolled over and looked at Ditric.

'Go on,' she muttered. 'Tell you if something's happening, yeah?'

After a slow retreat down the hill, Avesta led him on a tour of the provisions they'd prepared for the potential battle. The bulk of the League of Revance's force was still ensconced in the valley that hid them, their weapons readied but their minds idle. Ryza knew just how frustrating that type of waiting could be, but it was a better feeling than the alternative.

The plan was a loose one at best, and heavily dependent on what the Scythes did, and what the conditions were. Ideally, the Scythes and whatever they were quarrelling with would devastate each other, allowing the League of Revance to simply come in and scoop Origin up from the wreckage.

But nothing's ever that easy.

A sandstorm came before their chance to strike ever would.

Another day had come and gone. A billowing blanket of dust had rolled through the night, forcing the amassed forces of the League of Revance to shelter under the low chassis of their hidden vehicles.

With the morning's rise, the gale had subsided, but a pink and orange haze lingered in the air to hamper all visibility. Their watchpoint from the ridge was useless. Having a Reythurist burn an axiom to cut through the haze would only give them away, and sending one up to scout the skies would do it quicker, something Elya only accepted once Vhoze and the others threatened to weld her into a box to keep her on the ground.

Midday was signalled by the first burst of sun and blue sky appearing directly above them. Ryza looked up at it with trepidation. He could hear Ditric grinding her teeth next to him. At least that was what it sounded like.

The dust-filled air not only muffled all but the loudest of noises but also choked out any breath they tried to take. It had been a long night wearing a vent mask, one where Ryza had struggled to sleep, but even after half a day of sucking in pitiful breaths through the damn thing, he still couldn't settle the nerves raised by the mask's signature *hiss-click*.

'Fuck it,' Ditric's smothered voice said. 'We should've gone hours ago.'

'We would've shot each other to pieces before we even found the Scythes,' Ryza grunted back.

Ditric shook her head, loosening yet another coat of gathered grit from her stubbled scalp.

'Still got the small plan. You and me. In and out, Ryza.'

'You sure you want it to be me?'

Ditric's chuckle came through as a crackling rattle. 'No one else's crazy enough.'

'Ruka would be,' Ryza challenged. 'She'll be in there. You ever killed a friend?'

'Tah,' she growled. 'But if it were you over there. In blue with the Scythes. Would you be asking her the same thing?'

'She wouldn't know we're coming.'

'I'm sure she does. She'll make that choice when she gets to it. Same as the rest of us do. No point making it ahead of time.'

Ditric turned away from the blank view across the ridgeline and went stomping back down the slope to their base of operations. Ryza followed with her, his hand unconsciously at his holster, massaging the grip of his rifle.

CHAPTER TWENTY-SEVEN

THE ACCELERATOR

THE ENGINE SPAT AND protested as Ditric tested its throttle. Exposed valves flashed with bursts of fire and unignited oil. The drips of the latter ran down the roughly welded sides of the housing and across the new struts that fixed it in place. A gnashing network of mismatched gears drew it into their teeth to use as motion-smoothing lubricant before a stray spark of friction sent a pinwheel of flame out from the workings.

The vehicle was no longer a lead-better. Its engine was the only uncorrupted portion of the vehicle, yet with its chassis now stripped of so much of its initial weight and rebalanced, it shook with an unbridled power that was never meant for it. Its connection to the ground was down to one wheel which was connected directly to the engine by a single chain belt, positioned right at the fore of the rig. No axles, no gear differentials, nothing to stop it from delivering raw, roaring power.

The majority of the weight came from the armour reaffixed to the craft. Three other lead-betters had been freed of their heavy plates, and they were now arrayed across the front of the vehicle like an armoured shell or a low-slung sail. Rigged under this was a central skeleton for a driver and a passenger to lie in on their stomachs. The ground was to rush below them, their dug in, steel-capped boots acting as rudders and the only means of steering.

It was to be an insane, one-way trip for the vehicle, and Berlic couldn't be more proud of his creation. It was him who helped Ryza down into the left side, only speaking with him for long enough to tell him that he'd taken to calling the newly birthed vehicle the "lead-shell" and for him to hold on tight.

Ordinarily, Ryza would've refused his help, but the half hour Ditric had given them to prepare for their strike had weighed them both down with a staggering amount of munitions. Avesta had equipped them both with three of the small devices she'd made out of the pipe cuttings. Her part in this battle was well behind the frontlines and with the mortar-equipped treadhulk.

The veterans who'd gifted them the war machine would be crewing the workings of it, but it had been Avesta's idea to turn the workings contained in the handheld pipes into arcanites, allowing her senses to travel with them. At the push of a button, she'd know to order the mortar crews to unleash a volley of fire, targeted precisely wherever they threw the damn thing.

Once Ditric was out of earshot, Avesta had tucked a fourth pipe into the pouch on Ryza's armoured chest, this one bearing a red marking along its length.

'You remember that shard of a rebel sun we recovered from the drifter?'

'I do,' Ryza had said. 'Is this...'

'Last resort. Only if it's something you ain't coming back from. No tricks this time either. If you want it, you got it.'

'Got it.'

Ryza's and Ditric's bodies were now as armoured as the lead-shell that was about to carry them into battle. Vent masks and tightly secured goggles hid their faces, intended to protect them both from the haze and from whatever atmospheric traps the Scythes might try on them. Body armour had been dug out from the depths of the veterans' carried stores, not thick enough to stop a rifle slug, but when it came to a slashing blade, the Scythes' weapon of choice, it might buy them an extra swing with one of their own.

At their wrists was another familiar feature. A steel wristband featuring a dial that would point to Origin. Berlic and the others hadn't been able to replicate the enchanted miracle that'd been given to them aboard Revance, with this cobbled-together version only able to point the way if they were close, but it was better than nothing at all.

They each had been equipped with a pair of sawn-off rifles. Ditric had requested them specifically for herself, saying she was taking a note out of Ryza's book. What this meant was yet to be seen, but it was another convoluted vote of confidence that lifted Ryza's hopes a touch.

With the two of them packed into the lead-shell, the vehicle had been wheeled right up to the ridgeline where Ditric had finally been given the go-ahead to crank the engine's ignition.

The motor-driven roar pumped in Ryza's veins, eliciting a cool focus that he hadn't felt for a long time. His vision sharpened, his grip tightened around the handhold within the vehicle that was the only thing securing him in place, and his muscles tensed like a coiled spring.

I'm ready.

'Ditric!' he roared through his vent mask.

'There he fucken is!' she called back.

'*FUCKEN PUNCH IT!*'

She shunted the throttle forwards without another word needed, and the engine screamed with the same vicious cacophony that was burning in Ryza's chest. His skin pulled and stretched across his face and shoulders as the sheer force of the acceleration yanked at whatever it could reach.

The lead-shell ripped through the low rocks of the ridgeline and howled as it hurtled through the air, smacking the rocky slope on the other side with a bone-rattling crunch. The lone forward wheel kicked loose pebbles up into the chassis. They plinked off the metal over Ryza's and Ditric's heads like a volley of fired slugs, only relenting when the wheel found purchase on the rough ground and sent them rocketing forwards with renewed gusto.

Ryza's toes bounced and clattered off the ground behind them, so he tensed his thighs to tuck them further into the lead-shell's fuselage. Even the slightest contact with the ground would hurt their speed or cause them to turn, and right now, speed was the only thing working in their favour.

He could see the ground rushing past through the narrow viewport cut through the lead-shell's armour. They were going fast, but Ryza couldn't help feeling that they could be faster. He had a line of runes readied under his thick leather gauntlets: an axiom primed to take command of the lead-shell's metal the moment Ditric lost control of it. But the runes had to be saved for later, for the moment when the chaos would truly begin.

Ryza glanced across to see Ditric rocking in her prone seat, trying to shunt the throttle lever a fraction of an inch further. She was giving the machine her all, her withdrawn leg furiously working at the pressure pump that'd been installed under her left foot. It was connected to the long, narrow fuel tank that was welded in between them, the result of two regular ones taken from lead-betters that'd been hastily joined.

The outside of it was streaked with leaking fuel, stained so heavily it might as well have been dipped in oil in the first place. The fuel tank had only been filled minutes before they'd launched the damn thing, and a carefully aimed kick from Ryza's right foot produced a half-empty clang.

We don't need this thing for long.

Ryza didn't need to pass this assurance on to Ditric. The Scythes' camp was in view, starting with their anchored dirigibles. The grounded crafts were covered by massive canvas sails that'd been thrown over them to protect them from the dust storm, giving the gathered sand at its sides the illusion of being a solid dune.

'Go through the bastards!' Ryza roared over the engine.

There was a distinct snap of metal, and Ryza looked over in time to see Ditric with the broken-off throttle lever in her hand, the mechanism connected to it stuck at full. She threw it aside and grabbed the lead-shell's frame with both hands to brace herself. As the line of canvas hills sped towards them, Ryza did the same, jamming his feet into the rear struts so his shoulders were wedged against the forward ones, turning his body into a rigid part that was one with the machine.

The lead-shell punched through the sheltering sail of canvas and everything hidden beneath it like one enormous artillery shell, passing clean through the other side without losing a single ounce of speed. Screams and blasts of unleashed gas followed in their wake as the vehicle penetrated the next one, wreaking just the same destruction again.

But it seemed Ditric wasn't satisfied with that. A burst of heat came from Ryza's right, and he twisted as best he could within the lead-shell's confines to see Ditric had gotten one of her hands free. Her leather gauntlet was gone, burnt to a cinder by the billowing trail of fire that was vomiting from her palm.

She's used an axiom!

Ryza twisted further, snagging a look back at their trail of utter havoc as her trailing line of fire caught within the billowing sails and detonated. A column of flame shot to the sky as the shockwave swept across the loose sand. The thrashing wave of dust overtook them, shaking the lead-shell, adding to its already uncontrollable acceleration. The next pierced dirigible exploded as they shot through. Ryza couldn't hear the screams. He didn't need to. He knew well what that type of burning agony sounded like.

Sharp crashes and bumps shook the lead-shell as they plunged through the tents that came next. The fabric of them tore quickly from where it caught on the armoured skull of the lead-shell, and then they were through the camp, the hazy silhouette of the ruins now before them.

'Gotta steer, Ryza!' Ditric shouted. 'Right up the middle!'

Their pre-emptive ram raid had thrown their course, and they were now hurtling towards one of the exposed skyscrapers on the right side of the valley. Ryza kicked his legs out from where he'd wedged his feet and held on tight as he dug his toes into the ground. The speeding ground slammed his heels against the inside of the lead-shell, and it took a few more sharp kicks for the toes of his boots to properly get any purchase in the rapid sand.

Once he did, he had to grit his teeth against the pain of it. Despite the rigidity of his armoured boots, it still felt like his ankles were about to be ripped clean from his shins. The effort was paying off. The lead-shell began to drift leftwards in a slow arc, cutting their course back towards the centre of the ruins, their path now heading under the enormous white archways.

The destination of their "small" plan lay at the other end of the ruins, right at the highest point of the dead-end canyon. With the high ground, they could draw the Scythes forwards into the ruins, holding them off with well-timed mortar barrages thanks to Avesta's beacons, while the rest of their force swept in to assault the Scythes' abandoned camp from behind.

Of course, this was all under the assumption that the Scythes wouldn't be able to simply fly up to greet them. Their fleet of dirigibles may've been on its way to ashes, but the many Reythurists among them could still take to the air themselves. Ryza could only hope that whatever it was about the ruins that was currently keeping them at bay would also keep them on the ground.

And that it won't fuck us up, either.

With the lead-shell nearing the centre, it was Ditric's turn to dig her feet in, straightening their path. Ryza gave the fuel tank another kick, and it rang nearly empty. Whatever fuel was burning in the engine was all they had left to carry them, and they hadn't even reached the first archway. Ryza mentally prepared himself to take over the machine. The next archway was about a hundred metres after the first, with a steep incline of blank sand between the two. If they were to run out of fuel, that was where they'd be stranded as the enraged Scythes gave chase.

'Ditric, I'm going to—'

But before he could do anything, Ryza's words were shoved back down his throat as they passed under the first archway and a sudden burst of acceleration yanked the lead-shell forwards. The engine whined as the lone wheel it supported suddenly spun faster than it could drive the chain belt. The valves and pistons sputtered and cracked, taken aback by the sudden reversal of torque.

'Ryza! This ain't me! What did you—'

Another eye-popping burst of speed urged them faster, and despite travelling up such a steep slope, they were now going faster than ever before. It was just too much for the engine. The piercing crack of splitting metal nearly made Ryza fall straight out the exposed rear of the lead-shell, where his tumbling body would've been followed by both shattered halves of the now defunct engine. The broken engine blocks cleaved through the centre of the lead-shell's innards one after another, the first gouging through the frame of the fuel tank and the second demolishing the remnants entirely.

They passed under another archway, another burst of speed practically lifting up what was left of the lead-shell as it doubled in speed once again. The ground beyond the viewport was nothing but a hurtling blur, but Ryza recognised the sudden disappearance of skyscrapers from their surroundings. They were a third of the way into the canyon, but somehow they were still picking up speed! The canyon wall at the end of it that'd once looked so distant was now only seconds away!

Ryza tried to jam his toes into the ground again, to do anything to divert their path from passing under the next archway, but he only managed one attempt before the next punch of speed throttled him. He wasn't even sure if his feet had touched the ground that time, but he didn't get another chance before they were under another archway, doubling their speed once more.

His body and everything within it suddenly felt compressed beyond repair. Like his organs had been ripped from his chest, through his shoulder blades, and jammed back in through his ribs in no particular order. All he knew to do was to hold on, to stay in the armoured confines of the lead-shell as it rocketed towards its demise.

'Out!' Ditric managed to roar. 'Get—'

Her last word disappeared as she did the same, her entire body slipping from its place within the craft as if she'd been yanked by her ankles.

Get out!

Ryza finally rebelled against his instincts to stay in the comet of a vehicle and relinquished his grip within the lead-shell. His own body was snatched out, just in time to avoid going through another archway, yet he still had enough speed to skim on his chest like a low-thrown pebble across the smooth slope of sand before it caught in his armour. He flipped and tumbled in a chaotic mix of jarred limbs and bodily thumps until he finally ground to a stop in a crater of settling dust.

He was on his back, his goggles miraculously unshattered, yet his vision still seemed wrong. The blue and orange-hazed sky was not complete, a bar of solid white pieced through the middle of it from the top of his eyes.

Am I blind?

Ryza moved his head, causing a shooting agony to course through his neck, but at least he realised that white bar was just the legs of one of the archways looming over him. He gathered his wits and his jumbled bones as quickly and painfully as he could and stood up. He'd ended up just three paces from the archway's enormous trunk where it met the sand. Three paces and he would've been splattered against it like an insolent bug.

An exploding crash echoed through the valley, and Ryza realised it was the lead-shell crumpling against the back wall of the canyon. It had been louder than anything he'd heard before in his life, and he'd come under fire from Revance's main cannon that fired shells larger than the damn lead-shell. As the dust and boulder-sized hunks of rubble fell away, there remained a clean punctured hole at the end of the canyon, a blue dot of sky visible all the way through.

That thing must've punched through a hundred metres of solid rock...

He looked around, turning with his feet rather than his jarred neck as he searched for Ditric. Even though she'd ditched the lead-shell only a fraction of a second before he had, she was still nearly a hundred metres down the dunes. At least the haze wasn't as harsh up here. It lay as a blanket across the stretch of land spanning out before Ryza. A solid border between faint orange and the pure blue of the sky.

Beyond Ditric, Ryza could see the Scythes' camp in flames as the scattered figures within it rushed to their battle stations. After that, the dozen or so vehicles brought by the League of Revance were prowling across the ridgeline, still just out of sight to the warrior-scholars.

He kept low, cringing as he raised his arm to wave at Ditric to signal he was in one piece. Ditric didn't wave back, instead jabbing her finger at the damaged canyon wall behind him before scrambling sideways to shelter behind one of the archways.

Ryza turned and had to dive to the ground behind the archway leg nearest to him as one of the boulders whipped past. If not for her warning, he would've been pulverised by it. The air cracked as the next few rocks rushed past, all picking up more and more speed with each archway they passed under. Some failed to keep their course as they reached the exposed heads of the skyscrapers, hitting them with enough force to shatter every remaining pane of glass. One skyscraper near the bottom of the canyon was even less lucky.

A larger boulder, twice the size of a man maybe, passed through every single archway on its rolling journey. It was glowing red hot and trailing flecks of molten stone as it punched clean through the fragile tower.

What the tower had withstood in the cataclysm that'd wiped those-of-glass to their extinction, whatever it had survived in the thousands, if not millions of years since then, was no match for the sheer kinetic force that had just been delivered to its structure.

The skyscraper detonated without a single hint of flame. Pylons of hyper-machined steel shot in every direction. Those that took to the sky may as well have flown beyond the blue itself. Some made it the half mile or so to the Scythes' camp, further devastating their scattered forces as they tried to recover, distracting them from the threat still lurking at the ridgeline.

But the metal that came Ryza's way was far more dangerous. The severed hunks rolled and spun faster and faster as they ricocheted between the archways, cleaving in and out of the intervening skyscrapers like sharpened blades through waiting flesh.

Ryza made to scramble around to the other side of his sheltering archway, but as he staggered through it himself, his feet were yanked from under him as he was thrown into a running pace. He regained his balance, ten paces past where he was aiming to be, and was left with the only choice of throwing himself bodily to the ground.

The air snapped hard as the steel blew past his head, now the second loudest sound he'd ever heard. Before he could uncurl his near defenceless body, a wave of glass particles washed over him, clattering harmlessly where it hit his armour back and stinging where it found the flesh on his neck.

Ryza stayed down until the chaos subsided, swearing under his breath with each crash and blast that came echoing to him from up and down the canyon.

When it finally ended, he got up with caution, limping slightly as he skittered to the cover behind the leg of the archway. He peered around it, spotting Ditric in a similar position a hundred metres down on the other side of the canyon.

She was sitting with her back against the white metal, more flames dancing from her hands as she worked quickly to pull the smattering of glass from her exposed arms before her blood stained the sand too badly.

Throwing caution to the wind, Ryza bolted from his cover, ready this time for the way the archway hurled him into a running pace. Between that and the sprinting momentum of heading down such a steep hill, Ryza crossed the hundred or so metres in ten seconds flat.

'That's why they didn't go in, eh?' Ditric grunted, her teeth stained red.

'Do they know?' Ryza said, still out of breath. 'They must, or...'

Ryza trailed off. He'd just glanced beyond the shelter of the archway at the Scythes' camp. Some of the blue-robed warriors had taken to the air, soaring towards the archways in pursuit of their attacks.

'Fuck me, they don't know...'

'Then cover your fucken head!' Ditric spat back.

But Ryza could only watch in horror as five of the airborne Scythes passed through the first archway. The first hadn't been ready at all. They pinwheeled as if they'd been swatted out of the air, crashing into the sand below and throwing up a lethal cloud of dust. The next two had tried to avert their flights, plunging downwards in an attempt to avoid the archway entirely, but they failed and were shot into the ground where they threw up dust clouds twice the size.

The remaining two Scythes stood brave in their path. They passed through the first archway with barely a wobble, holding steady in the air as they belted towards the next.

They're going to try and ride it out.

They would fail. The first made it through three archways before a stray antenna from one of the skyscrapers caught them, slicing them clean in half.

The last of them remained high as they picked up more and more speed. Flecks of fabric, then ripped patches of skin, fell away from their speeding form as they passed under the midpoint archway of the ruins. It was too late for them now. There was no stopping even if they wanted to. Three-quarters of the way up, they flashed and burst into flame. As they hurtled over Ryza's and Ditric's heads, their body disintegrated, sending hunks of flesh and bone spraying through the bounds of the next archway, where they were taken so quickly that Ryza completely lost sight of them.

The only thing left of them was the thin streaks that their fractured bones had gouged into the sand and the muddy red stains that their blood had left against the back of the canyon.

CHAPTER TWENTY-EIGHT

HOW REVANCE ONCE FOUGHT

As Ditric worked on searing shut the scratches that the thrown glass from down the canyon had left on his neck, Ryza drew his rifle and held it tightly. Despite the clearing haze, he kept his eyes unfocused. Between each sting of burning pain Ditric produced on his skin, he was letting his memory flicker through the brief visions he'd caught of the camp as they'd torn through it.

Had they carried rifles with them? Something else they could shoot with? Ryza had been assuming not as they'd formed this insane strategy. Vorric had made his abhorrence for guns and similar weapons clear as they'd flown in towards the mess that'd become Iroka all those months ago.

They're a crude weapon of a bygone age.

But with Ruka at their helm, things could've changed. As they'd churned through the charnel camp of torn tents and broken, burning bodies, Ryza hadn't seen a sign that answered either way.

How many Scythes had there been? How many had survived? How many were warriors like those he'd expected to fight, and how many were innocent supporting men and women that were never meant to see this type of death and destruction at all? His thoughts drifted back to the League of Revance's own supporting soldiers, who were still hidden, lying in wait in the valley that had sheltered their vehicles for so many days.

They were just as defenceless, so Ryza had to hope that the League of Revance's pincer-like attack would draw attention away from them, and that the second wave of the offensive wouldn't be overwhelmed, either.

Ditric slapped him on the back to signal that her work was done, and with bloody hands, she drew her own rifle. The two of them crouched low at the edge of the archway's trunk, creeping forwards with step after careful step to not trigger the sudden lurch of pace that seemed to take advantage of even the slightest movement.

'Ditric,' Ryza whispered. 'How many?'

She pushed him aside slightly to get a bit closer, for what little good it did, and squinted down at the advancing, blue-robed forms. They were on foot. The example of what had happened to their compatriots had been a firm one, and even if they avoided the archways, they likely wouldn't be risking flight any time soon.

'Twenty. Maybe thirty. But that's just the first wave,' she grunted. 'Must be half-a-hundred, maybe even a hundred of them still trying to deal with the camp.'

'Reckon we've done what we need to?'

'Nah. We're too far up, and I don't want to fight these fuckers without a skyscraper to hide in.'

In the span of only a few tense minutes, they made it a third of the way down the canyon, only one archway away from the nearest intact skyscraper. They were yet to come under fire, either because the Scythes weren't armed like they were for their own hubris or were yet to reveal their own ranged weapons out of caution.

Nevertheless, the first wave of Scythes had continued their own progress up the canyon just as free of fire. Ditric had gone to snap off the first shot in their general direction, figuring the sheer force of the fired slug once it had passed through the intervening three or four archways would be enough to obliterate the unlucky bastard it hit and scare the shit out of anyone standing next to them.

But Ryza had stayed her hand. Beyond the canyon, the League of

Revance was launching its attack. The motor roars of their engines was a distinct echo that reached them over the strangely whipping winds as the sound passed through the archways. The vehicles looked slow from the distance Ryza and Ditric were watching them from. Like toy pieces being pushed by an invisible child's hand across an orange blanket towards the still-recovering camp.

When they hit, the lead-betters weaved in and out of the fray, too agile to be taken down, yet too fast to do much damage themselves. It was a distraction manoeuvre, allowing the trailing treadhulk to dispatch another half-dozen former conscripts unnoticed at the far perimeter of the camp. They'd be able to flank the defenders by surprise, yet if Ditric's eyes had counted right, they'd be outnumbered seven-to-one.

Ditric reached the skyscraper's glass a few steps before Ryza did, and by the time he'd caught up, she'd already made short work of bashing out a glass pane where the building's walls met the sand. This created a half-buried opening, and the pressing sand quickly began draining into it.

'Wait,' Ryza hissed, grabbing her arm before she went through. 'Don't know if it's safe.'

'You want to check yourself? Stick something in there that you don't need,' she said with a chuckle, smirking towards his crotch.

Ryza ignored the joke despite giggling internally as he checked his pouches.

'Need everything we brought with us,' Ryza said, shaking his head.

'Oh you fucking idiot,' Ditric muttered.

Ryza wasn't sure if this was directed at herself or at him, but as she bent down to scoop up a handful of sand, he realised it had been at both of them.

Ditric took a step back to wind up her throw, then pelted the gathered dust through the freshly broken void. It hissed as it hit the hallway wall opposite, and Ditric didn't waste time following it in. Ryza went in after her, crouching below the upper rim of the window that stood at waist height and shuffled forward.

The glass that remained intact below the sand line snapped and shattered as he put his weight on it through the heel of his boot, unleashing a flowing wave of sand into the skyscraper that carried Ryza ass-first into the hallway.

He collected himself quickly as Ditric dug herself out from the knee-deep wash that he'd caused. They shared a nod as they readied their rifle and began to move further into the building.

Ditric went first, holding her sawn-off rifle like she would a normal one, close to her chest and mindful of snagging the muzzle on a corner that she'd misjudged the depth of. Following her, Ryza kept his own weapon low at his hip. He knew how fast he could level it. He'd had plenty of practice. These days, walking around with it raised meant he was on the verge of panic or just making a show of it.

The sand subsided beneath their feet to reveal an ancient, smooth carpet. It was white like the coat of a beast unfortunate enough to stand out as an albino of its herd, and smooth like its fur had been freshly clipped from its hide for clothes-stuffing. Where the sand fell upon it from the various cracks and breaches in the windows, the grains didn't truly touch it, instead hovering a fraction of an inch above the ancient fibres.

Ryza glanced downwards as he purposely pressed down on a step in his boots. It felt solid, like he really was stepping on it, but as he watched Ditric's heels, he saw it not to be true.

Seems normal enough.

The dismissal was one he wanted to tell Ditric, just in case she was on edge about it, but the tenseness that was squared at her shoulders kept him quiet. She stopped. Her head turned slowly, and her eyes met Ryza's in the corner of hers as they grew wider and wider with doubt.

Now Ryza heard it too.

Clanking.

Clanking metal.

They weren't alone.

Frozen on the spot, Ryza did his best to take inventory of his surroundings as his mind raced. If he and Ditric hadn't been detected yet, they still had the element of surprise. If they had, then whatever was waiting to strike them was close by. Too close.

The hallway was a narrow one. They'd only come down twenty paces of it, but the flowing line of sand outside had reached high enough so only a crack of light came through. Still, the place was well-lit, a sourceless light coming from empty divots in the white ceiling above.

On the right, three paces beyond where Ditric stood, was a doorway that led further into the skyscraper's guts, but they were too far away to try peeking around the corner without risking another step. Ryza leaned to the side slightly, close enough to the wall that his ear was almost pressed against the garishly blue-painted surface, and he listened.

It was metal that he was hearing. He was certain of it. Clanking metal like only an arcanite made by a Kretatic could make. He'd seen the machines of those-of-glass in action. They were smooth. Slick. They didn't clank. They hissed.

Ryza refocused his eyes but still didn't budge. While they'd been unfocused, they'd caught a glimmer of movement. He let his eyes dart rapidly back and forth across the hallway to find where it had come from, but the place was empty. The hallway stretched for another thirty or so paces before it began a rounding right bend to connect it to the next hallway, the sand line outside subsiding there to expose the harsh, sunburnt sands outside.

But then Ryza realised the movement hadn't been in the hallway at all. His eyes had lingered back on the dark, buried glass on Ditric's left. If he didn't know any better, he'd say it was a view of the night out there, but that only served to make the glass as reflective as a mirror.

A mirror that allowed him sight of the metal, human-like form waiting for them just around the corner.

Ryza stiffened, practically paralysing his entire body through the sheer force of his muscles to hold in a scream. It wasn't a man that was around the corner. It was armoured like one, more heavily than Ryza and Ditric put together, complete with a helmet that covered almost all of its face.

The portion left exposed wasn't flesh that needed to be protected, however. Like everything else, it was metal. Steel. Dark grey and impossibly sculpted into the sharp bones that would make up the eye sockets of a skull had a Kretatic been asked to sculpt them from memory. In each of those hollow pits was a green glow that had no fire or fuel to light it.

That was what Ryza had seen out of the corner of his eye. The green glow made by a Kretatic who'd gone far beyond the limits of his axioms. He'd seen it in Tyrag when he'd taken control of Revance, in Maligar when he'd bragged of his manufactured minds in the tunnels under Kyrea, and in Origin when the tiny arcanite had first been freed of its fortress-sized burden.

Ryza raised his rifle, keeping the muzzle of it pointed through the walls but his muscles tense enough as he held it that his rifle didn't brush against the walls. The arcanite twitched. Its head had moved, its hands too, along with the weapon held between them, but it hadn't gone beyond its resting state.

He did a double take as he caught sight of the weapon again. It was a familiar one. A bolt-lock. The weapons that Origin had equipped Ryza and the rest of the conscripts with before they'd faced down Tyrag and the full might of a flying Revance. Their pitfalls against the rifles Ryza had first fought with was their lack of range, but they made up for that in their ability to fire off rapid volleys of sharpened iron rods without the need for blast powder or a reload. This close, within these ruins, Ditric and Ryza didn't stand a chance. Not if they fought with rifles alone.

The bolt-lock was pointed through the doorway. If they were to take another step, their bodies would be pressed against the muzzle of it. They couldn't move. Ryza knew it, and somehow Ditric had sensed it as well.

The arcanite jolted again, this time taking a purposeful step forwards as the clangs of unleashed bolt-locks echoed in from beyond the skyscraper's broken glass. Other machines must've been awoken by the Scythes' presence and were now engaging them in the same combat he and Ditric were about to face.

Yet they couldn't fight like the Scythes could.

Claps of wind came in glass-shattering waves, and the furthest windows of the hallways exploded inwards from the pressure. The arcanite took another marching step forwards, then turned on its semi-hooved heel, priming itself to move through the doorway where he and Ditric would be just a metre away. More clanking came from within the room, more green glowing eye sockets appearing in the reflection beyond the terrifying visage of the first.

It has to be now!

Chapter Twenty-Nine

Origin's Army

RYZA PUMMELLED DITRIC TO the left with the nub of his arm as he surged forward, turning the corner at the doorway with one smooth pivot of his heel as it landed. Suddenly he was face-to-face with the arcanite soldier. At least face-to-chest. He looked up at the contraption's blankly glowing eyes as he realised, too late, that the glass behind him that had provided the reflection was curved outwards slightly, warping the image of all it showed, making the arcanite look smaller.

Could be twice my height for all it fucking matters now!

The arcanite drew its bolt-lock across its chest, winding up to swing the butt of it directly down on Ryza's skull, but Ryza was quicker. An axiom had already burned in his hand, and he slammed his palm into the armoured shell of the arcanite's chest plate.

He knew what resonance he'd find. He knew that the creation was Origin's the moment he saw the bolt-lock in its hands. That was why he knew he'd be able to use the axioms he'd prepared to take over the lead-shell on the arcanite instead.

Ryza's resonance flooded through the joints and machinery of the contraption, purging Origin's own control with an expectant ease. If the clanging sounds of battle he was hearing outside were anything to go by, there were hundreds of these things now emerging from their hiding places within the skyscrapers. Even a being as immortal as Origin wouldn't notice or have the focus to battle against the corruption of just one of them.

But as Ryza's own control began to weigh heavy on his mind, he gained a true appreciation of just how impossible Origin was. Ryza had held the walking fortress of Revance in his mind before, hoisting that same burden that Origin had carried for centuries, and he'd only lasted a matter of seconds before he'd needed a network of thousands of autominds to assist him.

Controlling this lone arcanite in all its quasi-human complexities was just as difficult as the fortress had been, and this time Ryza didn't have a battery of autominds to aid him. All sensation in his own fleshy body ceased. The arcanite's legs stood as his own collapsed. Its eyes watched as Ryza's own went blind. Its hands, both of them, clenched firmly on its weapon as Ryza dropped his own.

The only thing he had left to feel was the pulse of his thrumming heart, but even that seemed to be getting confused with the whirring, clinking mechanisms that pounded away within this arcanite's chest. He had become the metal. He had become the machine. A fate for Kretatics comparable to Reythurists and their terror of dying away from the sky.

And I can only watch as it happens.

It felt like his emotions were being dulled and blunted as he watched indifferently as his body crumpled on the white carpet. A let down, considering how strongly they'd just fared as he'd raced into battle. But now he didn't need to feel them. He wasn't even sure why he was controlling this machine in the first place.

Maybe he could just relinquish this, as well, and be free of it all. The temptation was only further fuelled as the metal itself grew numb. It was no longer his body, but the decaying bones of what had never been such a thing. This armour did not protect him. Instead, it caged him. There was nothing left to fight for, so why had he become this fighter at all?

And Origin survived like this for all his life?

If these were to be his last thoughts, at least Ryza would go knowing that Origin didn't want to be immortal. That he hadn't once been some power-hungry bastard like Tyrag or Maligar. That whatever form of limitless life had been inflicted upon him hadn't been by choice.

As Ryza's own senses within the machine began to fade, one last feeling came from his flesh. A prodding. No, it was a grip. It was difficult to tell when he didn't know how soft he was supposed to be. He forced his ebbing magnetic resonance to look through the arcanite's glowing green eyes once again and was met with a sight that made his entire spirit flare back into life.

It was Ditric. She'd stowed her own rifle in the face of a machine that would eviscerate her in a second and had instead picked up Ryza's limp form and hauled it over her left shoulder. A squiggly vein bulged in her forehead as she struggled against the deadweight of his limp body, drawing an embossed line through her shaved hairline and across her scalp.

'I dunno if you're in that thing, Ryza,' she said to the machine, 'but you better do something about those bastards before they figure out what's happened!'

His magnetic resonance gained yet another burst of control, and he spun within the arcanite as if it were his own body, barely noticing as the left arm disengaged from the machine from the elbow down and fell to the floor.

A dozen more arcanites just like him had emerged from alcoves embedded in the oddly crenelated walls of this sweeping, circular room. They held bolt-locks of their own, but only across their chests. They still had no idea where to point them, the focus of their controller called to the running battle outside. Ryza stowed his own bolt-lock by hooking it into a purpose-made latch in the machine's right hip. Steel bolts were all well and good when it came to piercing smelter flesh, but they'd simply bounce off the metal hides of these mechanical warriors.

The opposing arcanites stomped at their heels and turned on the spot like a well-drilled squadron to face Ryza, finally bringing their bolt-locks level to aim at him.

They haven't realised I am the machine!

A rapid-fire series of clangs echoed through the massive room as bolt after sharpened bolt flew through the air and glanced harmlessly off Ryza's heavily plated chest. If this arcanite had a voice, he would laugh, but he settled for a grinding hum that some redundant mechanism in the arcanite's neck could make.

'Too fucken close, Ryza!'

He turned within the arcanite to find Ditric backing away from the doorway, her face stricken with panic as she tried to check Ryza's fleshy form for wounds. Most of the sharpened bolts had hit his mechanical chest, but those that'd missed had pierced the glass in the hallway beyond, sending in another wave of orange sand.

Easing his control of the arcanite for just a moment, Ryza found his real voice.

'Run.'

When Ryza returned to the arcanite's eyes, he was met with the relieving sight of Ditric doing just that as she scrambled up onto the sands through the newly created breach. He turned back to the other arcanites as they loaded and fired another volley of bolts, this time spreading his metal arms wide on the off chance they would catch a few more bolts that were meant for him or Ditric.

He still wasn't sure how he was going to deal with the rest of the arcanites. They were evenly matched, after all, and neither of them had weapons suited to destroy the others. Then suddenly they all went limp. Their heads were now hung low, the glow of their eyes almost absent.

It can't've been that easy...

The thought was right. The intensity of the clanging and clanking battle outside suddenly doubled, and Ryza turned in the arcanite and rushed outside as fast as he could on the unfamiliar metal legs.

The world outside looked hazy to these metallic eyes. Before he'd entered the skyscraper with Ditric, the haze of last night's sandstorm had been lifting, and it had almost become what he'd consider a clear day. But now it was as if that haze had returned, the strange speckling of a green aura sparkling like distant stars within it.

He could barely see thirty metres beyond where the arcanite stood, and he realised it was not a fault with its eyes, but that the eyes never really existed in the first place. All he was seeing and sensing was from the metal itself. Whether or not he had a head didn't make a difference. If he had the spare brain power he could designate to wondering about it, he'd question why Origin had built these things with heads in the first place.

Everything beyond his senses just looked to have been engulfed in the sandstorm that had passed hours ago. Just a wall of orange that nothing could be seen through. Nothing except metal itself. And there was plenty of it.

Entire battalions of mechanical soldiers were now marching in tightly squared-away formations down the sloping dune of the canyon. They were clumsy as they navigated around and between the skyscrapers that remained to peek their heads out of the sand, some of the arcanites having to march in place to keep their formation as the rest moved to get around an annoyance of a corner or an obstacle without breaking ranks.

From within this metallic mind, it made perfect sense. Controlling one of these machines was hard enough, so hard in fact that designating to them enough free will or individual attention to act as true soldiers would be all too taxing. Perhaps Origin would be able to do so if he trimmed his army down to a force of two dozen, but then he would lose the frankly absurd numbers advantage he currently held.

Each marching machine showed up in Ryza's magnetic resonance-fuelled vision as a stick-figure-like cloud of green glowing dust. Perhaps he'd show up just the same to Origin, if he could spare his mind to look for him. But there were other shapes in the misty orange beyond.

The archways.

Their metal trunks glowed solidly white as if Ryza were seeing it with the eyes he was born with. He could see the highest peaks of the structures and even follow them down through the ground as they plunged deep below the sands to the undercity that'd spawned the skyscrapers. Were they themselves arcanites, or were they something else entirely?

It was a question for later. Ahead, Ditric was still running down the hill, putting as much distance from the skyscraper that they'd just attempted to explore as she could, even if that meant putting herself closer to Origin's marching legions. Ryza spurred his arcanite's metallic legs into action and sprinted after her before she grew too distant for his machine sight.

As he caught up, Ditric started barking words at him, half out of breath and caught between whether she should yell them at the arcanite following her or directly into the ears of the body she was carrying.

'—hundreds of them! Scythes have 'em tied up good... Using the archways to throw shit at them to bowl ten over at a time. Even our fighters have come up to—'

She cut herself off and ducked, throwing Ryza's flesh body to the ground. He felt the impact on the sand distantly, almost as if it were a rude slap in the face that he couldn't identify the justification of, but before he could find his mouth to ask, one of the League of Revance's lead-betters flashed into his limited view as it careened sideways up the canyon. It disappeared from his sight as fast as it had appeared, but Ryza was relieved that, through the arcanite at least, he hadn't sensed anyone onboard the doomed buggy.

The sound of the explosion from it hitting the canyon's wall came barely a second afterwards, and the arcanite's throat whirred again as Ryza imagined a second, near identical hole in the cliff face next to the one that the lead-shell had punched.

Ditric found her feet quickly, waving her arms as if getting the attention of the battle below was a good idea, yelling the entire time.

'Archways! Stay away from the fucking—' She spun on the spot, her face contorted in surprise as if she'd just remembered something. 'Rocks!'

Fuck.

From within the machine, Ryza couldn't see them coming. Even if he managed to find safety or shelter in this form, his true body would be left out in the open, along with Ditric as she tried fruitlessly to haul him to safety.

Fuck!

Instead, Ryza dived forwards within the arcanite, only just avoiding crushing his and Ditric's delicate bones with the half ton of steel that his were made of, and wrapped his body around them as best he could. With the ground already thundering with super-accelerated rocks, he braced for impact.

The benefits of being within an arcanite like this, with this level of control, was that his sight wasn't just constricted to what was in front of his face, but that he could see everything around him. The downfall was that he had a front row seat to his potential obliteration as he watched each of the man-sized boulders rocket past. They whizzed and cracked like whips as they tumbled through the air, barely skimming the ground for the fractional moments that Ryza could sense them.

He could feel Ditric wiggling under him a second later, and he took it to mean that the danger had passed. He stood up, drawing up the arcanite's entire nine-foot-tall height as he focused his vision on the legions of metal soldiers below. He might not have been able to see the rocks themselves, but he could certainly see what they did to the arcanites.

Their tight formations rendered the machines helpless victims as the boulders blitzed through their ranks. Ryza only saw them as their glowing green outlines, but he still felt his fleshy lungs gasp in shock and awe as the mechanical soldiers were utterly obliterated by the impacts.

Some flew in every direction, reduced to nothing more than summary components. Others were flung so far that they passed through the next set of archways, picking up more speed as they turned into projectiles in their own right that careened through the next formation of their machine kin. Ryza thought he even saw one go pinwheeling up into the sky, same as the steel pylons from the first skyscraper to suffer similar damage.

The archways! That's how I can destroy them!

He found his mouth for another moment to whisper the instructions to the increasingly befuddled Ditric, but she obeyed without question. With Ryza's mechanical help, she hauled his form onto her shoulder and began a staggering run back up the canyon slope towards the nearest archway. Ryza followed, drawing out his arcanite's bolt-lock again and levelling it.

The other arcanites were beginning to spill out of the skyscraper he and Ditric had breached. They were still gathering in their formation, but Ryza could guess that as more of the arcanites in the battle down the canyon were destroyed, Origin gained more free mind power to send reinforcements into action.

Walking backwards, Ryza passed around the outside of the archway as he felt Ditric lay his fleshy body down in a shelter there.

'I don't know what you're planning, but it'd better work, because these fuckers are starting to square up.'

'Archway,' Ryza whispered back.

He relinquished control of his mouth once more as Ditric looked up at his metallic face, and he used it to nod out towards the open, hefting his bolt-lock slightly to indicate that Ditric should ready her own weapon.

She got the gist, and together, they strode out into the open. Two dozen of the arcanites had assembled outside the skyscraper's breached window, yet they still hadn't readied their weapons. Perhaps they still didn't see Ryza and Ditric as a threat. They hadn't yet shot at them, and Origin's focus was likely still tied up with the battle that was still raging down below. By what Ryza could feel and what Ditric had told him, the Scythes had figured out how to take advantage of the archways.

Now it's our turn to do the same.

'I see what you're thinking,' Ditric said coyly as she levelled her sawn-off rifle. 'Good thing I brought a few solid slugs, right?'

Ryza raised the bolt-lock effortlessly, and he felt the lips on his true face smirk.

Not as good as what I got.

Still, he allowed Ditric to take the first shot as a courtesy. The rifle kicked in her hands, but the slug fired from it flew far faster and harder than it had any right to. If someone had wanted a rifle to fire like that without the aid of the archways, then they likely wanted a set of shattered wrists as well.

The slug pounded one of the arcanite soldiers in the ribs, entirely collapsing its chest cavity and sending it dropping back on to the next rank of machines, broken beyond repair.

Then it was Ryza's turn. Pulling the bolt-lock's trigger was as simple as thinking it, not as satisfying as the hard-earned *click* that a rifle required, but it more than made up for it with the resounding *clang* that it emitted with each shot.

The bolts, weightier than a slug by a tenfold factor, utterly devastated the arcanites. It blew clean through the pelvis of the first rank to embed in the inner workings of the second. By the time Ryza had finished firing the full volley of ten bolts contained in the bolt-lock's stores, only two arcanites were left standing.

'I've always wanted to...'

She didn't need to say more. Ryza caught sight of her, both arms outstretched, a rifle in each hand and an insane leer on her face. She fired both at once, her arms nearly windmilling upwards from the unrestrained recoil, but then she roared in victorious exhilaration as both arcanites collapsed.

Within the bounds of the metal, Ryza couldn't find it in himself to enjoy the moment with her. Mainly because he suddenly couldn't feel large chunks of his body. Little did he know, but another arcanite from somewhere down the ruins had gained its revenge, even if it was by accident. His thoughts were instantly rapid and panicked as his armoured torso lurched sideways off his hips and collapsed to the ground.

His instincts took over. His legs sprinted for cover. His arms dug wildly at the sand as it flowed and collapsed around his chest. His bolt-lock, discarded somewhere a few feet away, clicked and twitched as it attempted to fire wildly, clanging incessantly despite not firing a single shot. All these things were happening separately, and suddenly his metallic body was spread all over the side of the dune.

Another colossal blast hit him, and what remained of his body shattered. Fragments of his metal limbs were writhing in the sand, skittering uselessly away from each other as Ryza tried to find a mouth within the arcanite to scream through.

But there was nothing.

Chapter Thirty

Shifting Allegiances

Pummelling slaps and roared demands for him to live guided Ryza's senses back into his true body. He felt shrunken within it as Ditric continued smacking him back to consciousness. Like he was a bug wandering inside a shell that'd been discarded by a giant creature. He found the tips of his two smallest fingers, but they were forgotten as he was suddenly thrust into the bones behind his right kneecap. They creaked and popped as the leg that stretched out from it flailed and wobbled. A tenseness punched into his throat as the entire world suddenly rocked and shifted sideways.

Everything jostled and bumped as Ryza's flickering sense of himself grew slowly to fill out all the limbs and bones that he'd left behind. His eyes came last, light flowing into them in a series of brief, painful flashes until he could force them to both stay open and focus on the wildly shifting ground that was moving below him.

Ditric's swearing and the sharp cracks of iron bolts speeding overhead got mixed up in his ears as he caught sight of the shattered arcanite he'd once been. The blood rush borne in his body was forgotten as searing grief replaced it. It had been such a brief life within the machine, but nevertheless, such a full one. Those few fleeting minutes where he'd had total and utter control over every single one of his faculties and total certainty of his purpose.

That arcanite had been built to be a warrior, just as Ryza had built himself up to be from the second he'd accepted his place within the walking fortress of Revance, but that arcanite hadn't needed to figure out what it would do after the fighting had ended. It wasn't a part of its creation. It existed to fight, and beyond that, there wasn't a single expectation for it at all.

It did not need to find its fights. It did not need to pick its battles. It did not need to leave the battlefield. It did not need to want to return to it. It was free of needs and wants, for it was a machine.

Just like Origin...

The little robot's name lingered in Ryza's mind. It was a realisation he never could've reached on his own. Not until he'd controlled a machine entirely. Until he'd died within it. What Origin had become wasn't a way to preserve his life but an attempt to shirk it entirely.

But he'd failed.

Ryza was thrown bodily against the glass wall of a skyscraper. Ditric collapsed next to him, heaving in each breath like she was attempting to steal the air for herself. The time for pondering was over. Higher pitched clangs were sounding off across the sloping canyon, coming closer and closer as they both tried to ready themselves for the next assault.

'Less of 'em... But they're...' Ditric ran out of breath again. Carrying Ryza was something she could ordinarily do with ease, but whatever had her this spent must've been worse.

'Smarter?' Ryza suggested. Even he had to pause for a moment as he readied himself for his next words. Limp as his body may've been while controlling the arcanite, it was his mind that felt battered. 'Figured it would happen... Origin was controlling too much.'

'You reckon it's him?'

Ryza nodded. 'Felt it. His resonance. Saw it from in the metal... It's all him, Ditric, and he doesn't want to be found.'

'More reason to find him before the Scythes,' Ditric grunted as she shoved slugs back into her pair of spent rifles.

Ryza pushed himself up a few inches against the glass wall so he was sitting properly, first checking there wasn't another of the soldier-like arcanites lurking on the other side within the skyscraper. As Ditric did her best to explain what had happened after his arcanite was shot to pieces, Ryza took in their surroundings.

They were back at the foot of the skyscraper they'd originally broken their way into, this time on the side closest to the canyon wall, which was only ten metres or so from the nearest point of the glass. Not much could be seen if he looked up and down the valley from here, not even the broad white trunks of the archways themselves. Down the hill, the shapes of the flying Scythes dipped in and out of view as they nimbly dodged their way up through the ruins.

They must've worked out that it was only the archways that they couldn't fly through, but they still didn't risk ascending too high, and the storm of iron-tipped projectiles still clanging out from the arcanites was keeping them distracted.

'League's taking a hammering. Scared there ain't much left of them, but I can't get a better look out there without something flying past and nearly taking my head off. Scythes drove them back to the ridgeline, but ain't pushing further.'

'Too busy with the arcanites?'

Ditric nodded, swallowing hard. 'Reckon you were right about before. Wish we hadn't hit the Scythes so hard now. We ain't got the firepower to deal with that many of the metal bastards, and the Scythes might not either.'

Ryza pushed his legs against the sand, driving his body up the glass until he was standing. He patted down his chest. The armour there still felt as chunky as when he'd first left his body, still carrying all the armaments and munitions that he'd charged into battle with. Ditric watched and did the same, pulling out one of the pipe-encased beacons that Avesta had given them.

'Don't even know if the mortars are still ready to go…'

'Ditric, if you throw that, we'll collapse the place! We'll lose Origin! If a single mortar hits an archway on the way down—'

'Go look, Ryza!' she barked. 'They're moving fast now. They'd probably dodge the bombs before they hit.'

Ryza pulled his rifle from its holster and kept it low as he edged his way to the rounded corner of the skyscraper's darkened glass wall.

Without an archway to shoot through, he wasn't expecting a single slug to do much more than make a charging arcanite flinch, but it was better than nothing.

This view only afforded him a look at half of the battlefield, but it was still enough to gauge the turning fortunes of the machines. Most lay collapsed and dormant in the ranks where they'd stood, piled atop one another like a half-hearted attempt at a mass grave. However, the few that did move were fighting forces in their own rights.

Ryza could only count a dozen of them in total, a number he doubted for how quickly they darted through the battle. Their stomping, semi-hooved feet pounded the sand hard enough to leave small craters in their wake as the arcanites sprinted through the combat. Their strides looked more like leaps, and their bolt-locks clanged loud and infrequently, though each echoing slam of metal within magnetised metal was guaranteed to fell a Scythe no matter how they spun through the air to avoid it.

The blue-robed figures had been forced back into the accidental ramparts left by the chunks of the demolished skyscrapers from earlier in the battle as the arcanites they outnumbered sprinted up and down the length of their defences, probing for a weakness or a way in. An archway stood near this fortress of ruins, but the arcanites assaulting it knew well to avoid stepping foot through it. Without the help of super-accelerated projectiles, the Scythes struggled to hit their metallic attackers, let alone wound them.

Then their tactics changed. Someone within their ranks must've been clever enough to realise they didn't need to wound them. They just needed to get them out of the fight.

Feigning a two-step retreat into the bounds of their defences, the Scythes were suddenly exposed on their right flank, a pathway into their midst suddenly unblocked. One of the arcanites seized on the moment before Ryza had even noticed the opportunity. It belted forwards with great, bounding steps with its bolt-lock ready to fire, but before it had the chance, the air snapped around it with a deafening crack that nearly threw Ryza from his feet.

The sand beneath the arcanite dropped and shunted to the side, swallowing the machine entirely before another wash of sand buried it for good. But the Scythes weren't done yet. Another blast of wind flattened the newly churned ground until it looked as flat as polished stone, and one of their number charged out. Flames streamed from their palms, and they slammed the inferno down on the sand, melting it and turning it into unrendered chunks of glass in seconds. The surface of it splintered and cracked as that Scythe retreated, but nothing buried under the freshly turned sand moved.

Ryza edged further out from the side of the skyscraper as he watched the idea take hold across the battlefield. It must've been burning through most of the ink and runes the Scythes had set out with, but it seemed to be the only effective way of countering the agile arcanites. But as Ryza watched another dozen of them rise from the dormant piles of their metal comrades, he felt his stomach drop.

No way anyone has enough ink to deal with that.

Ryza stepped back in case he drew the ire of one of the machines and muttered under his breath as he tried to count just how many there were. Must've been hundreds. Hundreds of Origin's creations, with more stashed away within the reflective glass walls of the skyscrapers.

'Told you,' Ditric said from behind him. 'Origin has got smart. Once they're done with the Scythes, they're coming for us, so we ain't got a choice.'

Ryza looked up beyond the current battlefield to the ridgeline where the leftover and battered forces of the League of Revance now sheltered. The fight there was a strange mirror of what was happening nearby. Only five or so Scythes, nimble on their feet to the point that they were flying, darted back and forth along the peaks of the rocks as they threatened to encroach on the League's desperate defences.

'Then we need to be quick,' Ryza said. 'Before they take out the mortars. If we can point them at the piles of arcanites out there before they all activate, then we can—'

'Take out the reinforcements,' Ditric said, finishing his sentence. 'Easy. Just have to make sure the Scythes don't take us out on the way.'

Ryza opened his mouth, knowing what he was about to say was a cheap shot, but Ditric read his thoughts and cut him off with a barked profanity.

'I know! I shouldn't've done it, but that's the past, and there ain't no point—'

Ryza cut her off, slamming her in her armoured chest with the grip of his rifle to knock the words back down her throat. He'd heard something over the din of the distant battle. Something close. He kept his closed fist pressed against her chest as he clamped his eyes shut, listening harder and harder for anything beyond the incessant ringing the last hour's blasts had left in his ears.

It's metal, but it's…

He opened his eyes and nodded quickly from Ditric to the glass wall next to them.

'Can you see through that?' Ryza whispered.

She glanced over, still confused, then froze. The muscles in her face went limp, and her mouth cracked open, slack beyond horror. Ryza squinted desperately at the darkened glass to see what she could, but the sun's pounding rays rendered the surface a mirror.

'What is it?'

Ditric didn't reply. Didn't even look at him. Instead, she reached up to the satchel on her chest, withdrew one of Avesta's beacons, and pressed her thumb down hard on the button. Ryza lurched away from her like the roughly cut piece of metal pipe itself was going to explode. Avesta hadn't said how long a gap there'd be from the moment the beacon was activated and when a storm of ordinance would rain down upon them.

'Ditric! What are you—?'

With a quick, jarring shake of her head, she cut him off. Her next words weren't even whispered. They were mouthed.

'Right fucken there.'

Now Ryza could truly embrace her sudden panic. It would only require a stray thought for Origin, for him to simply notice that they were here, and one of those arcanites would probably be able to burst through the wall of glass and mutilate them.

'Go!'

Ditric's shouted order came as she spiked the beacon down into the sand. Flaring spears of mortar fire shot up over the ridgeline as they started sprinting. A second later, a rapid-fire series of blasts caught up with the sight to snap in their ears. It was loud, but not as loud as the rapid pounding of their feet as they fled from the skyscraper and towards the next. Ryza glanced up in time to see the mortar shells howling across the sky, trailing tails of bright red fire as the munitions themselves wobbled in flight.

They reached the apex of their arching path before they'd even passed over the first archway. Ryza looked over his shoulder. It was like the skyscraper was still right behind them. They were too close! He sprinted faster, the sand collapsing under his feet until he was barrelling out of control towards the bounds of the nearest archway. Ditric, carried by her sheer mass, overtook Ryza, but there was no chance for either of them to slow before they were to be hurled forwards by the archway's strange effects. They could only embrace it.

In the metre before they were due to pass under it, Ryza and Ditric both leapt into the air, kicking their feet out in front of them as they prayed that whatever was about to happen wouldn't shatter their ankles. The archway took hold of them while they were still in midair, yanking them forwards with enough momentum that they flew another ten metres before they hit the ground. The force of it knocked the wind out of Ryza, and he had to fight his legs' instincts to kick and flail and find purchase, instead leaning harder into his armoured back so the metal could slide smoothly along the sand.

The small waves in the dunes bumped and rocked against his body, but he fought to keep his muscles taut as he careened towards the next skyscraper downhill. Ditric, still a few metres ahead of him, skidded to a stop before she crashed into the glass wall, diving into Ryza's path to stop him from shattering through the glass.

He'd barely recovered his senses when a snapping series of cracks sounded from high up within the archway that'd just thrown them forwards.

The mortars!

Still flat on his back, Ryza looked up as the shells pounded the walls of the skyscraper they'd just fled from. The glass didn't even shatter as each iron-tipped bomb shot through it. The sheer force of them was enough to blast entire chunks out of the exposed floors within, but the detonations that followed more than finished the job.

Entire hunks of the skyscraper fell away with each debilitating hit, exposing its delicate innards and its battalions of dormant arcanites to the next incoming shell that demolished them, in turn. Ryza and Ditric curled and cowered as shrapnel, rubble, and shards of glass pelted them from above. By the time the volley had finished, the only thing left of the skyscraper was the void where it had once stood and the sand that was rapidly draining into it.

He and Ditric rose to their feet in staggering starts, grabbing each other as their heads swam from the blasts. His feet felt unstable, like the sand itself was shifting around him, but when Ryza looked at the ground, he realised it was no illusion.

Uphill, the shape of the dunes was starting to warp. The furthest reaches of the valley lost the ridges of their dunes as the sand seemed to liquify and flow towards the newly created pit it had no chance of filling. What lay directly uphill of the void was fated to go into it, but the rest of the land was still on the move, slowly gathering into one enormous wave.

'Fuck! It's going to wipe out everyone! Ditric, what do we do?'

But by the time Ryza looked back to her, she'd already withdrawn another beacon and slammed her thumb on the button.

'Fucken RUN!'

CHAPTER THIRTY-ONE

SHIFTING SANDS

THE MORTAR BARRAGE HIT when they were only halfway to the next skyscraper. It was across the canyon instead of down, so the whole time they'd been sprinting, Ryza and Ditric battled the sand itself as it sifted across their feet and gathered momentum further up the hill. Stray bolts of iron flung across their path, snapping the air itself with loud cracks having passed through multiple archways to get to them.

If they were any closer, Ryza was certain that these bolts would've impaled them dead in the chest, but Origin's arcanites, for how efficient they were as machines of battle, still couldn't quite calculate the exact effect the archways would have on their fired projectiles.

It's fair enough. I don't have a chance of it, either.

The mortar blasts made the ground quake viciously, sending them stumbling a few paces before they could regain their speed. Fifty metres to their right, as they continued their sprint across the canyon, lay a pile of Origin's dormant soldiers. Ditric withdrew her third and final beacon without breaking stride, but before she primed it, Ryza called for her to wait.

'The sand's moving! It'll eat them!'

The limp arcanites, already half-buried by the sand where they lay, were beginning to float across the surface of it towards the recently torn hole in the ground where the second bombed skyscraper had stood.

Further down, the cacophony of clanging war stopped at the Scythe's battle lines. The arcanites there had also forgotten their fight, Origin's focus now drawn to the slowly shifting legions that were attempting to find their feet. But there were far more of the arcanites here than there were at the skirmish below.

Each one's clumsy and stumbling steps came with the screeching rusted joints, their movements mirrored across their collapsing ranks regardless of how successful they were. Soon they could only thrash in unison as the ground devoured them.

Once again, there were too many under Origin's control. Too much complication within the machines for him to save them all. Ryza and Ditric ran on, and Ryza kept looking over his shoulder to watch as rank after rank of the arcanites disappeared down the bottomless sinkhole that they'd left behind.

With the last ranks flailing on the cusp of doom, a new wave of energy seemed to burst across the beleaguered arcanites. Their movements suddenly became crisp and quick, purposeful and unique, and in no time at all, they were digging themselves out of the sand that was dragging them down and charging towards the skyscraper Ryza and Ditric had just reached.

'Ditric! He's on to us! Throw it!'

Ryza hadn't even finished his desperate shout when the silver pipe was sailing through the air. It glinted of the sun, spinning end over end before it landed in the sand fifty metres short, somewhere between them and the charging arcanites.

'I thought that would've gone longer!' Ditric shouted. 'Go! Run!'

The beacon had been lost to sight before Ryza got his straining legs into gear, consumed by the loose sand. Wherever it was, Ryza just had to hope that the arcanites would be with it when the mortars hit. He still had the runes up his sleeve to control another one of them, but if his mind went inside one of those machines again, he was certain he wouldn't be coming out.

As the distant array of artillery boomed out again, the force of arcanites simply collapsed into the sand. Ryza stared back at them as he jogged the last few paces to the next skyscraper, utterly bewildered.

They'd just escaped their mechanical demise at the hands of the hole that would've sucked them deep into the ground, only to give up.

'Ryza! Gimmie one!'

Ditric crouched next to the glass walls of the skyscraper, an almost entirely round tower that was taller than the others despite the significant slant it possessed, facing largely downhill. She'd already smashed out one of the glass panes with the muzzle of her sawn-off rifle, having used it like a hammer, and was now gesticulating with an outstretched hand for Ryza to hurry up.

Something's wrong...

Downhill, the Scythes were making short work of burying their now dormant attackers. They dashed out in efficient pairs to scoop the sand out from under the metallic corpses before they were sealed in with a layer of superheated glass. That would take care of their immediate threats, but there was still the matter of two more entire piles of inactive arcanites that lay on the sands, along with whatever else was hidden in the skyscrapers.

Ryza looked up at the skyscraper in front of him again. It rose from the ground an entire forty metres before its peak simply diffused into a mess of wires and antennae, but he knew it plunged so much deeper, a gateway to the undercity itself. The place where Origin would be hiding.

'Ryza! The sand's coming! Come on!'

He ran over to her but refused to give her a beacon. Even when she reached over to grab one from the pouch on his chest, he squabbled with her to ward her off.

'Origin's down there! The more we blast the place, the bigger the risk is that he gets buried!'

'We'll dig him up after!'

'You know how deep it is? How long it'll take? We need to go down there and find him.'

Ditric continued to argue, but the deafening thunder of the oncoming wall of sand simply erased her words from the air. Tendrils of dust reached ahead of the encroaching wave like slapping arms to claw more of the land into its ravenous bounds, now stretching sixty metres skyward. If they were caught in it, it wouldn't just buffet them like a sandstorm would. It would crush them entirely.

Ryza glanced back to Ditric's face. The dumbstruck, wide-eyed expression stretched across it a sure sign that she'd relented in her destructive whims. They didn't need the skyscraper intact to make their way down to the undercity.

It was their only chance of survival.

They both bolted in through the broken window, crouching low as they scurried along the darkening corridors bordered with glass, searching desperately for a way deeper into the heart of the tower. It didn't matter if they found arcanites in there. They were just as likely to kill them as the sand was if it caught them against the glass.

The sky outside was blotted out completely. There were only seconds left before the sand hit. They dashed around another corner, Ditric leading the way, and finally found a doorway. They dived headfirst through the door, then thrashed their way forwards as they hit the white-carpeted floor inside, throwing away all sense of caution or thoughts of checking the room for ticking men of metal.

The entire skyscraper quaked like it was on the verge of collapse as the wall of tumultuous sand engulfed it. Glass shattered across its every face with a single, earsplitting crash and torrents of dunes rumbled as they invaded through any doorway they could find, or, where they couldn't, bursting through cracked walls with sprays of rubble and artificial stone.

Ditric was pulling Ryza to his feet by the scruff of his collar as her head spun wildly, searching for another path to safety. The sand hadn't come as a single, sharp hit. It was still filling the room, sloshing loose around their feet and threatening to swallow their ankles.

The walls of the wide room they'd found themselves in weren't straight, instead they were tilted and slanted at strange angles, up and down, and they groaned and flexed as the pressure of the sand built upon them.

Ancient, untouched furniture began to shift from their fixtures as the weight of the sand uprooted them. Some sparked and flashed with bright red flares of light and fire as they were separated, then began to shrink as they were carried off from their resting places.

Ryza and Ditric backed into the walls to avoid an elongated chair as it flowed past. It may've looked innocent and unobtrusive as it went shrinking away, but Ryza could only imagine the same thing happening to him if he touched it.

'The room's filling,' Ditric said. 'Gotta go up!'

'No, down! Before it's blocked off!'

'You're crazy!'

'That's why you wanted me here, right?'

Ditric burst with a sudden bark of laughter and tamped it down as quickly as it'd come.

'Lead the way!'

If only I knew where to go...

He almost didn't have a choice in his path. The sand was now lapping across his knees. His legs were forced into a stumbling motion as he followed the flow of the red sand. He stowed his rifle, freeing his hand to grab on to whatever he could reach to keep his balance, but recoiling as he instinctively reached for one of the shrinking bits of furniture as it passed him.

The smaller it got, the faster it was carried through the room towards the other doorway the sand was disappearing through. Ryza glanced over his shoulder. There weren't any more of bits of debris like that.

At least not that I can see.

Shrinking chairs were the least of his problems. The oscillating indents of the walls bulged outwards as they strained to hold back the greater volume of sand. Cracks crept their way across the seams that'd once been indents. Small holes that'd already given way to the weight now spurted constant fine torrents of dust into the room. There were only seconds left until they burst.

Still staggering, Ryza reached the doorway at the other end of the room. He slammed into it with his chest, clamping his arm around the edge of it as his feet were picked up from under him and thrown around the corner into the corridor.

Ditric came next, stomping with high knees as rapidly as she could, only just managing to stabilise herself in the corridor before the flowing sand could carry her out the broken window. The walls that now separated them from the first room still had some time left in their resistance against the sand, though the sound of grinding steel from the first set collapsing told Ryza that it wouldn't be long.

Momentarily safe and with stable feet, he breathed hard as he surveyed the rest of the valley. His stomach dropped. Waves of violently thrashing sand were still thundering down the length of the valley. The other skyscrapers he could see were groaning under the strain just like the one that he and Ditric were in.

One of the furthest towers was beginning to sag from the barrage. There were four archways before it, and the sand seemed to have clumped up into temporary boulders, gaining so much momentum that they punched straight through one glassy wall and out the other side.

The legions of Origin's arcanites were nowhere to be seen. Sucked under the shifting sands and buried. The remaining Scythes looked to be going the same way. Those who still remained within the bounds of the ruins were the sources of echoing claps of summoned wind as they attempted to cut their way through the sandstorm towards shelter.

Ten metres below Ryza's lookout, a squad of seven of them had just dragged themselves to the lower glass walls of the embattled skyscraper and were currently breaking their way in.

Further down the way, another squad of them succumbed. Either they'd run out of axioms or the sheer force of the sand was too strong for them. If they'd been higher up in the valley, they would've only needed to withstand the barrage for a short while. The land had to run out of sand eventually.

Those beyond the ruin couldn't count on such relief. The Scythes' camp had been completely obliterated. The dirigibles had been picked up by the endless flow and swept off with the rest of the sand for another kilometre or so, where they were settling as crumpled wrecks. Only two had managed to take off, though one was ailing rapidly. It skimmed over the surface of the absorbing wash, its gondola dipping in and out of the flowing dust until it was eventually consumed.

The last remaining dirigible hovered over the scene as a tragic witness helpless to aid those still stuck in the ruin. The battle between the Scythes and the League of Revance had died down, with the latter saved by the slope that led up to their defensive ridgeline.

The skyscraper groaned again, and Ryza felt the floor start to slant beneath his feet. He and Ditric exchanged a panicked look.

'It ain't going to hold, Ryza! We gotta go up! Get above the—'

'No! Down! We get Origin!'

'There's Scythes down there now!'

The walls at their backs began to creak as well, adding to Ryza's argument. Even if they managed to climb further up the tower, it just left them with further to fall when it inevitably collapsed. Downhill, one skyscraper did just that, its upper levels severing from their place and grinding forwards, leaving no trace of where it had once stood.

'Fine! But ready the mortars! It's the only thing we've got left to scare those bastards!'

Ryza nodded, stowing his rifle, producing one of the beacons and striding past Ditric to take the lead as they searched for a way down. They moved with haste. More walls were starting to crack on their left as they skirted the glassy perimeter of the tower's innards. They soon came across a collapsed wound in the tower's flank, an ancient breach that would've once been hollow if not for the sand now vomiting through it.

Ryza stood at the edge of the floor, swaying slightly as the tower continued to teeter. The way the sand washed through wasn't a consistent flow. It came in lapping waves that undulated up and down, covering between one and three of the floors below them as it did so. Lowering himself into a crouch, Ryza readied himself to drop. He felt Ditric do the same next to him, having already figured out what he planned to do.

'How far?' she shouted over the barrage of sand.

'As far down as you can, just don't break your legs!'

She yelled something back, but Ryza didn't hear it. He'd already jumped.

He plummeted for barely a second, but even as he landed in the shifting sands, it still felt like he was falling. It sucked in his legs instantly, pulling them down further as the surface of the sand fell with the current. The first floor shot past him, something he hadn't been aiming for with how far inwards its ledge was positioned. The sand then smashed his heels against the second, buckling his knees and shocking his mind enough that he lost his place entirely.

For a moment, he wasn't sure if he was upside down or if he'd already been carried out of the tower by the flow of the sand. He thrashed out with his right arm, his gripping fist covering the button at one end of his held beacon in case he accidentally activated it, and caught his elbow against a sharp ledge.

His breath hissed out of him like a pneumatic machine as he tensed his shoulder and core, hooking all of his body weight and the dragging force of the sand against it. The sand kept flowing, the surface of it falling by another foot and putting more weight on his arm as it finally freed his legs. His elbow began to slip, and Ryza knew that if he straightened his arm now to get more of his grip onto the solid fragments of floor, he'd skid away entirely.

The sand came back with a rumbling roar, rising rapidly and densely enough that instead of absorbing his legs, it pushed them upwards, nearly breaking his grip anyway as his body was yanked along with the current. It spun him around, and he used the momentum to twist his body and throw his left arm onto the ledge as well.

Another gasp of pain escaped him as he slammed his nub of scar tissue down on the hard surface. It was like the remnant of bone within had just stabbed through the flesh itself. The sand continued to rise, lifting his legs so they were level with the rest of his body, and Ryza scrambled forwards. He only had seconds to find his feet and scan around for Ditric. Finding no sign of her, he looked out at the ruin beyond, fearing that he'd see her being washed away by the unrelenting flow.

'Ryza!'

He looked up, seeing Ditric standing on the ledge a few metres above him.

'I'll come down, just—'

'No! Go in! The sand—'

A roar from the barraging dunes cut him off, and the rising sand began to flow around his feet, forcing him to sprint further down the next corridor before he was washed away by it.

CHAPTER THIRTY-TWO

DARK ROOMS

T HE SAND RUSHING THROUGH the skyscraper's wounded side continued with its deafening howl as Ryza retreated away from it. This took him into darkened halls that muttered and groaned against a stress its architects had never intended for it to withstand. The corridors weaved and twisted without need for sharp corners or branching paths. Doorways sprouted in the walls as portals of glass without handles, and Ryza didn't dare touch them.

The light came and went as the sand that'd carried him down here rose and fell, and it was only when Ryza was well beyond it that he knelt down for a moment to gather himself. He placed the mortar beacon on the ground, holding it in place between his knees as he gently ran a finger across the activating button at the top. It still had some tenseness left in its internal spring, which meant it still hadn't been activated.

Hopefully.

Ryza swallowed hard at the doubtful thought. Maybe he was only seconds away from being pounded by a different kind of barrage. Under the surface, there was a good chance he wouldn't even feel it over the strife currently rocking the buried tower. But Ditric would. She was still on the floor above him, potentially still exposed.

Nothing I can do about it now.

If there was anyone that would survive something like that, it would be her. She'd find her way down, Ryza reassured himself. As long as she didn't run into the Scythes along the way. Ryza held his breath as he tried to remember where he'd seen them breach the tower, but with how fast the sand had been coursing around them, it was impossible to tell if it had been at his level, Ditric's, or somewhere else.

It was another thing he couldn't change, he decided. After blindly fumbling through the various pouches and satchels affixed to his armour, he produced the small, tubular torch he'd made for himself weeks ago.

It was a miracle the delicate, slapdash little instrument had survived the drifter's crash, and it had been a last-minute addition to his kit for the battle. He gave it a few shakes, unable to hear the rattle over the roaring sand outside, but the green glow emerged from its cracked glass tips, nevertheless.

He slotted it back into a pouch on his chest so one end was pointing out, providing just enough light for him to see a few metres ahead. He waited another thirty seconds, hoping his eyes would adjust to see more, but all he could make out beyond the rim of the green glow was a thin haze that wafted in and out of existence. It wasn't raised dust or anything suspended in the air. It was more like the little spots that showed up in his vision if he accidentally glanced at the sun for too long.

Picking up the mortar beacon again, he stood. He blinked as he went, enough time for Archarus to appear three paces ahead of him. Ryza's thumb twitched on the button of the beacon, and his feet darted backwards, carrying him far enough that his torch's light lost Archarus' visage. The heavy *hiss-click* of his vent mask came and went as he waited for the shadow dancer to reappear, to step forwards from the shadows, but it seemed that Archarus was too stubborn for such a thing.

Another part of his fucking games.

Ryza knew he'd have to let Archarus win this one. He stepped forwards and saw the shadow dancer grinning back at him.

'I ain't got time for this,' Ryza spat through his mask.

'You don't want my help?'

'Help!? Your *help* is always some scheme that's meant to kill me!

Origin told me about your vain obsession a long time ago.'

'And now Origin is the one you hunt,' Archarus said back, his tone level. 'So, who would you trust?'

'No one.'

Ryza walked forwards, following an instinct to roughly shove past Archarus, but he simply passed through the shadow dancer's form, who turned and followed him with a stalking gait. The carpet muffled Ryza's footsteps, making them almost as quiet as Archarus'.

'But you trust yourself, don't you?'

Ryza saved his breath, the *hiss-click* of his vent mask being his only reply.

'It's a question you've already answered, Ryza, even if you did not know it. You still controlled Origin's soldier. You nearly became it, for a moment. If not for your friend, your flesh would've died, and you would've only had until your concentration within the metal broke to live out the rest of your existence.'

'Is that the life that Origin lives?'

He glanced over his shoulder to see Archarus shaking his head slightly. 'Origin lives. That is a fact in itself. You should be wary of challenging it.'

'But why should I believe you? Why should I believe him? Why should I believe anything at all? If I followed the truth of what I saw around me, if I let everything be as it should, I would've never escaped my father. I would've never destroyed Revance, never stopped Maligar... I would never have lived. I only exist because I am impossible! That's a fact you told me yourself! And now you come to challenge it?'

He looked over his shoulder again, breathless from his rambling, to see that Archarus had stopped following him. The shadow dancer lingered at the edge of his torch's light a few paces behind, his expression almost crestfallen.

'What?'

'I'm sorry for causing you such... consternation.'

'Conster— What!?'

'Trouble. Trouble in your mind. But it's necessary. You already know why.'

Ryza paused to breathe, his vent mask's clicking threatening to break his thoughts. 'Doubts,' he eventually said. 'You need me to keep doubting.'

'All do. All the Droughtlands,' Archarus said quietly. 'For your doubts are unique. They may be the only thing stopping molten flux from reaching its final, logical conclusion. Stopping my misguided work from destroying all that there will ever be, and all that was after it.'

'To salvage your legacy,' Ryza replied, echoing another set of Origin's words.

Archarus nodded, then disappeared.

As always, the shadow dancer's philosophising visits left Ryza shaken, but if that was their true purpose... He shuddered, unchaining himself from the thought. If he was to believe Archarus, then he'd have to distrust him, but that would require him to renege on that initial belief.

The two ideas were so contradictory that when Ryza's balance began to sway, he forgot entirely that his left hand wouldn't be there to catch him when his arm reached out to steady himself on the smooth and ancient wall.

His shoulder slammed into it with an armoured clang, and his right fist punched into the wall on instinct, providing enough recoiling force to throw his weight back onto his feet.

'Dammit, what am I?' Ryza grunted in frustration.

'A paradox,' a voice from the darkness ahead replied. 'An anomaly, potentially.'

Ryza thrust the mortar beacon forwards in his clenched fist like he was brandishing a weapon. The *hiss-click* of his vent mask was suddenly too rapid for him to discern if the beating pace in his ears was his panicked heart or approaching footsteps, but when Vorric came into view, he realised it could only be the former.

The hazy light of Ryza's torch caught as gleaming flashes across Vorric's sharply angular vent mask. Vorric held his sword pressed by the flat across his chest, compact but readied to lash out. His blue robes, tattered and dusty beneath his silver armour, billowed around his feet which hovered inches above the forgotten carpet. The pulsing rush of air emanating from them kicked up little cyclones of dust that spun for a moment before the hovering forms of the Scythes flanking

Vorric disturbed them yet again.

'Stay back!' Ryza snapped, thumbing the beacon's trigger.

'You'd destroy us all so simply?'

'It's what you thought I'd do, ain't it? That's why you sent me away on a set of wheels powered by a piece of a fucking rebel sun! Well, guess where that is now, Vorric!' Ryza waggled the beacon for good measure, and two of the three flanking Scythes around Vorric danced back a few floating steps. 'I won't just flatten this skyscraper. I'll turn it all to slag.'

'Was that your plan?' Vorric replied, his voice still cool, but now a touch more forceful. 'To butcher half of my people, fail to fight a flanking action, then activate these metal warriors to surround us once we'd given chase? The only thing I don't understand is... despite it being a perfect trap, why stop? Why direct your bombardments at the buildings instead of at us?'

'Why...' Ryza lost his words. Then it dawned on him. 'Why did you come here, Vorric?'

The question sent a wave of unsettled glances between Vorric and the other Scythes. Another half a dozen of them had emerged from the shadows, and Ryza could recognise Ruka among them.

'Ruka, why did you come here?'

'Because I'm with the Scythes now,' she answered.

'No, why did you, the Scythes, come here?' Ryza pressed, his thumb still ready on the beacon.

She looked to Vorric, who nodded back at her. 'We were following you, Ryza. We were tryin' to—'

'How long?' Ryza said quickly, cutting her off. 'How long have you been following me?'

'You'd be a fool for thinking we wouldn't,' Vorric said. 'We wanted to see where your journey would take you. To study it to see what instincts you followed when left to yourself and what effects you'd have on the flux when you believed you were unobserved.'

'Impossible. I would've seen you. Felt the metal in your kits.'

'You didn't,' Ruka said. 'If you had seen me, you would've talked to me, at least.'

'Ruka, you've...?'

'It's been a lonely few weeks, Ryza.'

Ryza's instinct was to apologise, but that was snubbed as Ruka spoke again.

'You were going all over the place. I tried figuring out the maps that I'd set off with to track where you were going, but it was more like you just wanted to get away from something. Thought you were going to Kyrea, then suddenly you ended up in the Scraplands where you found Origin, then you just abandoned the drifter and went north. North and north and north and then...'

'This place,' Vorric finished. 'You've been productive. In a week, you've created all these arcanites, but for what?'

Ryza couldn't focus on Vorric's question. He was still staring at Ruka, watching her eyes go wide as a shared realisation breached both their minds. Ryza spoke slowly as Vorric waited for an answer.

'I didn't go north from the Scraplands. I... I went west.'

'No,' Ruka said quickly, throwing a panicked look at Vorric. 'No! You went in that cave and then you came out. Like you were scared! Running! And you just kept running. For days and days. I didn't believe it. Couldn't. I thought you'd drop after the first few days, but you just kept going, so I kept following. I knew you'd changed and all after... after everything, but—'

'That wasn't me,' Ryza said. 'Ruka, I only got here with Ditric and the others from the League of Revance yesterday.'

Ruka pushed through the Scythes between her and Ryza, staring him dead in the eyes, her own wide as she searched for some kind of imperfection, some untruth that would make the next words she said the right ones.

'I saw you go in here, Ryza! It was you! The you I've always known!'

'The me that Holm knows as well. That the flux knows.'

'We've been led into a trap,' Vorric muttered to himself. 'Then what is the truth here, Ryza? Is it...? Are you...?'

'The real Ryza? It's too late for it to matter. There's nothing that I could tell you, that I could do, that the flux wouldn't already know you wanted to see and hear. So, you can trust me or not. What I say will still be the same.'

'Then why are *you* here?' Vorric asked, putting an uncomfortable emphasis on the word.

'To find Origin before you did. Because he is the last remaining truth created before molten flux, and if you get your hands on that truth, then the flux will be able to understand it through your eyes.'

'I see you've had plenty of time alone to think about this.'

Ryza brushed off Vorric's barb and returned one of his own.

'I have. I had help. But so did you, right?'

'Less than you'd imagine,' Vorric said after a time.

Another ripple of discontent crossed the ranks of the less than a dozen Scythes, but they all knew this was a situation too dire to challenge their leader.

'If I trust your answer and walk away, and let you find Origin, can I trust you with possession of this "truth" of yours?'

'I guess not,' Ryza replied. He glanced past Vorric's shoulder and grinned beneath his vent mask. 'But I'd trust her.'

Vorric tried to spin, but he was too late. A flash of blinding light all but erased the corridor from sight, leaving them stunned and shouting as they tried to find the source of the thundering set of bootsteps coming from further down the corridor.

When their vision collectively returned, another had joined their number. With one arm tightly wrapped around Vorric's neck, Ditric's vent mask rattled as she chuckled, the muzzle of her sawn-off rifle pressed hard into Vorric's temple.

'Good to see ya again, Vorric. Sorry 'bout your little camp and all that, but you were in the way, and I reckon you would've done the same to us. Just like you do to all those poor bastards coming to Breggesa to help, eh?'

'Ditric, we're in a trap,' Vorric hissed.

In response, she pushed on the rifle harder, breaking the tension of Vorric's neck and tilting his head to the side.

'Yeah, yeah, I heard it all. But that don't change much, does it? Don't change how many people got marched into the wastes of Kyrea like they could ever clean it up?'

'Vorric, what's she talking about?' Ruka asked.

'Things that needed to happen,' Vorric grunted back. 'Things we can kill each other for later. And your hands aren't clean, either. I should rip your lungs out for the unprovoked attack you and your mercenaries mounted today. But we won't have a chance at doing so unless we work—'

'Work together?' Ditric spat. 'Wouldn't even listen to us, would you? Because you need to be in control. You know what's right! What's meant to happen! Even if you grind everyone else's blood into the dust!'

'He hasn't got a choice,' Ryza shouted. 'Put it down, Ditric. We're here now. So is Origin, along with a force he built to stop anyone from finding him and a version of me that's already had a week to try. Origin's still our only chance at stopping the flux. I don't know how or why, but that's probably the only way it's going to work.'

'A certainty in an uncertainty,' Vorric said with a stifled voice.

'How do you know those words?' Ryza snapped. 'They were only said to me by—'

'Certainty, Ryza. That's how.'

CHAPTER THIRTY-THREE

DISTRUST

RYZA'S THOUGHTS HAD STRAYED into the territory of "understatements" many times, but to call what followed between him, Ditric, and the Scythes an uneasy alliance was a redefining moment for the phrase.

Even though it had been him who'd told Ditric to lower her rifle, complete with twitching trigger finger, from Vorric's dented temple, he'd been tempted to turn back on the request when he glanced the murderous look in Ruka's eyes. It wasn't one directed at him.

Vorric likely felt Ruka's blue eyes burning into the back of his head as Ditric finally relinquished him, but with Ditric still so close, so ready to kill, it wasn't something he could address.

Ryza knew that kind of look. The disbelief of the deceived. It inspired a guilt within himself for inadvertently allowing Ruka to go off following a flux-born copy of him for so many weeks. It was something he wouldn't have been able to control, but his anxious mind still toyed with ways he could've prevented it.

Vorric was responsible for her fruitless pursuit, and as such, the fall of the Scythes into this trap set by either Origin or the flux. His hidden motives, his clandestine gambit, it had all led to this violent and fumbling battle between the League of Revance and the Scythes.

As Ryza, Ditric, and Vorric quietly corroborated their differing perspectives of how their paths had crossed, Ryza felt a niggling realisation grow in the back of his mind. Something Vorric had said earlier was still bothering him. Just a few words.

A certainty in an uncertainty.

They were almost the same as something Archarus had said to him weeks ago, when the shadow dancer had continued to probe at the edges of Ryza's reality. But they'd been alone then. Just Ryza and Archarus. If Ruka was to be believed, she'd already left to follow the false copy of himself that'd emerged from the Scraplands.

But how could he have known?

Five words were few enough to chance a coincidence, but no degree of luck could've ever produced the piercing understanding that had come from Vorric's eyes when he'd said them. Vorric's own nameless shadow dancer must've been spying the conversation, yet this was something Archarus would've surely detected unless he was also in league with Vorric's phantom.

And yet the word "certainty" still rang in Ryza's head. He couldn't stop it from doing so, by how many times it had been said to him in the past weeks. But if that certainty was something Vorric was relying on, then did Vorric already know what was going to happen this day? These past weeks, even? Did he assemble his compatriots in a camp, awaiting the destruction that Ditric would burn a path with, because that was the vision of the future that he'd had whispered to him?

Why let it happen? All the death and destruction? If he knew of it, why not try to prevent it? Maybe those were the same questions that Ruka was silently asking of Vorric now and getting no reply to. Ryza couldn't find a way to ask them, himself. There was no answer that Vorric could give that would still allow him to call the man an ally.

At least that gave him something else to ponder aside from the clone of him that'd wandered the Droughtlands. The League of Revance might've already have dealt with the Ryz-ain'ts, but they treated them has hollow copies of what they were truly waiting for. Maybe that was why Ruka was so easily deceived. She only saw what she saw, not what should be. The same doctrine that now had her questioning her very loyalty to Vorric.

With Vorric and Ditric deeply ensconced in a terse discussion of differing plans, Ryza took the opportunity to slip away from the conversation. The other Scythes had arrayed themselves through the rest of the corridor, standing guard at either end, or at the sides of doorways, as they waited for more mechanical foes to leap out.

The rumbling of the sands above had lessened, but not enough to ensure that the lands had settled. This was the subject of Vorric and Ditric's current debate. They had no idea what the surface looked like, nor what remaining battle was still being fought. As far as they knew, Avesta still had the mortars primed and ready to fire, a fact Ryza kept in his mind as his thumb strayed ever closer to the beacon's trigger.

But below, the possibilities were endless. Deluged with loosened sand, limp and swallowed arcanites, and the wreckage of shattered skyscrapers, whatever trap or complex Origin or the molten flux itself had waiting for them would be in disarray. It was as good a time as any to raid its depths, Ditric kept saying, as the forces working against them would be off-guard.

Vorric's caution couldn't be suppressed, despite his reluctant agreement, and he steered the course of the argument to the matter of how they'd perform the descent.

Their heated bickering overrode the sound of Ryza's soft bootsteps as he approached Ruka, and he caught her by surprise as he cleared his throat. She turned with a start, then nudged the other Scythe, a much taller woman standing with her, who departed with a nod, but not before regarding Ryza with a long and wary look.

Ryza made sure to stare back before taking her place next to Ruka, guarding the far end of the corridor from where he'd entered it. They didn't look at each other. They just stared into the darkness that hovered thickly a few feet ahead of them.

'I shouldn't have left. I was stupid for thinking it was the right thing to do. Stupid for trusting Vorric telling me as much,' Ryza said quietly, his words almost staying trapped behind his vent mask.

Ruka heard them, nonetheless. It took a while for her to reply.

'I didn't know about the refugees. Or I did, but... not about Kyrea, not whatever else. Can't tell you what it was like in Breggesa from inside the Scythes and the Academy. The whole time, I knew I wasn't meant to be there. I was barely getting together all the letters and stuff on learning to read, but at the same time there was always something else happening. Somewhere else Vorric needed me to be. I was just... I was just blind to it.'

'Not because you couldn't see it, but because there was just too much to see, right?'

'Yeah, that's about it.'

Ryza tilted his head slightly to glance down at her. She still stood as stoically as she could. A soldier's instinct that still hadn't left her.

'I got tricked into the Locusts in the same way.'

'That was a whole fucking mess,' Ruka said, her ensuing chuckle coming through her vent mask as a metallic rasp.

'Yeah,' Ryza said softly. 'But it had to happen, didn't it? I wouldn't have found out about Origin, or lost him down in the ruins, or—'

'Lost Gry,' Ruka said, cutting him off.

Ryza swallowed, but not hard enough.

'You saying he needed to die?' Ruka asked tersely.

'No,' Ryza replied quickly. 'Still wonder how I could've saved him, apart from never bringing him into those ruins in the first place. But it's just how it played out. Maybe if he didn't... if he didn't...' Ryza sighed as he steadied himself, sparing another glance at Ruka. 'Could've been someone else, you know?'

'Could've been all of us. We're still here, though.' She paused for a moment, finally turning her head, not to look at Ryza, but to catch sight of Ditric, who was still ten paces away and suitably distracted. 'She right about everything?'

'I trust her. I ain't seen Kyrea myself, but Ditric ain't one to lie. Too stubborn to, I reckon.'

Ruka chuckled again, but it was short-lived.

'Makes me wonder about Vorric. I know he's got a reason, and I believe it's a good one, but that's a lot of lives to end...'

'You talking about the refugees?' Ryza asked quietly. 'Kyrea?'

Ruka nodded. 'I still gotta trust him. Even if I don't right now, I still gotta trust him.'

'You're right,' Ryza said. He glanced past his shoulder to make sure no other Scythes were close enough to listen. The few that nearby seemed too distracted anyway. Their ears were focused on detecting something that wasn't words. 'He should've seen us coming. The League of Revance, I mean. We were camped out behind you over the ridge for a whole day, and he didn't have a single scout patrolling.

Vorric's not that dumb. He ain't a bright-eyes like we were when we got pulled aboard Revance. He let this happen, Ruka. Let all those Scythes get killed before leading the rest into a battle that would tear them to shreds.'

'He did it on purpose?'

'I think so. And he wouldn't do it without a reason.'

'A real fucking good one,' Ruka growled through clenched teeth.

Before the animosity could sprout further between them, Ditric's call split the air, making them all flinch. It was the loudest sound they'd heard in the last ten minutes. It was something that felt forbidden in a place that already had such a tenuous grasp on reality.

'Ryza! Over here. We need you.'

He turned and obeyed, giving Ruka a nudge that he hoped could be interpreted as friendly. Vorric and Ditric watched him as he approached. They didn't look impatient, but something close to it.

Unsettled.

It was enough to make them both leery of meeting his eyes, a hesitancy they hid by scanning the darkened reaches of the corridor's branching rooms. Ryza felt no such fear himself, and the three of them stood in silence for a moment as he waited for them to break it. A few heartbeats later, Ryza got impatient.

'We're just friends now, are we?'

'You have a twisted idea of friendship, Ryza,' Vorric replied. 'Though with your past, I can't say it would be fair to expect anything else.'

'We ain't fucken friends. Well, you and me, Ryza, but—' Ditric shut up before she could drag herself into the minutiae. 'We're going to go down. We're finding Origin.'

'And who gets him?' Ryza asked, glancing at Vorric.

'She does,' Vorric replied. 'I'm not sure what she plans to do with the arcanite after that, but if that's the way matters must be...'

Ryza's brow twitched, causing the upper edges of his cheekbones to dig into the edge of his vent mask. 'And you'd know that for a fact?'

'Know what?' Ditric asked.

'How things are meant to be. It's like you've been clumsy, Vorric. Even just now, letting Ditric sneak up behind you. Surely something you would've sensed, right?'

Vorric didn't answer. Staying silent, Ryza could almost hear the man counting out the seconds in his head, so he interrupted before that count could finish.

'No, you know more than you let on, but I know that you can't tell me, can you? You can't risk putting another idea in my mind. But I still can't tell if this is leading to another trap of yours.'

'We're already in one,' Vorric retorted.

'Yeah, whose?' Ditric said.

'That's exactly what we need to find out. But it isn't mine. I can promise you that, even if it is something you can't trust. The only way you can find out is by moving forwards, which is why we need you, Ryza. The flux will just kill the rest of us if we face it alone. But it wants something more from you.'

'The flux doesn't want,' Ryza said quickly.

'But you want it to want. That's why it copied you, did it not? Led Ruka to this place where Origin ended up, as if the flux sensed that, deep down, you needed our help.'

'It's fucked, but he's right,' Ditric added.

'I agree with the first half of that,' Ryza muttered. 'I'll lead the way.'

'And put the damn beacon away,' Ditric said. 'Don't even know if Avesta's still up there, and fuck, I hope she is, but the last thing we need is half a rebel sun burning down on our heads.'

A part of Ryza wanted to disagree with her. He still didn't trust Vorric, especially with how reticent he'd been when prompted to reveal the full extent of his knowledge, but a look from Ruka as he walked past her and into the lead was enough to convince him. She had to trust Vorric, even if she didn't fully know why, just like she now had to trust Ryza as well.

He stowed the beacon safely in the small satchel on his armoured chest and replaced its weight in his hand with his sawn-off rifle. He paused at the next corridor corner to fiddle with it, swapping the loaded shell for a red-marked incendiary one, then held the weapon level as he rounded the bend.

He found nothing to shoot at, but that wasn't much of a relief. Being in the thick of the action meant all he needed to do was react, to rely on his wits to survive. If they failed, at least he wouldn't have time to think about it.

Here, his mind analysed and challenged every single decision. Each step was a potential failure, not just by where he placed his boot but by how it landed on the dusty carpet, as if that would make the difference between safety and triggering an unexpectedly inscrutable response from the ruins.

He glanced back to see Ruka and the taller Scythe that'd stood by her side earlier following him. Their blades had been swapped out for other strange little handheld instruments of brass and copper. Dials and needles spun within their shells, alternating in the direction they pointed for all manner of inexplicable reason. But these instruments were only a distraction from the careful way they eyed Ryza's own movements.

Each step, even each hissing breath, was copied meticulously by them, an act that was passed down the line of Scythes until it reached Ditric, who was bringing up the rear and paid no attention to such a performance.

Ryza continued to lead the slow and careful circuit of the ruin's corridors, pausing before doorways that lay open to let the air emanating from them breeze across his exposed forehead, deciding based on how it felt on his skin whether that path was safe. Most weren't.

The first stairwell he came across looked promising for a descent, yet as Ryza lingered at the threshold of it, he remembered to look up. Upside down, sand had gathered in a sloping wall like the underside of the cliff above, but only trickling tendrils a few inches long managed to interrupt the smooth ceiling it formed.

Ryza moved on, and the Scythes followed without protest. A hissing wash of sound trickled from the next set of stairs they found. Inside, sand from above flowed across the steps as an obscuring blanket, looping down the twisting triangular landings without so much as a single grain leaping stray from the path. If Ryza's eyes weren't as good as they were, he'd mistake the dust for a stationary dune. He glanced back at Ruka.

'I can find another one.'

'Can you?'

'I could. But this is the best we've got, and I ain't sure we're going to get better.'

She nodded and stepped forward, surveying the staircase from his left side.

'I'll go first, then.'

'No.'

But it was too late. A rune must've burned in her palm, because another wave of air pulsed over them, lifting her feet a few inches above the ground. The only way Ryza could've stopped her before she hovered her way in was if he shot her in the back with his rifle.

Instead, he had to watch helplessly as the tips of Ruka's boots skimmed over the flowing sand. She leaned down and squinted at the shifting surface, the angled tips of her vent mask close enough to it that her exhaling breath fluttered against the sandy surface as it clattered out the forward valves.

There she hovered, as still as the air in Ryza's unbreathing lungs, seeing something that he could only strain to recognise himself.

'It goes up.'

Ruka's words rattled through the workings of her vent mask, the first full exhalation of breath since she'd lifted her feet from the ground. The gentle force of it was enough to impact the flow of the constantly rushing sand, imprinting a depression in the surface that was quickly washed away by the current.

Just as she'd said, it went upwards, swooping around the corner of the landing before disappearing into the darkened depths above. Once it had gone, Ruka straightened up and floated back to Ryza. He stepped out of the way to clear a space for her feet to land, and the *hiss-click* of her vent mask briefly hit a rapid pace as she caught her breath. A Reythurist's magic stole the very air from their lungs, so speaking while employing such a manifestation shortened the time it could be held on to.

Ruka didn't wait for words to return to her as she continued to demonstrate the discovery. She drew her sword from the sling at her hip and held the point over the flowing sand. A few quick dips of her wrist carved a series of divots into the stream, all of which were carried up the stairs as predicted.

'Why would it do that?' the Scythe at Ryza's side asked. 'Vorric. Your thoughts? I believe there's a record of something similar.'

The other Scythes stepped aside for Vorric to come closer, Ditric following with a disgruntled expression and the muttered reprieve of 'now what?'

Vorric only risked a quick glance up and down the odd stairs before pulling his head back from over the threshold.

'You're right, Pastina, but watch your words.' He glanced at Ryza, then focused back on the stairs. 'It's an effect of the ruins, though likely not a purposeful one. There's potential that recent acts of destruction could've triggered it, but why it would take this form...'

'Could be a defence,' Ditric suggested. 'Keeps sand out of the undercity by shooting it all back up.'

'But would it end up anywhere?' Vorric replied. 'No... I think it's something else.'

Ryza glanced between the pair of them, sensing another bickering session about to start. 'Whatever it is, what do we do with it?'

'Your call, Ryza. You're leading our way,' Vorric said.

From behind his vent mask, Ryza sighed, making the mechanisms rattle. It had been easier to follow his instincts when he was alone, but now there were so many sharp minds to consult, some of which he even trusted, he could barely do the same for himself. Steeling himself, he pushed through the hesitation and stepped through to the rushing stairs.

The sand fizzed with envy as its course broke around his ankles. The grains were fine, fine enough that he'd likely be inhaling them if not for the vent mask, yet they still couldn't find a way in through the tightly strapped leather beneath the armoured plates of his boots. The disruption caused a lull beyond it deep enough to reveal the edge of the next step. Ryza lifted his left foot, careful to avoid losing his balance, and pressed the arch of his boot's sole against the unbroken stone edge. It held, not even creaking as he pressed more weight against it.

'Your thoughts, Ryza?' Vorric asked.

Ryza looked back to Ditric and the Scythes, all waiting with a studious curiosity. Whatever he said next, they'd believe. Maybe that would be enough for him to believe it, too.

'Sand falls. It covers what lies below. That's where we want to go. We follow the sand. Up.'

Chapter Thirty-Four

What Lies Below

RYZA KEPT HIS MIND focused as he led the journey upwards. All stray thoughts were erased in a bombardment of blind faith that what he was doing was correct. The concept of it being correct didn't matter, because at this point, he'd come closer to the flux than anyone else in the Droughtlands ever had. Maybe closer than even those-of-glass, despite it being their creation.

Each doorway or torn void in the walls that would've led to another perplexing layer of the skyscraper was a struggle to ignore, but Ryza pushed on despite the way the upwards-flowing sand dragged his feet towards exploration.

Ruka was the first to follow him, and the hardest to keep out of his mind. His solace of travelling alone, of not risking the life of another Reythurist he cared about, was once again gone. The dozen or so Scythes that followed her, still backed up by Ditric, may've shared equal stakes in their fear of dying away from the sky, but at least Ryza knew they'd always had some kind of choice in their ventures.

Ryza's interpretation of Ruka's story was that she'd always been a child of her circumstances, and in a way, he felt a kinship with that. The way that they'd grown up and been moulded by a world of unkindness around them. It wasn't a thought he could share with her, however. He knew the differences she'd point out. The reels. The power. The blood that soaked his hands. But it had still pulled them towards the same destiny aboard Revance. Towards those treacherous ventures into the cities below the sands.

Ryza couldn't tell if Ruka's current venture was another one of circumstance for her. Had she followed Vorric back to Breggesa to join the Scythes because she felt she had no choice? Why hadn't she joined Ditric in the formation of the League of Revance?

Ryza glanced back at her, catching view of Ruka just as she glanced back at her own compatriots. Maybe she'd finally had a choice, after all. It was just bitter to his mind that she'd chosen Vorric instead of him and Ditric.

That bitterness wasn't a grudge. Ryza kept telling himself as much as he tried to cement the new alliance with the Scythes in his mind. It was another circumstance they could not avoid. Just as Ruka now couldn't avoid following him below the ground.

The stairs were growing wider and broader in shape as the climb wore on. They became grand enough that the flowing sand struggled to leap over the next rise to continue its journey. Soon only scattered grains crunched under Ryza's boots, trapped between battered leather and impossibly polished stone that shone like mirrors.

Slits of glass appeared in the walls as narrow, arching windows. Whatever lay beyond them was too dark to make out, unless Ryza was foolish enough to press his face to its surface, but their forms reminded him of the glowing gouges that had painted the walls in the tunnels below Iroka.

The similarities were uncanny, but Ryza didn't draw conclusions from it. He couldn't. To do so would be too dangerous.

The sand had all but subsided now. The stray grains that Ryza could spot in the dim glow of their collective torches and glow orbs were the idle ones that'd fallen from their clothes. Up ahead, the stairs had stopped at a final landing, a place flanked on both sides by a pair of low walls. Their smooth surfaces were made up of square metal panels where once white paint peeled from their connecting edges.

Ryza hesitated after drawing near enough to observe the decay. It was a strange thing to see in the world left by those-of-glass. The objects those ancient, extinct people had built were practically eternal, be it through impossible workmanship or unknowable magics. Ryza's hand hovered close to one of the flaking edges of the paint. He still held his rifle, so it was only with his outstretched index finger that he could touch it.

Gently, he slid the seam of the leather at the tip of his gloved finger under a flake the size of his thumbnail. He tried to pull at it, but only the leather of his glove bent, tugging it across the rest of his fingers. He pushed in his index finger and tried again, exerting more force than could possibly be needed for such a thing, but his bones and tendons relented before the paint chip did.

It was strange. Just an hour ago, the once dormant weapons cobbled together by Revance's now dead armourers had been enough to topple entire skyscrapers through the very ground that had hidden their bulk, but now his own hand couldn't chip away at the ongoing decay within.

Maybe that's how I expected it to go...

Ryza moved on before the others could question his findings. If they did, they might just arrive at the same conclusion.

Ruka and the others didn't follow him as he edged up the last few steps. Where Ryza had emerged was no longer within a building. There was a ceiling, but that was only a flat sail of metal held up by five unequally dispersed pylons, a mimicry of the roofs within the skyscraper. No walls, windows, or doors separated Ryza from the undercity now. He turned back to the others and waved his fist twice at them, signalling for them to wait.

When he was sure they'd gotten the message, he began to explore. Tentatively at first, telling himself that he wouldn't stray from their sight, but each step forwards revealed another tantalising view of the undercity's reaches, along with another razor-straight band of sunlight. Ryza eventually emerged from under the false ceiling and had to stop himself from gasping as his eyes began to feast on the scene.

The sunlight was not a trick of the undercity. It was natural. Their sun from above. The bottomless pits that'd been left in the surface of the ruins turned out not to be bottomless, for their end was now where he stood. The cavern's ceiling of rough and jagged stone continued to crumble gently around the sites of the puncture wounds where skyscrapers had once breached through. Sand trickled in as light billowed past it.

The latter caught in the former like a torrent of silent sparks. The remaining skyscrapers surrounding them, more numerous than they'd been above, crudely reflected the sand falls as blurred, vertical beams of orange light. It might've been that Ryza's eyes were still struggling to absorb the sheer perspective of it, but the reflections didn't seem to lie on the glass itself, but instead from deep within the hearts of the silent skyscrapers.

The towers themselves were pristine. Untouched from the moment they'd been completed, despite the colossal lumps of debris that sat among their number. They were the graves of the skyscrapers that he and Ditric had destroyed. Chalky dust swirled in the air over their undulating wrecks like the spirits of those who'd once lived in them.

The wide archways of above had not been affected by such destruction, yet they weren't entirely immune to it. The enormous beams of white metal narrowed and converged as they drew closer to the ground, where a scaly rash of rust pickled at their exteriors. Even though they'd spanned the width of the ruins above ground, the space between the pairs shrunk to only be broad enough to be a metre in width. Each pair still kept the same spacing from the next, however, so the series of them formed a strange avenue that ran straight down the centre of the undercity.

Ryza squinted as if it would help him see what lay at the other end, but it was no use. The breaching rays of sunlight weren't angled to illuminate it. Even if they could, the fresh sand dunes that now gathered throughout the undercity had come in swooping waves to block the view from the ground. The surface of them looked more orange than usual, perhaps owing to the contrast provided by the polished stone on which it sat.

Sand didn't gather around the bases of the narrowed archways, however. Clear stone exploded out either end of the rusted opening, so if one were to look at it from above, it would take the pattern of an hourglass' silhouette.

Before he could stare too long at the nearest archway, which stood around fifty metres away, Ryza turned back to beckon the others out of the stairs.

They waited for Vorric's order to do so, and when they moved, they moved as a cohesive unit. It was a well-drilled dance, to the point that Ryza could tell each of their steps were measured, as some of the shorter members among the Scythes were taking notably larger strides as to not lose pace with the others.

Ditric rushed out after them, her sawn-off rifle held high and ready, all of the gracefulness having been sucked out of the air before she could've helped herself to a bite of it.

'What about the arcanites?' she barked at Ryza. 'Where are they? Why aren't they attacking us? We've invaded their...'

'It's not their city, Ditric,' Ryza said quietly. He pointed towards one of the nearer dunes, a large hill that'd gathered in the sun under a rent in the cavern. Inert metal limbs stuck out from the surface, yet the sand itself was smooth. The arcanites hadn't moved an inch since they'd fallen. Had Origin fully relinquished control of them or was he waiting to spring into action?

Ryza began to make his way towards the half-buried bodies. Hissed calls to retreat came from the Scythes as he exited from the bounds of their perimeter, but Ditric bellowed at them to shut it as she followed him. Her voice, the words now indiscernible, was still echoing through the cavern when Ryza knelt in front of the nearest arcanite. Strangely enough, the sound had become a higher pitch than anything he'd heard Ditric's mouth produce, too.

He looked up at the archways before going back to the arcanite. Maybe it was something to do with those? The closest was now a few paces away, though the void within it didn't face them. Ryza caught himself staring at the rust that coated its surface. It was a layer separate from the white metal itself. As he ran his eyes up the length of the archway, he could pick out the thickened veins from which the rust itself sprouted and snaked out from. It wasn't a part of the archway. It was a parasite.

Ryza glanced back to the arcanite. Only a chunk of its shoulder and its upper arm remained above the sand. The machinery was just like that of the contraption he'd occupied in his mind, yet he still had to look closely and think slowly to distinguish all the little wires and workings that would've made the arcanite operable.

It was one of those strange things about being a Kretatic, Ryza thought to himself. They had all the ability in the world to move metal with just their minds, but the focus of their experience was in finding any other way to do so. The less metal that *they* needed to move, the less stress on their mind, which was why such complex mechanisms commonly occupied arcanites' guts, even if they were time-consuming to create.

Ryza knew well why Origin would do such a thing for this defeated army of arcanites, but the question that plagued him was how? Not in the terms of the execution or construction; Ryza had faith in Origin's abilities as a fabricator of machines. How had Origin had the time to create all of them?

Unless there was more than one of him.

With a growing sense of noxious dread, Ryza looked up at the rest of the fresh grave that entombed the fallen arcanites. Could they be more than just mere arcanites? He'd wondered for a long while if there was another version of Origin out there, but he'd never considered that there could be thousands. Had there always been or was the creation of these immortal iterations recent?

Maligar.

Ryza's mind flashed back to what had once been his desperate final moments in the tunnels beneath Iroka, where a gloating manifestation of Maligar from within the molten flux itself had shown off the replicas he'd created of Origin's bones. There had been thousands. Ryza stowed the beacon and used his free hand to sift aside the sand covering the dormant arcanite's faceplate.

And now there are thousands here.

But why weren't they doing anything? Why had so many of them given up in the midst of the fight? Ryza straightened up and returned to the supposed safety of the Scythes' perimeter. Ditric followed, battering him with questions.

'No flux, no Holm, what the fuck's down here, Ryza? Where's Origin? I thought this place would be more like the other undercity with all the—'

'Doesn't matter that it ain't,' Ryza said. 'Can't take anything as a given here. Nothing's ever going to be like you thought it was before, I mean. That's how these places work, right, Vorric?'

Vorric nodded. 'They may've been created by the same people, but the intention behind them has been so long lost that their purposes have been warped.' He dropped his voice to a quieter register, for what good it would do. 'You've observed the rust, Ryza?'

'I have.'

'Have you ever seen rust in a place like this?'

Ryza shook his head as he held Vorric's gaze. It was the only thing stopping either of them from looking back at what coated the archways' white metal.

'Why would it decay?' Vorric asked.

He glanced sideways at Ditric, who'd also been near enough to hear the question, but she looked to Ryza for an answer, as did the others.

'Either it's been used or forgotten. If Origin came back here, he would've had a reason more than it being a hiding place.'

'So, he's using this place for something?'

Ryza nodded at Ditric's answer, then pointed to the far end of the ruins.

'Over there. Has to be. Everything behind us is stone and glass, but it hasn't been destroyed by anything hurling through it like what happened above.'

'I was foolish for letting my people fall victim to that,' Vorric muttered to himself.

'Were you?' Ryza asked pointedly.

Vorric returned his gaze but didn't see fit to reply.

'Come on,' he eventually said. 'We need to chart this place.'

Vorric doled out orders to his Scythes with a series of waving hands and halted words, splitting the remaining party of them into an even number of scouting guards and cautious scholars, the latter producing compact scanning devices from within their robes. Ryza kept glancing at them as they walked, his eyes drawn by the strange glows they emitted and the little metallic pings they made when waved too close to a wall of unbroken glass.

He didn't trust them. He knew his own instincts were better. But whatever comfort the rest found in their faithful machines was a pleasure he couldn't bring himself to snatch away. It was something he'd once had. Something he now dearly missed.

With each archway they passed, Vorric instructed them all to stand far back as he carefully threw a handful of freshly scooped sand through its bounds. The results were as disconcerting as they were ordinary, the sand failing to accelerate as it would above. Ryza privately theorised that it was something to do with the rust that sometimes stretched as high as the cavern roof itself, yet the fifth archway they tested was clean, disproving the idea.

Maybe it's the sunlight. Maybe it's that we're expecting it. Maybe it's for no reason at all.

Ryza's impatience bubbled beneath his skin with each experimental delay as another theory came to his mind. These things were a distraction. Just like Origin's army. Just like everything else. A curiosity to delay him from reaching a conclusion he'd been on the cusp of all along.

When they reached the seventh archway, Ryza didn't stop with the rest of the group. Vorric called for him to halt. Ditric demanded. Ruka even followed him enough to plead. But Ryza was deaf to it, for he could finally see what lay at the other end of the undercity. A place he'd sworn he'd never go again. A place he knew the others would not follow.

The tunnels.

CHAPTER THIRTY-FIVE

A LIMITED LIFE

THE GRANDEUR OF THE ruins fell away from Ryza's peripherals as his legs walked as if they were stilts towards the stretching maw of the tunnel. It was as broad as the entire undercity and tall enough to almost touch the cavern's ceiling.

Just as I remember it.

That was what the archways were leading to. What they'd been built for. With great speed, they could fire an object down through these enormous passages, covering months' worth of travel in minutes. Ryza turned to face the undercity again, the forms of his uneasy comrades now only stubble on the face of the fallen sand. Something didn't make sense to him.

Why build a tunnel above ground?

Because these skyscrapers, these grand pillars of glass and steel, they must've once been above ground themselves. It would be absurd to build as if this cavern had already existed, and even if these places were already absurd beyond belief, this seemed a step too far. Which meant that this tunnel, this grand excavation that possibly spanned under the entire length of the Droughtlands, had been created after this ancient city. Perhaps even after it had been destroyed and abandoned.

But why? Why connect these places after they were dead and gone? Why create such vast and enormous tunnels only for them to be hidden beneath the sands with dead ends at either side? It was inexplicable. A purpose warped and twisted and decayed far beyond an original intention, but the core tenet must've still been there. A crumb of it. Anything.

'After them, but before us,' Ryza murmured to himself. 'After them... Before us...'

He turned to stare back into the beckoning tunnel. He was close enough to see the threshold where the stone of the undercity turned to steel. Upon the tunnel's walls, he could see the familiar arching gouges that rose and fell along its length. Further along, just at the point that the darkness swallowed any light cast into it, Ryza could see the beginnings of the slope leading down.

And a single, tiny, metallic figure.

Origin.

Beyond him was a familiar shoreline. One of smooth, reflective silver. It did not flow or break with waves, it just grew deeper and deeper as the tunnel continued to recede into the depths. All that interrupted it was a rickety footbridge that was as narrow as Ryza's feet if he stood with them pressed together. It was almost identical to the footbridge Origin had left him standing on the last time they'd met. As Ryza approached the shoreline, he saw that it sank into the surface of the flux like anything else would.

This tunnel wasn't always filled with flux. Not until after Origin got here.

Ryza lowered himself to a crouch, then allowed himself the short fall back to sit before Origin. The arcanite remained standing. The glow in his little green eye sockets remained dim, but stared piercingly at Ryza, nonetheless.

'This is where you came,' Ryza said. 'A place we could not find you. Not without fighting.'

Ryza waited for an answer, for Origin to reach into his mind from afar and insert a few more cryptic words to his already jumbled thoughts, but his mind remained empty. After all this time, Origin still needed to touch him.

He held out the end of his left arm, and Origin approached it. His clothes had been ripped in the battle, so there was nothing between his nub and the frigid air. He watched idly as the arcanite slowly sidestepped around it, searching for the right spot before reaching out, tapping at the scarred flesh hard enough to make Ryza wince, and forcing his resonance into the inert metal plate beneath.

The fatigue of the battle instantly caught up to Ryza as a wave of sheer exhaustion rippled out from his left arm. His bones felt like they'd crumbled to powder, held in place only by ancient muscles and flesh that'd petrified in a momentary eon. His mind slowed to a crawl, and he basked in the relief of it, feasting on Origin's words as they rang through his senses, one by one.

A reluctant test. Determination is key. Though there is no prize.

A slow smile crept across Ryza's face. He'd forgotten the strange pattern Origin spoke with. Almost missed it. How purposeful was it? How long did it take him to conjure the right words?

'You're probably right. I don't know how you'd help now. So why wait for us?'

Origin's head swivelled on his body until it had rotated to face backwards, to look out over the shoreline of patient flux. Ryza looked with him, his eyes focusing on the point where the footbridge disappeared into the silver surface.

'The flux has trapped you. Turned your escape to a prison.' Ryza paused for a moment. The words had made him think of Revance. It was a fond memory. 'You found certainty.'

The arcanite's eyes swung around to face him at a blinding speed. A rapid ticking of inner workings had come with it, the closest thing his metallic, expressionless face could portray as panic.

I'm forced to be this. This certainty is binding. Do not embrace it.

A dark chuckle took Ryza's voice before he could answer. When it subsided, his throat tickled until he coughed like a wounded man.

'Another warning?' Ryza said as his lungs recovered. 'They're always too late for me. The flux is faster.'

And magic is, too. Think of what flux must mimic. Does it become it?

'Of course it doesn't. It's still flux, it's just hidden. Waiting to turn back.'

But what lies beneath? What about pure resonance? You've long had this thought.

Origin's words echoed Archarus', but they didn't get Ryza any closer to an understanding he did not already have. He stood up and allowed himself to pace, ignoring the tinkering little footsteps of Origin's flat feet as he tottered along in his wake.

Out the corner of his eye, Ryza was aware that the others had approached to survey the conversation. Ditric had had the good sense to hold them back from drawing too near and interrupting, but Ryza knew that from the distance, he'd only look like a muttering lunatic.

They only heard one side of the conversation, but for them, what difference was that from the way they needed to speak with him, anyway? Ryza knew that his mind was a constant internal battle. He knew it was one of strife. He knew that what little trickled out his mouth as words were the staggering survivors in a war of decisions and doubts.

Maybe it was better to let them think of him as a madman. This instability was what Vorric had put his faith in when they'd ventured together into the depths of Iroka. It was what Archarus lauded in him now. What Origin was warning him against relinquishing.

'It's not that simple. I won't know the flux is gone.' Ryza paused for a moment, stopping his pacing long enough to chew his upper lip, a difficult thing with the vent mask. 'Not without a sign.'

A quick scrape of metal came from behind him, somewhere near his knees, and he turned to see Origin's jaw had dislodged and began grinding against itself in a mimicry of him. Ryza was half tempted to aim a kick at the arcanite, but he didn't have the energy. Each burst of Origin's words wore heavy on his body like the thoughts were lead weights.

Signs you'd call a trick?

There was a short pause before Origin continued. Time enough that Ryza could register something else in the magnetic resonance aching from within his arm. Something beyond the ancient exhaustion. Regret.

I believed I had won, once. I trusted the flux.

'But why try stop it? I thought flux was made *from* you. When you were alive.'

This fabrication... It's what Archarus told you. It's convenient.

Ryza ground his teeth, a sound audible through his mask, and did his best to suppress his rage for the shadow dancer.

'He's always lying... But you let me believe it? People died for that!'

If you had known... I had failed like he had... would you have saved me?

The question was an important one. Would he have brought Origin back up from the depths of the city beneath Twin Rings? Origin's question repeated through Ryza's mind again and again, leaving him unsure if the inner chanting was his doing or Origin's. No matter which it was, Ryza still gave the idea all his focus. He shut his eyes, even going as far as to stow his rifle so he could press his thumb and forefinger into the bridge of his nose until the darkness beyond his eyelids sparkled.

Origin's version of the story made more sense than Archarus', now that Ryza thought about it. Why would an immortal man of flesh and blood surrender himself to a metal prison so willingly? And once it had all gone so wrong, why not find a way out, or a way to stop it, if he really did control the flux? If he really was the source of it?

But if molten flux had come before Origin, if Origin had been the one attempting to put an end to it... then it put Ryza in the arcanite's tiny metal shoes, didn't it? Countless thousands of years later and the failure of an ever-living ancient was to be rectified by the efforts of a battered ex-conscript.

Yet Ryza still couldn't understand the full nature of Origin's question.

'There aren't enough words for how I can't understand...' Ryza said slowly. 'Can you not say more?'

Unlimited life... It calls for limitations... To give it meaning.

'But you've said that's false. That meaning's an illusion.' He grimaced down at Origin before crouching down, pulling off his gauntlet, and holding his free hand out to the arcanite. 'Tell me. Just this once?'

Origin approached his offered palm and bent slightly so his hollow eye sockets better stared into it. He stayed like this for a while. His head swivelled slightly, this way and that, as if his non-existent eyes were tracing a path across the scarred lines on Ryza's palm. When Origin's spindly little arm finally whirred as more of it spooled out to place his hand in Ryza's, another wave of his ancient resonance dulled Ryza's senses to the bone. Now his only experience of this life was Origin's deep and distant voice, echoing to him through an impassible darkness.

If you knew I was not key to the flux, that I couldn't stop it, would you have come here?

Would I have been your beacon of hope?

Your distraction?

What else would you have done? Where else would you have gone? Do you now see this as a metaphor for what the flux has done to me? That the flux blinded me to the truth it sought to conceal?

This world, the flux, this matter, it's far simpler than you believe it to be. Because for you and I, for Archarus and all the rest who died attempting to truly know the flux, we all craved complication because it allowed us to believe it.

To you, the truth is a machine. The more moving parts, the more actions and stages and gears it has, the easier it is to believe in its extraordinary results without understanding its parts or processes.

But if this engine of life was stripped down to a single function, to one single movement that achieved the exact same result as its complex cousin, would you still trust it to produce such a thing? For this is the comparison, the divide that exists between molten flux and pure resonance. The mimicry and the magic. This was the purpose of my original warning.

You control machines.

Not in the sense of you as a Kretatic, or as your hands on the inputs of metal contraptions, but in humanity's innate need to create complex structures to fill the void to a point of strain where a simple one would fit comfortably.

Think of your factories beneath Kyrea. Of the walking fortress of Revance. Even of the skyscrapers that surround us now. All these places, these things, they were created to feed a hunger to produce more than ever could be consumed, yet this result was only capable of continuing its cycle rather than being directed towards what truly matters.

Life. Love. Happiness. Fear. Joy. Everything I have lost over this eternal lifetime within this prison of metallic flesh. Everything we attempt to preserve by stealing it from others. Everything you have forgotten in a quest to follow the instincts you have been attempting to rid yourself of since birth.

This machine will control life.

Molten flux was just one representation of my warning. It was not the thing that dominated the Droughtlands for your entire lifetime, but the greed of those who could exploit it, and the acceptance of all others who believed in the machine that was created by this greed. That believed it too complex to simply dismantle, even with the guns and violence they employed to contain it.

These machines warped all expectations, all fates, all ambitions, around themselves as a protective armour. Any attempt to destroy, dismantle, or disregard them was misguided from inception because they were all fomented from the concept of the machine's implicit eternal existence.

Do not control it.

It was a trap I fell for myself. I believed the flux to be a permanent, existential problem that needed to be seen to. You believed Revance a threat to the Droughtlands that had to be stopped at all costs. But ask yourself this, Ryza. What would've happened without you? Without the resistance? Without the battle that destroyed the fortress? Without you being a part of that machine?

Tyrag would've arrived to an empty Iroka, collected his autominds, and continued his rampage across the Droughtlands for the few days he had left before the flux consumed him entirely. But even if that had not happened, even if he had lived, what good, what result, what possibility could've come from his control of Revance?

More autominds? More factories? More weapons of war? But what war would there have been left to fight? What demands would be left for the factories to whirr and clank to fulfill? What use would a horde of autominds be in a world where they outnumbered the living? For that was Tyrag's goal. An infinite profit. Yet even if it weren't, how could a power like that which he'd acquired be dismantled from within a machine, one worked by the smelters and the Locusts, that was determined to uphold it?

If left alone and without purpose, the machine would have consumed itself in its complexity. It is something Cardan, the flux-trader, discovered in the factory he created below the place you call Twin Rings. Something Vorric will himself one day discover as Breggesa continues to burst at its seams by virtue of being the only city that exists while no others do.

It is even what those-of-glass eventually learnt in their final days. I watched them as they fought and fell. Their wounds were nothing compared to the anguished pain of realising all they'd created had been for nothing.

These skyscrapers mean nothing. These tunnels lead nowhere. They are remembered only by their baffling futility, a memory that can only be insulted by the minds that observe it while they fail to learn from it themselves.

This is my plea to you, Ryza. Not only to learn, but to forget. To see things as they are and not as they should be. Not in the sense of believing your surroundings and your instincts, but to look at the broader picture of what will come of it.

It is not shortsighted or naïve to ask if these actions will improve life. Failure to ask these questions, both from yourself and from others, led to the battle and the slaughter that you witnessed and took part in today and all throughout history.

You have lived a life obeying the rules of the machine you were born into. You believed its complexity gave it reason, even when you learnt that those reasons where either cruel or indecipherable. You fought from within its whirring workings, believing that you, yourself, were not just another cog in its construction, and when it was revealed to you, the only action left to you was to become a machine yourself.

Just as I did.

Look back on those who've followed you to these depths. They watch your every move, waiting for you to provide another input for them to respond to. They have welded themselves in as the workings of your machinery without being aware of it, because they believe that your complexity, despite it being inscrutable and beyond their understanding, is the only thing that can destroy molten flux.

Would they still do this if you told them that it was simpler than they believed? Would they still fuel your own beliefs with their trust? Would you still need that trust to enable your own pure resonance, if you knew it was unnecessary?

That is the true purpose of my warning. It was something the scholar Rettic came so close to understanding when he was confronted with molten flux, until he obeyed the rules set by the machine that is the Academy of Breggesa, and followed the curiosity he believed was innate and compulsory.

This is why you, Ryza, have a unique chance of succeeding in destroying the molten flux where I and all others have failed before you. You, your life, and your experiences were forged purely from within the bounds of the machine created by molten flux, so to destroy it, you only have to imagine the impossible.

A life without it.

You already know pure resonance as a magic that is the momentary impossible. You have already experienced it, and continue to do so, to this very moment. All you must do now is look upon the machine that surrounds you and close your eyes to it. To walk away and experience not just a life beyond it, but a total emptiness within. A void where nothing that has ever occurred may finally happen.

It is not a task that requires your death, though I will envy you if you choose it. It will be difficult to imagine yourself beyond the machine that embraces you, given your lust for purpose, but I wonder if you can find a purpose in a total lack of it.

That is what true freedom is, I've been told. It's something only discovered by those whose sense of certainty for their lives has sealed them off from ever attaining it.

Those like me.

Chapter Thirty-Six

INSTINCTS

THERE WAS A PRESSURE building in Ryza's head. Somewhere behind his left ear, an inch below the plate of his skull. It wouldn't be worth the exaggerated effort to reach across to massage it away, and he doubted if he could, in the first place. It was a common echo for him now. Two months had passed since he'd last seen Origin below the bizarre archways that'd been left by those-of-glass. The arcanite's words still rattled in his head, along with the crisp vision of what he'd done next.

The trance Origin's words had put him in must've been a deep one, because there was no other way he would've let the arcanite snatch the mortar beacon from his front pocket and push the button. The battle that followed had been brief. Ryza could still count in his muscles the amount of tugs he'd attempted to remove the deadly beacon from Origin's arms.

Two.

Only two.

It was all Ryza had been able to afford, and even those had been in vain. The metal of Origin's form had somehow become welded tight to the body of the beacon, so it hadn't taken long for Ryza to realise the futility of it. From the moment he'd started running, he'd wished he stayed to fight.

That was the last thing burned into his mind. That one look back at Origin he'd spared. He'd just been a speck against the backdrop of the yawning tunnel, watching as Ryza and the others had fled, knowing that it was, in fact, Origin's intention to die.

To be obliterated.

It was something Ryza still felt. Two months in a stone cell would do that to anyone, but it didn't help that Ryza had wrestled with the sentiment before. The potentially world-changing revelations Origin had left him with had fallen on Vorric's deaf ears once they'd finally made it to safety.

There'd been nothing left of the ruins they'd fought over, and with it, nothing left of Vorric's patience for Ryza's erraticism. Just a burning pit of fire and rage. Ryza still didn't know how many Scythes Vorric had lost that day. No one had visited his dark and cool cell to tell him. He didn't know what had become of Ditric and the rest of the League of Revance. Or Ruka. Their fates were unknown, like everything else in Breggesa.

That was where Ryza assumed he was. There'd been a span of three entire days after he'd emerged from the ruins where he hadn't seen anything but the inside of a tightly woven sack. It had been coarse on his skin. Grating against his nose and the tips of his ears, knotting up with his lank hair as it had shifted around.

He knew he'd been stripped and forced to purge himself of the rest of his runes. He knew he'd been airborne for a matter of days at a time. When he'd asked questions, a new voice always answered them. A new set of unforgiving hands to shove him around or tend to his other needs.

Now, alone in this little subterranean room, he could only wonder why they'd not yet killed him. Parcels of food were delivered once a day, but there was never enough light to truly determine what was contained within them. Ryza was sure that a few times he'd spent hours inadvertently gnawing on parts of the cloth wrappings themselves. Still, that was better than some of the things he'd choked down aboard Revance.

Whenever Ryza woke, whenever he slept, whenever he waited, whenever he threw the series of seven stray pebbles that he'd found in the carved room at the opposite corner to pass the time, he'd only been able to feel confused. Vorric had never come to ask what Origin had said to him. He couldn't be dead. He couldn't be simply too busy. Origin had been the key to stopping the flux, and after finding him, Vorric didn't want to hear the last words that the little arcanite had said?

Maybe he didn't care for them. Maybe he didn't need them. The thought had occurred to Ryza before, but it wasn't a hopeful one. What if Vorric had found a way to rid the Droughtlands of molten flux without him?

Ryza resigned himself to thinking that Vorric was justified. The thought cast him into a pit of guilt for all the destruction he'd wrought, but it was the only thing he could wallow in if he wasn't to leave his mind a blank slate.

Even if Vorric did come for him, Ryza knew that what he had to say would be of no use.

'I've made a mistake. Origin never mattered. It was always me.'

Ryza murmured the words aloud with an unpractised voice and shut his eyes to listen to their little echoes as they bounced off the small walls. Soon only the light wisp of his breath was all he could hear.

'What's Origin?'

The only other voice Ryza had heard in weeks answered his quiet confession. Still sitting on the bare floor, Ryza slid over to the small crack in the wall to hear it. Once close enough, he ran his fingers back and forth across the surface until he found the hole through which a faint breeze blew. He pressed his lips to it, pausing to savour that slight movement of air, relief from the staleness he'd been breathing, and spoke.

'Foll?'

He had to check. Sometimes she was there, sometimes she wasn't. The name and the voice of the smelter he'd captured while hunting down his father hadn't left his mind since the day he'd last seen her, abandoned in an isolated little cell in the Academy of Breggesa. How she'd come to end up here was something Ryza hadn't yet asked. He was afraid if he did so, he'd find an answer that would make him doubt her existence entirely. The feeling was strong enough when she didn't answer.

He asked again and then waited another tantalising minute to get a reply. He never pushed her on this. She'd likely been entombed in this prison for longer, and that wasn't good for one's health or alertness.

'Yeah. I'm... I'm here.'

'Origin was an arcanite,' Ryza said quickly. 'Old one. Was a man, once.'

'Can that happen?'

Ryza's lips twitched into something that was close to a smile. 'Lot of things can happen.'

'Are you that old?'

This time Ryza managed a chuckle. The sound grated in his throat. It had become unfamiliar. 'Never could be. Origin is... Origin was old. Older than those-of-glass. Probably older than whatever came before them. I could feel it when I touched him. His magnetic resonance... Now I think about it, he was probably from a time before magnetic resonances, a time when...'

'When what?'

'Don't think about it,' Ryza whispered quietly.

'Empty minds?'

Ryza felt a flash of alertness surge through him. 'Where did you hear that?'

There was a long pause. Longer than Ryza liked, but he still didn't push past it. His patience was a penance. An acceptance to know there'd one day be things he would not be told. Today, however, was not that day.

'You said it. A while back. When you found me.'

Ryza let out a small sigh of relief. There were times where he was sure that Foll's voice, her presence, it was all just another trick of his mind, and times after that where he worried those thoughts would make it so.

'That's right... That's right. I wish I hadn't.'

'Said it?'

'Found you.' Ryza paused for a moment, licking his upper lip with the very tip of his tongue as he weighed his next words. 'I'm... I'm sorry.'

Foll's reply came after another long pause.

'What for?'

'Bringing you in. Getting you stuck up in here. Like me.'

'I was already dead out there, Ryza. That's what being a smelter is. Dead without a choice. Same as Revance, eh? I almost joined. Thought I was too young, though. Guess I was wrong. Maybe we would've seen each other.'

'More likely you would've died,' Ryza replied. 'There were days I'd get sent out with ten or twenty and come back alongside only two or three. They were just... just dumb, vicious fights that didn't have no plan, no means, no prize at the end of it. Just a bunch of dead bodies that I knew... that I *knew* were going to end up being autominds.'

'Bodies like mine?'

'Yeah. Well, if it weren't for the collars around their necks, I wouldn't have been able to tell the dead of ours from the smelters. I remember this one raid we did on an ore-collecting village. Me and two others had been fighting on the outskirts. Watched the whole fight go to shit for us. Bright-eyes just running round corners and getting blown away by rifles just like what we were holding. I couldn't go in to help because then smelters would've been able to run up right behind us, but what good was covering our asses when our faces were getting pummelled?'

The question was rhetorical, but Ryza still waited in case Foll wanted to answer it. She didn't. He continued.

'All the shots stopped after a while and the last three of us decided to give it an hour, then move in. I... You ever seen what happens to sand when it gets too much blood in it? It gets chunky. Looks like hunks of freshly dug up iron until you stick your boot through it and it turns to mush. Turns out that day was an even battle, despite the losses we took, because all we found in there was a pile of corpses and the last living smelter that'd dragged them all into the middle of the village.'

'Did you kill them?'

'Maybe I should've. Weren't no need. Don't know what happened to him exactly, but he looked like he was in a worse state than the dead. Half his jaw hanging loose, and a chunk taken out of his shoulder, too. I still wonder if it was the one slug that'd done it to him. Just been crouched wrong, and it'd blasted straight through him. But it hadn't stopped him. He'd still dragged up the dead to be turned into autominds. He'd just followed his instincts. Just wish I'd followed mine.'

'What were yours?'

'To burn the dead. Bury them. Drag 'em back to Revance to stop them from ending up in another factory.'

'I mean... bigger than that. Back then. What did you... What were your instincts?'

Ryza found himself chewing on his upper lip for longer than he realised. Maybe that was why Foll fell quiet sometimes. It was hard to tell how long he'd been thinking when he'd not seen the sun for so long.

'To kill 'em all.'

'You didn't kill me.'

'I changed.'

'Are you still changing?'

'I...' Ryza let himself pause. 'Let me think about that...'

He moved away from the crack in the wall, and his breathing quickened. Suddenly it was like he'd just come out of a sprint, despite having not moved his legs more than a twitch in days. His hand scraped around at the ground he was sitting on. Loose sand picked up from the tiled stone and stabbed into the soft flesh under his fingernails. He pushed his palm flat against the ground as if it would purge the sand, but instead it only gouged the grains deeper into the fleshy parts of his hand.

It was just like those seconds after he'd been torn out of the vent suit after Iroka. When he'd come free into the air screaming and spewing flux. He could feel it in his throat now, seizing his breath and crushing his windpipe. Something was suddenly grasping it from the outside. It was his own hand, once again clawing at the flesh of his neck, caught in a spasming instinct between ripping the flux out of his throat and tearing the metal collar from around his neck.

He was trapped. Trapped in this cell. Trapped in his mind. Trapped in this machine. These were not things of his own making but things that he'd never decided to escape. Things he could only claw at the edges of and plead and scream at the creators of them for freedom, for mercy, for anything that signalled that he'd been seen, that he'd been heard, that they would just reach down and crush him like the tiny insignificant bug that he was.

His jaw snapped open as wide as it would go, and he stuck his hand in his mouth to rip it off further, to yank at his bottom teeth to widen that silent scream, to maybe, to *finally* give voice to that constant rattling terror that he'd lived for his entire life.

But no sound came out. No sound ever came out. No sound could possibly be summoned to incapsulate the years and years of unsaid protest that his mind had whirled and blended about.

'Ryza?'

The sound of his name snatched him from his seizure. Foll's voice had been faint. Fainter than usual. All panic forgotten, he scrambled back to the crack in the wall and pressed his ear to it, holding his heaving breath just in case it obscured a single precious word.

'Ryza?'

'I'm here,' he said quickly.

'Are you still changing?'

He felt himself nodding quickly. Her question had been the weakest her voice had yet been.

'I am. I am, Foll.'

'Good,' she said, her breath a soft exhale. 'I hope I do, too.'

No more words came.

'Foll?'

Nothing.

'Foll?'

Still nothing. He jammed his fingers as deep into the crack as they'd go, wriggling them to dislodge whatever silently fallen stone had blocked the way, tearing up the skin around his well-chewed fingernails in the process.

'Foll?'

Nothing.

CHAPTER THIRTY-SEVEN

RELEASE

'**R**YZA?'

The voice was unfamiliar. Though any sound that hadn't come through the crack since he'd last heard Foll's voice was unfamiliar. It was as if his mind was purposely voiding any stimulus that wasn't her. He'd stayed close to the crack since her last words. He could almost still hear them coming through.

I hope I do, too.

The thought made the sides of Ryza's lips stiffen, but it wasn't to smile. He hadn't felt that way since he'd lost Holm. Did that mean he was still changing, himself? Or was he still the same? What was he in the first place?

'Ryza?'

The voice came again. It wasn't through the crack, but Ryza still shuffled so his ear could be closer to it as he leaned against the lilting stone wall. He'd lost track of time again. Of how much had passed between the calls of his name. Of how long since he'd slept. Of how long silence had reigned after Foll's last words. Of how long it had been since he'd been entombed in this blank and blackened cave.

There was an odd smell coming through on the small breeze spouting from the crack. It wasn't death. Ryza knew it wasn't death, even if it was a knowledge overridden with hope. It was something else. Something that defied description or definition. Ryza stayed near it, inhaling it deeply as the voice from somewhere beyond the rocks kept calling his name, until the scent was so utterly embedded in his lungs that he could no longer detect it.

'Screw it, get him out of there.'

The voice sounded disappointed. Bitter. Much more close by, as if it were on the other side of the featureless stone walls. Ryza's eyes momentarily focused on the wall opposite where he sat. Now he thought about it, it was rather strange that there wasn't a door in the subterranean cell. Not even a slot for the food to be pushed through. In fact, food generally just seemed to appear and be waiting for him whenever he woke up.

'There's still air in there, he could still be awake,' another voice said. It was gruffer. Older.

Followed right on my thought, too.

'Don't care. We need him awake. Can't wait no longer.'

Ryza's faded mind was on the cusp of recognising the voice when a deafening grinding of stone made him lurch. His legs attempted to shoot out from under him, to get him standing upright, but they only threw his back into the wall hard. A gasp knocked the air out of him, and all he could do was shield his eyes as a shower of dust spattered out from the wall to his right.

It was *moving*.

At first the flat surface retreated, staying upright and revealing inch after inch of hidden gouges in the floor. It was a track that the false wall ran along as it moved. Though it didn't do so for long. When the first cracks of light clawed their way around the edges of the revealing wall, the entire surface of the stone tilted on its base and began to lie flat.

Ryza kept his eyes shielded as more was revealed. He knew the light beyond was not a bright one, but to his deprived eyes, it was still enough to pierce his skull with physical pain. The clanks and rattles of tensed chains came to him over the grinding of the stone.

Pulleys.

Ryza knew the sound well. Beyond the mystical powers that Origin had gifted the fortress of Revance, most of the heavy lifting was done by overengineered systems of pulleys. As painful as they were to his ears, they at least didn't squeak as much.

New iron. No rust.

Fine dust coated the inside of his nostrils and throat, but he could still smell how fresh the welds on the chains were. This prison was his and his alone.

The racket of shifting stone eventually stopped, but Ryza refused to move. To even lower his hand. Just under his raised wrist, he could see the forms of legs. Of waiting guards too cautious and too afraid to approach.

'Ryza?'

Without the stone to obscure it, the voice was unmistakable. It was Ruka.

Ryza remained silent. His jailor was a friend. A former friend. It spurned a pit of betrayal in his guts, but no anger followed it. Just a moaning sadness he could not give voice to.

A few footsteps approached, and he felt her presence draw nearer. She crouched next to him, dropping her head slightly to look him in the eye from under his obstructing arm. Ryza's own gaze remained unfocused.

'We need you.'

Her words snapped his vision into a clear focus. She was still herself. Still young and battered. But hidden under a softly rattling vent mask, there was a new desperation about her expression. One that worried for others instead of herself.

'Then why lock me up?' Ryza said quietly, his voice rusty. 'Why throw me in a hole with the rest of the smelters?'

'That's just it, Ryza... We didn't. Come on, get up. I don't think you figured out what's happened.'

She offered him her hand. He stood up without it. The two Scythes standing behind her, their faces entirely hidden by newer, more complex vent masks, recoiled. One of them went to draw their sword, but Ruka hissed at her before she could.

'Leave me with him.'

'Not possible,' the woman said, her hand still at her pommel. 'Vorric's order.'

'Go,' Ryza whispered.

Ryza felt something happen to his face as he stepped forwards out of his stone cell. Something contorting across his skin that made it stretch in a way that verged on cracking. But it was enough. Enough to make Ruka stumble back. Enough to make the two closest Scythes turn tail and run. They barked panicked orders to the other Scythes as they went, and suddenly Ruka and Ryza were alone.

Ryza sucked in a deep breath as he took in his surroundings. The air was still stale, that of a cool cave a little less polluted with the stench of his festering body. But something else was there. That other scent he'd faintly smelt through the crack in his cell. He could better pick out the flavours of it now. It was sweet.

His current surroundings made his release less of a relief. He was still within a cavern, even if this one was ten times as large. The carved stone slabs that'd made up his confining walls and ceiling stood behind him, alone and tiny in the centre of a natural rocky floor. Glow orbs were laid out across the floor in a precise grid, so that their humble light just barely connected to the reach of their neighbour's.

The only way out of the space was a narrow tunnel twenty metres ahead that the Scythes had fled through. There was no longer any sign of them. No light from the tunnel mouth, either. This place was deep. Only the multitude of glow orbs lying scattered across the ground illuminated it, and the light couldn't reach the ceiling.

'Vorric said you'd have questions,' Ruka said, trying to keep her voice steady. 'Said I'd better answer them first. Better than telling you.'

Ryza looked at her again, frowning slightly as she recoiled again.

'What's wrong with me?'

'In... in what way?'

'The Scythes ran away. I've never seen them run away. Why are they scared of me now?'

Ruka looked confused for a moment. 'That... that wasn't the question you were supposed to ask,' she muttered to herself.

'Then what was?'

'I dunno. "Where am I?" Just... Look, Vorric said you'd—'

'I don't care what Vorric says,' Ryza spat.

He went to start pacing around the cavern, but Ruka stepped into his path, stopping him dead.

'Why not?' she challenged. 'Say it, Ryza!'

'Because he left me here to rot!'

'And where's here?'

'It's Breggesa, ain't it!? Deep under the Academy with the rest of the smelters your lot picked up. That's what you've been doing, right? Burying them without even killing them. That's what Foll told me.'

'This ain't Breggesa, Ryza.'

'Then where!?'

'I can't tell you!' Ruka retorted. 'Not yet, alright? You gotta trust me, Ryza.'

'What, because you've got a plan, too?' Ryza spat back. He shoved past her and moved away from his stony cage, turning to survey it with disgust. 'Everyone's had a fucking plan for me! You, Ditric, Vorric, Archarus, Origin, my father, even... even Holm! They all wanted me to be something they wanted! All wanted to use me like I was a fucking tool because I thought I wanted to be that, but what's that led to? Death! Everyone's fucking dead and the blood is on my hands!'

'Then what do you want?' Ruka shouted back.

She'd followed him as he'd began to pace again, moving quick enough to herd him back and forth so he remained in front of his broken cell.

'I want it to stop.'

Ryza stopped walking for a moment to draw in another shuddering breath of stale air. He shut his eyes as he did so, feeling his eyelids flutter against the darkness. When he opened them, his gaze fell upon the nearest glow orb. It was just sitting there on the ground, unfixed among the pebbles that stopped it from rolling away. His hand began shaking as the instinct to grab it overwhelmed his restraint.

Ruka glanced from his hand to the orb. 'Take it,' she muttered.

He did so and began pacing again without a second thought, rubbing the corner of his pointedly gnawed thumbnail against the orb's surface.

'I tried to stop it. Stop it all,' Ryza muttered, Ruka still following him. 'You saw me. I fucked it all up, I know, but what else could I have done? I used to think if I killed enough smelters, it would be over, but that's what they wanted, right? More bodies for more autominds. A war that fuelled itself. But then I realised they didn't have a choice. Just like me.'

'That's why you brought Foll in,' Ruka breathed, her words a revelation. 'You... you saw what she'd gone through. Same as you. She just hadn't got lucky.'

'Nah,' Ryza said, shaking his head heavily. 'It ain't that. Ain't pity. It's... It's...' He paused to take a breath, looking over Ruka's head to the side of the cave she was keeping him out of. 'Why was she brought here? You... the Scythes and Vorric and all, you wanted me alone here because you thought I was too dangerous... but her?'

Ruka's expression sagged as she caught his eyes. 'That's what Vorric said you'd ask,' she said softly. 'Wish you hadn't.'

'Why? It's not her, is it?'

Ruka looked down, her eyes following his thumb as it circuited the glow orb.

'Ruka!'

'Vorric told me not to tell you. I want to... but he's right. You'd trust me if I told you the truth, right?'

Ryza felt himself hesitate. He wanted to say yes. He was scared of what it meant if he couldn't. But he couldn't.

'Yeah. Knew it,' Ruka said despondently. 'I guess you gotta see it.'

She turned and led him around the back of the stone cell's exterior. Ryza followed, three steps behind. The phantom scent of sweetness grew stronger in the air until Ryza could recognise it for what it was. Why Ruka had kept her vent mask on.

There was no other cell at the rear of his own. Just the outside of the flat wall with a body slumped next to the crack he'd spoken to it through. Ruka nodded towards it.

'Go look for yourself. Just don't touch it.'

Ryza moved closer, gripping the glow orb tighter and tighter as he fought his sense of revulsion. The corpse was Foll's. There was no doubt of it. Ryza couldn't mistake her narrow face, or her still splint-bound arm. But her skin had turned grey. It was impossible to tell how long she'd been dead. Silver veins throbbing with molten flux made sure of that.

Decayed patches of skin had been filled in by wobbling pools of the liquid across her chest and her stomach. It had eaten away at the rags that'd once been clothes, or emerged as fine threads from the wounds to replace the fabric where it had failed, weaving silvery flesh into the garment itself.

Some parts of her had practically dissolved. Her legs were little more than bones held together by ichor-like strands of flux. Her unbroken arm wasn't even there. It just stopped shortly below her shoulder. Ragged strands of meat and flux hung from it, twitching slightly in response to a command that was never there.

Ryza leaned closer still, holding the glow orb to her frozen face. Her jaw hung slack, but the teeth inside were... Ryza almost retched. They weren't teeth. There were indents carved into the line of them where the gaps should be, but each one was fused to the other like a solid piece of metal that'd been cast from a mould.

He finally looked in her eyes.

Flux. Couldn't be anything else.

'You killed her,' Ryza growled. 'You brought her here to kill her. Just to fuck with me!'

'You really think we'd do that!?'

Ryza rose to his feet and bore down on her. 'Yeah! Yeah, I fucken do!'

'Then that's why she's here,' Ruka said. 'That proves it.'

'Proves what?'

'The truth.'

The answer came in the form of Vorric's voice, a distant one from the other side of the cavern. The sound echoed as Ryza searched for its source and Vorric revealed himself, stepping from the shadows of a natural alcove positioned on the opposite side of the tunnel. Ryza stormed towards him, fury burling in his guts. He wanted nothing more than to tear his precious vent mask off and knock out every single one of his teeth.

'No more fucking games, Vorric! You've had me here for two months—'

'Eight days,' Vorric said curtly.

'No, no it's been—'

'Eight. Days.'

'He's not lying, Ryza,' Ruka said. 'We couldn't tell you anything.'

'Why?'

'Because you have been experiencing pure resonance for far too long,' Vorric replied.

Ryza sneered at him. 'Then I'd be dead! A shadow dancer! I *survived* it, you stupid fuck!'

'The forces of the League of Revance had been routed and captured by my Scythes by the time we had emerged in the undercity. We'd destroyed the treadhulk bearing the mortars that supported you and had incapacitated the crew controlling it, even finding and disarming the shard of the rebel sun that'd been encased in one of the shells, and yet you still managed to cause the weapon to fire as if none of this had happened.'

'But... but it was Origin that triggered it. He took the beacon from me. He pressed the button!'

'Because you believed it was there. That it would fire. That's why we had to take you the way we did. What if you'd discovered this at the time? What would've happened in that moment of doubt? You're no longer just a danger to yourself or those around you Ryza. You're an existential threat to the Droughtlands.'

'Then why's telling me now any better?' Ryza asked. He looked back to Foll's flux-ridden corpse. 'What does killing her have to do with it?'

'Because now there's proof. Undeniable because you've seen it and accepted it before you knew it. We just had to hold you for long enough for it to appear.'

'Appear?'

Vorric took a step towards Ryza, the tip of his vent mask only inches from Ryza's nose.

'Foll is still alive and held far away in Breggesa. Mortar mail confirms this daily in messages coded in a way you couldn't possibly imagine or mimic. The thing that you have created... that you've been speaking with...'

'First showed up two days after we locked you in here,' Ruka said. 'Just a mouth. Then ears. Then a face. Three days ago, it was an entire body. It lived. It breathed. It couldn't see us, but it could hear you. And then it started to just... die.'

'You told it you were still changing,' Vorric added. 'What does that mean?'

Ryza opened his mouth to answer, then paused. 'I don't have to tell you, do I?'

Vorric and Ruka exchanged a confused look.

'We need to know, Ryza,' Ruka said.

'I don't care.'

Ryza threw the glow orb aside, watching as it clattered and bounced across the cave's floor. It came to a stop near one of the others, disrupting the perfect grid that'd been laid out.

'You understand what's at stake, don't you?' Vorric pressed. 'You are a danger to—'

It only took a silent little smile to cut Vorric off. There was now fear in the eyes of the leader of the Scythes. The same kind of fear Ryza had seen in the Academy's Archives.

'I am a danger to a machine.'

'A *what*!?' Ruka said, looking around rapidly for an arcanite.

'You control machines. This machine will control life. Do not control it,' Ryza recited. 'Origin told me what he really meant when he said it to Rettic. To Archarus. Even to me. We all missed it. Molten flux was never the machine. It was what we created from it.'

'The autominds?' Vorric asked.

'No. Think harder. A machine, Vorric. It turns one thing into another. Fuel into force. Raw into refined. Life into death. All the parts that make it up have a choice in their actions. Work or break. They know no other life. They only have the forces that act upon them. If they break, then the rest of the machine sees to it they are fixed. The flux trade is a machine. The Academy of Breggesa is a machine. The Droughtlands is a machine. All in response to molten flux. To the magic that those-of-glass left behind. That's what Origin told me. That's why I could never destroy the flux by fighting it. Because then I'd be accepting it exists. That it has a power over us. Everything that has happened is because we have responded to the flux.'

'You suggest we do nothing?' Vorric shot back.

'Imagine if we all had. If we all could've just turned away from all it promised us. But we couldn't, because that's the world that we exist in. One where we explore and interpret and respond, and everyone else either has to be a part of it or be discarded.' He looked to the false corpse of Foll. Its disintegration was accelerating. 'She was discarded.'

'But, Ryza, that's not her!' Ruka said.

'But she was to *her*,' he said, pointing at the corpse. 'She was made real and the way she was because of me, the same way the actual Foll was made real and the way she is because of the Droughtlands.'

Ruka grimaced under her mask, shaking her head. 'I don't get it anymore, Ryza, I really fucken don't.'

'Take your leave, Ruka,' Vorric said quickly. 'You've done enough.'

She took a few backwards paces towards the cave's tunnel out before she turned. 'Just... treat him right, okay?'

Ryza watched her go, making sure a minute had passed since she'd disappeared up the tunnel before speaking again.

'Is this still the way things are meant to go?' Ryza asked Vorric. 'You had a plan, didn't you?'

'A machine, as you call it?'

Ryza nodded.

'It's not my plan,' Vorric answered. 'It's his.'

Vorric raised an arm and pointed to the dark space on the cavern's floor from where Ryza had taken the glow orb.

A silhouette stood there.

But it wasn't Archarus.

CHAPTER THIRTY-EIGHT

THE SIEGE OF KYREA

V ORRIC WAS WAITING FOR him at the mouth of the cave when Ryza finally emerged. He'd never seen the man looking so impatient. The pacing, the balling of hands into useless fists, all the things that Ryza had come accustomed to doing himself whenever he was forced to be "out of the know." Vorric caught sight of him and approached quickly, navigating up the rocky path that led down from the cave's mouth to open brown-orange clay, deftly crossing the pointed stones, sometimes only balancing his heel on the pointed tip of particular steps.

A route well-worn.

Whether it was day or night, Ryza couldn't tell. The sky was blinding enough, and his eyes refused to focus on anything further than what his hand could reach. If this was how bad his vision had become after only eight days sealed away, he couldn't imagine how blind he would've been if it were the two months he originally believed.

The conversation with Vorric's shadow dancer companion had dissolved away all spitefulness that Ryza should've held for Vorric,

Ruka, and the rest of the Scythes. It was a dialogue even Vorric hadn't been privy to, having been sent away with nothing more than a silent gesture from the shadow dancer he so revered.

Ryza had kept his own questions curt and closed, not even asking the shadow dancer's name. It was bad enough having Archarus' in his head. It had been the subject of his first question, in fact. Why had he not shown himself to Ryza during his time in isolating stone? The answer had been the same as what he'd seen in the Scythes.

Fear. Just as they fear me now. Fear I might change things. Fear that I might change, myself.

They were right to hold such reservations. The shadow dancer had said so. They'd worded Ryza's presence as: 'A difficult time of uncertainty. One I am always forced to repeat.'

The meaning was cryptic as ever it was with shadow dancers, but Ryza could solve such a puzzle himself. This was the nature of Vorric's plan. Of fates and futures and certainties. Things Ryza himself couldn't be privy to, unless he was to risk inflicting that certainty on himself.

Because then I wouldn't be able to keep changing.

'You spoke?' Vorric asked, standing before Ryza.

'We did,' he replied. Vorric was still an expressionless blur, but there was a certain droop in his shoulders that belied disappointment. 'I can't say more, can I?'

'I suppose you can't. I was always meant to draw my own conclusions, to settle my own fate by my own hand, so it was a consistent one, but knowing this had only created more indecision as to if I'm doing the right thing. I can't imagine how you could possibly tackle such a thing.'

Ryza felt a smirk crack across the skin of his worn lips. 'Try not to think about it.'

'It's impossible. I'm still grappling with the havoc that this course causes. I wonder if it's all necessary. But I'm told it is.'

'And you believe it?' Ryza said. 'You'd be a part of that machine?'

Vorric's expression, now slightly clearer, tweaked at this.

'I now worry I've addled your mind by imprisoning you. Are you even aware of where we are?'

Ryza was still struggling to make out the surrounding lands. He could not see the outlines of mountains on the horizon, where a dark sky of either dusk or dawn lay, but the clear blue air above should've been blazing orange if it were the start or end of a day. Movement and bustle spread out across the ground before him. A camp or a town, a large one or a small one, respectively. But there were no walls. No towers of newly erected grey stone.

'This really isn't Breggesa, is it?'

'I would've been insane to take you there,' Vorric said. 'No. If your eyes can't see it, take another guess. Think of the journey I sent you on.'

Ryza kept blinking against the burning sunlight. It was a bright white pinprick directly above, its pointed heat lancing as a sharp ache into his mind.

'I still can't see a fucking thing, why do you want me to guess?'

'Because you don't trust me, do you?'

'Of course I fucking don't.'

'Then why ask me? What would you take my answer for? A lie? What happened to your doctrine of simply not caring? Has it already faded in the little time that's passed? Besides, I take it you already have your answer. You know why I've taken you here.'

'Because that's how things are meant to be...' Ryza paused for a moment as more of the surroundings came into focus.

There were siegeworks and long-wreckers lined around the place. The mountainous tracks that cut a trail through the natural battlements had their rocks long churned to dust. The crews that lingered around the firing batteries looked weary and deafened. They could not walk without obstruction, instead having to wade through the pools of spent brass shells, each one as thick as their legs, as they sought to resupply their guns for the next barrage.

'What are those guns pointed at?' Ryza asked quietly.

His answer was the roared order for them to fire. It echoed up and down the never-ending line artillery, lulling to silence as the guns clanked, their gunners shoving another shell into place before loosing a ground-shattering volley of firepower. The air beat faster than Ryza's heart, throbbing in his chest and knocking him a step back. The plumes of bright orange fire rippled back and forth across his vision as the long-wreckers continued their barrage. The flashes burnt off into clouds of black smoke. The dark haze lingered long after the call to cease firing had been heard, and when it finally faded, Ryza could see where they were.

'It's Kyrea, Ryza.'

'I thought it got wiped out... Why... why shoot at it?'

Vorric's grim and stony face was the only response Ryza got as he was handed a brass scope. He took it in his shaking right hand, but his first attempt to hold it to his eye was fruitless. He needed to steady himself. Crossing his left arm across his chest, he used the tension of his elbow pushing against his right forearm to better stabilise himself as he held up the scope again, this time gaining a clear view.

His jaw clenched. At first, he'd thought the scope was faulty. That one of the lenses or mirrors within it had slipped and rendered him only a vision of cloudy silver, but as he'd lowered his view to the land, he saw the source of the grand plumes of blazing flux

It billowed from the yawning tunnel mouths of Kyrea in great, coughing waves. Lakes of molten flux flowed forth in waves that crested and crashed with violent frothing force. They spilled out in spanning ripples that crossed the massive, once empty pits that had marked Kyrea's buried mass upon the land. And from it, Ryza could see the bodies emerging.

The thousands and thousands of autominds rose from the lakes of flux with each wave that carried them ashore. They came with no grace. No sure steps. They washed up in ungainly writhing piles that fought meekly to disentangle themselves before they rose and began hobbling forth. They did so with filled hands, carrying the very rifles their lives had produced in Kyrea's factories.

They marched in their legions, in their disordered rabbles, with no mind for the smaller craters they waded through that'd been filled with molten flux. With no mind for the pounding volleys of artillery that shattered their ranks and deposited their broken bodies in freshly dug craters.

Because they had no mind. They had no want. They only had the machine they'd been born from. The one that manufactured death and destruction because that was what their entire world had screamed out in need of.

Ryza lowered the scope from his eye, but he could still see so closely the blank and burned faces of the autominds that marched their way. The armies of them spread out across the desert plains between their firing position and Kyrea, a battle line as wide as the horizon.

Ryza looked back across the battlements he now stood behind. The earthworks that hid the long-wreckers from view were substantial. Well-built over a course of months, yet unscarred from even a single barrage. The supply lines that stretched behind them were gouged deep into the rock and widened to the point that lead-betters could rocket up and down their lengths as they ferried supplies and munitions towards the frontlines. Ryza took off following one such trench, walking along the edge of it with Vorric silently tailing him. A lead-better rushed past in reverse, its payload emptied as it headed back to the larger camp from whence it had come.

He'd only caught a glimpse of the driver. An angry and desperate man with a glance of pain across his face from how he had to twist his neck to negotiate the lead-better on a difficult journey it had made a hundred times in the past week. Strangest of all, he was old. Old, frail, and soft. Not something Ryza was used to seeing in a soldier.

He stopped following the trench. He'd seen what he needed to. He waited at the corner of a crossroads as another squadron of conscripts jogged past. They were armed with the very same rifles as the autominds they fought. Were they relics of a time when Ryza had held one himself? Or were they reluctantly looted trophies from this battle?

Vorric caught up to him.

'Do you want an explanation yet, Ryza?'

'I don't need one. You gave them a machine. The autominds, the flux... you gave them something to fight against, so they'll just keep fighting.'

'An unintentional necessity,' Vorric spat. 'Kyrea was a lost cause before the Scythes even reached Iroka. A dozen or more autominds were emerging each day, armed and hostile, and those we'd tasked with the effort to contain this place had already taken to clashing with them. We've tasked multiple expeditions with planting a rebel sun like we did with Iroka. All have failed. It has exhausted our stock of viable rebel suns, so no more attempts are possible. This is all we can do, Ryza.'

He turned to Vorric, his heart strangely unbothered by all of this.

'Then why do it at all?'

'Why? Why!?' Vorric roared. 'Don't you see what they are? What they'd do? Any time they make it within range, they open fire without a care for their lives or ours. Am I supposed to just let them wander out across the Droughtlands? What if they reach Breggesa? The city's walls can barely withstand the masses that've flocked to its gates, they'll crumble the moment a single gun is pointed at them.'

Ryza ignored him for a moment as he thought, then began making his way back towards the front line. Vorric followed, badgering him despite his usual aura of restraint, stopping only as Ryza stepped up and over the parapet.

'Get back here, you fool! Get back here now!'

'No! Not until you see what you've created, Vorric. It's a war machine. That's what I see. But the one thing I don't see is a single set of blue robes on the front lines. Where are the Scythes in all this? Coordinating this effort? From everything I've been told, you've taken all power in Breggesa and beyond to respond to this "threat," right?'

'Another necessity,' Vorric growled back.

'Then you control this machine!' Ryza shouted. He was loud enough to elicit the poked heads and pricked ears from some of the other gunner crews up and down the parapet. Ryza pointed broadly across them, keeping his eyes on Vorric. 'You see all these people here? Where'd they come from? Where are their homes? Do they even still have homes? Do you even know?'

'There are thousands here, Ryza! How do you expect me to know? Now get—'

'Then this machine controls life!' Ryza cried out. He came a few steps back to Vorric, standing atop the parapet so he could tower over the man and look out over the length of the battle line. The orders to fire were once again chorusing up and down the gunners' ranks, but it felt silent when it reached those in Ryza's earshot. They were all staring at him. They all knew who he was. What he'd done. Whether that drew within them fear or courage, it didn't matter. He just needed them to hear him now.

'You, Vorric! You of all people should've understood how the flux would respond to this. How it would rise to clash against you. It ain't the fault of everyone else here that this battle is still going. They're just a part in your machine. If they break, fail, or rebel, they'll be replaced with another. They have no choice. They *believe* they have no choice! They've trusted you, taken your word that this war you've started will spell the death of all across the Droughtlands, so they've followed you into battle as you try your very best to make this true.'

'Then what else was I supposed to do!? I did exactly as you tried to do in Iroka before I came to your aid!'

'And I failed! I lost all those who followed me. I lost Holm. I lost myself. And you failed to learn from it. Just like I did, you controlled this machine. This machine that controls life. Do not control it, Vorric. That's what you always should've done. But now it's too late for you. Just as it was too late for Archarus, for Rettic, and for all the rest. All you can do is let your machine fail and get ready to pick up the pieces.'

'You'd have all these people die!?'

'No,' Ryza spat. 'Just me.'

Chapter Thirty-Nine

A Dangerous Question

R YZA NEGLECTED TO SHARE the finer points of his plan with Vorric as he made his requests. Primarily to hide the fact there weren't any finer points in the first place. But that wasn't something Vorric needed to know. His trust in Ryza was absolute to the point of naivety. Perhaps that was the same kind of trust he placed in his own shadow dancer.

There was something Vorric had once said to Ryza that seemed pertinent in a moment like this.

I worry there will come a day when I must decide the way things shall be, rather than accept the way they are.

Maybe Vorric's time under the shadow dancer's command was a means to escape such responsibility, even if it had resulted him in commanding this enormous battle. However, Vorric had been more than compliant in bending to Ryza's wishes.

Scared he was already making those decisions.

He'd ordered the gunlines to pause their endless volleys. In response, the waves of autominds had stopped coming. They still emerged from the massive pools of flux. Still marshalled themselves for battle. But they took not a single step closer than they'd already made. A delicate ceasefire, where each side couldn't possibly understand why the other would follow it, so could only follow it themselves.

Ryza was confident it would hold for a while. Long enough for him to make his preparations and embark on his final journey into Kyrea. The lines of the autominds held around a mile and a half from the battlements built by the living, and there was precious little left to fight over in the lands in between. The raining of shells had cratered the land so much that the rock had somehow become smooth again.

At least in fighting the waves of autominds, Vorric had been smart about it. Ryza shuddered to think the lives that would've been lost had they been engaged with rifle-toting soldiers at close range.

If his own plan didn't work, they'd be lost anyway.

Ryza kept pushing this from his mind as the days crept forwards. Vorric had promised him everything he'd need, but he hadn't been able to promise that it would come quickly. Each second was a crawling hour in his mind, and to keep himself from becoming distracted and doubtful, he'd taken to retreating into the cave where he'd been held prisoner.

He never checked behind the stone walls of his cell for what had become of Foll. Instead, he sat in the corner he'd become accustomed to for most of the time the sun was up, emerging only when he thought it was gone. Sometimes he caught sunsets. Sometimes it was the dead of night.

At least at these times, the battle line was largely vacant. The ceasefire had drawn the majority of the gunners and supply staff back to the reserve camps, so only the sentries remained in their positions splayed out across the line. Ryza could pace between their positions at night in peace. The dark meant their attention had to be fixed on their supposed enemy, not him.

If he was lucky, he'd find an empty sentry nest. They were delicate little towers whose floor only had him standing another length taller, but it, along with the well-loved scopes he found there, afforded him a full view over Kyrea's surface tunnels. He'd surveyed them in peace, and whenever the errant sentry did arrive hurriedly to their post, it only took a knowing glance to convince them to be a little bit later to their station.

Ryza's attention rarely went to the massed line of autominds. They all stood silently. They numbered beyond thousands now, and Ryza wasn't sure he could count that high if he tried. He could only wonder where so many bodies had come from in the first place. Either Kyrea's factories had churned through more autominds than he could've ever imagined, or they, like nearly everything else here, was a production of the molten flux, in one way or another.

Instead, his focus was drawn to the tunnels themselves. There were only a few he could see before the haze of the blazing flux became too thick. One was large, as large as that which Ryza had found under Iroka. The other three, interspersed across the land, were smaller, carved out from the rock instead of steel like that which had been left by those-of-glass. They were auxiliary tunnels created for the purposes of the factories, venting or alternate supply routes, and what Ryza would be aiming for when he journeyed in.

As of that moment, molten flux was not flowing from the tunnels. The autominds didn't even seem to be crowding around them, either.

Ryza did his best to avoid thinking about them.

'What does it mean to not control a machine, Ryza?'

Vorric had waited two days to ask the question. He'd withdrawn from the frontlines himself, an action Ryza had first interpreted as Vorric's efforts to see to his requests, yet as he'd seen more and more of Vorric's lieutenants arriving to deposit neatly bundled sacks of supplies at the mouth of his cave, Ryza had begun to draw his own conclusions.

The other conspicuous absence among the Scythes was Ruka, but that wasn't a point Ryza was ready to press. It was a miracle she hadn't been killed yet, and Ryza wasn't about to implant any ideas in Vorric's head that he needed Ruka to follow him into danger.

Vorric's eventual return had been carried aboard the back of a lead-better as it rumbled through the now often-vacant trenches of the dusty battle lines. Having dropped off Vorric, the driver of the scrappy buggy had looked almost relieved to have something to do, but was more than happy to throw his gears into reverse after catching sight of Ryza. This left Ryza alone among the silent long-wreckers with Vorric and three other Scythes, along with the metal crates they'd purposefully unloaded.

It took some time, but Ryza eventually recognised one of the other blue-robed figures as Lucia. He hadn't seen the woman since they'd escaped Iroka, but her presence made sense, considering the cargo they'd just delivered. Ryza realised he'd never seen her beyond the confines of a bulky vent suit, so for her to be sporting an equally bulky figure was a shock to him. She had shortened brown hair and a set of blue eyes that were always narrowed so as to almost hide their colour, and she was intent on never properly meeting Ryza's eyes.

Vorric's hand was stilled at the lid of one of the crates, unable to open it until he had his answer.

'Well?' he prompted. 'I'm not looking to clear my conscience, but I still struggle to understand your meaning. Not for my own ends, but to better interpret the meaning that Rettic and the others failed to see. That is what you're referencing, yes?'

'It is.'

'Then what does it mean to *not* control a machine if all our actions and their consequences seem to create them? I feel as though you've simply asked us to do nothing in the face of an existential threat.'

Ryza chewed his upper lip as he thought, pacing and watching his stunted shadow wobble across the ground next to him. The definition of Origin's warning had been clear when it had been communicated to Ryza, an idea fully formed as it was dropped into his mind, but doing the same with spoken words was a great deal harder. The task had taken up most of Ryza's mind for the past few days.

'I don't think that the warning is meant to be a personal one,' Ryza eventually said. 'More of an overall thought...'

'A philosophy,' Lucia suggested.

'Whatever that is, sure. It's to... look at the machine, not from inside it but from the outside. To see that it exists but then to see that its existence is not some undeniable thing, that it's an ordinary thing with causes and effects like everything else. Something that'll just stop if you just stop feeding it, but the act of doing that seems so... so impossible because there's so many parts of it that *want* to be fed. Parts you can't deny.

'Essentially... the machine draws too much of our attention, and then everything we do is done in the context of the machine. That's how these things get power. That's how things got as bad as they are. It took me a while to understand, but to not control a machine was not to find yourself empty of purpose in relation to it but to find a purpose beyond all it could ever be. Impossible for you, because you still live. The machine still, and always will, threaten your life. Impossible for the shadow dancers, because they still must dwell in this land, a land scarred and wounded by the reach of molten flux, but for me...'

'It comes back to pure resonance, doesn't it?' Vorric said.

The other Scythes didn't flinch at the mention of such a thing, but they stared intently at Ryza, waiting for his answer.

'I think so,' Ryza said, nodding slowly. 'It's the last thing beyond molten flux. The thing, I think... that I know I've been living through for... for months now. There's nothing that the flux can do to pretend to cater to my needs, to my wants, because pure resonance has beaten it to it.'

'You're just going to go in there and...'

Lucia trailed off, and Ryza wasn't sure what words would follow if he were to say them himself.

'Not... not quite.' He looked aside to the other crates for a moment. 'Probably wouldn't need all this if I could, right?'

'No. Likely not,' Vorric said.

Vorric finally pulled back the lid of the crate he'd been withholding. The metal scraped, and light spilled into the box, its contents nestled in a supportive metal frame.

The sight of a vent suit's helmet made Ryza's heart seize for a moment, but he knew this was what he needed. Maybe he could survive the atmosphere of blazing flux without it, but he didn't believe in it as strongly as he did the vent suit.

'It's been through a full purge and burn cycle three separate times,' one of the other Scythes said, pointing to the scorch marks across the helmet's metal frame that they hadn't been able to polish away. 'The glass, the leathers, everything that wasn't metal got incinerated... It's all been replaced and reinforced, and then we've added more armoured plating where we could. Might be a bit heavier, but...'

Ryza reached into the crate, running his thumb down the surface of the glass visor. His face was reflected there, imprisoned by the structural bars that housed the vertical slats of glass. He blinked, and for just a moment, his reflection's eyes were black. Another blink and they returned to normal, and Ryza wondered if there'd come a time when they'd never return to green.

'What is your purpose, then, Ryza?' Vorric asked. 'What still keeps you human? I know it's a dangerous question, but—'

'Do you really want an answer?' Lucia challenged.

'I do,' Vorric replied.

'It's Holm,' Ryza said.

Vorric and the Scythes recoiled.

'Her? Really? But why? Through all our reports, *your* reports, what you told us... I thought you'd want nothing to do with her,' Vorric said.

'I had thought that,' Ryza admitted. 'But she kept appearing before me. Walking out of the flux itself or in my dreams. Sometimes creating copies of me to taunt me or my friends. Or to replace me so I may live in peace. And I thought that it was due to the molten flux showing me what I wanted to see, deep down, but after what you showed me with Foll... it tipped the scales in my mind on something I'd been doubting for a long time.'

'Pure resonance, again?' Vorric suggested.

'In a way. Foll must've been real... She must've been my... creation. The flux that came after that was just it trying to provide reason for what had happened. Because that's what flux was originally for, I believe. To give reason to magic, to impossible things. That's why I now believe it really was my father that I brought to you.'

'Perhaps he was merely bluffing when he was intimating that we knew each other.'

'I think so, too. But that's not why the flux came out of him. I think that was because of me. Because I thought it was so impossible that I'd finally get to make him fucking pay for what he made me into.'

'You now accept that it was him?'

Ryza looked back to the vent suit's helmet again, where his reflection's eyes were still green, then looked back at Vorric. He nodded in response.

'Without a shadow of a doubt. But that's why I need to find Holm again. Just as I couldn't accept that I'd killed my father, I still haven't been able to accept whether or not Holm is dead. Maybe it was under Twin Rings that it happened. Maybe it was when Maligar's flux got into her when we were fighting Revance. Maybe she ain't dead at all. But that's what I need. Certainty. And that's beyond what molten flux can give me now, and far beyond any machine that it can create. That's why I have to go in there. That's where she'll be.'

'You're sure?' Lucia asked.

Ryza glanced down at the helmet's glass again.

'I'm certain.'

His eyes were black.

Chapter Forty

One Man's War

AFTER BEING GIVEN THE full tour of the improved vent suit, having to swallow his own brewing fear for the thought of getting back in the damn thing, Vorric and the other Scythes took him back to the larger camp to show him what else they'd been working on.

Sending Lucia ahead, Vorric and the other Scythes escorted Ryza on foot down the length of the gouged trench. The near-mile-long journey took half an hour of weaving through blind turns and deserted checkpoints. The latter took the form of twin sets of steel gates that were bracketed by bridges that larger vehicles could cross. Small firing ports and sentry nests were built into the upper corners of each gate's housing, though Ryza wasn't sure what good they'd do defensively if the enemy horde of autominds had penetrated the defensives that deeply.

They did little good now, considering they weren't crewed and stood open. Maybe the defenders had become lax with the few days of respite they'd been granted from the ceasefire. Or maybe it was an order from high above them to abandon and open their posts to better promote the idea of the supposed peace among the troops.

One thing that did strike Ryza's mind as he followed Vorric through the trench network was what would happen if molten flux spilled into the trenches? It would expand and multiply until it filled the entire defensive network, a fact its architects surely would've been aware of when gouging paths through the ground.

It had to be the result of the war machine that'd sprung up so rapidly in this place. They'd followed their instinct to dig in and hide from the rifle shells that would be flying overhead without giving thought to the possibility that they were digging their own potentially flux-filled graves.

He realised they reminded him of the tunnels left by those-of-glass. Those massive caverns bored through the core of the Droughtlands itself in response to a danger that would only be aided by it.

They are not tunnels. Catacombs, past and future. Reborn as trenches.

Ryza chuckled to himself, then shook his head at Vorric when he looked back in curious half-alarm. Ever since his last moments with Origin, he'd caught himself thinking in that same strange poetic pattern that the little arcanite spoke with. Exactly why it was like that was still beyond him, but what stayed with him was Origin's reason for doing it.

Unlimited life... It calls for limitations... To give it meaning.

Limitations were what Ryza's life verged on lacking at that very moment. It was why he was grateful for Vorric taking his requests so seriously.

When they reached the main body of the camp, it was also deserted, and Ryza realised why.

'They're afraid of me, aren't they?'

'They're not,' Lucia answered. 'It's a precaution for the future.'

She'd been waiting for them at the final set of open gates and joined them as they headed further into the camp, her short, coarse brown hair looking a good deal more windswept. She would've taken to the skies to get here fast enough to evacuate so many people.

Few of the tents that Ryza was used to seeing were blue. Most were grey, propped up by poorly cut beams of iron that'd been hastily rammed into the ground in stretching rows. Large, silo-like workhouses interrupted them at disparate intervals. Laterally rolling walls that acted as doors, left open for Ryza to see through, revealed the multiple lead-betters and long-wreckers that sat in each one, all in various states of repair or modification.

Other storehouses overflowed with ammo or with spent casings that piled towards the neighbouring ammo presses where they were to be recycled into live munitions. They were positioned closest to the trenches, separated from having a direct path down to the lines by blast-resistant steel walls that were reinforced with earth-driven struts.

Ryza paused for a moment in a clearing to take in the full sprawl of the camp before looking back to Lucia. She'd followed at a distance, staying ten paces away.

'What do you mean, "precaution for the future," anyway?'

'Think about it, Ryza,' Vorric said from closer by. 'What happens if you do rid us of the flux? What do we tell people? The truth? No, it's impossible. It's insane. It'll cause more havoc across the Droughtlands than molten flux did. Imagine if everyone knew about pure resonance. That it was really possible. That you *lived* through it.'

'Then what are you going to tell them?'

'The truth. One they'll be able to believe.'

Vorric continued on, leading him towards the only silo that was sealed shut. The sand near it was smooth, footsteps conspicuously absent from all around its walls, yet Ryza could still hear work coming from within. The thrill of sparks from fresh welds and the frustrated beatings of a hammer against a part that didn't fit. Lucia and the two other Scythes followed Vorric's nod and began pulling back the wall-sized sliding doors to reveal the works within. Ryza gasped when he saw who was carrying them out.

'Ditric? Avesta? What the fuck are—'

Ditric turned at his call, a snarl on her soot-stained face that twisted the fresh and welted line of black ink that ran down her left cheek, from her eye to jaw. The others looked up to Ryza's presence, facing him with a grim determination void of any elation, all bearing identical marks on their faces.

They stood among a series of buggies. The vehicles were beyond lead-betters. A lead-better's armour was a joke compared to those things. The chassis of each machine was stacked with armoured plating, the cockpit itself a mess of glass and hastily welded rebar.

The front armoured plate had been lowered so it would scrape along the ground, and its form had been hammered into a concave, scoop-like shape with a pointed prowl in the centre. If it built up enough speed, Ryza was sure the vehicle would be able to drive through a mountain and brush the resulting rubble to the sides without slowing.

Even the wheels had been replaced by a complex network of interlinking tracks, a shrunken version of a treadhulk's means of propulsion. The vehicle's engine had been ripped out of the front and welded into the rear, with another smaller engine stacked atop it for good measure. It was an excessive, desperate abomination, and from the sight of the piles of yet-to-be-affixed scrap iron plating, they weren't close to being done with their additions.

At the back of the workshop, half hidden in the fume-streaked shadows, were rack after rack of vent suit pieces. These didn't look to be nearly as well-repaired as what Vorric had just presented to Ryza, but once again, this hadn't stopped Ditric and the rest from making their own additions.

There was a mezzanine above where more of them were still working, still attempting to remedy the desperate state of the equipment they'd been given. Ryza could even spot some of Holm's old R-Three prototypes hanging on racks with the rest of the surplus rifles they had to work with.

Wiping the grease from her hands, Ditric approached slowly, keeping her eyes trained on Vorric, waiting for the slightest hint that she was about to step out of line so that she could do it anyway. Ryza scanned the marked faces as she approached, frowning when she stopped a few extra paces away, the tips of her worn boots at the edge of the undisturbed sand ring.

Nearly the entire League of Revance was crammed into that prison of a workshop, spare a few faces that Ryza could only assume hadn't survived the battle against the Scythes. Ditric was the only one of their number that Ryza had even seen after the battle, and even then, they hadn't had a chance to say a single word before Vorric ordered a bag to be thrown over their heads.

Ryza thought he'd be relieved to see them all alive again, but there was something about the grim stare they fixed him with that reminded him of the way the conscripts started to look aboard Revance after they'd gotten over being terrified that they were about to be shot by one of the officers.

'What are you... what are you doing here?' Ryza asked Ditric, still bewildered.

Before answering, Ditric glanced again to Vorric, who nodded stiffly.

'We lost the battle, Ryza. How the Scythes see it, at least. They ain't killed us for it yet, but...' She glanced away again, this time towards the wall of blazing flux that painted the sky silver to the west.

'We have taken the mercenary company known as the League of Revance prisoner,' Vorric declared, his tone dour and akin to a public denouncement. 'For the assault and murder of scholars of the Academy of Breggesa, their lives are now forfeit. A punishment of summary execution was withheld in the face of extraordinary circumstances, so those who assist in the final expedition into the cordoned zone of Kyrea may be spared should the effort be successful.'

'Yeah, but being successful means we're all dead,' Ditric muttered to herself.

Vorric continued as if she'd remained silent, his words now so precise they seemed to have been pulled from a legal decree. 'The black mark upon their visage will remain with them for the rest of their lives. It will be a warning to all that they must not be provided, traded upon, or otherwise furnished with runic ink, water, or any other ingredients involved in the creation of runic axioms, or be marked themselves under the order of the Academy of Breggesa.'

'I've seen refugees with that mark,' Ryza said. 'That a crime now too?'

'Doesn't matter,' Ditric replied. 'Way things are going, we're all going to be marked like that.'

'Watch your tone,' Vorric said cooly. 'Besides, this matter is not the one concerning us right now. Please explain your mission to Ryza.'

Ditric scowled at Vorric one last time before looking back to Ryza. 'We're going in with ya.'

'You'll die. Vorric, you'll kill them!'

'It's what he wants,' Ditric growled. 'The fucking state of the vent suits we've got, we'll only have about twenty minutes before they bust a seam.' She jabbed her thumb back at the squadron of armoured vehicles. 'The ram-raiders ain't looking much better, neither.'

The thought of them dying like that, sent into their own slaughter after all that time, sickened Ryza. He stomped up to Vorric, bellowing in his face until the man was forced to flinch. 'Vorric, I don't need them! I don't want them coming with me!'

'It doesn't matter what you want,' Vorric replied quickly. 'It's what the Droughtlands needs. If you do manage to stop the spread of molten flux for good, then it'll be known as the deed of Ditric and the League of Revance.'

'And you actually have to kill 'em for it!? Actually have to send them in there and kill them?'

'I should've buried them already for how many of my people they've killed,' Vorric snarled back. 'At least they get a bit more use out of their quarrelsome little lives. It's a sacrifice that needs to be made, that *will* be made, whether you like it or not, and if they live, then that's the story they get to tell.'

Ryza felt his fist clench, ready to lash out and puncture straight through Vorric's guts, but suddenly Ditric had appeared between them, her own resolve outweighing his fury.

'Don't. Ryza, don't. Fuck, I wanna let ya, but don't. We already know we're dead. We ain't gotta like it, but at least we can do it as close to our own terms as they'll let us. One last big fight. The way it was always meant to be. Besides, I hate it, but he's right. The Droughtlands can't know about you. Not more than they already do.'

'It ain't right! It ain't fucken fair!'

Ditric nodded, pushing against his chest with one planted hand to gain some distance between them and Vorric. 'I've lost track of the number of times I've had to kill you. Things that looked like you. If we don't do this, then that's how you'll be remembered. A ghost that came out of the flux wherever it was found. If I can give you anything, it's a chance to be forgotten. A chance for no one to need you.' She lowered her voice again, leaning closer to Ryza so she was whispering straight into his ear. 'We know what we're doing.'

She pulled away, giving a tight-lipped nod as she slapped him on the shoulder, then retreated to the bounds of the silo she and the others were imprisoned in, giving Vorric the same nod as she went.

'You don't have to send them in, Vorric,' Ryza said, still shuddering with rage. 'No one knows what happened at Iroka and that's fine.'

'I cannot,' Vorric said quietly, drawing close so only Ryza could hear. '*I cannot.*'

The emphasis on the word made Ryza hesitate, catching his response in his throat. 'That's the way things are supposed to be, right? That's why you couldn't kill them after we fought. Just so they could die here.'

'And you know just how dangerous it is for you to know that. You'd best leave it, Ryza. You have to let this fate play out.'

'Then you have to let my fate play out, too.'

The comment was enough to drive Vorric away, though not too far. He and the other Scythes lingered as Ryza joined the rest of the League of Revance to aid in their preparations. One of the ram-raiders was meant for him, so Ditric took great pains to explain the modified workings of the vehicle.

Despite the fact they'd be encased in their own vent suits, the cockpits of the pilot's compartment were as airtight as they could make them. Sitting in the driver's seat, Ryza could already see that it had been modified for him.

The steering yoke was offset to the right slightly, with the engine's choke, clutch, and igniter relegated to dual sets of pedals down by his feet. This allowed for a deeper window of banded glass to run along the front of the vehicle, giving Ryza a view out as low as his knees. The armoured scoop at the front was the only thing that cut it off, otherwise, he'd probably be able to see the ground below him as well.

The door was a slab of steel and glass thicker than his leg, and after making sure he wasn't about to lose any extra limbs, Ditric let it drop.

The door swung down and landed in its latches with a loud thud that made Ryza flinch in his seat. A scraping of hand cranks and locking bolts further sealed it in place, and Ryza had to pay careful attention to the corresponding hand cranks within the vehicle that spun with Ditric's actions if he were ever to exit it himself.

Once Ditric had fully sealed him in, the only thing he could hear was his breath. It wasn't as bad as being stuck in the vent suit, as it only began to echo once it hit the offset console in front of him. The seat itself had enough room for Ryza to slide around in, and his feet didn't reach the pedals if his back was resting against it, but it was likely extra room to accommodate for the vent suit he'd be wearing.

Another spin of metal came from somewhere behind, and

Ryza turned, following his ears. Ditric was climbing into another compartment to the rear and left of where Ryza was now sat. Only a small corridor of open space joined the two elements of the cockpit. It was about three inches wide, not even enough for Ryza to see how Ditric sealed herself into her own compartment.

'You ain't coming with me, Ditric,' Ryza said.

She finished her work on the door before she answered, turning to him with a wry grin.

'I know. Figured you wouldn't need a gunner with what you're up against, but it's been easier to make all these things the same.'

She pointed up at the bracketed controls that seemed to orbit her head.

'Crazy what we've done in a few days. Fynis got a rifle that'll load itself attached up top. Won't do much against how many autominds are out there, but makes the rest of us happier.'

'You're happy with this?' Ryza asked flatly.

'Yeah,' Ditric replied, grinning as she leaned forwards. 'We got a plan. Couldn't tell you out there, Vorric would hear it in the air, but he can't in here. We always knew you weren't going to need us all the way into Kyrea. Shit, I wasn't even sure you were actually going to come out of the cave they put you in. Vorric ain't telling us anything, and I reckon you're going to be keeping it that way, right?'

'You're right. On everything. I don't need you. I don't need any of this.'

'You'll need the artillery to clear a path through all those fucken autominds. You just going to walk out there and ask them to move?'

'No, I—'

'I mean, fuck, the shit I've seen from you, you probably could.'

'No. That's stupid. I'm just going to plough straight through them. That's why you built these things like this, right?'

But Ditric shook her head. 'Nah, you'll gum up the works too fast. You ever run over a bunch of smelters? Throws your course too hard after the first three. No, you let the big guns clear the first line, then we'll help you punch through to the tunnels.'

Ryza contorted his face into an expression that he hoped would display how absurd he found Ditric's casualness when it came to this plan. It did little to dissuade her.

'You're crazy,' he said. 'And what do you do after that? Get out and start brawling with whatever comes out of the flux?'

'If it comes down to it, you fucken bet.'

'Why do you wanna go for the tunnels, anyway?'

'That's where you're going, ain't it?'

'No, why do *you* want to—'

Ditric's wry grin cut him off.

'You remember a while ago when Vorric said there were a bunch of reels stuck in there?'

Ryza forgot to breathe for a moment. 'Ditric, I'm crazy, but you're—'

'Gonna get enough reels that Vorric won't be able to put another fucken finger on us.'

She was holding back laughter as she said it, rocking giddily in her seat with her teeth clenched and bared.

'I know where they are, Ryza. I started asking around the second we left the Academy that day, and I reckon I've got it scouted. When the Scythes started cutting the smelters loose with these marks,' she pointed to the fresh line on her face, 'I knew I'd have plenty of ears to ask, none of them loyal to their flux-trader masters no more, and more than happy to sell them out just to fucken spite them. We get those reels, we make things right. Not in the way that Holm wanted, but for real. I'm gonna help those fucken refugees, Ryza. I can't stop thinking about anything else, because if it wasn't for you and Revance, I'd be one of them, or one of the autominds we're about to blast our way through.'

'I don't know, Ditric. Can't you just run?'

'Then what? Just run out of fuel and start wandering around the Droughtlands? That don't do no good. You gotta trust me, Ryza.' She paused. 'Do you?'

It was Ryza's turn to pause. He chewed on his words carefully before he spoke, letting them out one by one.

'I don't. I can't. But it doesn't matter if I do. It's whether you trust me.'

'Trust you? I fucken trust you more than... Fuck, you know what, Ryza? If you ain't figured it out by now, then I'd say that the only reason you ain't gone pure yet is that you're too fucken stupid to.'

Ryza sighed, the only way to hide his chuckling response.

Chapter Forty-One

Engine Control

ANOTHER THREE DAYS OF preparations passed by. Ryza savoured them. He knew they'd be his last.

The vent suit was hot and itchy on his body. It focused its ire on his neck and around his knees, so all he could do was keep each joint as locked and stiff as possible as he trudged towards the ram-raider designated for him. Someone —likely someone who'd been around for the battle of Iroka— had daubed a layer of still-drying yellow paint across the armoured scoop at the vehicle's front.

It was set apart from the others, who were twenty metres ahead, with the rest of the battle line's force stationed even further away up and down the lines. Once again, they were manning the guns. Once again, they were readying themselves for war.

The League of Revance stood by their vehicles as they watched him approach. Ryza had ensconced himself into his vent suit separate from the others, from inside the cave where he'd been held captive. Only Ruka had been there to help him. It was at his request. There were many people he still held his trust for, but Vorric and the rest of the Scythes weren't one of them. That was the problem with having a determined path. Why trust a man who didn't think of rebelling against the machine he'd become a part of?

Ruka walked with him now, caged in her own vent suit. She'd

been wearing it the whole time she'd been helping him, which meant their final words took the form of silent looks shared through the thick layers of tinted glass of the helmets. She'd been mournful. Ryza couldn't turn to see her now. He couldn't bring himself to.

The door of the ram-raider was waiting raised and wide open for him. He paused before its shade. The way the sun beat down on the armoured metal of his vent suit made it a walking oven, and getting in the vehicle would only make it worse. But the heat wasn't why he hesitated. He patted his gauntleted hand over the outside of his vent suit, making sure he still had everything he was sure he wouldn't need.

A sawn-off rifle was holstered on the outside of his right thigh, with a second one, even more sawn-off, strapped across his chest. A bandolier of slugs, both standard lead-bodied and incendiary, were strapped across the remaining space on his chest, covered by leather pouches that could be flipped up at a moment's notice.

At his back, welded on somewhere he couldn't reach and hidden between the networks of pressurised air tanks and valved filters, was another beacon similar to what Avesta had given him before the beginning of the battle with the Scythes and Origin's arcanites. Though this one wasn't to call down a strike of mortars upon him, but instead to help the others in their ram-raiders keep track of him as he punched further and further into the depths of Kyrea.

Considering that they were meant to be leading the way, clearing the path before peeling off, it didn't quite make sense to Ryza. Perhaps it was so they could be sure that he really was following them and hadn't abandoned them, rendering their coming sacrifice as one in vain.

I know the feeling.

That was if their sacrifice was to be a true one. Ditric's steadfast refusal to discuss her plans outside the confines of a ram-raider —whose engine was even sealed from the outside air, instead relying on long, pressurised gas tanks fitted within the undercarriage— had worked. Vorric would've had his suspicions, but he was powerless to stop them without knowing what was planned. And if he did know, then he'd be forced to let it come to pass.

Ryza stepped softly as he turned to look back. Vorric and a few of the other Scythes watched on from the distance, perched atop the mound that contained Ryza's cave. He'd spent a great deal of time over the last few days wondering how much of Vorric's life, of his actions, were determined by what his shadow dancer had told him.

But wasn't that the same for himself? Hadn't his actions all been the results of being led on by the words of others, whether or not they'd been true or false? Ryza shuffled again, this time turning the narrowed view from within his helmet to face the storm of blazing flux they were about to assault.

The reach of the billowing grey clouds had expanded further towards their battle line. Now all of Kyrea's tunnels were obscured. Maybe they weren't there anymore. Maybe there were even more of them.

Scouts from the morning had already reported sightings of autominds becoming more present within the metallic mists. It was uncertain if they were armed, for the autominds hadn't yet strayed out into the open. There had also been a few stray reports of other things moving within the wall of blazing flux. Larger than humans. Sleeker than machines. Things they could not identify.

But Ryza had an inkling.

Best not to think about it.

His mindset in the lead up to that moment had been one of meditation. It was the first time in the hours before a battle or a sojourn into the depths of an undercity where Ryza hadn't darkly hoped for Archarus to appear in order to guide him. Perhaps Archarus already knew. Perhaps Vorric's shadow dancer was playing a part in holding him back. Either way, Ryza needed to keep himself steady.

Right then, he feared no death. He feared nothing that may or may not happen to the desperate remaining members of the League of Revance. He feared nothing that the molten flux could reveal to him, reflect within him, or trigger a revelation from him. Fear, despair, hope, and regret, they were all emotions he was saving for when he was deep within Kyrea.

For when I find Holm.

He knew she'd be in there. It was the last place she'd be safe within the flux. As far as Ryza was concerned, all other collections of molten flux, no matter how large or isolated they were, had become tainted. The minds of others had made sure of that. Ryza's own infamy was what they now saw reflected in the liquid metal. That was why his form had become the omen that emerged from the flux.

To the people of the Droughtlands, he was the conscript who'd become it. He just needed to find his way to the heart of Kyrea to make it true.

And it had to be the heart. The very depths of the tunnels, the darkest corners of the derelict and abandoned factories that had shaped and tainted so many lives. The edges and outskirts of Kyrea would've fallen folly to that same tainting that the rest of the flux on the land had, something proven by its response to the call for battle Vorric's involuntary army had shouted to it.

Now Ryza's theory was that those effects would lessen the closer he came to the centre. Diluted as the purest forms of molten flux fought to remain true to what it was supposed to be. What Holm wanted it to be.

Her request for Ryza to simply leave the flux alone, to walk away and let her put things as they should be, was one that he could no longer obey. It had been another lie, another manipulation, and he'd foolishly believed the deceiving flux had finally told the truth. But the truth had never been what he'd wanted. Not until now.

Once more he turned on the spot, and he slowly raised his arm to Ruka in a half-salute, limited by the overly armoured vent suit's carapace. She responded in kind, but made no action to lower her hand when Ryza did. She stayed, stock still, resolute in seeing him off, as if it would cleanse her of her good-willed betrayal in joining the Scythes.

Ryza turned to the Scythes. Only Vorric saluted among them for a while, until the others caught on and mechanically copied the gesture.

Finally, Ryza looked back to the League of Revance. He saluted with all the vigour he could, and they did so in return, performing the action quickly, those among them who'd served aboard Revance doing so with expertly jolting movements. As Ryza lowered his arm again, he watched as they hauled themselves into the cabins of their ram-raiders, two to a vehicle, and sealed themselves in.

Their engines sounded as a rising chorus, each one a roar of a slowed tempo like a pair of metallurgists hammering at an anvil in an alternating fashion. It sounded nothing like a lead-better engine's whining scream.

The change came from the extended pistons in the ram-raider's engine block, made to suck in and then push out more air than normal, hopefully making the most of the limited reserves of compressed air that each vehicle carried, because they didn't know for how long the engines would be able to operate if they were sucking in pure blazing flux.

It was a miracle that Holm's lead-better had worked for as long as it did when it had saved Ryza's life in the tunnels under Iroka, and it had been spitting pure fire from its exhausts the whole time.

The roar of engines was also the signal to begin the fresh wave of bombardment, and even through the thick glass and steel of the vent suit, Ryza could hear the call echoing up and down the line. He lowered himself quickly into his ram-raider and pulled the door shut, actioning all the stiff levers and even stiffer valves to secure it in place and seal himself in.

The first volley rumbled across the sky, making the loose parts within the ram-raider's compartment rattle violently. High above, on the backdrop of blue and all-consuming metallic grey, arcing spears of fire cut through the air. They disappeared as soon as they hit the wall of blazing flux, returning a few seconds later as bright flashes of yellow and fiery red deep within the mist.

The ground rumbled as the forward party of ram-raiders took off. The League of Revance had gotten a total of seven other vehicles up and running in time for the assault on Kyrea, each crewed with a pilot and a gunner. The latter was charged not with thinning the numbers but with repelling the autominds that survived being ploughed through.

From within the tight confines of the vehicle's cockpit, Ryza knew it would be a hard job, but it was better than nothing. He wasn't accompanied with a gunner himself, another request of his. He didn't need them. What he was attempting to kill wouldn't be slain by mere slugs.

The ram-raiders quickly shuffled into their formations. A leading arrowhead trio churned up red sand as they lurched towards the recently excavated gap in the strongpoint's natural ramparts. Ryza kicked hard with his left foot at his ram-raider's ignition pedal.

The engine coughed, but nothing followed.

Fuck.

Another arrowhead of ram-raiders was already filtering through the narrow gap ahead, one of its three vehicles having already broken out into a clanking sprint to catch up to the first three. Ryza pumped the pedal again, but the engine still disobeyed him.

I should've tested out the damn thing before—

A movement across the forward glass view ports made him look up from the offending pedal. It was Ruka. She was arm-deep in the workings, an impressive feat considering the bulk of her vent suit. Ryza banged on the glass to get her attention, but it wasn't until the next volley of cannon fire faded that she heard him.

He waved for her to step back, to get away, that he was certain he could get the damn engine working. He had to. Ditric's ram-raider, the last of the seven, had already rocketed through the breach and onwards to Kyrea. There was no way of turning them back now.

But Ruka shook her head as best she could from within the vent suit and withdrew her hand, revealing the loose piece of twisted metal that she was clutching. She waved her other hand across her neck, indicating that his ram-raider was as dead as the League of Revance was about to be.

Ryza didn't have time to figure out if this was the result of a sabotage or Ruka's last-ditch effort to save him. Within the gauntlet of his vent suit, runes were already sliding into his palm. He knew the skeleton of a lead-better well enough. He just had to hope that the ram-raider wouldn't be so different in its means of control.

The first sparks of his magnetic resonance reached out from under his chewed-down fingernails and into the curved shells at the tips of his gauntlets. It lashed and wavered against the tempered metal, as hesitant as Ryza was to control an arcanite again. He'd been reluctant in painting runes on his skin one last time, tempted to test just how readied his access to pure resonance would be in his final hours. But runes had been a constant in his life, in the lives of almost all those in the Droughtlands. If they helped him make sense of one last bit of magic, then so they should.

I can save the insanity for Holm.

He clenched his left eye shut as he forced his magnetic resonance to stream harder from his grip, embracing the layered carapace of his gauntlet and shooting down the steering vane he was gripping tightly.

When his senses reached the chassis' floor, he was momentarily lost. The extra armoured cladding and the excessively airtight welding had crafted a new landscape around him. A lead-better was one of simple beams and straight-line paths. This was a coagulated mess of a dozen different machines still struggling to form a cohesive mass despite its united appearance.

Ryza's magnetic resonance skittered back and forth over the folds and under the creases in the newly forged metal. He wasn't brave enough to hop from one piece to another, lest he lose the way back to his body. He needed to leave a trail for himself as he sought out the engine block.

Ruka had already shown the broken connecting rod that would've kicked it into a grumbling gear, but Ryza didn't need a physical connection to its ignition mechanism. He could detour around it, travelling through the manifolds and gaskets until he could plant the spark that was needed.

An erroneous turn shunted him into the networked treads on the ram-raiders left flank, yet Ryza found it hard to double back on his path, so he was forced to waste more time journeying to the back of the chassis and through the top of the vehicle's frame. Not that he knew how much time was being wasted. Controlling metal or an arcanite was funny like that. Time didn't matter when there was no flesh that could die.

Not being able to double back on his own resonance was a more novel problem. It was like he was trying to turn his head to look over his shoulder, but his spine had been fused in place. Like everything he was leaving behind had already become the property of a stranger Ryza no longer was.

It would cause problems in the future, Ryza was sure of that, but he couldn't afford to think of it. He'd just tapped into the engine itself through its dual-layered intake valve, steering clear of its tightly sealed flaps for fear of sabotaging them.

Another form of metal suddenly joined the fray, and Ryza felt his magnetic resonance hesitate halfway down a piston as he tried to work out what else he'd just snatched control of. If he had the space left in his mind to do it, he would've laughed.

That's why it felt weird.

It was another metal gauntlet. One made for a left hand. With one eye still squeezed shut, Ryza forced the other to focus, looking out the front view port. Ruka was still leaning over the engine as best her vent suit would allow, elbow-deep in the engine's workings on the same mission as Ryza.

It wasn't a sabotage.

Ryza shut his other eye and returned his focus to the still-thundering path of his magnetic resonance. It had looped through four of the piston's cylinders, but he still hadn't found the ignition mechanism. He plunged deeper into the engine block, bringing his senses closer to the back of it to near where his feet now rested, and finally found the flywheel.

It was likely the oldest part of the engine, older than the rest of it, having been transplanted from another rusted motor. The teeth on its surface were no more than gentle bumps, and Ryza didn't have the spare wits to work out what order the related cogs needed to turn.

I have to move on.

With the majority of the engine now under the purview of his magnetic resonance, Ryza finally realised he didn't need the flywheel at all. He snaked his resonance out to seize the sixth and final piston in the alternating row and shoved them all into gear. They argued with the crankshaft for a moment, a few of them even managing to properly strike the jutting spark-blocks at the peak of their motion to ignite the fuel in the cylinders, but little more came of it.

Another motion momentarily distracted him, the sudden withdrawal of Ruka's gauntlet as she leapt back from the ram-raider. She wasn't gone for long. Her fingers were back on the intakes, attempting to jam the closed valves open to allow a gasp of filtered air into the engine's working, but the gauntlets were too thick. There was no way she could do it alone.

Ryza grabbed her gauntlet with his magnetic resonance, focusing all of his mind there so he didn't accidentally crush her fingers, and locked the metal in place. He could feel her recoiling, struggling to get away from the engine, but he only needed to hold her there for a moment as he skipped his resonance back into the intakes' valves.

These things were more complicated than the engine itself, a compliment to Ditric's team for manufacturing such an advanced valve under the circumstances. Ryza relinquished his control of Ruka, allowing her to stagger back, and tested each valve carefully, making sure they'd work on their own before jamming both layers of them open.

He shunted the pistons into motion again, and the entire engine roared in delight, spinning up so fast Ryza felt like his entire body was being twisted. He relinquished his control quickly, lingering briefly on the valves to ensure they'd continue to work, then returned to his body.

It was hard to see for a moment. His vision was darkened, but his first, rattling breath brought it pulsing back to life. He hadn't been breathing. Any longer in the engine and he would've suffocated inside the vent suit.

Clumsily, he stomped both feet down on the respective accelerators for the ram-raider's left and right treads, sending the vehicle rocketing in pursuit of Ditric and farewelling Ruka with one last billowing cloud of red dust.

CHAPTER FORTY-TWO

BARRAGE

RYZA KEPT THE COURSE of his magnetic resonance rippling through the inner workings of the ram-raider as he urged it to go faster, sending the dual treads into whining overdrive as they struggled to keep purchase on the loose ground. Either he or the engine was exerting too much power on the recently forged workings, but he had to catch up.

Another chorus of cannon fire rocked the air behind him, washing over the shell of the ram-raider like a gale. If Ryza had a sail, he was sure it would've carried him to the lead of the assaulting convoy. He let vision return to his eyes for a mere moment to watch as the burning lines traced a path overhead. The wall of blazing flux was tall enough it reached beyond the sky. It rippled as the artillery punched through it, parting in anticipation of the blow, then clenching the gap shut before anything could be seen through it.

The ground quaked again as the artillery hit. Sprays of fire and dust rose into the air beyond the barrier of blazing flux, signalling the end of the final barrage from Vorric's battle line. From here on, they were alone in their journey.

Ryza didn't need to imagine the fear and thrill throbbing in the hearts and heads of the others piloting the ram-raiders. It was something he'd experienced so many times that there was no longer a care for death to go along with it. That was part of the thrill he now missed. That they *could* die, but that they also *could* live.

With both the power of his stomping feet on the accelerators and the talons of his magnetic resonance still clutching the ram-raider's engine, Ryza urged the armoured vehicle forwards, bringing his path level to Ditric's so he could cruise along at her right. A protective mesh stopped his eyes from seeing much of her vehicle when he turned his head, so instead he peeked at it from within the controlled metal itself.

Her ram-raider was running like a dream. The forward-facing intake valves that rose just above the armoured scoop flared and gasped in concert with the backwards facing exhausts just behind the gunner's compartment, where they burped and spouted fire with each unnecessarily shifted gear within the engine.

Ryza eased his ram-raider even closer, nudging the tip of Ditric's armoured scoop with his own, transferring just a drop of his magnetic resonance to it, before duking leftwards to avoid an errant pillar of sun-bleached rock.

As his resonance probed its way through Ditric's vehicle, Ryza checked in with his own body. He could feel his lungs gasping again, tight and empty for want of air that the vent suit couldn't provide quickly enough.

Flesh and machine... Can't do both at once. But what if I didn't have to?

Ryza relaxed his grip on his own ram-raider's engine, letting the torrent of fuel being injected into it do the work, and refocused his magnetic resonance on his vent suit. The entire point of the damn thing was to pump clean, pressurised air back into the suit, so why not take advantage of that? One of the oddities of wearing such a contraption was that it always felt like the air itself was being pressed by invisible cupped hands into his mouth if he pumped the handle too much.

With another carefully placed axiom, he gave the pressurising pump lever its own command, one which it would obey until Ryza told it to cease. It might risk over-pressurising the suit, but at least control of his own breathing wouldn't take up much more of his mind. The lever began to creak and hiss off its own accord, and Ryza could feel his lungs responding in kind. With relief, Ryza returned his focus to the metal of his arcanite.

The force of his magnetic resonance was still spreading across Ditric's ram-raider. He held back from taking control but remained near enough to observe the pair of vent-suited soldiers crammed in the cockpit, to hear and translate the faint buzzing voices filtering out from their suits' voice boxes. Ryza had a hard time discerning who was riding along as Ditric's gunner, mainly due to the torrent of swearing radiating from Ditric.

'Don't know what he's fucken playing at! Ding me like that? Tah, and I'll get him back! Thought he wasn't even with us for a— Ah shit, we're about to hit the flux, get the rifle ready!'

Ryza felt the housing mechanism above her gunner's seat swivel to face the oncoming wall of blazing flux and a jarring clack of spring-pushed metal as the mounted weapon was primed for action.

Retreating again to his body, Ryza opened both his eyes, this time exhaling heavily. He made a note to slow the pumping lever at his side a touch, because it was jamming too much air down his throat. Maybe it was a good thing. He was only seconds from hitting the wall of blazing flux, and the sight of that alone had already stolen his breath.

Grey sparkling tendrils of billowing smoke lanced out from the rippling surface to seize the ram-raiders and pull them in. Ryza could feel the deluge of chittering voices clashing against the metal armour of the ram-raider as it probed for a way in, digging their gnashing little teeth into the edges and gaps between the plates.

Ryza felt himself grunting in agony against their bites. It wasn't like a wild animal sinking its fangs into his flesh, more like the needles and spines of a creature's sharp fur grating against him, pulling and pulling and pulling against his skin until it threatened to tear apart like slowly roasted meat.

The ram-raider rocked and shuddered on its path as it fought through the buffeting gusts of blazing flux. His eyes couldn't see more than ten metres ahead of him, something he could hear Ditric swearing about in the next ram-raider over. Even his senses through the metal were stymied. The land around him shivered and jittered, folding in on itself and reforming as the influence of the flux attempted to recreate an expected image.

Soon the silhouettes appeared in the mists ahead.

It was the autominds. Stood in disorganised ranks of their thousands, they crowded across the barren and obscured plains as a wall of reconstituted flesh. Vorric's barrage had done nothing to thin their lines. The blasts had only created craters that the autominds had filled with their own bodies before having more stand atop them, packing them down with sheer weight until those of the former group had become the land itself.

Ryza could sense their blank stares as they lowered their rifles to aim at the onrushing ram-raiders. Their inert fingers as the rifles pulled their own triggers. The uniform backstep against the recoil that they took as they unleashed a volley of momentarily fabricated slugs.

Hundreds of slugs battered the front armour of the ram-raiders, with thousands more flying overhead, but it didn't slow down the vehicles at all.

The first trio of ram-raiders hit the autominds, and predictably, they blasted through them. Through the chittering haze that the blazing flux left in the air, Ryza could feel their bodies being scattered like kicked pebbles. But they didn't stop moving once they hit the ground. Before the next line of ram-raiders could follow through, the scattered autominds had found their feet. They were now braced and ready, their rifles held out before them like blocking polearms as the next three ram-raiders thundered in.

It was like the ram-raiders had hit pure rock.

Metal twisted and screamed. Fuel pumps overloaded as the engines backfired, driving a hungry inferno back into the fuel tanks of the offending vehicles. Secondary blasts went off again as the igniting heat struck the reserve air tanks beneath the vehicles' chassis, launching them with force high into the air.

The crews of all three ram-raiders were ashes before their vehicles even hit the ground.

Ryza lifted his feet from his own vehicle's accelerators and jammed them down on the brakes, using the magnetic resonance he'd imparted in the metal frame of Ditric's ram-raider to do the same. They both ground to a halt, stopping only a few feet short of the barrier of braced autominds.

The kicked-up cloud of dust that'd been following their assault caught up and washed over their vehicles, carrying over the autominds' lines next. When it cleared, Ryza looked into their glassy silver eyes. The expression around them wasn't blank. It was crunched upon their scarred and burned faces. It was a determination Ryza could no longer match.

In the other ram-raider, Ditric was swearing louder than ever, yanking at the release handle of her door so she could get out and brawl with the autominds herself. Ryza didn't doubt how many she was saying she could take down, but he forced his resonance into the door and sealed it shut anyway.

They couldn't afford to fight now. They needed to think. They'd already lost three-quarters of their force.

Going fast didn't work. They expected it because we prepared for it. It's what these vehicles were built for.

The clinical nature of the thought struck a secondary blow in Ryza's heart as the initial grief finally hit. He didn't know exactly who'd been in the other ram-raiders. In which order they'd died. But they'd known which one he was in. That they were doing this for him.

Because of him.

'Fuck! Ryza! I know you can hear me,' Ditric shouted from within her ram-raider. 'We gotta fucken MOVE! Come on, punch it!'

Ryza eased his feet back towards the accelerator pedals, keeping his eyes open to watch the autominds as they raised their rifles again, his ears tuning out the engine as he waited for the next volley of shots. That close, the layered glass protecting him didn't stand a chance, especially not now that he believed as much.

But the autominds didn't fire. Ryza hadn't accelerated yet. He could feel Ditric stomping valiantly on her own accelerators, demanding her gunner to open fire as she did so, but Ryza had already unconsciously jammed both mechanisms in place.

'I don't want to fight.'

The words came out as a whisper, but one of the autominds seemed to have heard. It was in the second rank, slightly to the left, hidden behind the flesh-eaten shoulders of two others, but still visible enough for Ryza to watch as it lowered its rifle.

'This expectation's not mine.'

More of them began lowering their rifles, some dropping them entirely. Ditric could see it happening now too, and her swearing had taken on an air of disbelief.

'Fear is not a want.'

Thousands of rifles thudded into the sand. They hissed as they fell against each other, dissolving into molten flux which then boiled off in tendrils of blazing flux which attempted to reach the ram-raiders but dissipated into the greater mists before making contact.

The autominds hadn't moved.

They watched Ryza.

Their expressions had eased, but there was still some sort of anticipation about them, like they knew what he was about to do next. Ryza's feet hovered over the accelerators. He didn't know how many of these autominds were real, that had existed before the flux had polluted Kyrea or had been conjured by the expectations of those who'd tried to clean it up. Maybe some of them were the bodies of the cleanup crew, those that Vorric had forced to their deaths because he'd seen no other way to get to this future.

Ryza let the weight of his feet rest on the accelerators, using his magnetic resonance to force Ditric's ram-raider to do the same. Both vehicles grumbled restlessly but began grinding forwards. The autominds refused to move. Refused to look away. Ryza could hear Ditric screaming in his ear to either stop or to go faster, to at least let her control her own damn machine, but he blocked her out.

She seemed to feel no pity for the Scythes when she'd ploughed a scorching path through their camp in the opening moments of the battle they'd baited themselves into. At least Ryza had that now.

Pity for the thousands of lives wasted in this wretched factory town.

Pity for the thousands more that'd been conjured to feed the fears of insurmountable numbers.

Pity for the bodies that couldn't feel, couldn't run, and couldn't die as they were knocked down by the armoured scoops of the ram-raiders and squashed beneath their relentless tracks.

Their shins broke first, pierced and punctured by the sharpened lower edge of the scoop. The metal blade then scraped across their chests, tearing away at what little flesh, flux, and dignity was left to reveal their innards, some of which remained in their original forms, desperately continuing to operate despite the ill-mannered workings of the neighbouring, flux-constructed organs.

It didn't matter anymore.

The crushing tracks of the ram-raiders pressed them flat into the ground, spreading the last of their true bodies across the sand as the flux that'd sewn it all together drained into the depths.

The autominds that'd avoided the tracks still faced a painful fate. The pressurised air tanks beneath the ram-raiders' chassis rolled across them, further flattening them until they were spat out the rear, their limp bodies bouncing slightly from the ground as they were suddenly freed.

Out the back of his vehicle's workings, Ryza could sense them as they began to move. They stood up, first pushing themselves upright with shattered arms before wobbling onto shattered legs, the molten flux within them and from the air around them knitting quickly to provide some sort of stability, even if what resulted resembled nothing close to the automind's original form.

Those unlucky survivors were left with stunted, triple-jointed arms that'd formed too long or too short depending on how they'd righted their battered torsos. Their crushed and subsequently elongated heads wavered on necks that had shifted across their bodies until they'd sprouted from chests, backs, and shoulders. The legs were the most sickening.

Extra knees had populated up and down the length of some, alternating backwards and forwards, twisting round and round like a bone-driven spring. Others had been gifted with spikes of solidified flux that'd shot out from their shins and hit the ground as flat pads, making it so their posture was constantly leant forwards. The forms of flesh even melded with that of the machines these lives had been sacrificed to run, crafting wheels, pistons, and cantilevered gears that the autominds now stood with.

The only constant among the autominds, spare for those who'd lost their heads and had found them attached to the hips of those who'd been run over next to them, was that they managed to turn to watch the ram-raiders continue their slaughter.

On and on it went, until Ryza lost track of how many he'd flattened. He reached a nervous tendril of his magnetic resonance out from the safety of his ram-raider's chassis to see how many more autominds were left and if they were purposefully gathering in his path. But the chittering resonances within the blazing flux snapped at him, forcing him back.

He could only watch out the front viewport as more and more autominds were knocked down and crushed under his ram-raider. Every face was different. Not a single copy among them.

They're all real. All of this is real.

Accepting this only made the nauseating horror curdle further in Ryza's stomach. It was so sickening, he wasn't even surprised when the ram-raider hit the overturned wreck of one of its fallen brethren. It was one of the first trio's ram-raiders. Ryza's vehicle pushed it aside with ease before crushing the two vent-suited figures that stood numbly in his way.

When the parade of bodies before him finally ended and the two ram-raiders rumbled out across clear ground, Ryza couldn't see what lay ahead. The faces of the autominds still clouded his vision.

Just like they always have.

AS THINGS SHOULD BE

THE MISTS OF BLAZING flux lifted not long after the ram-raiders cleared the masses of autominds. Laid before Ryza was the tall plateaus that hid the bulk of Kyrea's tunnels, along with the narrow, rocky ramps that led up to their heightened roads. Pools of molten flux dotted the cratered floor before him, though they showed no sign of turning into blazing flux. Through the thick glass of the ram-raider's view port, Ryza could barely tell whether the air above them shimmered.

The sky above was as blue as it had been before Ryza and the rest of the League of Revance had crashed into the barrier of blazing flux. The grey plumes instead formed an enveloping fence surrounding the land at their backs.

But why not here?

If Ryza was right, he was in Holm's territory. Her last bastion against the differing strains of flux that'd been polluted across the land by the ideas of those who'd seen it. Maybe she was keeping the last of the pure stuff to herself, hidden away in Kyrea's tunnels, and that the barrier of blazing flux, along with the autominds they'd found within it, were precautions to keep the living away from it.

But then Ryza remembered Holm's mission within the flux.

Put things right. As they should be.

He looked across the remaining pools of molten flux. Maybe they wouldn't expand. Maybe they'd soon be absorbed into the ground or erased entirely as Holm completed her vision of how she remembered Kyrea. One day, the protective ring of blazing flux would expand, absorbing all that'd been touched by the flux or the machines spawned from it, and leaving behind creations from a time before everything went to shit.

But it would only be in her mind. As it was from within the machine of flux that she was born.

Ryza let both ram-raiders roll to a halt and relinquished his grip on the metal. His body heaved and thrashed as he tried to breathe, regaining control of the action on the wrong tempo. The air he swallowed went straight to his gut, but before he could burp it out, the vent suit's pump forced another breath down his throat.

His lungs burned with the mismatch, and he clawed at the various latches around his neck, failing to free himself of his helmet before he calmed down. With his breathing finally stabilised, he allowed himself a few measured gasps before he began unsealing the door of his ram-raider.

Tiny droplets of silver liquid trickled out of the various levers and valves as he pulled and turned them. A sign of how close they'd come to getting into the ram-raider's cockpit in the first place. He left the vehicle's engine running as he kicked the door open and hauled himself out.

The sandy ground absorbed his boots when he planted them down, and he had to shift his weight carefully to avoid being sucked in up to his ankles. He bent over to look down as best he could from within the vent suit.

On closer inspection, the sand itself was teeming with molten flux. Its chittering chorus became apparent to him, and he turned, seeing his deep footsteps already filled with the silver liquid. The shape of the impressions were already warping, growing distinct toes pre-emptively creating their own footsteps of where it thought he'd walk.

The vent suit's voice box crackled in his ear, and Ryza never thought he'd be so relieved to hear Ditric swearing at him. It'd taken her a few sturdy kicks to open the door of her ram-raider, and her passenger still couldn't get themselves free.

'Don't tell me who it is,' Ryza said quickly as Ditric stormed over.

'Why!? Fucken everyone else is dead! Back there, I swear I just ran over Vhoze, and after him—'

'Don't!' Ryza shouted, the word coming back to him as a shrill whine within his vent suit. 'I know... I know everyone's... dead.' He pointed to Ditric's ram-raider, where the gunner's door was quaking under a rhythm of more desperate kicks. 'But they aren't! It could be any one of them! I didn't know who you brought with you, what the crews were going to be, Vorric wouldn't let me. That means I can just think that all of them lived.'

'You're fucken crazy!' Ditric snapped back.

'Just give me this much,' Ryza pleaded.

'Why? They weren't your people! They're mine! And I led them into this. They believed in me as much as I believed in you, but they only ended up this far from Breggesa or wherever else they came from because I asked them to! I knew we were all gonna die in this, but... fuck, not this fast...'

'You're not,' Ryza said. 'I know you'll live, Ditric.'

'What do you—?'

'I *know*. You and whoever else is in there, but I don't want to find out who else it is, because then I have to accept that the rest are gone. At least this way... Fuck, at least this way I can think it could be any of them. Just give me that much.'

Ryza saw Ditric's stance freeze as the realisation hit her. She quickly stomped back to her ram-raider, making it to the gunner's door in time to shunt it back down before it opened. She tapped on the glass, then made a hand signal at whoever was inside for them to stand down before returning to Ryza.

'So... You *know*, huh?'

Ryza nodded slowly from inside the vent suit, a gesture that rocked his whole body back and forth on the spot slightly. 'I was told. I believe it. I know.'

'And the reels?' Ditric asked hopefully.

'I believe it,' he repeated. Ryza pointed at one of the smaller ramps set into the side of the cliffs ahead. It was narrow, only reaching about halfway up, and the tunnel it led to could've been mistaken for a fold in the rock face. 'That's your in.'

'It's not on the map,' Ditric said after squinting at it.

'There's going to be a lot of things not on the map,' Ryza said grimly. 'Just be ready for it.'

'And what about you?'

Ryza turned to her, silent for a moment.

'Do you... you know, *know*?' she asked.

'I don't,' Ryza said. 'Maybe it's better that way. Better that you don't know, either.'

'I ain't going to see you again, am I?'

'I'd be worried if you did. Means I won't have done what I had to.'

'You figured out what that is yet?'

Ryza sucked in a deep breath, and something within the vent suit squeaked in response. He ignored it, looking up at the ridgelines before returning his gaze to Ditric.

'I'll know it when I see it. Until then...' He pointed up the nearest natural ramp in the chalky cliffside. 'Just need to follow the path.'

'Really are going up there to die, huh?'

'I'm living a life without limits, Ditric. Need to make a few of my own.'

They would've shaken hands, or hugged tightly, anything to farewell each other, but any contact, even now they were supposedly clear of the mists of the blazing flux, was a risk to the integrity of their suits. They could only wave, walk back to their vehicles, and watch as the other sealed themselves in as they readied themselves for a journey they were certain they'd complete.

Ryza sat still in his ram-raider as Ditric's rumbled off towards the small ramp he'd indicated. Vorric's shadow dancer had refused to offer him foresight as to his own fate, with good reason, but was kind enough to tell him that of Ditric's. Ryza now just wished he'd asked after the fates of the others so that maybe he could've saved them. But then he'd be changing things to a way he thought they should be, the very thing he'd come here to stop.

Ditric's tracks left a pair of deep, flux-filled trenches in her wake, so Ryza figured it would be best to start moving before his own ram-raider was absorbed into the sand. The ram-raider's engine roar felt distant and disconnected as it accelerated without the help of Ryza's magnetic resonance. Twin sprays of flux droplets and dust kicked up behind him as he veered the ram-raider towards the larger of the natural ramps, the start of the slope positioned in the opposite direction of where Ditric had headed.

He had to swerve occasionally to avoid suddenly appearing pits of flux, some of which he swore hadn't been there a moment ago. The damn things were hard enough to see in the first place. It was almost unfair that they were appearing on their own. But then again, that was what Ryza was expecting, wasn't it?

The mental dissonance didn't have time to resolve in Ryza's head when he hit the start of the ramp. Trickles of flux ran down its length in small rivulets, but the sloping ground itself was solid rock, pounded down by constant processions of automind-carriers ferrying their cargo up and down the trail. The ram-raider trundled along happily as the ramp grew steeper and steeper, its engine spitting fire gleefully from the dual-valved exhausts.

The path grew narrower, leaving the leftmost tip of the armoured scoop on the ram-raider's fore dangling over the edge, while the right scraped a new, trailing indent into the cliff walls. The grating screech of metal on rock chilled Ryza's spine, but turning slightly to relieve it would send him plummeting back into the pit.

The gentle leftward curve of the trail as it contoured to the face of the cliff brought the barrier of blazing flux back into view. Ryza could barely see it, having to twist out of his seat and jam the front panels of his vent suit's helmet to the view port, but he could pick out where he'd come from. The deep tracks still lingered in the sand, deeper than they'd been when he'd left them, with cracking tendrils sprouting in all different directions from the two lines as the flux carved its own trenches.

Autominds were emerging from the mists of the blazing flux to follow the path he left. None had retained their human shapes. They all hobbled, staggered, or rolled on whatever limbs their twisted and confused regeneration had provided them. From far away, Ryza couldn't tell if they were armed, but he didn't doubt that they'd be able to conjure their rifles at a moment's notice.

Just as it was when it came to exploring the ruins left by those-of-glass, Ryza could not count on the flux to play by any kind of rules. He knew his expectations would be twisted, either by the flux or his own pure resonance-fuelled doubt, and attempting to play them off against each other would only result in a more stunning abomination.

When Ryza's ram-raider crested the ramp and rolled onto the connecting plateaus above Kyrea, he found exactly that. He jammed the vehicle to a halt and began blindly yanking at the door's unsealing mechanisms, not taking his eyes off what lay ahead in case it disappeared.

But I destroyed it!

The door opened after a few more kicks, snapping a few of the sealing mechanisms, but Ryza didn't care. He staggered out of the ram-raider and only stopped when he was at the edge of the next massive pit. He barely even saw the drop.

Lurking over in the distance, its massive legs motionless like pillars clamped upon the land, was Revance. Ryza had forgotten just how gargantuan the fortress had been. It was practically on the horizon itself, but that didn't stop the mechanical beast from towering over him.

It wasn't as he remembered.

The entire hind section of the fortress was missing. The upper portion of the motor pool, the back decks he used to skulk about on when he needed to be alone, all of it was gone. Instead, spines of flux that flashed silver and black in the sun protruded from it like it was a massive, open wound. The rashes of needles covered other sections of the fortress too, constantly writhing as they attempted to knit themselves into a more solid form.

Where the legs met the land, the ichor-like plague of molten flux continued, spilling downwards into the massive pit itself to cover the entire floor of the basin. The surface of the massive lake of flux bubbled and thrashed as it attempted to form waves and currents, choppy in its indecision. Ryza couldn't tell if the flow was originating from the newly rebuilt Revance, or from the gaping, dark tunnel that lay against the back wall of the sunken basin.

Observing the currents, it became clear that they were duelling against each other. The flows of flux spewing from Revance's rear was not pure silver liquid. Hunks of hastily materialised vehicles, scraps discarded from the fortress, and other rusted and discarded parts bobbed up and down as they followed the flux's slow fall down the cliff walls. Once they fell into the basin itself, they were quickly absorbed, sometimes re-emerging with different shapes or armaments that could never have belonged to their originals.

The flux flowing from the tunnel had a similar problem, though what it produced was vastly different. The strips of metal that emerged were gleamingly silver, untouched and exquisitely manufactured. Ryza couldn't even begin to identify what kind of building or craft or vehicle they'd go into because every time the pieces sunk too far below the surface, they began to change. What resulted was a messy, slow-moving whirlpool of detritus that had no idea what era it wanted to belong in or what technology it wanted to utilise.

These overengineered abominations washed up on the shores of the basin a hundred metres below Ryza's feet. He leant over to look down at them and was instantly reminded of the piles of junk in the Scraplands.

No one had any idea where the detritus of the region had come from, what purpose it could've possibly served, or why anyone would've thrown away so much damn metal in the first place, but maybe there'd never been a reason for it, at all. Maybe the Scraplands was another result of molten flux's misfortune, a catastrophe that'd come and gone long before the time of the Droughtlands as Ryza knew it.

So I can do it again.

Maybe Holm wasn't in control of any of this, at all. Maybe no one was. Not even him. He risked clenching his eyes shut for a moment, trying to remember precisely what Origin had said to him.

What would've happened without you? Without the resistance? Without the battle that destroyed the fortress? Without you being a part of that machine?

Ryza chewed his upper lip. It was hard to do within the tight confines of the vent suit's helmet, but he forced himself to do it anyway. His mind was weary, beyond strained, and worn out from a lack of sleep. Could Origin really be right? Could he have told Ryza the truth, even if he had lied to all the others as a means to ward them away from finding molten flux?

That was the nature of what those-of-glass had left behind. The flux and the magic, they were both lies that needed to be accepted as truths in order to not destroy the minds of those who heard them. Ryza had worked so hard to see them for what they were, then to reject them as falsities, but now, after all this time, how was it possible to ignore them both entirely?

There was a movement in the pit of the yawning tunnel that caught his eye. From his distance, it was no bigger to Ryza than an unfortunate worm that'd burrowed up next to his boot, but he knew its form instantly.

It's Holm's war serpent.

It slithered out from the tunnel's shade and into the sunlight, the bright orange rays glinting off its steel-scaled back as it followed the tide of the flowing flux. Ryza was sure it was looking up at him as it swam. Sure that he could see a rider upon its back. Certain that it was Holm, beckoning him to give chase.

The war serpent paused, unnaturally still against the tide, then turned and began swimming against it, disappearing into the tunnel now that Ryza's curiosity was piqued. He knew that he should ignore it. That it meant nothing. That it likely only appeared just so he'd pursue it. But knowing only that wasn't enough.

Ryza turned and marched back to the ram-raider, not even bothering to shut the door before kicking the engine back into gear. The piston-driven roar was all the goading he needed, and he angled the ram-raider to launch it on a new path, one that would skirt along the cliffs overlooking the basin and towards the foot of Revance itself.

CHAPTER FORTY-FOUR

SKELETON CREW

REVANCE HADN'T MOVED BY the time Ryza brought the ram-raider to a skidding stop next to one of its forward legs. A small miracle, because he'd spent the entire journey over to it swearing under his breath, praying that the damn thing wouldn't just take off.

The fortress' presence still perplexed Ryza, and no matter how much he forced his mind to ignore the problem, he couldn't help wondering why it had shown up there of all places. Tracing Revance's original route, it had never walked directly into or over Kyrea. Its avoidance of the place was likely one of the only reasons that the conscripts hadn't been sent in, wave after wave, to purge the very factories that manufactured their rifles and munitions.

Ryza had previously heard tales from some of Revance's old guard that there'd been attempts to do just that. Without the supporting bombardment of the fortress itself, it was impossible to breach through the tunnels once the smelters entrenched themselves within their mouths, let alone hold the subterranean ground that lay beyond.

Ryza spared the yawning tunnel at the bottom of the basin one last look before climbing out of the ram-raider. The mimicries it was producing had become more complete in their form as he'd come nearer. They now resembled carved-off hunks of skyscrapers or other strangely shaped buildings left by those-of-glass. Things festooned with antennae, oddly angled metal dishes, and walls entirely clad with mosaics of golden, hexagonal tiles.

Good thing Ditric isn't here, she'd probably want to go pry those things off to sell.

There'd been many aboard Revance who would've done the same, Ryza thought to himself. Such greed was how Maligar had whipped up so many to join the Locusts in order to betray Revance's command. Whether Maligar himself had held that same, simple greed in his heart was harder to determine. After watching him die twice, Ryza was sure that the man had always been hungry to control the flux itself, that the picture of greed was only a means to an end.

Yet that greed could only be construed as something natural to all those who'd worn the conscript's collar. No one had joined Revance's ranks for a reason that didn't boil down to the sack of reels they'd been promised if they survived.

The refugees that'd flocked to Breggesa likely would've been the next generation willing to staff Revance's now non-existent corridors. Maybe that was why the fortress had reformed in this place. It needed to exist so everything that relied on its influence could continue to thrive. The factories that armed its soldiers. The smelters that fought against them. The downtrodden, the drifters, and the urchins of the Droughtlands that had no other choice but to join up and fight.

Revance was a machine, both in metal and concept, just as Origin had said, that served as such a vital part of the Droughtlands that its re-creation was an inevitability.

It wasn't Holm's doing. Wasn't Ryza's, or anyone else's. It was a manifestation of a need that could not be ignored. Maybe that was why Origin said he'd created Revance in the first time. Ryza wasn't sure how much to believe this, however. He was still weighing up if Origin had actually been a person that was still in control of his consciousness and his grinding, metallic voice, or if he was a more complex result of molten flux's creation.

Ryza hauled himself out of the ram-raider, letting the engines die one last time, and ambled over to the massive foot this version of Revance had sunk into the plateau. He had a feeling he no longer needed the vehicle. It had served its purpose. When he turned to look back at it, jagged spikes of molten flux had already sprouted from the rocky ground to begin dismantling it. To incorporate the new ideas that it had been starved of within this desolate place.

'You can have it,' Ryza said to the flux. 'They made it because of you, so that's as good as you making it yourself, isn't it?'

At his words, the probing spines of flux lurched away from the chassis, repulsed by the very concept. Ryza chuckled to himself.

'That's right. No new ideas here! We're stuck! That's probably why you can't come after me, ain't it? Because I've *seen* you. I know what you are. If you take me, then you're stuck being just that.' Ryza allowed himself a dramatic gasp as another realisation struck him. 'And that's why I keep coming out of the flux as well. Because you've *seen* me! But I'm not like you. *I* can change on my own!'

'Then prove it.'

Ryza screamed, and the vent suit's voice box crackled back violently. The damn thing made it near impossible to figure out where sounds were coming from, but on a well-honed instinct, Ryza spun and found the source of the words.

'Archarus!'

Fuelled only by spite, Ryza whipped the sawn-off rifle out of the holster on his thigh and fired it straight into the shadow dancer's flickering chest. The incendiary slug was more than happy to abide the order, sending out a lancing spear of blinding white fire. The inferno sprayed in all directions as the air itself ignited, producing a combination of blackened smoke and the gently tinkling sound of scorched flux as it fell to the ground.

The air cleared, and a trail of miniscule silver needles lay along the ground between Ryza and the shadow dancer. Though it may not be as visible as the clouds of blazing flux he'd passed through to get here, it was apparent that some flux still lingered in the air.

His breath heaving in his chest and rifle still held outstretched, Ryza stared Archarus down. Predictably enough, the shadow dancer was entirely unaffected by Ryza's shot. Considering the scorching pit burning in the leg of Revance beyond him, the slug had passed straight through his ethereal body. Archarus made no move to respond. He just stood there, his hands hidden behind his back as always, his deep black coat of embossed silver runes motionless, and his expression nonplussed.

'Why?' Archarus asked simply.

'Made me feel better,' Ryza said as he jammed another incendiary slug down the breach of his rifle. 'Where the fuck have you been? Of all the people it would've been helpful to talk to—'

'I was withheld.'

'You can be anywhere! Anytime! No one can stop you! Who could've—'

'I've been told you met just who could've held me back,' Archarus snapped, cutting Ryza off. 'Most shadow dancers wouldn't risk quarrelling with another of our fate. Too costly to the both of us. But the one you met... Well, they have a different price to pay.'

'Then why are you here now?' Ryza asked.

'Because this place, this moment, it's one of those few unique ones where the price paid by the shadow dancer you met is far greater than what I can ever risk.' Archarus walked past Ryza, beckoning him to join him at the edge of the cliff overlooking the basin. 'They spoke of fixed fates, of sureties and certainties, yes?'

'They did,' Ryza answered, having joined Archarus at his side.

'That's not something that pure resonance caters for. Especially not in the form you've stumbled upon. They are afraid of this place. This moment in their history. Where the impossible is already happening. Where it can happen again.' Archarus looked to Ryza, his black eyes boring straight through the protective layers of glass separating them to make Ryza shiver. 'They do not know your fate. Cannot know your fate, rather, because to do so would be interfering in the actions you take at such a consequential moment.'

'Wouldn't they want to try make things better? They've told me they can't, but I don't get why...'

Archarus thought for a while, eventually coming out with a slow-paced answer.

'A known fate is a certainty, one of the key aspects of pure resonance, yes? They... they know all fates. All except a few that are too delicate, too complex, too dangerous for them to know. If they interfered and changed them now, would the rest of that which they know, of futures now and long beyond this time, still be worth it? Or would they tumble into uncertainty and create something like...' he waved out across the basin, where at the centre of the flood of flux, the swirling trash heap was piling up to be half as tall as the cliffs surrounding it, '...like this?'

'But you still showed up. Does that mean you're a part of whatever's about to happen?'

Archarus shrugged. 'It's all down to instincts now, Ryza. But remember that yours are truly unique.'

'How?'

Archarus smiled grimly at him. 'You're no longer trying to survive.'

But Holm is.

As soon as Ryza had the thought, Archarus vanished. Ryza didn't bother calling after him. The shadow dancer may've been right, but it did little to change his mind or course of action. He stumbled back to the nearest leg of Revance, pumping the pressurising lever of his vent suit for good measure, and assessed the best route up there.

The flux had done an impressive job of replicating the many gaps and crevices in Revance's rivet-strewn skin. With a sigh followed by a few deep breaths, Ryza picked his starting point and began his ascent. The route almost seemed similar to what he'd climbed up way back when he'd first found Origin and had been forced to sneak back aboard the fortress in the dead of night.

At least this time it's not moving.

The only hazard he had to deal with was the patches that the flux hadn't gotten around to finishing. Those lay as open wounds upon the surface of the rusted metal. Silver strands of flux bristled sharply within, the points of the spines retracting as Ryza drew near. If he wanted to be cocky, he'd begin to think that the flux was afraid of him, but too much of his mind was focused on climbing to bother with that.

The ill-fitting boots he'd originally climbed all over the fortress with had been ill-fit for the task, but at least Ryza had been able to feel the surface of the metal through them. The vent suit's metal boots were broad and lacked a single sharp edge around their soles, so there were very few gaps large enough that he could jam them in that weren't the curving rungs of a partial ladder.

The gauntlet wasn't much better, and with only one hand to keep his unbalanced body from falling away from the metal surface, Ryza was rapidly finding himself exhausted. Each step up required him to carefully scour his surroundings for another stable handhold, difficult enough with the limited view the vent suit's helm provided, then whip his hand towards it and pray that he caught a secure hold. Without the ability to test his weight against it, each move came with a heart-leaping creak of slowly warping metal.

After clambering over the final edge and onto the upper housing of Revance's rounded foot, Ryza allowed himself to flop in a heap. It took him a minute to push himself to his feet. The only thing more painful than the irony of falling now would probably be the impact at the bottom.

Ryza drew his rifle from his thigh again and began carefully making his way up the narrow walkway that ran along the top of Revance's extended leg. There was no guardrail, just like it had been with the original, but the way the metal groaned and bowed underfoot made Ryza wish the flux had added one.

At the other end, Ryza found a way inside by means of a nearby hatch. An entrance like this would usually be bolted shut. It was a constant decapitation risk, being positioned in the path of the leg's oscillating joint, but it was safe enough for Ryza to squeeze through.

He landed in what should've been the corridors around the small munition stores, but as he clanked down the narrow passage, he found room after room that he was certain shouldn't be there. One was an infirmary that belonged on the other side of the fortress, just a few corridors down from the motor pool. Another looked to have grown too large for its allotted space, somehow invading the bounds of the next chamber over, signalled by the jarring change in the floor's texture and pattern as the initial forge room warped into crew quarters.

The next looked to have never belonged aboard Revance in the first place. The floor went from plated, overlapping metal at the threshold to strips of flat wood. These followed a straight line for a few metres, but then swung jarringly to the left, shrinking and converging until they all met in the room's back as a handspan-wide strip of spackled brown that proceeded to run up the corner of the metal walls like a supporting pillar.

Ryza kept moving, eerily aware of how empty the fortress felt. Revance wasn't itself without its people. Without the vital parts of its machine. The thought made Ryza wonder about the nature of

Revance's creation. If Origin had simply created the fortress and let it loose upon the Droughtlands, who had been the first person to board it? To weld and bolt on so much metal that it was impossible to tell what it had originally looked like?

What would they think of it now?

His mind continued to probe the topic as he entered the motor pool. It had been a twisting journey to get there. Some parts of the walkways and passages had been completely absent, forcing Ryza to double back or precariously clamber across what little remained of them. With the wind blowing in from the motor pool's open back and rustling against the vent suit's voice box, Ryza discovered he was no longer alone.

The place was just as he remembered it. It was almost entirely cleared of its vehicles. Sitting on the barren deck plates were a crowd of conscripts. Their skin was a mix of silver and flesh, the colour only broken where unscabbed wounds and fresh bruises made themselves known. Similar inconsistencies came with their battered greatcoats, some of which trailed across the floor for far too long, while others seemed to wear the coats more as tunics, robes, or even dresses.

The garments quickly rearranged themselves, correcting the error, each time Ryza spotted one. Ryza struggled to recognise any of the faces there. He should be able to. By his count, many of those who'd ended up at Iroka, or had come along for the journey with he and Ditric thereafter would've at one point been sat in this place as well. But try as he might, he couldn't force his memory back to that dark day when Revance had first fallen to the smelters.

It was as if the vision was blocked off. Imprisoned within one of those damn black blocks that Holm had insisted on showing him in those dreams. The conscripts on the floor didn't make it any easier, either. Their heads hung low under the weight of their iron collars, they refused to look up. All except one.

Me.

CHAPTER FORTY-FIVE

BACK FROM DEATH

Ryza's memory finally snapped into place. He could picture exactly where he'd sat with Ditric beside him, hissing and swearing, while he did his best to hide Origin from the guarding Locusts that patrolled the beaten-down captives.

But there were no guards in this version of the motor pool. No one else standing, aside from Ryza, clad in his vent suit but feeling too naked, too exposed, as the copy of himself stared at him. The clone moved, and Ryza brandished his rifle at him, but the clone did not hesitate as he stood. The other conscripts shifted carefully to create a path between the twin figures, glancing around as if the guards really were there.

Ryza could see Origin hanging limp in his clone's grip. The arcanite's arms dangled and clinked, a sound Ryza was surprised his vent suit could pick up on.

'Drop him!' Ryza called out to the clone, twitching the muzzle of his gun towards Origin.

'No,' his clone replied.

'Is he a part of you?' Ryza snarled quickly. 'That why you can't let him go?'

The Ryz-ain't's face broke into a tilted grimace, the kind Ryza knew was the result of his own expression when he was trying for something more well-humoured.

'Well, that's why you're here, isn't it?' the Ryz-ain't replied.

'Can't let this moment go?' another voice from the captive conscripts asked, also sounding eerily like Ryza.

'Still regret coming back here?' a third called.

'I'll make you fucking regret it!' Ryza roared back.

He launched his stride towards the false copy of himself, rifle still raised and fully ready to take back whatever version of Origin the flux had summoned out of sheer pride, but he only made it one step. One single step before the entire captive mass of conscripts suddenly rose to their feet. As one, they turned on him, and he froze, all their faces suddenly a mirror of his.

'If you'd stood up,' one of them said.

'All of them would have,' another finished.

'You could've won this fight, Ryza.'

The last words were spoken by the Ryz-ain't holding Origin, but all the rest joined in to say his name. It echoed through the motor pool, coming straight back through his vent suit as if he weren't wearing it at all.

'That's only what I thought!' Ryza protested.

He jammed his foot forwards and managed another step before the crowd of his copies pressed in again. All he could do was try to elbow his way through the field of his clones, but the gathering throng turned into a thrashing mob. Their pummelling fists bounced off the armoured exterior of his vent suit as he fought valiantly forwards, but their goading taunts cut deep beyond his flesh.

'But then Revance wouldn't have fallen!'

'Tyrag wouldn't have gotten all the autominds!'

'Maligar wouldn't have controlled the flux!'

'Holm wouldn't have controlled it, either!'

The mention of her name shot a bolt of fury through Ryza's body. It yanked at the muscles in his still outstretched arm as he was wrestling it out of the grasp of three more, instead bringing it down, elbow first and devastatingly hard, into the core of one of the Ryz-ain'ts. They responded with roars and whoops of exhilaration. A fight was on, and no matter what, Ryza was going to win it.

Ryza whipped and slashed his sawn-off rifle like a sabre, staving in several copies of his own face with each swing. More arms lashed out, right hands grappling with his own, their grips too strong for Ryza to appreciate the flux finally recognising the truth of his body. Suddenly he was backpedalling; it was the only way to free himself, even if it was sending him teetering towards the edge of the motor pool.

A few more quick steps extracted him from the crowd of his mirrored faces, and he spun on the spot, paying the price of momentary dizziness to get a view of how far the fall was into the pit below. It was maybe a hundred metres or more to the bottom of the flux-filled basin, where a surface of nothing but writhing silver liquid waited for him.

Facing the Ryz-ain'ts again, Ryza swung the muzzle of his rifle between them, searching for the one holding Origin as the others crowded around. They did not hesitate out of fear of death. Their grins were hungry, the same kind of hunger Ryza knew he'd felt in his heart when he'd jammed the flux injector needle into Tyrag's spine. They wanted to hear his last words. To see his last actions in such a moment of defeat.

The Ryz-ain't he was searching for stepped forwards. Origin was still held in his hand, and he raised his arm to display the arcanite to Ryza, placing it between the muzzle of his rifle and his own leering face.

'There was a time when finding Origin would've solved all your problems,' the Ryz-ain't taunted. 'Many times. But why not now? Why not weeks ago under those ruins?'

'You know what he said to me?'

'Of course we do,' the Ryz-ain'ts chorused. 'Because we said it to you.'

'You don't know that!' Ryza spat back. 'You only think that because I think that! Because I only have room for doubt, and doubt only leads me back to the flux!'

The leading Ryz-ain't cocked his head, appearing out from behind Origin and meeting Ryza's eyes with his own green stare. 'But does that make it any less true?'

'No. But you can't change the past. Fuck, I tried. You watched me try. You tried to help me, didn't you? But what would've happened if I did? How much more would've been lost? How long would the

Droughtlands have lasted before you were let loose across it?'

'Me?' the Ryz-ain't asked.

'The flux!' Ryza shouted back.

'No, Ryza. Us.' The Ryz-ain't took another step closer, lowering Origin to the ground where the arcanite simply dissolved into the deck plates. 'You.'

Ryza forced a grim chuckle through his gritted teeth, moving forwards slightly to press the muzzle of his rifle into the Ryz-ain't's forehead. The clone resisted the force, the muscles of his neck stiffening as they braced, but Ryza could still feel the way the metal of his weapon gouged into the manufactured flesh.

'Don't play this game with me,' Ryza growled. 'I've already played it for long enough.'

'We know that well,' the Ryz-ain't responded. There was a certain gloom in his voice. An admission of ignorance. 'Molten flux wasn't made to be questioned. Not to the extent that you've done.'

'Are these your words as the flux or my thoughts being vomited back to me?' Ryza grunted.

'Both would be the same,' the Ryz-ain't replied simply. 'The flux was to be a replacement for pure resonance. An accepted solution to a problem that could not be solved. It triumphed over curiosity. Over greed. Over patience and over superstitious fear. But not you, Ryza. What are you? It's not a question you can answer, yet it's one you've tried. Just as the flux has tried. Just as I have tried.'

The Ryz-ain't's face began to morph. It twisted into a snarling rage as the nose shrunk, the eyes puffed and then recessed, the skin simmered, and the form shrunk. Soon, in an audience of her creations, Holm stood before Ryza.

She was perfect.

Every inch of skin, every dint from old scars, the scratches that hadn't yet healed, the imprints of the vent mask across her cheekbones, it was all perfect to the way Ryza last had seen her. She looked to him with pity for a moment, then to her left arm.

Inside the brown greatcoat she'd summoned for herself, it still hadn't grown back. Ryza unleashed a snapping bark of laughter at her.

'You tried so hard to please me that you forgot yourself!'

'Just as you did to me,' Holm replied.

Her lips twitched with a silently spoken word, and the hollow sleeve instantly filled, a silver-skinned hand shooting out from the cuff.

'But I think you know why that happens,' Holm continued. 'An overreliance on another's mind to form an idea of who you are. I thought I was better than it. Better than you. I should've known better.'

'Should've?' Ryza said. He waved across the crowd of his copies, then out at the still brewing basin of flux behind him. 'How were you supposed to know any of this!? That's the problem with the flux! That's just it! It makes you fucking arrogant! How have I never realised this before?'

He muttered the last words to himself as he turned to look out from the edge of the motor pool. If not for the clouded wall of blazing flux, the scene might've been serene. Now he thought about it, he was probably the first and only person to ever stand aboard Revance while it wasn't in motion. Holm appeared beside him, having taken a few steps and now looking up at him with a raised eyebrow. Ryza continued, his tone bitter.

'The flux wasn't made to be questioned,' Ryza said, repeating the words that'd just been said to him. 'It was just to give confidence, but isn't unquestioning confidence just arrogance? The same kind that led everyone else to their deaths?'

'I don't understand,' Holm said innocently.

'Oh, you do, don't give me that,' Ryza replied. 'Think of it... Think of it like this. The flux is a machine—'

'One of Origin's machines?'

'—that provides answers. Yeah, sure... It provides answers in the face of uncertainty to *make* certainty. It...' Ryza was still grappling with the thoughts as they came to his lips, but he pushed on, doing his best not to stumble over his words. 'This machine worked all well and good right up until it met me. Or anyone who spent too long looking at it, just like pure resonance. But with pure resonance, if you get to it, you just die, right? You just turn into a shadow dancer and that's it. No more of that unlimited magic, you're just waiting for the end with the rest of them.

'But not me. Not after my pure resonance, because the molten flux let me live. And unlike pure resonance, molten flux doesn't have a way to kill off someone that thinks too hard about it. It... it can blaze, find new ideas, overwhelm whoever's been asking it tricky questions by finding more people who aren't, but Holm, when you jumped into the flux, when you made it about me... when *I* made it about me... then there was no stopping it. There was no way to answer my questions, my instincts, because I was... I still am nothing but doubt. So how does molten flux answer to that doubt of truth?'

'By lying?' Holm suggested.

'And what if I doubt that?'

'Then the flux lies again.'

'And then I doubt that as well! Don't you see it, Holm? An infinite cycle, one contained within another, where the flux has to keep becoming more and more bizarre and unhinged in the face of *me*, the very thing it's structured itself around, where it can only expect another answer the same as the first. The flux is so... focused on getting to me because it has yet to satisfy me, it can't "want as I want" because I don't want the truth! I want lies! I want lies that I can never believe so I can want even bigger ones to pick apart and doubt! And because the flux has become so obsessed with showing me that, that it's even gone on to show the lies meant for me to everyone else, then everyone else expects the flux to be based around me!

'That's why Revance is here! That's why I am here, why you are here! It's even what Origin said to me! "I'm going away. A command it must obey. It wants nothing else." If the flux was to truly spread across the Droughtlands, it would have to hide in plain sight just as pure resonance does now. Inside every rune and axiom, beneath every grain of sand. But it can't do that. Not as long as I'm around. Not as long as it's so focused on me. That's why you came to this place. Why you needed to draw me in alone. Because this machine is nothing without me. If I found a way to live beyond flux like Origin truly said, like you truly said to me, all of this would collapse. It would be gone.'

'And you trust that?'

Ryza grinned, a movement that would normally be imperceptible from within the vent suit, but it made Holm bristle all the same.

'Of course I don't. You can't trust me not to change. You'll have to keep changing with me, but how long can you keep that up? How long can you cater to my doubts until you doubt yourself? How long until the molten flux that you've become experiences pure resonance?'

'You think that I could?'

'I wouldn't want to stay here to find out,' Ryza said.

He turned, realising that Holm wasn't standing at his side anymore, having instead shifted behind him. His heart jumped. He knew this moment. That indifferent expression on her face. The next words she was about to say.

'Suit yourself.'

'Holm, no—!'

Without warning, Holm shoved him square in the chest. Ryza felt the deck plates disappear from under his feet, and suddenly he was plummeting into the abyss.

WORDS SO FINAL

RYZA COULDN'T REMEMBER THE fall. He wasn't sure if he wanted to. He felt that his body was flat on the ground, but as he scraped his hand through whatever was supporting him, it seemed to slosh between his fingers. He opened his eyes, waiting for the blurry mass of grey to solidify into something else, but all he could see was the intense spiderweb of cracks of his vent suit's visor.

He gasped, then held his breath for what little good it would do him. To the left side of his face, one of the glass panels was gone. Grey-looking sand had flowed into the helmet, the grains dancing across the inside of the flat glass pieces with every shuddering breath that Ryza blew out from his pursed lips.

Slowly, Ryza pushed himself off his stomach and onto his hand and knees, keeping his head tilted to drain the sand from the wounds in the vent suit's protective layers. As he began to stand, he kept his head bowed, still shaking out little falls of sand.

The ground below absorbed the grains happily, resolving into a flat plane of grey that struggled to remember his footprints. Ryza didn't need to look up to know where he was. It was a place well beyond the vent suit's protection. The shattered glass of the helmet didn't matter anymore.

His fingers ached as they scrabbled against the clasps of the vent suit's helmet. The gauntlet's mechanisms were stiffer than usual, likely jammed from the fall, but Ryza still didn't have the brain power to think of how far a fall it had been. He was just focused on the relief of having an excuse to take the damn helmet off.

The working latches came apart with subtle clicks. The damaged ones, bent by the impact or eaten away by the corrosive fangs of blazing flux, either crumbled when forced or snapped like bone. Once the helmet was free, Ryza jammed his fingers through the gap in the cracked visor to get a grip, then yanked it off in one grand motion. He dropped it to the ground at his side, where it hit the sand with a dull thud, throwing up a low mist of it that lingered for a bit too long.

Ryza watched as the helm's steel plating dissolved, running off into the ground as unwoven strands of wire, and tried not to think about the same happening to his armoured boots.

He was now in the depths of the basin, his back a few metres from the cliffs and an island of grey sand inexplicably under his feet. High above, the rear lip of Revance's motor pool still hung out over the rocky edge. The twin falls of flux that came from either side, festooned with jagged scrap metal creations, fell as a slow ooze. It almost looked like these contraptions were being gently lowered into the basin.

Not much point. Doesn't matter if they break, they're changing three times before they get down here.

The machines that'd reached the bottom of the basin bobbed idly up and down through the stretching surface of the silver liquid, temporarily bristling with blackened metal spines from the first moment they emerged. They flowed towards the centre, the current steering them away from a narrow path of chalky sand that cut ahead of the island where Ryza now stood.

I guess that's for me as well.

Now things were starting to make sense in Ryza's battered mind. Holm and the flux knew they couldn't continue on without him, but they couldn't keep going if he was wandering around freely, either. Not while he could go and see anything he wanted, to doubt whatever he was shown.

They needed to trap me so they could tell me the right kinds of lies.

Ryza checked the rest of his vent suit. It was largely intact, and he still had the rifle that was strapped across his chest. He checked his thigh for the other one, but the welded metal band that'd been serving as a holster was empty. He'd probably lost the damn thing in the fall, if he could call it that. Ryza looked up at Revance again. Surely it had to have been a hundred metres. How had he survived?

It needs me alive. It needs me to play its game. But I will win it.

Pulling his rifle from his chest, Ryza began stubbornly marching forwards, following the weaving, narrow band of sand across the lake of flux. The liquid metal lapped against the twin shorelines in gentle little waves, bringing with it small trinkets, odds and ends, parts of machines that never existed, and twisted scraps of metal that collapsed upon themselves the moment Ryza set his eyes on them.

He spared a look over his shoulder, prompting a swelling wave to surge away from him across the surface of the flux. It crashed against the rocky walls with a spray of silver droplets. When the flux retreated, the perimeter of junk was reinstated against the bounds of the temporarily bare cliffs.

The place had become more bizarre than the endless factory that'd been founded beneath Twin Rings. More enslaved by rationalism than Maligar's tunnels below Iroka. But Ryza knew what it now mimicked. It was the dreams that Holm had shown him. The dreams that had drawn him back to her.

Even now, the falls of flux coming from Revance's legs were attempting to attune themselves to the vision. Spiny lattices of flux sprouted out from the legs and reached into the air, thatching across itself and then reaching back to gain support from the cliffs, knitting together like rippling fabric to form a ceiling as it attempted to cross the basin.

But it only reached twenty metres before it began to sag. Flux from the more solid sections of what had already been established dropped from place, contorting itself into a series of struts and beams, but they didn't make it to the cliff face before they collapsed and fell into the basin. They landed with a splash, and a confusion took to the surface of the flux in the basin.

Some of it fought valiantly to remain as the support structure it had momentarily demanded itself to be. Other hunks were quickly absorbed, sprouting little wheeled machines that bore strange, ladder-like heads of their own. Still more of them were stuck as the ceiling they were trying to create, floating around as small impressions of the pockmarked basins that lay across the surroundings.

Ryza looked back up at the surviving ceiling as it rapidly reconstructed itself. This time it was smarter, first forming massive, coiled bands that tethered themselves to Revance's hide before extending too far across the void. The reconstructed portions were once again reflecting the land, creating silver imprints of the basins and valleys.

It's trying to trap me. To make sure all I see is molten flux.

Ryza turned and quickened his pace. Even if the flux was successful at covering the basin, he didn't trust it to hold up for long. The shoreline path was widening out as he scurried along it, but it was only to make way for the new colossal wrecks that were washing up from the surface of the flux.

Hunks of debris the size of treadhulks hauled themselves from the flux, carried by legs and wheels that sprouted from all sides. They trundled across the sand before Ryza, momentarily halting his retreat away from the constantly collapsing ceiling before they slopped down into the flux on the other side.

The constructs became more detailed as Ryza neared the centre of the massive basin, but it didn't make them any more comprehensible as they went about their newly imagined duties. Some even managed to float on hastily constructed hulls when they reached the other side of the sandy pathway.

Cracks of gunfire made Ryza flinch, and he pulled his head as low as the remains of his vent suit could allow as slugs hissed over him. The rusted constructions floating on the lake of molten flux had suddenly grown arrays of twisted little cannons and were doing battle with each other.

A swarm of a dozen or so metallic conjurations, each no bigger than a large bucket filled with appropriately lethal scrap, were picking away at something that'd taken the form of an elongated automind-carrier. It even had stumbling human forms wobbling up and down its narrow decks as it attempted to fend off the attackers.

They shot back with a mix of rifles bearing too many barrels and R-Three copies that sprouted from their arms. The swirling current carried the floating skirmish away before Ryza could see if any of the forms taking part in it had stolen his face as well, with more melees breaking out across the lake.

It is a distraction! It's fucking bait!

Ryza tore his eyes away from the pointless battles, focusing on the narrow path of sand ahead. It led down the yawning dark tunnel itself, the very one he'd seen Holm's war serpent disappear into.

Re-holstering his rifle, Ryza pushed himself into the fastest jog that the vent suit would allow. The sand puffed and sank with each footfall, dragging him in, and cursory shots from the surrounding battles began pinging off his armoured back.

Ryza ignored them all. He knew the flux couldn't kill him. He could doubt everything else there was that the flux could show him, but he knew beyond a shadow of a doubt that it needed him alive.

My pure resonance is better than theirs. For now…

The path of grey sand split in two and skirted around the edge of the whirlpool at the basin's centre. Grains were constantly ebbing from them, sucked into the vortex of silver liquid, only to be added to the opposite trail. Ryza hurried along the left path, glancing into the depression of the liquid. More constructs were rising from it, but none of them were ramshackle creations like before.

It had to be the technology left by those-of-glass. It began as a pointed spear of pure white metal as it rose from the opaque depths. Supporting struts followed, connecting the pointed spine to a blunted cone of bronze with a surface of spiralling contours.

The rest of it followed as a perfectly straight cylinder, then arms… no, wings, like that of the rarest insects, unfurled from points across its exterior. Where they connected was delicate, a joint barely more than an inch thick, but the blades of the wings themselves unfurled once their tips were free from the flux.

Their feathers were long, black, and made of curving glass that occasionally glinted gold along its edges. The wingspan of this new metal creature was wide enough to span half the basin's radius. Ryza made it to the other side of the whirlpool as it continued to emerge, the metal sentinel now almost as tall as the surrounding cliff walls.

He turned his back on it and ran on. It was another curiosity offered by the flux. Another thing he did not need to know. To waste his mind on comprehending or doubting. Even as a roar of fire tore through the air from behind him, Ryza did not turn. Even as droplets of flux sprayed past him, prickling against his armour, he did not turn.

The tunnel was close. Fifty metres, maybe less.

In there the flux couldn't lie. It couldn't summon these theatrical visions. It was another thing Ryza was certain of. Kyrea's sordid history would make certain of that. If, like at Iroka, the flux took ideas from the land itself when it ran out of living inspiration, then Ryza was sure that he'd find nothing but the factories of his nightmares.

The industry he'd been born to fuel.

As the infernal roar of the flux's creation faded into the sky above him, the echoes of the tunnel's clanking factories hit Ryza's ears. In the tunnel's mouth, he could see into the gloom where the remains of hovels stood guard. Molten flux still flowed across the floor, adding to the basin both in liquid form and with the fabricated offerings of unseen technology. Ryza slowed just enough to observe the strange weapons that floated past. He recognised some of the components. He'd seen them as a part of the contraptions that'd been fabricated in the factory below Twin Rings.

One factory becomes another.

As the darkness of the tunnel mouth clenched in around him, he spared one last look back at the calamitous basin. The scene had become frozen in time, spare for a few juddering details that were rebelling against the stasis. The ceiling that the flux was trying to construct over the land remained in a half-complete, half-collapsed form. It echoed the geography Ryza had seen in his now distant dreams, but drops of molten flux leaked and dripped from the very highest and deepest crevices of its lands.

The droplets blew in the absent breeze, suspended on impossibly fine strands that held the fallen chunks of ceiling like puppets. They did not move with their controlling threads, gently swaying like they should. Instead, they stuttered back and forth in their place, inch by inch, like the vibration of a thrumming engine had taken it, a sight barely perceptible with how far away it was.

A pyre of halted flux spines rose out from the centre of the valley. They were blackened at the tips of their bloom, a gravestone marker of whatever the flux had shot into the sky to distract him. Ryza didn't know where that thing had gone. Even if he'd seen it go, he wouldn't have believed it.

Blazing flux in a physical form, maybe. Hunting for new ideas beyond the skies themselves, or an echo of how it had come to be in the first place.

But the origins of molten flux didn't matter now. What had once been effective against it, what it had once been and why it had been made, these were all things that had been changed an infinite number of times by each tiny, chittering machine within the liquid metal itself. What was important was what it was now. These precious, present moments where it struggled to cater to his doubts.

And then I will catch it in a lie.

Ryza turned his back on the open sky. On the Droughtlands and on the life he'd lived before. Kyrea waited for him. And within it, Holm.

CHAPTER FORTY-SEVEN

GASP, SCRAPE, SHUNT

T HE TUNNELS OF KYREA were not dark, but they remained gloomy as ever. Ryza felt a fight on his lips as he worked to suck in each breath of air. It prickled on his tongue, in his throat, and down into his lungs. The *hiss-click* of the vent suit's helmet was long gone, but a sound just like it tailed him.

Another rhythm made itself present. It followed a pattern that was impossible to match, be it with his breath or his striding footsteps. There was a gasp of pneumatics, of long-worked pistons with a bore as wide as the silos of fuel they drew from, pushing power into machines that created without demand. Then a scrape as that mechanical torque was pushed onto worn forge presses, ore grinders, and cast metal extruders. The final beat of the toneless song was a shunt. A violent, brief crash of malformed iron as the projects of the endless factory were bullied into their next phase. Conveyor belts starting then stopping, collectors scooping up raw materials, and the final detail being put on armaments that would never find hands to carry them.

This was the song of Kyrea. A never-ending chorus that even molten flux itself couldn't do without. Ryza stalked further down the yawning tunnels with his rifle drawn. It hung loose by his hip, and he walked with an exhausted swagger. He was resigned to what he'd find down there. He knew he was meant to keep doubting the flux, to follow his instincts to declare it a deceiver, but he couldn't help the certainty that this finality was bringing to him.

Holm would be down there. Not hidden among the remaining hovels of years gone by or the reconstructed ones that the flux had put up in their place. Not among the manufacturing lines that stood over the graves marking decades of autominds. But further below, in the chambers created by the flux as they sought to expand her domain. She would've come searching for the same answers Maligar had found below Iroka. A way to be reborn from the bowels of molten flux. A feat that even those-of-glass had failed.

So what chance does she have?

None while he still breathed, Ryza decided. Whatever she produced, whatever imitation of flesh, blood, and spirit came forth, he would doubt it. And because this Holm, whatever iteration she'd become, relied on Ryza's mind to form itself, then she'd never be able to escape those doubts.

She just needs to see it. Then it will spread to the rest of the flux.

A green glow took to the tunnels as Ryza headed in deeper. It came from the arching gouges in the walls like that below Iroka, and he searched his memory to check if those gouges had always been present in Kyrea. It had been hard to tell, back when he'd last had the misfortune of coming to the same place. The walls were always covered in so much grime, so much random scrap and machinery, that he wasn't sure if he'd ever seen the walls at all.

He stuck to the main tunnels as he explored. They were clustered with overlapping networks of machinery and industry that frequently blocked his path, but he didn't want to risk the confines of the smaller side tunnels. No, these places were consistent because they were the ones left by those-of-glass, created before the flux, unlike the rough little side passages that the smelters had dug for themselves.

He passed massive intersections where conveyer belts converged and piled their excrement atop each other, creating a growing dumping ground that he had to scramble over before it grew so large it blocked the way entirely.

There were the crowds of autominds, left over from when their factories operated with purpose, still standing there, tethered to the last dormant machines in the place. Ryza glanced at the faces of each group he passed. They didn't look back at least, but more and more of them in each group stood as a mirror image of himself. He ignored them and kept moving.

His feet ached after what felt like a half hour of walking. His lungs stung from the thickly sharpened air, and his eyes struggled to focus on the shapes ahead as they emerged from the gloom. The tunnels became emptier. The constantly running processions of machines got spottier and more incomplete. Conveyor belts hummed and rattled with nothing to carry. Forge presses clanged, spitting out their parts onto bare floor. The crowds of autominds were no longer in their hundreds, but their dozens, sometimes even less, and rarely did they have a machine to call their master at the end of their slackened, levitating tethers.

Ryza knew his path hadn't curved. He'd been barrelling straight through any junction in the tunnels that he met, and where he couldn't, he circumnavigated the detour until he was on track once again. The ground beneath his feet hadn't slanted up or down, either. Wherever he was being led was beyond the norm of Kyrea. It was the flux's territory. It was where he'd find Holm.

It was as Ryza was crossing yet another largely vacant intersection in the tunnels that she finally made herself known.

'Did you doubt you'd find me?'

Ryza turned at the sound of Holm's call, looking to his left over the top of a waist-high conveyor belt that was burbling away with nothing to show for it. She was walking towards him with silent footsteps, her form appearing from the haze as a silhouette until she was only twenty metres away. Her stance was wide when she eventually stopped. Something was on her shoulder and hanging from her back, weighing her down and throwing her balance. When Ryza realised what it was, he raised his own rifle.

She was armed.

The bracketed barrel of a cannon rested over her left shoulder, its muzzle pointed firmly at him while its bulky firing mechanism acted as a counterweight between her shoulder blades, where a belted feeding system linked to an ammo haulage that was strapped at her lower back. The metal-buckled leather straps holding it all up pressed tight against her clothes.

She was back in her forge leathers, just the way she'd been dressed when they'd first met. A blackened leather apron that was reinforced by chainmail, with tools poking from its pockets that had no consistent form or purpose.

In the remaining gloom, her battered trousers and unstrapped boots seemed to blend into one garment, and Ryza couldn't make out if her hands were gloved or not. The only thing that was certain were her eyes. The green glow of the surrounding tunnels did their best to paint their pale hue to be the truth in there, but they couldn't stop Ryza from seeing the ring of silver that surrounded her pupils.

'You like it?' she sung to him, using the guiding handle in her left hand to twitch the slug cannon's barrel menacingly at Ryza. 'You never got to see it in action more than once in Iroka. Just think. If the smelters had given us another day, we could've all had one. And now you've given me so much more time, Ryza.'

'Too much,' he shouted back. He kept his aim steady as he stepped closer to the conveyor belt. It was moving fast. Crossing it wasn't an option unless he wanted to be unceremoniously hauled further down the tunnel, and crawling under it would make him an easy target for an unsatisfying death. With his hips pressed against the clattering segmented plates of the rapidly moving belt, Ryza pushed his right arm to stretch as far as he could. Even with the incendiary slug, he knew the shot would do nothing, but he wouldn't be able to stand the shame if he missed.

Holm stayed put, a grin exploding across her face.

'I knew you'd come looking for a fight. It's why I chose to appear like this.'

'The flux wanting what they want,' Ryza replied derisively. 'Why? What do you get from it?'

'Why should I need anything at all?' Holm said, continuing to leer at him. 'I already have all I need. I have you.'

Ryza's finger twitched against the trigger. He could barely feel the pressure of it through the gauntlet of his vent suit, but he wasn't ready to fire yet, so he steadied himself.

'I haven't walked into a trap. That's not what this is. I'm ending this.'

'How will you know when you have?'

'When I stop thinking I haven't,' Ryza muttered.

He yanked the trigger.

The kick of the sawn-off rifle was immediate and exhilarating. Even with the weight of the vent suit to fight against it, his arm was still thrown into the air. A brilliant gout of orange flame came from the muzzle as the incendiary slug hurtled towards Holm's pridefully displayed chest. The slug spat fat, flickering sparks from its body as it fought its way through the thickened, flux-laden air, but it would never reach its target.

Narrow, black needles launched up out of the floor of the tunnel from tiny pits that weren't there a moment ago, shooting into the slug's path until one got lucky enough to skewer it only a foot before it hit Holm. The needle didn't waver as it absorbed the velocity of the slug, but the sheer, burning heat of it caused it to begin crackling. The once smooth surface prickled and burst out with miniature spines of its own, until the delicate length of fake metal shattered into a burning heap on the floor where it continued to smoulder and thorn.

Ryza stood his ground as he whipped his rifle open, jamming it under his left arm and shoving another slug in, his eyes locked on Holm. She could've taken the chance to fire up her cannon, to pulverise him where he stood, but she instead bent low, keeping the load of her cannon balanced on her back, and scurried into a mess of forgotten materials to her left.

With his rifle reloaded, Ryza trained it on the place he'd last seen her. Seconds passed. His ears were ringing too hard to detect her footsteps. She could be anywhere in there by now. Ryza could spot a dozen places she could pop out from, and there were probably a dozen more he couldn't spot at all.

Let's see how you like being taunted.

'What happens when flux shows doubt?'

'It changes,' Holm replied. Her voice echoed in the tunnels, coming to him in three distinct waves and from all directions.

'Can it keep changing?' Ryza asked.

'You can.'

Holm whipped out from behind an overflowing cart of twisted pipes, bringing the fearsome weapon on her shoulder to bear. It whined into a scream as she yanked the trigger, giving Ryza almost enough time to dive under the conveyor belt separating them.

Thick slugs of lead flew through the air before he'd hit the ground, the first getting lucky enough to nick one of the air canisters at the back of his vent suit. It gasped and exploded, coming into Ryza's left ear as a small pop before the hearing there was replaced with a painfully high-pitched ringing.

Through his right ear, even though it was pressed to the ground and smarting from how quickly it had gotten there, Ryza heard the rest of the volley smash off the tunnel wall beyond him. He turned his head to watch as the slugs ricocheted a short way, not even denting the faintly glowing surface despite their piercing velocity.

The whine of Holm's weapon died, and Ryza listened hard for footsteps, but only her voice called out to him, taunting him again.

'You've changed a great deal, Ryza. You've become who you really are.'

'And what do you think that is?' Ryza snapped back. He used the moment to dip his head over the top of the conveyor belt, snatching a glimpse, but Holm wasn't there.

'Something beyond the machine you were created for,' Holm called back.

Ryza looked up in panic. Her voice had come from somewhere ahead of him, further down the tunnel where nothing but gloom and silver mist lingered. There was no cover. Nothing to stop an oversized slug from whizzing through the air and killing him before he was good and ready. The telltale hum of Holm's weapon began to ring through the tunnels.

Ryza lurched to his feet and hastily retreated as the sound became a volley, diving behind a series of sturdy-looking vats at the tunnel's massive intersection. Slugs hummed low over his head, the vats around him echoing with great painful thwacks from each blow they took. When the engine whine of Holm's cannon began to die, he jumped to his feet, wheeling about wildly with his rifle as he searched for a target.

The fighting itself was pointless. Ryza knew it and he was sure Holm knew it just as well, but he wasn't about to back down from it.

Before Ryza could spot her, there was another quick-fire whizz from Holm's cannon somewhere to his right. Metal clanged off metal, and Ryza suddenly found himself sprawled, lying on his left side with a painful dent in the armour at his right hip.

He kicked his legs to get himself moving again, looking down his body with his rifle still raised. Holm was there, jogging low towards him as she readied herself to unleash another volley. Ryza pulled the trigger, loosing a shot at her, only for the slug to again be deflected by a spine of flux that shot out from the tunnel walls.

His thrashing boots carried him around the corner before Holm could fire another volley, and he used the momentary respite to right himself and start running again. One of the smelters' tunnels that he would've previously snubbed now shone like a beacon of safety and he dashed into it, only slowing his pace after the first few twists of the passage were between him and the main tunnel. At least here, there were only two directions he could get shot from. In front or from behind.

He reloaded his rifle, pausing midway through the action while the weapon was wedged under his left arm to rub at his right hip. The dent was deep, something he wouldn't be able to excise out from the surface of the metal with only the force of his fingers. The way it jabbed into his bony side forced his walk to become a limp.

She can't kill me yet. But she sure can make me hurt. I'll give her the same.

A moment of hesitation made him consider doubling back. Maybe he could catch her by surprise, but just as he had the thought, Holm's voice scouted its way down the tunnel, washing over him like it had been whispered in his ear.

'I remember coming to this place,' she said softly as Ryza forged ahead. 'I followed you. You navigated it with ease. I know it was Origin that led you, but knowing about him what you know now, do you still think that's the case? Is the flux really lying if it led you to the truth?'

'But it wasn't the truth,' Ryza hissed back over his shoulder to no one. 'The old scholar... Rettic... the truth he told me was what the flux had shown him of Origin. It was only true to the flux.'

'What's true to the flux in this place is the truth,' Holm's voice responded. She sounded more distant now, but it was as if she were coming from up ahead. 'So what happens when the flux calls you the liar?'

'It can't!'

'Can't it?' Holm's voice purred. 'But what if it did? You asked me a similar question, yourself. How long until the molten flux experiences pure resonance? Because that's what pure resonance is, isn't it? A doubt about your own existence that spreads to a doubt about the world around you. That's what you're fuelling the flux with, Ryza.'

'It won't fucking work like that!' Ryza shouted back. 'The flux is a machine! It isn't alive! It can't create life!'

'Then let me prove you wrong.'

Chapter Forty-Eight

The War Serpent

Ryza's skin went cold. A remarkable feat, considering that wearing a vent suit was like walking around in a furnace in the best of circumstances. But the realisation of what he'd done, of the trap he'd walked into after all, far outweighed the way the vent suit intensified his body's warmth.

Holm was right. She was always fucking right. The more he doubted it, the closer the molten flux came to achieving pure resonance, and the twisting dread growing tighter and tighter in his guts only fuelled it more. Even accepting the concept now would be too late. The flux would not be tricked by his own performative doubts. It would be intent on displaying the pure resonance that he'd fled from for months, and after that, it was impossible to guess what could happen.

Ryza didn't know whether to step forwards or flee. He didn't get the choice. The ground beneath his feet began to rumble. A racket of metal clashing and scraping against the hand-excavated rock followed in the same rhythm, growing louder and louder until a ray of radiant green light faded in behind Ryza. He turned, looking back the way he'd come as the glow got brighter. For what little it was worth, he shoved the slug he was holding into his rifle and snapped it shut.

But this time he didn't aim down the tunnel. He kept the rifle held across his chest, angled so that it was only a few inches from his own chin with his arm close to his body. It would only take a flick of the wrist to point the rifle at this mechanical newcomer or at himself.

The source of the noise finally made itself known only a moment before it slithered into sight. It was a metallic roar. A klaxon of sound that assaulted Ryza's ears until they were fit to bleed. As the noise mercifully faded, the massive, angular face of a mechanical snake edged around the corner.

The war serpent...

Its head was large enough to fill the entire passage. It could be that the tunnels were never bored by smelters or smugglers or anyone who'd ever lived down in this wretched place, but by machines of battle and its brethren as they assaulted the poor saps tasked with defending it. It bared its teeth as it turned to face Ryza, its enormous fangs sliding from its jaw like unsheathing swords, long enough that they filled the path from top to bottom.

The hyper-machined barrels that slid out from behind them dripped gently with molten flux. The existence of them was brief, as they sizzled and turned to blackened gravel the moment they hit the ground. It was like molten flux couldn't exist in its basic form down here.

The war serpent's green eyes darted up and down his body from behind their cracked glass casings. They took him in as a hunter would when coming across game that'd all but volunteered to be caught. It was like it was asking him to run. Begging so at least there'd be some sport in the chase.

His ears already ringing with it, terror was the only thing Ryza felt now. A human foe was nothing to him at this point. They carried motives of fear or greed or a mix of the two when it came to a moment of battle. An animal was just the same, most of the time replacing greed with simple, base hunger that would be sated shortly after the battle was won, no matter who won it.

But a machine had none of those things. Especially one with no discernible master behind it. A machine would only react, either to their commands or the circumstances around it, and there was no amount of reasoning or pummelling that could sway them otherwise. That was why the war serpent had been created by those-of-glass, Ryza decided. Why flux had been created, along with it.

For the war serpent, there was no such thing as mercy. It was something Ryza would have to attain himself.

He flicked his wrist upwards, jamming the muzzle of his sawn-off rifle into the fleshy gap under his jaw. The sensation of pressed flesh was one he was all too familiar with. His finger brushed the trigger, halfway through the squeeze that would take his own life, but the war serpent was determined to take him before then.

Another deafening klaxon of a roar sounded, deafening Ryza once more, and the mechanical beast launched forwards. Its fangs, its teeth, and its flux-throwing barrels retracted, and the war serpent's unhinged jaw consumed Ryza whole. He was knocked from his feet, spinning him headfirst into the thrashing metal gullet. He smashed his elbow in the fall, an insignificant blow for the vent suit's armoured carapace, but it jerked his hand, and the rifle still gripped within it, setting the weapon off.

Ryza could only clamp his eyes shut as a cloud of infernal smoke engulfed him. His face burned hard, his throat and his lungs with it, as the air in them ignited, all while the incendiary slug rocketed down the war serpent's throat. The flames dissipated quickly, and the slug rolled back along what served as the creature's tongue to Ryza, and the red-hot pebble of lead bounced right down the neck of Ryza's vent suit.

He screamed as it seared him again, but he couldn't even focus on the burning pain as it wriggled down onto his chest. The war serpent was moving, thrashing its way through the tunnels so violently that Ryza thought his brain was going to be shaken loose from his skull.

The war serpent's jaws only clenched tighter as it travelled, snubbing any chance Ryza had to thrash his way out. Ryza didn't know how far it carried him, or how long for, but when he next drew breath, his vision was a darkened blur, and he was lying flat on his back.

His body squirmed slightly as he tried to recover himself, but he could not find the will to immediately get to his feet. The dent in his armour that dug into his hip was worse. It felt like it was crushing the bone itself. There was no way he could roll onto his side, let alone stand. He clenched his eyes shut, riding the pulsing waves of pain, waiting for a moment where they'd temporarily subside, but it never came. When he opened them again, Holm was standing over him, her silver eyes leering down at him.

'You're alive.'

'I am,' Ryza breathed. He wasn't sure how long that answer would hold true, but he couldn't help humouring her. There was something in her voice, a certain lacquered tone that she could affect in her words that forced him to answer to her, regardless of if she'd asked a question.

'Do you still think it's because I need you alive?'

No matter how sweetly the question was asked, there was no way Ryza could answer. Even professing ignorance wasn't enough. She let out a small, breathless sigh, then held her hand out to him. He took it without thinking, and she hauled him to his feet with an unsurprising ease.

Ryza wobbled on the spot as she asked her next question. His vision still hadn't come back properly. He couldn't see if her eyes were still silver, or if they'd returned to green. There was something wet inside his vent suit that twanged uncomfortably with each breath.

'Do you know where you are?'

'No...' he said, the sound slurring sideways across his tongue.

'It's where you came with Ferrick. Where Origin took you.'

Ryza tried squinting to better make out his surroundings. It really was the cavern where he'd met Rettic. It had to be. But the walls weren't bare natural stone. They glinted with blackened metal. Ryza couldn't make out the shapes it took. Maybe he wouldn't be able to even once his vision returned. Holm was walking away from him now, talking over her shoulder as she approached the shabby old hut that Ryza had found the old man in. He picked up his rifle from where it lay on the ground, holstered it at his thigh, and followed.

'I decided to call this place my home for the same reason that Rettic did. It's the heart of the machine that the flux created. In our time, in his time, and in the time before those-of-glass. Speaking of them, did you like the show I put on for you, out in the basin?'

'It was distraction,' Ryza muttered.

'It was a history lesson,' Holm replied. 'Molten flux may be a machine obsessed with the present, but I've still been able to see glimpses of the past through it. The wonders those-of-glass created... Molten flux is primitive in comparison. The dying gasps of a world that could only doubt itself. I suppose that's what we've become now.'

She'd stopped a step short of the hut's open doorway and nodded for Ryza to look inside. He approached her carefully, then peeked in. The old scholar's clutter was untouched out of what could only be veneration.

Rettic's corpse hadn't been afforded the same treatment. It lay as barely more than a skeleton among the mix of gravel and iron filings that made up his floor, his bones entwined with lattices of coloured wires that almost weaved into garments themselves. Where they left his body, they trailed off into nothing. Just frayed bits of copper and fine white thread that dissolved into fluff. Molten flux had consumed his body the same way it had consumed Origin's. This time, it had nothing to show for it.

'Is this another history lesson?' Ryza asked.

'No. A curiosity, and little more.'

'A curiosity?'

Holm nodded. 'Flux didn't do that to his body, Ryza. Not directly, at least. "Another mystery that will outlast time itself." That's what he said to you, wasn't it?'

'I know. Maybe that's what we will all one day be. All this. Hopefully soon. Just another impossibility for Vorric to burn and bury.'

Holm flinched at this. She must've been remembering the rebel sun. Ryza felt a satisfied grin on his lips, but he didn't let it through.

'You can hope, Ryza. But is that what you expect?'

Ryza let out a disgruntled sigh. 'You already know that answer. Why bother asking?'

'Because I don't need you alive anymore. I asked so I could enjoy you for one last time while I still *wanted* you alive.'

'That isn't true. You *know* that isn't true.'

'And you know it is,' she retorted. 'Have you learnt nothing from what you've seen? From what I've shown you? From what the flux has shown you? It knows you. *I* know you. I can have you, a thousand times, dead or alive, and each time it could be just like this. Each one of you could think you're the one that was born from a flux trader rather than from flux itself. I could fight you, debate you, love you, chide you... I could do whatever I wanted, and no matter what kind of doubt or certainty you threw my way, I could do it all again.'

She began walking once more, beckoning him to follow as she led him around the back of the hut as she talked.

'I know this because that's the nature of molten flux. Thousands of tiny machines making thousands of tiny guesses. Thousands of iterations of the same little world with such small changes between them. A test of every action to find the right one. The accepted one. The one that would work. Because that's what I've done with you, Ryza. This may be the first time *you* have entered the tunnels of Kyrea chasing after me, but it is far, *far*, from the first time that I've asked you to give chase.'

She waved at the back wall of the cavern, and Ryza looked upon her works. He didn't even have the spare breath in him to sigh. It was him. His body. His bodies, all lying there dead in various states of being beaten, bloodied, bruised, and bashed. They lay in one gargantuan pile, their limbs tangled with each other like overly competitive weeds.

Some wore vent suits like Ryza did now. Some were clad in the leather greatcoat of Revance's uniform, all in varying states of tatters. Some wore no clothes at all. The cavern wall beyond them, smothered by the coating of blackened, spine-laden flux, even supported a few dozen of the corpses on their spears, hanging them like a grim tapestry.

There wasn't a hint of rot on the bodies. If Holm were allowed to continue, they'd probably remain fresh until the end of time itself. How funny it was to see so many corpses in a place so filled with molten flux, yet not a single one stood as an automind. If Ryza didn't know any better, he'd almost be heartened by the sight.

'How can you stand this?' Ryza said in disgust. 'And you said you loved some of them? Just to keep the bodies on display? Not even as a display, just a discarded pile of scrap! All to practise for this moment?'

'Would you prefer the bodies be mine?' Holm asked, an eyebrow raised as if she were about to accomplish the unspoken request.

'No! I mean… Would it even matter? You've got me. I'm here, and… and there's nothing I can do about it. But this isn't creating life. These are echoes. Not of me or you, but of the idea of me that grew between us. I used to think that's how you'd stabilise yourself in the flux. To use all these Ryz-ain'ts—'

'A cute name.'

'—to fuel the vision of yourself, but then I realised that you'd only get an echo of yourself. Even if you did find a way to live again, it was never going to be you... Just this copy of a copy of a copy and then what remained of it all by the time you did come back.'

'But that's just the thing, Ryza. Remember your doubts. Remember that the flux will prove you wrong because you want to be proven wrong, just so you can doubt yourself.'

'That's what this is now, is it?' He waved across the mass grave of his own visage. 'All the times I was wrong just so I can come here and be wrong again? What's the end look like, Holm? For you and for flux?'

'There has to be an end?'

'All things end.'

'So why think about it?'

They both looked to the pile of corpses once more, a serene calm in the air that Ryza knew was about to break.

Why think about it at all?

His hand shot to his holstered rifle, drawing it and breaking its breach open in one fluid movement before he jammed it under his arm. His hand then went to his ammo pouch, but before he could find the slug destined for his own chin, the metallic rush of the war serpent was upon him.

The sheer mass of its tackling body hurled him forwards through the cavern, sending him sprawling at the foot of his own corpse pile. Before he could get up, the war serpent was on him, collecting him in the tight grip of its coiled body. Ryza couldn't even writhe against it. The force was beyond crushing, nauseating him as it carried him further up the burial pile.

Holm scaled the jumble of limbs and torsos to meet him there.

'It does matter, huh?' Ryza grunted.

'I'm not done with you yet, Ryza,' she said cooly. 'I still need to prove you wrong on one thing.'

'Yeah? What's...' The serpent squeezed him tighter, forcing his breath out.

'That I can live. That I can be true. That I can be real.'

Ryza snorted as derisively as he could from within the binding serpent's grip. 'Fuck off with that! You ain't been real since Twin Rings!'

Holm chuckled at him, looking over the pile of corpses again. She crouched low over one, cupping its vacant, upturned face with her left hand. Ryza wasn't sure, but he thought he saw the corpse's eyelids flutter at her touch.

'Still one thing you haven't worked out, then.'

'What?'

'Who I am... Who I became... It started long before that. It wasn't in that undercity that I first touched the flux. It was with you. That battle we fought... What a way to be born. Feeling Maligar's blood on my hands, then watching his failed attempts to do as I have now done. That was the problem, Ryza. People didn't trust what Maligar showed them in the flux. You united them against it. They truly believed that you would be the one to stop him.

'People trusted you while you doubted yourself. They *trusted* your doubts. They manifested them and then you doubted it again. In the end, you've performed the same trick that Maligar tried, but you did it all from within your mind. That's how it made you who you are.'

'It made me want to die!' Ryza screamed against the war serpent's tightening coils.

'It made you true, Ryza! It forced you to strip away the pieces of yourself that couldn't withstand the constant doubt, so all that now remains is what's true. What's real. That's why I needed you, Ryza! To let me take off the mask that I was born to wear. To breathe in everything I truly am, and to breathe out everything I never was. You think the molten flux is really corrupted? That it's broken beyond repair?'

Her voice was drawing closer, but Ryza couldn't figure out where it came from. His vent suit was creaking, the metal plates becoming jabbing spears in his ribs.

'Think on it! Really focus!'

'I... can't!'

The war serpent's body emitted a metallic screech, and the pressure suddenly released from Ryza's body. He collapsed, landing facedown on the pile of his own corpses in a heap, motionless for long enough that he might just become one of them.

Something grabbed at his right shoulder, and he was flipped onto his back. His vision spun for a long while after the jerking motion, and he could barely recognise Holm standing over him, let alone the rifle she had pressed against the end of his left arm.

'You were still Ryza after you lost your arm,' Holm muttered. Her voice was barely audible over the cyclical clicking coming from the war serpent as it coiled around them both, rearing its head to leer from over Holm's shoulder.

'What's that supposed to mean?' Ryza wheezed, despite himself.

'Look at the flux,' Holm replied.

She broke his gaze to do just that, and he couldn't resist following suit. The walls were slick with droplets that refused to fall and the black spines that they'd come from. The liquid was no longer that reflective silver that had plagued Ryza's life. It was black. Scorched by a flame that had yet to come, dark as a shadow dancer's eyes.

'It is still flux. It was just changed. It was made true. It was broken free from the machine it was born into. It was your doubts that did that. What remained... these beautiful, bizarre creations... are what the flux truly is. What it will continue to be. Change.'

As Holm pulled him into a limp, sitting position, the war serpent left them, slithering back down the pile of corpses with no care or pity for the limbs and bones its colossal body splintered and crushed. It curled up on the barren ground between the hut and the corpse pile, its clicking pulse puncturing the silent wheezing of Ryza's breath.

'Just watch,' Holm whispered in his ear. 'I know it's been a long time since you've seen me. Since you've really seen me. But I haven't forgotten that moment. You haven't either. When you reached into me and controlled the flux itself. You thought you were pulling it from her blood. But that was only what you wanted, wasn't it?'

'Oh... Oh fuck...'

'That's why I never struggled to take this form, Ryza. Because you remembered that moment so perfectly. The one moment in your life that you never doubted. The first sign of pure resonance, and the perfect way to have a full and exact map of what a life really is. What Holm really is.'

As the war serpent began to retch and quake, Ryza's eyes went wide in horror. Its panelling was beginning to break apart. The smoothly welded seams simply melted, and the plating, composed of alloys strong enough to shrug off a shell from even Revance's main cannon, fell away.

Soon nothing was left but the skeleton that supported the creature's skin. Its bones were slick with black ichor, that corrupted oozing version of molten flux that coated the cavern's walls, all of it stringing together to form a web that blocked out the green glow coming from within.

It wasn't all of its guts that glowed. Only about two metres of it. The source of the light diminished as it began to wriggle up towards what was left of the creature's clamped jaws. There was a creak, a few light and distant grunts of exertion as the thing in there fought against the weight of the fangs.

The jaws were finally pushed open from within, and the last thing Ryza ever expected to see crawled out. She collapsed as she hit the stone-cold ground. She lay there for a while, ignorant of the circumstances of her birth. The strings of black flux coagulated and then fell from her body like dust, blending into the floor like it was a shadow without a source.

Then she stood up and looked upon the monument to death made out to what had once been her lover. She gave a weeping gasp, putting her bloodied hands over her mouth, ignorant to the stain they'd leave on her lips. She looked further. Up at the copy of her own face, at the figure that was cradling her worn and battered love.

Then finally, at Ryza.

The sight of Holm's green eyes made Ryza's heart stop.

'What... Where...' Holm's voice stuttered as she looked upon him. It was like her brain was duelling as to whether or not to recognise the bruised, battered, and scarred face that Ryza had become.

'Holm... It's me...' Ryza said weakly. He shifted, looking up at the silver-eyed Holm as she leered from behind his shoulder. 'What... What have you done?'

'Life, Ryza. I give it to you now. Exactly how I was the moment I left it. The moment I became this.' Her embrace squeezed him tighter as she continued, an attempt at that of a lover's grasp, but it only served to make Ryza's armour dig in even harder to his wounded hip. He grunted in pain, but the silver-eyed Holm only took pleasure in it.

'You can take her. She... she can take you. Go off and be happy together. Free of the animosity and hate that brewed between you and I in Iroka. For that was never her. It was you. Your doubts. Your worries. Your fears all reflected back at you because you *wanted* to quarrel with her. Because you only understood conflict. It broke my heart to give you what you wanted. But she...' the silver-eyed Holm pushed her arm over Ryza's shoulder, pointing at her creation, '...she has her own wants. She *wants* to love you. Without conflict. Without fear. Without worries and without quarrel.'

'Does she even remember any of this?' Ryza said softly, still watching Holm has she took her first steps once again.

'Would you want her to?'

'No. Because then she'd be like you,' Ryza spat.

Out the corner of his eye, the silver-eyed Holm grimaced. 'Then you're in luck. She doesn't. She is exactly that moment you loved her the most. That moment after all that screaming vengeance was finally fulfilled. Never before have I felt such passion. Such a desire. Such a *want*. Maligar fell to that beneath Iroka. You manifested that moment of her life within me, and now I have created it again just for you.'

After all this time, all these years and compressed months, Ryza could no longer doubt what the molten flux was showing him. Every version of Holm he'd seen up until now had borne their own imperfections. Sometimes in their appearance or their manner. Sometimes by accident or by purposeful deception.

But this... this was Holm. The voice whispering these sweet nothings into his ear was right. This really was Holm in that moment after she'd killed Maligar, clad in the leather greatcoat they'd fought to the death in, her hands covered in the blood of the one she'd promised to kill. But now there was no flux. No fear of death for her. Only the confusion plastered across her fresh and unmarked face as she grappled with what was now around her.

'But I killed Maligar! I remember it because I just—' She looked down at the blood on her hands, then back to Ryza and the silver-eyed Holm that embraced him. 'Ryza... what did you do?'

'I'm sorry, Holm... I'm so sorry, I failed... I couldn't get the flux out of you and... and...'

The horror in this new Holm's eyes struck Ryza dumb as she gawped at the abominations surrounding her. At the massed burial of a thousand of his bodies. At the alien and finely articulated, torturous forms of blackened metal that coated the cavern's walls. At the broken jaws of the war serpent that'd regurgitated her.

'Where the... where the *fuck* are we!?'

'Kyrea,' the silver-eyed Holm called back to her, confidence in her voice. She beckoned to her. 'Come. There's much for you to understand.'

'Understand?' Holm roared back in disbelief.

She stumbled towards them, climbing up and over the trail of limbs and legs and chests and burst guts. An abhorrent rage thickened across her brow with each lurching breath she swallowed, her jaw grinding up the words of scorn and disgust that simply weren't good enough to spit in the face of this mimicry.

The silver-eyed Holm rose to meet her, pulling Ryza to his feet by only the grace of the arm still wrapped around his chest. She shoved him gently to the side and let go, allotting him as a bystander to witness this meeting of supposedly identical minds.

'Holm, this ain't you,' Ryza said, nodding to the silver-eyed copy. 'She's flux. It's all flux. Always has been. After Iroka, I—'

'Be quiet,' the silver-eyed Holm hissed back. 'Fresh minds, remember? Do not influence her. Do not give her doubt, or you might lose her all over again.'

'Doubt?' Holm growled in the face of her creator. 'I don't know what you are, and I don't believe it, either!'

'It's better you don't,' she replied.

'YOU. AREN'T. REAL!' Holm screamed back. 'None of this... None of this makes any sense! None of it is... is possible!'

'But neither are you,' Ryza said.

Ryza looked to her, and she met his gaze, still holding all the rage and fire that she'd embraced him with the night before they'd been besieged by the full might of Revance.

The silver-eyed Holm glanced between them in alarm, suddenly scrutinising every detail of her artfully composed creation.

'But she's complete! Perfect in every way! This is exactly who she was! Who you knew! Who you love!'

'Her eyes were green.'

Now they were black.

'Because I'm not real...' Holm breathed out. 'I'm not... I'm...' She looked down at her hands. The blood was gone. The scars, the welts, the calluses and the burns. Her hands were clean. She looked back up at her creator, a maniacal expression taking her face. 'I'm not real.'

Then a spark, a single green spark, sprouted from the faintest crease on Holm's right hand where her thumb joined her palm. The three of them watched as it flickered and danced across her skin, bouncing back and forth across the bases of her fingers at random until it gave a mighty hop, landing in her other upturned hand, this time bouncing back as a pair, both as bright as the first, both bouncing back and forth between her hands, multiplying again and again until the sparks became a revolving wash of particles, then the particles a flowing aura, then the aura a dancing flame that grew and grew as Holm spread her hands apart.

The pale green fire, white at its hottest core, stretched with her, arching into the air to keep her hands connected and bringing the image carved on the walls of the tunnels out into the centre of the space they supported so far below the ground.

Ryza tried to step away, but the mass of his own corpses below him was beginning to writhe against the heat and the blinding light that was beaming from Holm's hands. They reached up and grabbed at his legs, grabbed at each other, and moaned in pained fear. The silver-eyed Holm was backing away, too. The Ryz-ain'ts around her were rising in a more orderly fashion, attempting to act as guards for their master.

But as the band of light continued to grow in Holm's hands, she brought it down, clapping her palms together to bind the arc into a solid, orbiting ring of energy. It wobbled and rocked where it levitated, expanding outwards from the sheer spinning momentum it continued to generate until it reached Holm's chest.

It seared through her clothes and her flesh, and she threw her face to the covered skies as she screamed in an unending pain. But it wasn't just pain. Ryza could see the grin twitching at the edges of her wide-roaring mouth.

It was exhilaration and ecstasy.

She could feel it.

She was alive.

As the energy left her, still expanding its shuddering orbit while the bounds of its crackling band grew thicker and thicker, Holm pulled in a wrenching gasp. Her clothes somehow remained where the energy had burnt through her, marked by a bleached bar of white that wrapped around her torso and her biceps.

Still struggling to fight off the feeble grabs of his copies, Ryza ducked, practically surrendering himself to the pile as the ring of green fire passed overhead. Beyond the clawing grasps of his own hands, beyond the snapping conflicts of his own bloodthirsty and relentless magnetic resonance, he could feel the one that radiated from above. It beat down on him like a sun that was too close, a roar of retribution and righteous fury. Of passion and payback.

It was Holm's magnetic resonance. What she had become once she'd finally broken free of the maniacal chaos that she'd been moulded into from birth.

Ryza thrashed against the corpses as he looked up, pulling himself to his feet now that the orbiting energy had passed. The silver-eyed Holm was backing away as her creation slowly advanced on her. The severed bodies of the Ryz-ain'ts that'd been caught by the green light lay bloodied over those that were intact, and more of them were falling by the second. Nothing could stand in the way of Holm's energy. Not when she was finally putting things as they should be.

'Ryza,' Holm said, her voice shudderingly distorted by the hissing chaos coming out of the energy she'd produced. 'You... you need to run.'

'No! Not now! Not after how far I've come! I need to see this through!'

'So you can doubt it?' Holm snapped back. 'No. Get away before you do. Run. You don't have to trust the flux, Ryza. Never had to.' She turned to him, her eyes flickering between the brilliant green he'd first seen there and the black that would likely be the last. 'I don't need your trust now. Just like you never needed mine.'

Chapter Forty-Nine

Nothing's As It Seems

T HOSE WORDS WERE FINALLY enough for Ryza. With grunting vigour, he started punching his way out of the tangle of his own corpses, not sparing a shred of compassion or disgust as their faces caved in under his clenched gauntlet. He staggered down the burial mound, ducking again to avoid the green ring of energy.

It was almost the size of the chamber itself. Its orbiting band was thin like a slicing wire, roaring with its still accelerating furore as it began to carve away at the blackened, ichor laden walls. At the mouth of the cavern's entrance, Ryza looked back again.

More Ryz-ain'ts had pulled themselves from the burial mound to climb up, to attempt to tackle Holm and stop her as she drew nearer and nearer to her creator. The silver-eyed Holm was back against the wall, the ring of energy holding steady in shrinking inches between the two.

But before it could pierce the silver-eyed Holm's chest, Holm spread her arms and then swung them together, clapping her palms to her creator's temples. The orbiting energy gave a cannon-like snap and whipped back across the room again, piercing Holm's head and leaving another, far narrower white band around her skull before it snapped into place around the silver-eyed Holm's skull like a floating crown.

A low-pitched roar ripped through the cavern, loud enough that it threw Ryza back a few steps more. He took advantage of the momentum, breaking into a clanking sprint as he fled back down Kyrea's tunnels.

The glow was gone from the arching gouges set into the walls. Stolen by whatever force Holm had just summoned. Instead, hotly forged sparks poured forth from them, hitting the ground as fire, as molten metal, as anything hot enough to sear straight through the ancient steel floor of this place.

She's going to bury the tunnels! Just like Twin Rings!

This version of Holm that'd been birthed before him wouldn't have even *known* about Twin Rings, about Iroka, about *anything* that'd happened since Ryza lost her in battle, but in the whirlwind of doubt that the flux had caused by creating her, maybe that didn't matter. In the face of pure resonance, a concept this Holm shouldn't even be able to understand, what could the flux even do to sate it? How could it quell her undying disbelief in this utter unreality except by following her along for the ride?

Crowds of autominds screamed and burned as Ryza hurtled past them. Fire and molten metal vomited from their jaws, melting through their flesh and their feet at the floor where they collapsed. They turned into glowing puddles that Ryza had no choice but to run through, the sheer heat of their liquified remains searing at the soles of his armoured boots.

The slag heaps that had once blocked the tunnel intersections thrashed with motion and life, spitting debris and scrap like there was a beast having a tantrum in the middle of it all. They forced Ryza to double back and skirt around even more of the collapsing wrecks. Soon he was lost. Lost and alone and with no chance of a lead-better roaring down his way to ferry him to safety.

Smoke billowed through the tunnels. The ceilings were lost to the silver-laced clouds of black smog. The machines had fallen silent. All Ryza could do was wheeze and listen to his own struggles as he scouted down tunnel after tunnel, turning away from dead ends of fire and rubble and scrap.

Soon he was ready to surrender to the smoke. His legs were aching, his right hip had locked up completely, and his lungs were shot. Staggering over to a wall, he clenched his teeth and pressed his back against it. Sliding down it made him spit and hiss in pain, but the floor was a welcome weight off his battered knees.

It's done. It's over. Like it should always have been. For me and for her.

There was a certainty in this thought. It didn't matter what molten flux or pure resonance had to do with it. One would triumph over the other, and with both wielded in the echoed minds of a long-gone person, the dissonance could only lead to destruction.

Ryza shut his eyes for a while. The smoke was stinging at them, but his eyelids couldn't relieve it. When he opened them again, a silhouette was standing before him.

'I thought your kind couldn't come here,' Ryza said weakly.

Archarus chuckled. He swept aside his grand coat of impossibly black fabric and sat down beside him, just to his left.

'Not quite. We aren't meant to. However, the one to enforce this *cannot* be here to do as much, so why would I stop now? Why miss a chance to say goodbye to a friend?'

Ryza didn't protest the notion. Far worse people had called him friend before.

'I wanted to thank you,' Archarus continued.

'For what?'

He paused before replying. 'For proving me wrong. And then proving me right. And then proving that proof doesn't matter at all.'

Ryza's brain stalled as he tried to comprehend the statement, and Archarus mercifully explained.

'You figured out what molten flux really is. You discovered a way to discern it from pure resonance, then to meld it back into one. What you have done now with Holm is... a miracle. A true expression of pure resonance. You already knew that the molten flux would be vanquished. You didn't know how, but you didn't need to. You constructed a way for it to occur, and conjured it as if from thin air with the aid of the molten flux itself, then imparted that notion into the mind of another before you could doubt it yourself. Because you trust her. You don't need to, but you continue to do so.'

'That's love for you, eh?' Ryza said glibly.

'Even love has its doubts, Ryza. Don't use it to discount the feat you've achieved.'

Ryza waved a hand at Archarus, dismissing the sentiment. 'Doesn't matter now.'

'Doesn't it?'

'I'm meant to die in here,' Ryza said. 'I've accepted that.'

'You were meant to disappear, Ryza. That's different.'

'Is it?'

Archarus let on with a wry smile and held out his hand. 'It is this time. Just a simple once.'

A coy grin spread on Ryza's own face, a chortle rising in his throat that he had to cough out.

As the smoke continued to fill the endlessly collapsing tunnels, Ryza took the shadow dancer's hand. A blackness swept his vision. It blotted out the veil of destruction surrounding him, stole away the pong of acrid smoke and seared flesh, cooling the world around his body until his eyes opened again.

A blazing orange sky screamed overhead. It dazzled Ryza. He brought his now empty hand to his brow to shade his eyes and looked around. Archarus was gone. It could be for a day or a year, he'd only find out once he saw the shadow dancer again. If he ever did at all.

He wasn't sure if he'd moved. Daylight burned in from above, a late afternoon that was only able to cast shadows on where he now sat. They weren't tunnels any more. The ceiling was gone, leaving only vast trenches that transitioned from walls of smoothly gouged metal to raw rock that'd been torn asunder.

Where he sat now was the only place free of rubble, a narrow, hand-excavated pit in a trough of sandstone. Ryza rolled sideways and pushed himself up the wall bit by bit, gasping in pain but ultimately satisfied he was upright. A shadow dancer's magic couldn't move people, now he thought about it.

These must still be the tunnels he'd been in. They'd just collapsed after Holm was through with them, but Ryza couldn't be sure how long ago that'd been. The chunks of rock and sandstone around him were largely blanketed by the red sand that trickled in falls from the high walls above, it was just this particular spot he'd been sitting in that was free of it.

'Someone must've dug it up... Like they knew I'd be here.'

Ryza was too exhausted to think who that possibly could've been, or how they'd discovered his would-be final resting place. It was easier to put it down to a freak chance.

He started work peeling the remaining chunks of the vent suit from his body. It started with the latches around his left shoulder, the only thing he could reach with his right hand without bending down. The buckled pauldron fell away before Ryza had freed half the bronze-ringed fasteners, the relieved pressure opening a crack along the seam connecting the front and back of his chest piece.

From there, it was as simple as worming his gauntleted fingers into the gaps as they presented themselves and prying them apart. As one chunk of the vent suit fell from him with a clang, another creaked open, asking to be next.

Soon all he was left with was his armoured boots, which he kept in order to save his bare feet from the rough ground; the padded trousers that acted as the air-sealed underlayer for the vent suit; and the tattered shirt that hung loosely around his shoulders.

His wounds stung in the open air, but that was a good thing, Ryza thought. A gentle sting like that meant they weren't life-threatening. He looked down at himself and winced.

A pool of crimson bloomed from his right hip, but it was already dark enough to be scabbing over. He lifted his shirt tenderly. The gash was smaller than he'd thought. Maybe it had only become such a bloody mess from the constant jabbing of what had caused it.

Another line of blood ran down his front, starting from the end of his left collar bone, across his chest below it, before halting halfway across his gut. A small chunk protruded from under the fabric there, and he lifted his shirt a bit more to pull it out. It was the incendiary slug, the one he'd accidentally loosed within the war serpent's throat. He chuckled and stashed the memento, shoving it down the side pocket of his pants.

Climbing out of the enormous trench was a final challenge that Ryza nearly gave up on. He was clambering up the side opposite to that where the setting sun marked its boundary, so he might as well have been climbing in the dark of night, but the slope here was gentler, and he wasn't in the mood for any feats of acrobatics.

Nothing extraordinary needed to happen now or ever again, as far as Ryza was concerned. There was a simple life for him out there, whenever he'd ended up. One he could forge for himself, without worry for complicated questions about wants and needs. Without the endless mind games brought on by nightmares, shadow dancers, and molten flux.

It was all his to have, and as he finally clambered out over the top of the newly formed cliff face, he felt himself smile.

The flux was gone. The basin was clear. Nothing remained on its floor other than lone and level sands. But before that, on the edge of the basin itself, a figure stood.

Silhouetted by the setting sun, a shadow dancer was waiting for him. Her cloak shone with the silver-embossed runes of a thousand axioms, flapping gently with the passing breeze. She smiled back, a maniacal grin, her black eyes twinkling. A hand was held out, and Ryza approached to take it.

It was Holm.

Also By

The Flux Catastrophe
RISING FLUX: The Prequel Novella to Molten Flux (March 2023)
MOLTEN FLUX (June 2023)
BLAZING FLUX (April 2024)
CORRUPTED FLUX (August 2025)
The First Hytharo
THE HYTHARO REDUX (October 2023)
THE HYTHARO ORIGIN (August 2024)

Check out my website: **jonathanweiss.com.au** to find more great books that've since been published!
And if you're inclined, consider leaving a review online, either on Goodreads or from where you purchased this book, it helps massively in getting this book in front of other readers, meaning you'll have more people to talk to about it!

GLOSSARY

You can find the living, in depth glossary for this book and for the world of The Droughtlands on my website, at **www.jonathanweiss.com.au/glossary**

Also, if you need a refresher on the events of a previous book, you can also find them at **www.jonathanweiss.com.au/plot-synopses**

ABOUT THE AUTHOR

Jonathan Weiss is an Australian Fantasy & Science Fiction author of The Flux Catastrophe and The First Hytharo series. Ever since being a small boy he hunted for the best way to tell stories, dabbling in film and stop motion before eventually finding a passion for novel writing as a teenager. More than a decade later he'd gathered a bachelor's degree of Journalism from the University of Wollongong and a career in commercial cloud sales, yet they were never as satisfying as the time spent writing.

With the support of his artist wife and the cacophonic trio of their pet budgies, he's now dedicated himself to a full-time career as an author. When not writing, Jonathan can be found reading halfway through books and being so satisfied he forgets to finish them and working through the never-ending queue of unpainted Warhammer 40,000 models.

www.ingramcontent.com/pod-product-compliance
Lightning Source LLC
Chambersburg PA
CBHW031736180726
48283CB00005B/1539